The Thief of THAT

A NOVEL

David Ewald

ISBN-13 (trade paperback): 979-8-9889795-4-8

ISBN-13 (ebook): 979-8-9889795-5-5

This book is a work of pure fiction. References to real people, events, establishments, organizations, or locales are intended only to provide a sense of authenticity, and are used fictitiously. All other characters, and all incidents and dialogue, are drawn from the author's imagination and are not be construed as real.

Cover Design by James, GoOnWrite.com

for Emily

Your Great American Novel

You are browsing the new hardcover fiction section when you stop, surprised at what you see.

Someone has taken your title.

You reach for the book, pull it off the shelf.

The book's cover shows a deserted beach. Wind whips across the ocean's surface, white-capped waves crest and fall licking the shore. The waves lash out at a child's sandcastle that crumbles in the bottom left-hand corner. A sanguine sandal lies half-buried nearby. The sun peaks above the horizon, as if shy or perhaps scared. The early morning light illuminates a body floating face-down, wrapped in strands of seaweed. A murder yet to be discovered.

The title, *After Me, The Deluge*, is emblazoned above the sun in dark letters. In the bottom right-hand corner, in smaller print: A Novel by Justice Bitterman.

You cannot believe—

Open the book to the copyright page. *After Me, The Deluge* © 2000 Justice Bitterman

You turn to the back cover flap and observe the colorless

author photo. Rather than offer a frontal view of her face, Ms. Bitterman poses from the side—quite pretentiously, you think. Her mouth is a flatline. Notice the mole on her chin.

After Me, The Deluge is the title of your own book, your unfinished book that you have been at work on for the past two and a half years. The title, such a great title encompassing the book's scope and magnitude, your vision, helped you to sustain interest in the project.

And now you find the title belongs to Justice Bitterman.

You fear she has taken more than your nights, your mornings, your days, your time. Your life.

"Oh, that's a great one."

Look up to see a bookstore employee standing close by. She has short immovable hair, freckles and sharply curving eyebrows. She smells of oranges.

She points to the book and says, "I really recommend buying that. It's exceptional."

"You've read it then?"

She nods. "Super story. It's based on that Andrew Cunanan guy. You know, the one who killed Versace."

"He killed other people also." It's difficult to speak. What's been said sounds familiar.

"Well, I like that it's written by a local author who really knows the San Diego scene. It's set all around the city. That's La Jolla Cove on the cover. I heard they took a picture of Whispering Sands and superimposed the body into the ocean. Pretty cool, huh?"

"It certainly looks that way."

"I also read this interview with the author a couple weeks ago and she said she spent a whole year researching Cunanan, doing psychological profiles and stuff..."

This too sounds familiar.

"It's supposed to be pretty accurate, but it's still fiction."

Her words are salt to your snail of a mind. "Thanks," you say. "I'll think about buying this."

"Not a problem. Just a recommendation, that's all." She smiles and walks away.

Stand there and clutch the book. Just a recommendation. Andrew Cunanan, a San Diego native who frequented the Hillcrest district and briefly attended the University of California at San Diego. Murderer of five men during the spring and summer of 1997. His former lover, Jeffrey Trail, on April 27th in Minneapolis. David Madson, with whom Jeffrey had been cheating on Andrew, shot near a lake in Minnesota on May 2nd. Seventy-two-year-old realty developer Lee Miglin on May 3rd in Chicago. Finn's Point Cemetery caretaker William Reese on May 9th in Pennsville, New Jersey. The famous fashion designer Gianni Versace shot outside his Miami Beach mansion on the morning of July 15th.

You have memorized these names, these dates, these places.

You too are a San Diego native. During the week following Versace's murder, you and so many others living in the area feared Cunanan's return. He had traveled from San Francisco to Minnesota to New Jersey to Miami—why wouldn't he complete the circle of violence in his hometown?

Cunanan—whose words were "After me, the deluge" or "After me, disaster," a quote from the Sun King Louis XIV, the conqueror—would hit Hillcrest, or perhaps downtown's Gaslamp Quarter, or possibly the UCSD campus in La Jolla.

So many in San Diego awaited the deluge that never came. Cunanan stayed in Miami, where he shot himself in a houseboat on July 23, 1997.

The morning after Cunanan's suicide, you decided to write a thriller based on his life. This composite of Cunanan would grow up in San Diego before moving to San Francisco where he would live for a time before returning to Southern California to begin his killing spree. Your novel would capture the mood, the feelings, the situations of the people and places in your city had Cunanan actually returned.

Flip through Justice Bitterman's book, scanning chapters, skimming paragraphs. The plot of her novel is almost exactly that of your own. Certain locations, the same. The 'what if' concept.... But the book was *your* idea—you had it the day after Cunanan's death, undoubtedly before Bitterman decided to pursue the same project!

You decide to buy the book. It's an impulse buy, you know, but you need to read *After Me, The Deluge* to see what you could have done, had you done it sooner.

The employee with immovable hair, freckles and sharply curving eyebrows takes your purchase at the counter. "You won't be disappointed," she says. "It's gripping."

You agree, pay with your credit card, and leave the bookstore. On your way out you tuck the novel underneath your coat to protect it from the cold rain.

If it rains in San Diego County, it must be winter.

It is early evening on the last day of January in the first year of the new millennium. A Monday.

There's nothing to do now but abandon your version. Just give up, stop writing altogether. What's the point of writing anything when the only story you ever cared to put on paper was published without your name attached to it?

But that's going too far. You will start over. You will write something new. Your novel—when it is finally finished—will be better, you believe, than *After Me, The Deluge*. It will be published to great critical acclaim and fanfare. You will graciously accept America's Book Club's seal of approval and attend a much-deserved dinner reception in your honor. Your book will sell millions of copies, enabling you to move into a mansion in La Jolla, right next to Justice Bitterman. The two of you will be neighbors, and there will be no hard feelings. Once a week you will meet in Esmeralda's Bookstore in Del Mar to discuss literature and laugh at how you spent two and a half years writing a book that Justice ended up publishing first.

All this will be yours—after you finish writing the novel, of course.

Reaching your car you promise yourself that you will begin writing as soon as you step through the front door. And with that promise comes another: you will no longer spend more time in the bookstore than you do in front of your computer.

ONE

And with that promise comes another: you will no longer spend more time in the bookstore than you do in front of your computer.

Ravel's spindly pianist fingers, never having endured a piano lesson, hovered over the keyboard. He hesitated. *Think,* he thought. *Think. Think. What next what next what next what—*

"Again, Ravel?"

Alarmed he had not sensed the usual hovering at his back before hearing the voice, Ravel toggled quickly from the start of his novel to the sales development screen he'd had sense enough to open earlier. Although difficult on the eyes, this work screen now commanded his attention. Ravel typed random words—nothing new in this environment: anything to give the appearance of actual work. Fernando Casillas, one of the floor supervisors, drew in close enough to whisper.

"You can't keep doing this, you know."

Casillas had been eating corn nuts for breakfast, again.

"Five years here and you're still having these lapses," the

floor supervisor said. "You think no one's looking but we are. All of us are."

Ravel felt Casillas might sink in on him, like the roof of a storm-battered shed. *If he touches me with his belly*, Ravel thought. *If he—*

"Time's running out for you, Averof."

"I know. I understand."

"You understand. Actualize that understanding then."

Ravel glanced over the short wall of his cubicle to see Casillas walking off to harass other sales development associates. Checking to see they were developing sales, whatever that meant. Years in and Ravel still wasn't certain. Despite the floor supervisor's absence, Ravel dared not toggle back to the opening of his novel. Instead, he toggled to something much safer: the search engine. He typed in *spiros averof* and hit return.

His screen filled with images and words centered on a man in his late 50s. The man wore a Herringbone flat cap and sported a full beard resplendently silver. Weathered but distinguished, the man stood in one much-replicated image with his arms folded across his chest as he leaned against a railing overlooking the East River and the Brooklyn skyline beyond. The latest author photo, released to coincide with the publication of the new novel.

At least he's looking at the camera, Ravel thought.

Absently, Ravel fingered the amulet he wore around his neck. It had been his mother's, given to him on her deathbed. Hand-crafted in Bulgaria by one of her distant relatives, the necklace was square-shaped, opal, with a silver circle in the center, and dazzling in the sun. Yoana had sworn it would give her son good luck, far more than it had ever given her.

Touching it now, pressed as it was to his sternum beneath his button-up shirt, Ravel heard his mother's words: *Will you fill it? Will you fill the void?* before snapping out of his reverie.

His cubicle supervisor with the big round pink ears, like a pika's, Daniel, stood at his back, though not for long. When Ravel turned, Dan moved on. He had seen: worse, Casillas had reported to Dan what he'd seen and Dan had just now confirmed it. Off-task, irredeemably so. More and more of it had been occurring with Ravel Averof in the past year. They could stop blaming the pandemic: at this point, at the end of 2022, this was all on Ravel, who had started out so promising only to see his work ethic and output drop below the monthly review thresholds in the wake of the all-employee office return of summer 2021.

The higher-ups at Maguffin-Shrift were at last figuring out what Ravel wanted—and it didn't involve industrial parts distribution.

"What are you going to do," Ravel whispered to himself. "What are you going to do..."

He glanced over his shoulder to see Dan returning. No time! Within seconds Ravel had closed out the search results page that lauded his father's many literary and familial accomplishments, closed out his personal email account and the document containing the meager opening of his novel as well. Ravel answered his work phone on the first ring, aware that Dan was watching.

"Ravel Averof, sales development associate with Maguffin-Shrift, speaking."

"Ravel Averof. *The* Ravel Averof?"

"Uh. Yes. How may I help you, ma'am?"

Despite the 'ma'am,' the woman on the line's other end

was anything but. She was young. Ravel sensed from the softness of her voice, a voice that sounded familiar. A young woman, perhaps just out of college? College...

"You're not going to remember me, of course."

Dan at his back. Instinctively, Ravel tensed up. "Please hold for a moment," he said. He hit the hold button and swiveled with the phone still in hand.

"Ravel," Dan said, "when you're done..."

Ravel nodded and, out of habit, swept back his long bangs —not that there was much hair left up front to touch. Two years ago, when he turned 28 at the height of the pandemic, he discovered his hairline receding and grieved for a while. The hair loss made sense: his mother's brother was bald, as had been his maternal grandfather. His mother's bloodline. His father, the renowned literary titan Spiros Averof, would of course keep his full head of hair until Death finally claimed him at some impressively ripe old age.

Ravel waited for Dan to move on and then hit the hold button again.

"Thanks for holding."

"I thought you'd snubbed me," the woman said.

"I wouldn't do that. So...where were we?"

"I was just saying you don't remember me."

"Uh. I'm sorry. Is this a business call? May I ask your name?"

"It's Laney. Laney Greer."

"Laney Greer..."

"*Professor* Averof."

"Oh..."

"You know: Mothers of the Merciful College. Fort Collins, Colorado. My freshman year..."

It hit him. *The* Laney Greer. His former and best student from when he taught that single year-long class of freshman girls in the 2016 – 2017 school year, he a lowly graduate student who had no idea what he was doing.

"Laney!" Ravel exclaimed. "I do remember you. Of course I do. I…"

"I'm calling to order a part, Professor Averof—"

"Please. Call me Ravel. I didn't let you call me 'professor' back then. Just Ravel then, just Ravel now."

"Okay, Ravel. Can I order a part with you? You're in sales, right?"

"Not really. I'm a sales development associate."

"That's not sales?"

"It's…" He didn't know what it was, what he did for work. Typed. Searched. Keyed numbers. Maintained accounts.

"Well, I'm hoping you can help me," Laney said. "I saw you worked for the only company in Colorado that has the part we need at this very moment, pronto."

"How did you know I worked here?"

"LinkedIn. Your profile needs updating, Ravel. I took a shot figuring you were still at this Maguffin-Shrift place, and the receptionist put me through to you. *Voila.*"

"It's a small world after all," Ravel said with a smile. "What part do you need?"

"Can I place my order with you?"

"Sure. I guess. Why not?"

Five years in and Maguffin-Shrift's departments and titles remained interchangeable. Ravel brought up the appropriate screen, peeked behind to see that Dan had moved on, and asked what Laney needed.

"It's part number 095-432-252-13."

Ravel keyed in the numbers and brought up the part's page. His eyes widened. "Um, Laney, this is *expensive*."

"I know it's expensive, Ravel. I can see the price on your company's site."

"It's just it's never been ordered. I don't believe it ever has. It's—"

"Almost a million dollars? Is that what you were going to say?"

"Yeah..."

"Is it Maguffin-Shrift's policy to comment on customer's purchases?"

"No," a chagrined Ravel said. Again he peeked: no Dan.

"Just put it through then, Ravel. We have the money. It's not going to break the bank for us."

"You got it." Ravel initiated the purchasing process, the phone cradled in the crook of his neck. "What's your company's name?"

"You need that? I can't just order this under my own name?"

"I'm afraid not, Ms. Greer. It's company policy. We need a name, especially since I assume this is the first time your company's ordered from us."

"Fine," Laney said after a noticeable hesitation. "It's Chronoflex."

"Chronoflex?"

She spelled it out for him. Then, before Ravel could comment further, Laney gave an address in Boulder and her company's credit card information. For all her interest in and familiarity with Ravel early in the call, she now seemed eager to end it.

"Okay, Ms. Greer—"

"Call me Laney, Ravel."

"Laney. Okay, Laney. This order is in the warehouse now, it'll be to you this afternoon."

"Even with the snow the way it is?"

"It's just Denver to Boulder. It is a big part, but we have the truck for it ready. You'll be fine."

"Great. Thanks. Sorry I've been short with you. We just need this ASAP. I'm hoping to talk more with you at another time, in person."

I'm hoping. Talk more with you.

"In person, huh." Ravel rubbed his wedding band with his thumb.

"It's not going to be a date, Ravel. Just to catch up."

"I'd like that," said Ravel.

"Here." Laney rattled off her number, which Ravel tapped into his personal phone.

"I'll text you so you have mine," he said.

"Great. I gotta go. Let's get together s—"

"Time."

"Excuse me?"

"Time," Ravel repeated. "Your company has something to do with time, right? Chrono, chronos, the Greek root for time. But flex..."

"We manufacture time pieces," said Laney.

"Time pieces. You mean watches? Clocks?"

"Yes."

"But the part you just ordered, it's a graphene- and tungsten-composite shield panel the size of...That can't be for a clock, Laney."

"Best not to ask questions now, Ravel."

But I can ask questions later? thought Ravel.

"I'm just intrigued, Laney, you know."

"I know. But I have to go now. We'll talk soon."

The call ended. Dan was on his way back, this time looking even more insistent. Ravel sat up straight in his ergonomically-challenged company chair and swiveled to fully face his supervisor.

"What was that about?"

"Just took a sales call, actually."

"Oh really...?" Dan leaned in, a hand on Ravel's desk, the other hand holding onto the top of the low cubicle wall. "How'd it go?"

"Fine. Great, in fact. Some company we don't have on file. I already checked."

"And you think it should be in our system." Dan took his hands off Ravel's work area and stood with his arms folded, expectant. "Why is that?"

Ravel explained the order. A part that had never before been purchased and that came to a grand total of $985,900, a part used in extremely dangerous environments, environments involving ocean depths or solar flares, underwater search and recovery, or space travel.

"But they're in Boulder," Ravel said. "Which rules out the ocean, right? So, what? Aerospace?"

"Outer space." Dan grinned. "Maybe they're the new rival to X."

"The company's name is Chronoflex. The, uh, the client said the company makes time pieces."

"Watches?"

"Or clocks, or *something* having to do with time. But that part.... Maybe they make watches for astronauts, and they need the shield to place on the shuttle a clock is going into?"

"Weird," Dan said. "But intriguing. Time for you to prospect to see if they'll be a repeat buyer. Company size, so on. You know the drill."

Dan pointed at Ravel and then at Ravel's computer and keyboard. Ravel faced the screen and ran a search for Chronoflex, aware of his cubicle supervisor not budging. Soon Dan had bent down so that the supervisor's pika ear came close to brushing Ravel's cheek. Both supervisor and employee scanned the screen for promising links. Most of what the search engine returned were suggestions for other words similar to Chronoflex, but the topmost result was a link that took them to the homepage of a Boulder-based company called Chronoflex.

"This must be it," said Ravel.

"Nothing much happening there."

The site was still under construction. Nothing more on the white homepage than black text announcing that this was the future site of Chronoflex.

'It's not enough," Dan said. In his mind, Chronoflex was a two-bit operation that had placed a one-time order, never to be heard from again. True, the part had cost close to a million dollars, but even then the evidence of this being a repeat buyer was scant.

"But look at the address," Ravel countered. "It's in the same business park Dyvaflo's in."

Conceding the point, Dan nodded. He wished Ravel would stop bringing up Dyvaflo, which the sales development associate had stumbled upon soon after he started in 2017, but Dan could not deny the success Maguffin-Shrift had seen with that company, nor could he pass up a potential pay-off in pursuing its neighbor, this mysterious Chronoflex.

"Look into them," he said and pinched the point between his eyes. "But if they have under ten employees..."

Ravel waited for Dan to disengage. When his cubicle supervisor had departed, he picked up his personal phone and brought up Laney's number, a 970 area code, the northern Front Range. A piece of his past, Laney Greer. And she'd sought *him* out. Asked to be patched through to *him* directly. She wanted *him* to process the sale. Vaguely he found this reconnection strange, but his mind didn't linger on the why. He had work to do. Maguffin-Shrift protocol required him to follow up with the company, call to inquire about the number of employees, the kind of work being done, but Ravel had already made up his mind. He would forego protocol and go straight to the company's front door to see what they were up to in person.

In person, Ravel thought. *Laney would be okay with that. She even said...*

Buoyed by the anticipation he felt at the thought of investigating Chronoflex the next day (he would call in to say he had a morning doctor's appointment), Ravel felt energized—so energized, in fact, that the usual sheer crushing drudgery of the work he had to complete didn't weigh him down one bit. The drive from Sheridan in the south of Denver to the city proper in the north was particularly harrowing that afternoon because of the heavy snow and howling wind, but Ravel turned up the tunes, kept his speed to a minimum, and refrained from honking even when the obligatory nutjob swung into his path on the 85. Rav was in such a good mood that he stopped off at a King Soopers, and by the time he'd reached the apartment in Capitol Hill he held in both hands a bouquet of his wife's favorite flowers.

Deborah was at the dining table, her taut face buried in a doorstop of a book, the cover of which showed a castle surrounded by mist and high crashing waves. Ravel approached her cautiously, aware of how she could be when ensconced in her research.

At last his wife of four years looked up, weary but grateful at the sight of the flowers. The circles under her striking hazel eyes seemed to retract just a little, and the creases around her chapped lips smoothed out somewhat. Her deep brown hair remained pulled back and held in place by one of those plastic claws, and an image came to Ravel then of a sunny day years ago, in the pre-marital time, when he'd sat behind Deborah on her bed and braided her long hair, so free then, one bunch of strands folding over another until there was nothing left to twist.

"Rav," she said. "That's so sweet of you."

"I'm just glad they had tulips. They don't always."

He bent down and kissed her. She closed the book but kept her hand in as a marker, and she did not rise.

"What's the special occasion?"

"Nothing really. Just you."

"That's sweet. I love them. Thank you." Deborah assessed her husband, two years her junior, with watery eyes. "But I do need to finish this. Just a half hour more…"

"You got it," Ravel said. He turned and walked into the kitchen where he opened the fridge and took out the defrosted scallops, leftover pasta and asparagus. He'd gotten used to leftovers in the past year since Deborah had moved from coursework to her dissertation. What he hadn't gotten used to was her constant weariness, a weariness that was wearing him down.

As Ravel got dinner going, he glanced at Deborah and sensed her jaw tighten as she hunched over her book on Irish folklore, taking notes for a dissertation she swore to him she would finish next year, no matter what. And then what? Entry into the hyper-competitive field of folklore professorship? Publish or perish? Inevitable part-time work at more than one community college? True, Ravel's master's degree in English literature was of no consequence at Maguffin-Shrift, but at least he had not pursued this mad quest.

When the food was ready they did what they had so often been doing lately: dinner in front of the screen. Ravel understood his wife's need to decompress, and so he again acquiesced after pushing aside his insecurities. Why couldn't talking with her husband face to face help Deborah decompress? Did their eyes need to be riveted to the screen while they shoveled food into their mouths? It was all right, Ravel reasoned. Tonight the Nuggets were taking on the Mavs in Dallas, and Jokic was a player not to miss. Ravel, who had played ball in high school and for a brief time in college, had a good feeling about this season. It could be the first championship for Denver, which had seen so few glory days in the NBA since joining in 1976.

The game was live, so they had to suffer through the commercials. Ravel muted the ads. Deborah asked him if anything new was going on at work.

"Yeah, actually, there is. I'm going to see a new company tomorrow."

"Really? What is it?"

"I'm pretty sure they're into aerospace manufacturing."

"Aerospace? That's great, Rav. A step up from that rafting equipment place you had to check out in October."

"Yeah, that sure was a bust."

He was careful not to touch her fingernails as he held her hand. Deborah had never explained why she hated to have her fingernails touched, and Ravel felt the time for asking had long passed. He brushed the back of Deborah's hand over and over until his wife nestled her head in the crook of his neck and closed her eyes. She exhaled deeply. Ravel turned and kissed her forehead, then her cheek, her lips, her neck. Deborah kept her eyes closed, smiled slightly and made a sound of pleasure.

Dinner was done, and the Nuggets were going to lose the game. "Let's go to the bed," Ravel said, careful to make the distinction between '*the* bed' and just 'bed.'

"I think I can only do bed tonight, Rav," Deborah said, her eyes still closed. "I'm beat."

Same as last night, Ravel stopped himself from saying, *and the night before, and the night before that....* He had to be strong. He had to be understanding. Deborah had warned him about the mad quest she would be undertaking after she completed her master's degree at the University of Denver. They had met in a bar near Coors Field; the Rockies had lost again, but that hadn't stopped the patrons from slamming back drink after drink, and it hadn't stopped Ravel Averof and Deborah Parker from kissing later in the evening, after they'd had a few rounds. Deborah had been free then, she'd been spontaneous and far more fun. The fact that he, an undergrad, had hooked up with a grad student excited him. Time did not concern him then. Deborah's age wasn't a factor then. Ravel would graduate, go on to grad school and earn his own master's degree, publish his first novel, and the rest—finances and a family—would fall into place.

The screen black and the dishes put away, Deborah and

Ravel took to bed. Deborah had barely slipped on her thick pajamas and placed her head on the pillow when she drifted off, and Ravel was left to watch her. She was tall, five-ten, and so he took his time rubbing all of her backside. He could do this much for her, at least. She had a *slammin'* backside, he often admired. It was the backside he'd known early on he would want to see for the rest of his life.

He could not, however, go the distance by wrapping his arms around her and snuggling. Not yet. After some time, when he was certain Deborah had fallen into a deep sleep, he got up and padded over to the office. The wind continued to howl outside, the snow continued to fall beyond the frosted window. Ravel stood in the middle of the room, a Lumineers song playing in his mind, and stared at his laptop as if it were an enemy. Then he took a seat before it, opened a drawer and took out his notes for the novel he'd been trying to get going for years. All that chicken scratch on all those legal pages. It was early December, over two decades removed from 2000, the past. Should he change the time period? Ravel had been only a boy in 2000, in San Diego County. What did he know of Cunanan? They'd already made the direct-to-streaming film and, Ravel was certain, a documentary as well. What could he possibly contribute?

Ravel closed his eyes and pictured his father's string of author photos. Those dark eyes, that even darker scowl, as if Spiros Averof was judging him, the son he hadn't seen in 21 years. Ravel tried to concentrate on his notes, to get any ideas going for where to take his novel next, but nothing presented itself and instead he pictured a bookshelf filled with only those works written by the people who continued to intimidate him: the few slim volumes of poetry by his recently deceased, to-eventually-be-forgotten-by-everyone mother standing next to and subsumed by his famous father's slew of muscular novels, which in turn stood shoulder to shoulder with the two novels written by the elusive but lucky Tristan Boppana, both bestsellers, the debut tome containing on its dedication page the name of Ravel's former girlfriend, the one who had driven him to throw everything he had into writing, who had praised him when he needed praise the most. Such regret Ravel felt at even having met Maggie. If they had not crossed paths, Ravel would not be miserable—or at least so miserable—in his work. If he could have convinced Maggie not to dump him, his work would not be weighing him down, he wouldn't even be working at Maguffin-Shrift, he would be in a prestigious position of letters, an editor or a full-time writer. But there was no going back, no conceivable way to go back.

In one hand, over and over, Ravel turned his mother's amulet. Eventually he stopped and stared at the amulet's center, that 'O,' the void that needed to be filled. Yoana Kopecka had not succeeded, but her son would. He had promised her that much, at least.

Back in bed, he again observed his wife. The last time she had praised him for his writing had been years ago, when they had first met and she had believed in him, believed that he would publish a novel and launch his literary career. Perhaps she no longer saw him as a writer. Perhaps she still saw him as one—but, worse, not a successful one.

He scooted closer to Deborah and, at the grazing of his velociraptor toenail, she murmured, "Rav." He withdrew his foot and slid his arms around her body. She sighed and pressed into him. He ran his fingers down her body, over her breasts, through the thin fabric, and she did not wake up. Eventually, he withdrew to sleep on his side of the bed—but not before kissing her on the neck and saying, "I love you, D."

On his back, he felt his heart jump and turn: unnatural. He felt as if it were going to seize up, like the controls of a plane. Then it happened. "What the—" Ravel started. He lifted the covers to look down in darkness at his groin. He had wet himself, quite without warning. It was a considerable amount of urine. He had felt it rush out of him abruptly, a quick epic release. "Shit," Ravel murmured. He again got up and headed to the bathroom, stopping on his way there to fetch a fresh pair of boxers and pajama pants out of a drawer.

After cleaning himself and making certain he had nothing left in his bladder, Ravel returned to bed. Fortunately the urine had soaked through his underwear, pajama pants and collected on his body only, so he needn't have changed the sheets. *That was weird*, he thought. *Probably my sphincter, whatever that is. I'll get it checked, when I get insurance, when I get a big advance, when I sell, celebrated, celebration...*

Ravel's thoughts fell now like confetti, exactly what he was picturing now, confetti of all colors, a ticker tape parade, when he finally, finally took to sleep.

Two

The next morning Ravel had a recurrence: in the shower, while lathering his underarms, he quite suddenly urinated a little. Just a little. A spurt. He again felt his bladder—his *sphincter*, he thought—let go. He felt no pain. What he'd experienced once at night and now this morning was more of a nuisance than anything. *This is 30,* Ravel thought. *By the time I really need to see a doctor, I'll have insurance.*

He chalked up the curious loss of bladder control to aging. Perhaps his mother had faced it and she'd never told him. Or a family member on her side. Perhaps a family member on his father's side, though Spiros would never admit any physical maladies in his bloodline, and Ravel wasn't about to seek his father out for a talk about the Averof family's health history. More pressing than Ravel's health was the prize, the future, the road. Though I-25 had been plowed early that Wednesday morning, the main transportation artery of Colorado was slick and crowded, and on his way north Ravel had witnessed more than one morning commuter spun out on the shoulder.

Six years ago, as he was finishing up his master's degree program at Colorado State in Fort Collins, if anyone had stopped Ravel in the hall or on the street and told him that at the end of 2022 he would be on the I-25 headed to prospect for an industrial supply parts distributor under the nebulous title 'sales development associate,' he would have scoffed. Anyone would have. At that time, in the wake of the election that changed the country, Ravel had only two goals, one main and one secondary. The main: to be known, not just by everyone, though that would be nice, but by his father, Spiros Averof, and his rival, his contemporary, Tristan Boppana, who had published his debut novel with an up-and-coming press and his sophomore effort with a major publisher without attending a day of graduate school. A literary wunderkind, Boppana had been hailed. Worse, to add insult to injury, Boppana had married Ravel's college girlfriend, Maggie, an act that had devastated Ravel far more than he wanted to admit.

Then there was the secondary goal: to stay with Deborah. They had met, and Ravel, in his weakness, had soon let it slip about his involvement in the strange triangle—Tristan, Maggie, Ravel. Unsettled, Deborah had nearly dumped him. But Ravel had convinced her, through notes, letters, messages, texts, none of them plagiarized, that he loved her, he needed her, he wanted her, he knew, deep down, that if he gave up Deborah he would be pursuing his own mad quest, with no hope of return.

Now, at the end of 2022, Ravel thought of Tristan too much, Maggie slightly less so. They were living in New York (of course), and Ravel had to remind himself every day that he had his own married life, his own career, his own (bleak) future.

Just before nine he reached the business park in Boulder. Large nondescript buildings, shaded windows, dirty snow in piles on either side of entryways. On the surface, it looked as if very little business was conducted here. The lot was about half full. In the considerable amount of time he sat at the wheel, Ravel saw no one go in or out of any building. Eerie. Then again, this was the location of Dyvaflo and Oxian, two of Maguffin-Shrift's most consistent buyers. Ravel had to take the plunge.

He walked across the concrete threshold and tried one of the double-doors. It gave easily. In the foliage-laden lobby, Ravel stood for a moment and observed the list of companies engraved on a plaque on the right-side wall. Chronoflex was unlisted. Ravel checked the address. This was the place all right. Why no listing? Ravel's interest deepened. *Top secret*, he thought. *They're really flying under the radar because...they make clocks? Not clocks: time pieces...*

Ravel continued down the hall and turned to each door he passed by. At last, at the very end of the hall, he found the one door that was unmarked, no company identified.

The blinds covering the window to the side of the door were drawn. Despite feeling unwelcome, Ravel raised his fist to knock. Before he could, the door opened, and standing before him was Laney Greer, twenty-four years old, dressed in jeans and a CU Boulder sweatshirt. "Beat me to it," she said. "Come in."

"You were expecting me?" a flabbergasted Ravel said.

"I had a hunch you'd be here early. We know you, Ravel. The psychometrics don't lie."

"*What*?" The alarm in Ravel's voice was caustic. He had more than half a mind to back away from this place and his former student. They'd profiled him? Stalked him? He had found it odd that Laney'd checked out his profile on LinkedIn. What else had she checked out? He did back away.

"You're really going to pass up this opportunity without finding out what it is?" Laney challenged.

"Um..." Ravel froze in the doorway, on the threshold of an apparent opportunity.

Laney had already turned from him and jumped on her phone, texting now with abandon just as she'd done all those times in the intro to literature class Ravel had stumbled through at Mothers of the Merciful College.

Ravel inched inside, trailing after his former student.

Sight was Ravel's first sense, followed quickly by smell. Lime-scented disinfectant assailed his nostrils. The air reeked of it. The waiting room was certainly clean, but it was also bare save for a couple of chairs lined up on either side of the door. A magazineless coffee table was positioned in the center of the lobby, not far from the front counter. Laney took a seat behind the counter and remained hunched over, her eyes on her device. Ravel, accosted by the thick air, coughed, and Laney looked up.

"You're not leaving?"

"I want to know what's going on," Ravel demanded. "What do you mean psychometrics? You've been keeping tabs on me for some reason?"

"We're interested in you, Ravel. You're exactly who we're looking for."

"Okay..." Ravel folded his arms. "You want to, what, hire me?"

"God no!" exclaimed Laney. "What could you possibly do

for us as an employee? You'd have nothing to offer us in that arena."

"But I do have something to offer you, you're saying."

"That's right." The small sharp pert nose, the fair freckled skin, the green eyes, the blondish-red hair tied in a ponytail that graced her smooth long neck; the smile that could reveal too much of her teeth, to the point of both charm and laughter. He recognized the entire Irish-Catholic *thing* about her, Laney Greer, whom he never thought he'd see again after he'd finished teaching that freshman intro to literature course at the all-female Mothers of the Merciful College, received his master's degree from Colorado State and moved with Deborah to Denver.

"Since you're game," Laney continued, "I'll get Nicholas up here to meet you."

After calling up Nicholas on her phone, Laney set it aside. "Five years," she said. "And you're working at an industrial supply distributor. I thought you'd stick with teaching."

"You know I was never good, Laney."

"*I* thought you were. I gave you a good evaluation at the end of the year."

"Oh so *yours* was the one positive one out of all of them!"

"Come on," Laney said. "You weren't that bad. Give yourself some credit."

"I wish I could," admitted Ravel, "but the truth is I was so done with teaching at that point, by the end of that school year, all I could do was take my graduate degree and get out of town. Anyway, the job I have isn't bad. The money is really good. Incredibly good, and I'm married now, and we're talking children, as soon as my wife—Deborah—finishes her PhD."

"That's great," Laney said. "I'm happy for you, Ravel. And I take it you're completely satisfied?"

"Completely satisfied?" Ravel was taken aback by the question. He'd never heard it posed to him before. "I'm not.... I'm not *completely* satisfied. Who is? Are you?"

"No. Of course not," Laney said. "But with you, Ravel, I suspect you're far more dissatisfied than you're letting on."

Ravel looked to either side, as if Casillas or Dan were watching. "You're not wrong," he said. "I'd like something else."

"Could that something else be an adventure?"

"Depends on what adventure we're talking about here. Are you saying I should try out one of your watches, your clocks, when I blast off into space on one of your rockets?"

"One of our *rockets*?" Laney looked bemused. "What gave you that idea?"

"The part you ordered. What else? It's big, Laney. The kind of part you'd need for paneling in a space shuttle. So what does this have to do—"

"Ah, he's here," Laney interrupted. "Just in time."

Emerging from the hallway at the back of the reception area was a short slight bespectacled man of French-African descent. Ravel was unsure of the nationality until Nicholas announced it to him as he shook the sales development associate's hand firmly. "To clear up any questions you may have," Nicholas said, "regarding my accent, skin color..."

"Oh I—"

Nicholas waved off any words that might have issued from Ravel's mouth. "I appreciate your decorum," he said, "but there's no need. You are here, at last. Laney did her work. She got you here."

"I need to know what this is," Ravel said. "I need to know now. If you keep toying with me, I'm walking out of here for good."

"Are we toying with you?" Nicholas's eyes fell on Laney as he said this. "I don't suppose my assistant here gave you the scoop, as the Americans say?"

"I thought you wanted me to leave the scoop to you, Nicholas," a peeved Laney said.

"Yes yes," said Nicholas, his tone dismissive. "We wouldn't want our liaison leading the tour."

Ravel picked up on Laney's flared nostrils, her narrowed eyes. She bristled at Nicholas's words. "Everyone's in charge of everything here, Nicholas," she said, her voice low, lethal. "No liaisons, no receptionists. Your words. *I'm* the one who caught the fracture in the Chronoquantumogriphier's hull. Isn't that right, Czar Nicholas?"

Nicholas bowed low enough to show the back of his bald head. "I concede," he said.

"I'm sorry—did you say Chronoquantu...?" Ravel looked from Laney to Nicholas.

"Quantumogriphier," Nicholas finished. "Chronoquantumogriphier. Now is time for the tour, my friend."

"Okay..." Ravel half-turned. "Look. If it's just a clock, or a timer..."

"It's a machine," announced Nicholas.

"A machine. What—"

"Combine the word 'machine' with the word 'time,'" Nicholas said, "and what do you find yourself with?"

Ravel took a moment. "Uh..." Then it hit him. Hard. "Oh *shit*," he said. "This is a joke. It's not a.... You didn't—" He directed this to Laney. "You roped me in to find out about a—a..."

"You would call it a time machine, Ravel," Laney said.

"And you want me to, what, check it out? Go in it?"

The silence surrounding Laney and Nicholas spoke for them.

"You don't make watches," Ravel deduced. "You don't make clocks, you don't make timers. The time pieces you make—the *time piece* you make is a freakin' time *machine*."

"Well done, Ravel," said Nicholas.

"Are you with the government?"

"No, we are not with the government. We are a private start-up. Under the radar."

"I'll say. Is your company's name even Chronoflex?"

"Close," Laney said. "Chrono*trex*."

"Trex," Ravel echoed. "Oh I get it. Jesus...This is so unbelievably ridiculous."

Nicholas guffawed. "It *does* sound ridiculous, doesn't it? Time travel can't be done! It is theoretically, physically, all-around impossible, they say. The logistics make no sense, it's the stuff of dreams and fantasies and fiction." Here Nicholas paused with significant gravity. "Before the summer of 2020 I believed all that. But now, I say: *bullshit*."

"Bullshit."

"Bullshit!" Nicholas guffawed again. An edge of his fashionable spectacles glinted. "And to prove what they say is bullshit, I will give you now the tour no outsider has ever received."

"Before I...before I go with you, if I'm even going to go with you," Ravel said, "I need to know why me. I mean why *this* outsider, of all the outsiders in Colorado, in the world?"

"From what Laney told me about you," said Nicholas, "you are the one most appropriate to be the first human outside of Chronotrex's staff to try the Chronoquantumogriphier."

"You think *I* want to go back in time?" Ravel laughed loudly. "Christ, Laney, what gave you that idea?"

"What we talked about, more than once, in your office, Ravel. Remember?"

A flash: a memory. Seated in the office he'd been granted, Ravel across from Laney, discussing regrets. What he wished he would have done. If he could only go back and do things differently. Set a new course. H.G. Wells's *The Time Machine* was brought up. So was Michael Crichton's *Timeline*. *The Time Traveler's Wife*. Stephen Hawking. Albert Einstein. Kip Thorne. Laney remembered. And now Ravel did, too.

"Laney, bring out the release form and the bracelet, please. We at last will use them!"

Laney, doing as told, asked Ravel to hold out his right wrist. Around his wrist she secured a metal band that emitted a buzzing sound, vibration, and red lights, not unlike the device given to restaurant patrons waiting for their table to be ready.

"For security reasons," Nicholas said. "And now, please sign here. This is the release form, in which you skim through the legalese and ultimately agree to not say a word about what you learn and see from this point forward."

Ravel looked over the one-page form clipped to the board Laney held out to him. The writing was dense, the font miniscule. It would take him far too long to read and comprehend. His future—the past—was waiting. He signed and handed her the pen.

"Thank you, Laney," Nicholas said. "She's the face of our operation, for good reason."

Ravel glanced over his shoulder on his way out of the lobby. Laney was looking at him intently, her mouth tight.

As Nicholas led him through a door and down a stuffy hallway, Ravel noted the blank walls, more closed doors, a mop standing in a bucket of water in front of the men's room. At the end of the hall they stopped, and Nicholas pointed down to what looked to be an entrance to a cellar. He got on his haunches and punched in a code on an adjacent keypad while shielding the act with his body. "Excuse me," he said, pulling the doors up and open, revealing the top of a stairway that descended into darkness. "I have to make sure they're ready for you."

"I don't believe this."

"What don't you believe?"

"Is this where you keep the bodies?"

Nicholas's face of stone told Ravel his joke was not welcome. Nicholas started down the stairs, turned and halted Ravel from following him. "It won't be more than a few minutes. Please wait here." Then the doors were shut and Ravel was left to himself.

Get out of here, he thought. *All kinds of wrong. Whatever this is is not going to be worth it. I'll die going back in time, I just know it. Or anyway something very bad will happen.* Ravel had to admit, however, that he *would* consider going back in time, despite the certain challenges and dangers. What if he *could* change something? All that regret, all that wasted time. He could avoid Maguffin-Shrift entirely, perhaps, set himself on a path, with Deborah, that would make him happy. If

Chronotrex had figured out how to make time travel possible...

The cellar doors opened and Nicholas emerged halfway. "They're waiting for you," he announced.

"This is actually, truly, definitely legit?" Ravel asked.

"Why wouldn't it be?"

"What I mean is, whatever you're doing down there, it's not going to kill me, right? I mean I'm sure there's danger, there must be, but you've tested this thing. You've gone in yourself, right?"

"Of course!" Nicholas scoffed. "I and the other engineers have all taken turns."

"Be honest with me now. Be honest. Please. What is this I'm about to see? Tell it straight to my face. Please...just, what is it?"

After a brief internal struggle, apparent on his face despite his best attempts to suppress it, Nicholas said, "The truth, sir, is that we have successfully developed a certain kind of machine that aids in a certain kind of travel. Not through air, not through water, not through outer space. Through time. Through time."

"Time travel," Ravel exhaled. "It's real. It's possible."

"It is, Ravel. And it's down here. Come."

The maw of the floor, its tongue the stairs, awaited. Strangely, despite feeling immense excitement and tension over his discovery, Ravel did not feel the need to urinate whatsoever. Nicholas, making no further comment, descended, followed closely by Ravel. Lights went on immediately to illuminate the concrete stairway that extended farther than Ravel could have imagined. It smelled better down here, which was to say it did not smell at all.

"This way," Nicholas said. "Careful of your steps."

"You need a railing," said Ravel.

"I assume your company has the part we'll need? I'll have Laney make the purchase."

Nicholas stopped on the stairs, near the bottom, and Ravel nearly knocked into him. "What—what's wrong?"

"For you to proceed," said Nicholas with the appropriate gravity, "you must trust Nicholas Decant. You have signed more than a piece of paper, Ravel. You understand, correct?"

"I would like to think I do. I still don't believe what's going on here. If this is truly time travel here, then why isn't the government involved? Have they found out? What if—"

"Questions, questions, questions," Nicholas said. "And they will receive answers. But first, you must see the product!"

They had reached the bottom, and Ravel's eyes had fully adjusted. His mouth moved soundlessly as he stared. A massive room, larger than any basement he could have imagined, cavernous and cluttered. In the center of this room, flanked on all sides by a vast array of computer consoles and fabrication stations, R&D forebays, electrical generators and towers, pumps and tubes and wires and sparks and liquids and flame, squatted *the machine*. Spherical, its door open, its surface smooth and reflective, it rested in a cup-like base carved into the floor. As Ravel watched, his mouth still working silently, giant robotic arms lowered from the ceiling and lifted the spherical machine. Drones hovered nearby; with tiny arms, a trio carried hoses and tubes they inserted through the entrance. Ravel noticed other robot laborers, small but humanoid, bustling from station to station, forebay to forebay, briskly, on time and attentive.

"An army," Ravel whispered, surprised when Nicholas picked up his words and responded.

"No war, I assure you. If we get this right, Chronotrex will end war."

"By going back to the start."

"Perhaps not the very start, but not far off."

"What are they...doing?"

"Perfecting the pressurization of the machine's compartment, the comfort level of the passenger."

"How many can it hold?"

"Just one traveler. For now."

"And you've been inside it. You've used it successfully."

"Already a few times, yes."

Ravel stepped forward, but Nicholas shot his arm out to stop him. "You mustn't get too close," the head of Chronotrex cautioned. "Even if you were to go inside it now, you would be able to go precisely nowhere. To go back and beyond, you need *the portal*."

Ravel, aware of Nicholas's bemused expression, peered past the equipment, machinery and robotics. He scanned only blank solid wall.

"Oh," Nicholas said, "the portal is not here, not in this location, of course. It was discovered elsewhere."

"Discovered?"

"It's what makes it all possible," said Nicholas. "The machine is just the vessel. The portal is the true method of transport." Ravel turned back to Nicholas and found Chronotrex's chief nodding at him intently. "For the portal," Nicholas said, "you will have to be a very special person. Are you a very special person, Ravel Averof?"

"I'd like to think so. But...what would make me special for time travel? Why me?"

"Simple," said Nicholas. "We know you would go back without hesitation."

"You don't want hesitation."

"No. We don't."

"But there's danger. Definite danger."

"There's always danger, Ravel. Everywhere is danger. Every minute of one's life. You have to shrug away the danger. Are you in a position in your life that you can do that?"

Ravel closed his eyes for a moment. Opening them, he spoke: "I am."

"Then we have ourselves an understanding," Nicholas said.

At the front desk, having had the security band removed from his wrist, Ravel lingered over Laney, who was reading a well-worn paperback: *The Order of Time*. Carlo Rovelli.

"Weren't you a history major at MMC?"

"Mathematics and physics double major," she said without looking up. "But close."

"That's a heady read."

"What can I say? I have a big head."

"Have you already gone?" he asked.

Laney looked up. "No. Some of the guys have. The Bowtie Bros, I call them. And Nicholas, of course. I'm surprised you haven't asked what time, what area."

"You do you mean?"

"What time and place you can chrono-trek back to."

"Can't you just go back anywhere in time you want?"

"It doesn't work that way," said Laney. "The wormhole won't allow it."

"Wormhole?"

"The portal, Ravel."

"Ah. So…. When and where does it take you back?"

"We're working on expanding the time frame—and the landing area. But currently we're able to go back to 1980s Colorado."

"Nineteen-eighties Colorado? *That's it?*"

"Hey," Laney snapped. "Don't knock it. Let me know when *you* figure out a way to go back to *any* point in the past, even to a minute ago."

"Sorry. It's just…this is so surreal."

"Understandable. But it's very real. Believe it. You already believe it. And you're okay with it. You want it, just like I remembered you would. That's why you're here, isn't it?"

"Yes."

"Then just believe. We want you to go back in time—"

"To do something. To change something."

"No…"

"You want me to be some patsy. Some change-agent…"

"No and no, Ravel."

"I've gotten that impression, Laney. So, what, you're saying I'm just going to go back in time and, what, enjoy the ride?"

"Pretty much." Laney smiled and held out her hand. "We'll be in touch. Just remember: mum's the word. Remember that paper you signed. We take everything you sign here deadly serious."

Ravel, with so much more on his mind and so much left to say, made the wise move: he tipped his imaginary hat to Laney Greer, turned and exited the lobby.

THREE

That night, ten hours after first setting foot in Chronotrex and seeing Laney and the machine, eight and a half hours after arriving back at work and the grind, and an hour after fighting traffic to reach home, Ravel had dinner with Deborah and her father, Mick.

As they were eating, Ravel couldn't help but focus on the gun. It was there, in his line of sight, riding high on Mick's hip. Ravel had thought many a time in his first four years of marriage of asking Mick, an officer with the Denver Police Department, to not bring his gun into the apartment. Leave it in the car, okay. Or at least not have it loaded, if he absolutely had to wear it. Mick, of course, had to have the gun loaded. As one of the mayor's bodyguards, he never knew when he might get a call.

When it came to his father-in-law, Ravel suffered from doublethink. He admired and loathed Mick's career. The love of that gun. A man who took his gun with him to the bedroom, the shower, the toilet, as if terrorists would barge in on him while he was on the john. Ravel was grateful for and resentful of Mick's support. With Yoana having passed only a few months ago, Spiros everywhere but in Ravel's life, this was what Ravel was left with in the way of family: a hulking mustached monolith and his ivory tower-aspiring daughter who, at least on the surface, bore little resemblance to him. Ravel watched Mick bow to the fork instead of bringing it to his mouth, then he turned to Deborah who was watching him watch her father. Difficult to tell what she was thinking. Ravel smiled at his wife and took a bite.

"Delicious, Debbie," Mick said through his food, bits of which hung from his 'stache. Ravel tried not to look, but it was impossible given where the conversation was going.

"So, have you got through to your agent yet?"

The question was asked in jest. Mick didn't take Ravel's writerly ambitions seriously. No money would ever come of it, the officer thought, but Ravel was saved in his father-in-law's eyes because he'd held down a well-paying job for longer than a lot of Ravel's peers.

Ravel smiled and stared at his plate. He felt his wife's foot brush against his leg.

"Dad. Ravel doesn't have an agent, and even if he did it wouldn't be a sure thing."

"I've read about this business," Mick said. He wiped his mouth with a napkin. "Referrals are where it's at."

Ravel had no doubt that Mick's screenplay, which he'd written with two other officers and which he wouldn't let Ravel read, was true to life, full of gritty, hard-hitting realism and other clichéd adjectives. Deborah, who also had not read the script but had heard about it, had said it was about "three cops who uncover a terrorist plot to release the next pandemic virus here in America's heartland."

"Where? Kansas City?" Ravel had said.

"Topeka. You know how Dad loves that city."

Mick was well aware that Ravel, shortly after finishing his master's degree, had interned unpaid for one of the few literary agencies in Denver, an agency that specialized in screenplays, and so the officer believed that connection, though almost six years old now, would get him and his buddies somewhere fast.

"Sure, but even with a referral," Deborah was saying, "a lot of those projects get turned down. Ravel saw so many when he was working there. How many?"

"A lot," Ravel said without looking up. "And that was just people from Colorado. You should have seen the subs from Kansas, Nebraska, Oklahoma, all over really…"

"All I want," said Mick, "is to know you've gotten through to her."

He was looking directly at Ravel, which meant the son-in-law, the son, had better look directly back.

"I'm close," Ravel said.

"Dad, if you'd let Ravel read this thing then he'd have a better chance of convincing—"

"Maybe I will," said Mick. "Obviously the names, our line of work, all that isn't going anywhere so. What do I have to worry about? Let him see it. Let the work speak for itself, right?"

"Good!" Deborah encouraged.

Ravel was back to eyeing the gun. He had seen it only once disengaged from his father-in-law's body, and that was over two years ago, in the summer of 2020, when Ravel had found himself in the living room of Deborah's family home, staring at the service pistol lying nonchalantly on the nearby kitchen counter. Mick was outside, pushing his rage at his wife's death from Covid into the lawn as he mowed back and forth over the same ground again and again. Cassandra's funeral had been held the day before, and Ravel had seriously considered taking the gun and—and what? using it somehow—but for what? On whom? He wouldn't have used it on himself, and he certainly wouldn't have used it on Mick or anyone else in Ravel's new family. Tristan Boppana's second novel was set to be released that fall, but, unlike Boppana's first novel, there would be no national book tour. The sophomore effort making it onto the *Times* bestseller list would have to suffice. And Ravel, who had no publishable novel, not even the start of one at that time, had seriously considered, deeply thought about, taking that gun, driving from Denver to New York amid the pandemic and—what? He would not have been able to find Tristan Boppana. He would not have been able to make him talk.

The gun shifted before Ravel's eyes, breaking his reverie. "Gotta blow my colon," Mick announced. Deborah's father got up and headed for the head. When the door had closed, husband and wife looked at one another as if it were the virginal wedding night they'd not experienced.

"What are you thinking?" Deborah asked.

"Nothing."

"You can't be thinking of nothing. No one can think of nothing."

"I'll tell you," Ravel said, "later."

After Mick had left for his house in Cherry Creek, Ravel and Deborah did the dishes and retired to the bedroom where they got under the covers. Ravel stared at the ceiling, knowing full well his wife was watching him, knowing also that when she had asked him at the dining table she knew exactly what he was thinking, just as Ravel had known he was lying when he'd answered "Nothing." He had to have been thinking of something, because just the act of trying not to think about anything was in itself *something*. Ravel continued to stare at the ceiling, knowing full well that his concept of nothing had come from a children's book he'd read twenty years earlier. No originality existed. Every idea originated somewhere else. He felt it to be his wife's move now.

"There's no way it's going to happen, is there?"

For a moment Ravel thought Deborah had meant his success as a writer, and if not that then their unborn child waiting for his (or her!) mother to finish her PhD and land a tenure-track teaching position at a four-year university. He soon realized Deborah had meant her father's prospects.

"It's not," he answered. "I'm sorry."

"I just don't think you should've led him on, if you weren't even going to call what's-her-name."

"Maxine. And I *did* call her."

Deborah tightened her mouth and narrowed her eyes. She knew when a lie was afoot.

"I *tried* calling her," Ravel said, exasperated. "Would she have remembered me if I'd gotten through? It's been too long. I was only there for three months, and it was over five years ago! What do you want from me?"

"I want you," Deborah said, placing her hand on Ravel's chest, "to not feel like you have to impress him."

"I'd feel less the need to impress him if he wasn't wearing that gun in our apartment."

"I thought we talked about the gun already."

"Yeah, well, it still bothers me. Just looking at it makes me think, Obey. Do what he asks you. Isn't that the case with you?"

"Not fair, Ravel."

He threw off the covers and got to his feet, unable to look at her.

"Are you going to sulk again?"

"Yes," he said and left the room.

He entered the kitchen and got himself a tall glass of ice water. After quartering a lime, squeezing then dropping one quarter into the glass and taking a sip, he returned to the bedroom, feeling in the mood to apologize. On this way through the living room he paused, his eyes on the main bookcase, the one that contained all the novels. He drew closer to the shelves and scanned row after row. Who would he have been? Who could he have been? For the last three years he'd thought he could be only one writer, the novelist Tristan Boppana—if Ravel had somehow managed to stay with Tristan's wife, all those years back. If they had stayed together, it would have been Ravel—not Tristan—publishing his first novel at age 27, Ravel dedicating that debut to Maggie—not Tristan. Ravel would have gone on the bicoastal book tour that summer, taking in city after city, pampered, promoted, flush with possibility as well as money, reading his novel to enthralled audiences, Maggie watching in the wings. She would have helped Ravel write the novel; she no doubt had helped Tristan. Tristan's debut novel was Ravel's debut novel—could've been his debut novel, would've been his debut novel, if only…

It wasn't even a great novel, Ravel thought. But the

reviews had been warm to ebullient, certainly enough to launch Boppana's sales and therefore his career. Ravel had read most of the novel, skimming only a bit in the middle, feeling on every page that tenuous yet eerily intimate connection to the author. He and Boppana had never met, never exchanged words in any medium, it was almost assured Maggie had never so much as mentioned Ravel to Tristan, but the fact that she bridged both husband and ex-boyfriend was enough for Ravel to feel familiarity.

What wastes in wasted time, thought Ravel.

To go back in time and do it over again. Chronotrex. To go back in time...

He felt Deborah's hands around his waist, her lips on his neck.

"You'll get there," she said, her eyes on the books.

"I don't know."

"You will. We will."

She kissed him on the lips in such a way that he remembered why he'd married her. She had such faith in him—too much faith, Ravel feared. In that she was like his mother.

HE HAD both expected and wanted this: a message in his inbox from Dan, who hadn't been in his cubicle all morning. Ravel sunk in his seat. Today, the eighth of December, certain key managerial types—the hard-edged and harried Victoria, the cross and capable Henry—looked at him differently. They struck Ravel as *more* hard-edged and harried, *more* cross and capable, as if he was their target.

Let's meet now to discuss Chronoflex, Dan's email read.

Meet me at the foot of the stairs, first floor, front entrance side. Now.

The message had just been sent. Ravel could not ignore it. He could not fake having not seen it. He was compelled to go. Now.

Ravel closed out, locked his desktop and left his cubicle. It could go either way. Elements of the message, and the day so far, signaled a firing, but Ravel had been plenty paranoid without cause before. The first floor was where the Window-less Room lived, but it was also the location of the War Room. That Dan was meeting with him just before lunch could mean he was taking Ravel out, or it could mean he was letting Ravel go. As he approached the staircase, Ravel thought, *Dyvaflo. Oxian. Dyvaflo. Oxian.*

Before he was halfway down the stairs, Ravel saw Dan come into view at the foot. Dan smiled. A good sign? Ravel planted both feet on the garishly bright carpet, and Dan's smile dissipated. He asked Ravel to follow him around the corner, past the HR offices, past—Ravel was relieved to see—the Windowless Room, along the wall and then the floor-to-ceiling windows that stretched to the side and looked out on the courtyard where for the past five years Ravel had taken his brown bag or cafeteria lunch as if he were in elementary school. Inside, at their backs, the sales floor—a sweeping, seething pit of head phone-wearing workers busily taking calls, entering orders, and generally rushing around, raising hands, signaling immediate supervisors when help was needed. These sales desk worker bees were the front line in Maguffin-Shrift's war on the Darwinism inherent in capitalism, and Ravel had admired them even as he pitied. They, far more than the sales development associates one floor above, worked their asses off to the bone.

And then Ravel was on the threshold of the War Room itself. It was smaller than he'd imagined, and only Fernando Casillas sat at the circular conference table in the center. No glasses of water or refreshments of any kind, but to Ravel's surprise Fernando looked pleased to see him.

"Rav," Fernando said. "Have a seat, please."

Ravel took a seat across from Fernando and Dan.

"You're a valued member of the Maguffin-Shrift family, Ravel. You have been since you started—how many years ago was it?"

"Five," Fernando said.

"Five," Dan affirmed.

"Over five, actually," Ravel said, after hesitating a moment. "I had my five-year anniversary in September."

"So it's just past that," said Dan. "Wonderful."

"Thank you."

Fernando scratched his ample chin and inspected his stubby fingers before addressing Ravel. "Dan has been supportive of your work, and as long as your cubicle supervisor is supportive of your work, you get no significant problems from me."

Casillas's word choice. Ravel would be fooling himself if he thought 'supportive' was the same—or even similar—to 'positive' or 'enthusiastic' or any number of other reasonable and available adjectives the floor supervisor could have chosen. Something was definitely up.

"...at Maguffin-Shrift," Fernando was saying, "we do ask our employees on occasion to try on new hats, so to speak. This means we may ask you to take on a new role, in a new department, such as the warehouse, say. Now you were in the warehouse..."

Ravel remembered the warehouse well. In the week he'd been asked to provide extra lift to the binning and receiving department, he'd discovered that counting little bits of supply stock was even more mind-numbing than the work he did at his computer in sales development, and he learned that he couldn't count worth a damn—especially not at six in the morning. At least his tenure in the warehouse had lasted only a week.

Out of his memories now, Ravel heard Fernando say, "...sales floor."

"What?"

"We think it's time you try your hat on at the sales desk, on the sales floor," Fernando repeated.

"You mean...out there?"

Fernando looked at Dan, who in turn looked at Ravel, who in turn looked at his superiors with quick-dawning horror at the realization that he was to be transferred. No more sales development. Hello sales desk, sales floor. Sales only. No *development* whatsoever.

"*Why?*"

Dan found the table's surface to be of great interest as he spoke. "You've helped out in sales development, really you have, Ravel. For five years you've been a decent, dependable associate..."

"But you're getting rid of me."

"Not getting rid of you!" Fernando seemed genuinely aghast. "You wouldn't be here if that were the case. It's just that Dan and I feel it's time to give you a little more exposure..."

Exposed, Ravel thought. *They want me exposed. What I do. What I really want.*

"Starting tomorrow," said Dan.

"Tomorrow? The sales floor?" Ravel wanted to wipe Fernando's grin with a dirty mop.

"Believe me, Rav," said Fernando, "you've got nothing to worry about."

"And what if—" Here Ravel paused, debating whether to proceed. He had to. His life, his past, he realized, had been leading to this day. He'd been fooling himself—for five years and far longer he'd been fooling himself. "What if I choose not to transfer?" he finished.

An electrical current seemed to jolt both upper-crusts. When Fernando spoke next the shield of his pretense had cracked. "Then I would have the unpleasant task of informing you that we would no longer have a place for you at Maguffin-Shrift."

"I understand," Ravel said reflexively. "Then I'll be on the floor tomorrow."

BACK AT HIS DESK, Ravel felt as he had many times in the past five years. At the seven month marker, the one year marker, the sixteen month marker, the two year marker, he'd felt it, and each time he'd told himself It's not right, what I'm feeling, what I'm thinking, not right at all. In this country, in this economy, this job market, with an ivory-tower-seeking spouse and two cars to support, don't even think it. He couldn't not think it, of course—but he never acted on it. There had always been the year-end bonus to look forward to, pleasantly compounded after three years of service by the start of the profit-sharing plan. There had always been the year-end Christmas party at some swanky downtown hotel, the new faces, the fresh recruits helping to dull the memories of those employees fired over the course of the year. There had been the possibility of friendships, of promotion, the excitement of wondering who was going to take that vacant desk, that empty cubicle. There had been the cafeteria discount, the bad-mouthing and jokes at the higher-ups' expense. There had been all of that and more, so much more, and Ravel was going to miss it, he had moved his mind to missing it, because that mind was made up.

He lowered his head and listened to the message again.

"Hi, Ravel. It's Laney. Hey, we'd like to speed up the process. Nicholas is insistent. We figure you'd want to get things moving soon too. Sorry if this is all pretty creepy. It is. But out of all the professors I had..."

Ravel closed his eyes and bent his head to listen more acutely.

"...you were the one that stood out. Why? Because you were a human being. You seemed, well, scared. Scared of being in that room with us, like you didn't want to be there. And you probably didn't. But you really did teach me things no one else would about books, about emotions, I guess. And I just remember all the grief you expressed in your office over where you'd ended up. Now I'm not saying you can change things to exactly where you want them to be, but there's at least—anyway, I'm going to say too much. Give me a call."

Before his impulses could get the better of him, Ravel turned his phone over and placed it face-down on his desk. Not yet. Dan was at his desk, typing furiously. Ravel recalled the look and feel of the resignation letter he'd been composing in his mind since month seven of the job that he'd never once thought of as his career. The words came fast and lucid. It was the sharpest, quite possibly the greatest, page he'd ever written.

ATTN.: DAN FLECK, SUPERVISOR OF SALES DEVELOPMENT

COLORADO (LOCAL) TERRITORY

MAGUFFIN-SHRIFT DISTRIBUTION

DEAR MR. FLECK:

I AM WRITING TO INFORM YOU THAT TODAY WILL BE MY LAST DAY OF EMPLOYMENT AT MAGUFFIN-SHRIFT. AS WE HAVE AN OFFER OF AT-WILL EMPLOYMENT, I AM CHOOSING TO LEAVE NOW WITHOUT ADVANCE NOTICE.

I HAVE ENJOYED MY TIME HERE UNDER YOUR SUPERVISION, AND I THANK YOU FOR ALL YOU HAVE TAUGHT ME OVER THE YEARS. I NOW FIND, HOWEVER, THAT I HAVE AN OPPORTUNITY THAT IS MORE IN LINE WITH MY LONG-TERM GOALS.

I WISH YOU AND YOUR COMPANY THE BEST OF LUCK IN ALL THAT LIES AHEAD.

SINCERELY,

RAVEL AVEROF

Ravel unbuttoned the top of his shirt. His fingers moved to his sternum to touch the amulet. If he could have been assured of not being seen, he would have kissed this memory of his mother at that moment. Instead, he looked to make sure no one was at the printer at the front of the pod of cubicles. Seeing no one there, and assured that no employees were on their way to inadvertently pick up the letter that would have just been printed out, Ravel hit the print option on his document and listened as seconds later the printer whirred to life. He got up from his desk, left his cubicle, not looking at anyone. His focus was on the printer. Without anyone interfering, Ravel retrieved the two copies and returned to his cubicle. As he passed the pod's middle section he saw Dan glance up. Ravel shifted his gaze straight ahead. The two pages were folded over slightly, their contents facing their author's stomach. When he'd reseated himself, Ravel took one of the copies, folded it in half and placed it in his document folder. He then read the other copy over. Finding it satisfactory, better than expected, he signed above his printed name, got up again and, his head hammering with anticipation, turned the pod's corner to stand at Dan's cubicle. It was happening. He handed the letter to Dan, who took it with pika ears attuned and eyebrows raised. Ravel smiled. He had rarely been happier. He was quitting. He was quitting to save the idea of himself—not just his mental state and his emotional health but the *idea* of himself, of what he could've been and what he still could be.

Outside, headed to his car, he felt light-headed yet relieved. He could breathe again. The intermittent sun warmed him. Reaching his vehicle, he put on his sunglasses and took out his phone. He knew even before he put the phone to his ear that whatever was going to happen wasn't going to happen today. He had to be *somewhat* realistic. She picked up on the third buzz.

"Hello?"

"Laney. It's Ravel. Professor."

"Oh hey. Thanks for calling back. So..."

"I..." As he was about to say more, Ravel thought better of it and shut his mouth. He would not reveal he was no longer employed at Maguffin-Shrift. In due time, he would. It would do no good to be honest at this time, the rupture still so raw. Instead, Ravel asked what was up.

"Let's meet."

"We've...met?"

"No, I mean I'll show you it."

"What?"

"The *portal*, Ravel. Head west out of Boulder on the 119 into the foothills, and you'll see a turnoff for the Rambis Plateau. That's the place. The place where it happens."

"Ah. I—"

"Are you free this Saturday?"

Deborah would once again be holed up at the DU library for most of the day. Researching. Compiling. Writing. Ravel told Laney that yes, he would be free Saturday. They arranged to meet at Rambis Plateau at nine o'clock in the morning.

DEBORAH WAS HOME when he arrived. The usual stack of notepads and books surrounded her on either side of the dining table, never to be cleared off. The material had become a member of the family, Deborah's child, but Ravel too felt responsible for its well-being. Her success would be his success. He felt the effects of watching his wife work night after night, secretly in awe and fear of what she was doing, what she had done and what she was likely to do. Outwork him. Surpass him. Deborah's drive, her motivation, shamed Ravel. He lay awake at night thinking of what it means to be committed to something, dedicated to someone. He saw Deborah publishing articles in preeminent journals in the field, then going on to greater work. Books. Perhaps *she* would become the bestselling author. He pictured her signing books, growing her fan base, widening her literary circle. He had been so smugly confident they would end up the same, equal in their failure. And yet Deborah had fought. She'd taken a step back, assessed her strengths and weaknesses, what she really wanted out of a PhD program, and realized she had to pursue her true interests if she was ever to be fulfilled.

At the moment she was on her phone. Ravel placed his work folder on a corner of the table. He watched Deborah for a time. His eyes flitted to her laptop, all those pages and pages of words on the screen. At last she looked up and asked how his day had been.

Ravel hesitated. Not yet. Now was not the time. "Fine," he said. "Same as always."

Her gaze lingered on him. Was it pity he saw behind her eyes? He did not want to be pitied; that was not why he'd married her. To be fair, he had done his share of judging her over the years, his scorn of the ivory tower and the perceived mad quest of securing a career in academia. Ravel had toned down his disapproval significantly in recent months, as Deborah entered the all-but-dissertation phase of her doctorate, and a few times he'd even offered up an apology for his past demeanor. Deborah had dodged these expressions of regret, which made Ravel feel even more like a heel.

In a couple years (or longer) their guest room would be transformed into the baby's room, and he would delete those jejune stabs at stories, that half-written screenplay, the opening of *Your Great American Novel*. He would erase from his files if not his memory all record of his attempt to make it as an author.

It was the wrong past—his past. That was the problem. He needed another's past.

He stood in front of the bookshelf again, all too aware he needed to start dinner. He lingered on certain titles, certain names. As always he took notice of the spot in between two novels where Tristan Boppana's should have been, and then the spot where his would never be.

Or would it? Was it in fact possible? Certain names, titles now seemed to speak to him, his friends, saying, Me. Pick me, Ravel. He did not realize he was smiling. He had his pick, and for the first time in over five years, Ravel Averof believed he had power.

Four

Laney had been surprised by men before, but Professor A, Ravel, falling in so readily with Chronotrex's forward momentum had to be the most significant recent surprise in her twenty-four years. Up until this point the number of naïve, desperate citizens to find out about the company's machine and prostrate themselves before Nicholas, willing to do anything to take a trip, was precisely zero. Ravel, none the wiser, had broken ground. Nicholas agreed: the tall, lanky sales development associate at Maguffin-Shrift was their guy. "Charm him," Nicholas had told his employee. "Charm all fear out of him. Make him ours." Laney's past with Ravel led her to feel some small degree of guilt over what was about to occur, but she reasoned that Chronotrex was helping Ravel even more than he was helping Chronotrex. She knew her former professor wasn't happy, still wasn't happy after five years; Chronotrex would at least make him hopeful and perhaps happy, if only for a brief time. Now that Ravel was standing next to her on the Rambis Plateau, the wind whipping what was left of his hair back off his forehead, Laney felt no shame in what she was doing. She told herself she would be as up front with him as possible without scaring him off.

The sun was out, and the cold was tolerable. Through sunglasses Ravel scanned the terrain. He cleared his throat. "What did you mean when you said this is where it happens?"

"Just that," Laney said. "This is where we go back in time."

"Because this is where the portal is. The wormhole."

"That's right. Nicholas discovered it while camping here in the summer of 2020, when escaping from the city and every single person was the right idea."

"So where is it?"

"In the ground. I'll show you."

Laney headed off but stopped to catch Ravel staring at her.

This is crazy, he thought. He should return to his car and leave right now, this very moment, drive to DU and enter Deborah's cave in the university library, where he would come clean to his wife. He no longer had the means of supporting her at the time she needed support the most. To take a chance, though, to take just one chance for himself and see where it leads.... The temptation was too great. For an hour this morning, Laney would remind him of what he was—a failure, true, but when he last spoke to her he had been a younger, more alive and hopeful failure.

"Show me," said Ravel. "This just seems so impossible."

"I thought the same," Laney said. "But it works. Nicholas is a genius, the Bowtie Bros not quite on his level, but they're up there."

"And they developed the..."

"The Chronoquantumogriphier."

"That's a mouthful."

"I know. I didn't like it at first either. But say it enough times and it sticks."

"Look." The strength in Ravel's voice stopped Laney in her tracks. "You gotta explain how this works. If I'm going to do it, I mean. If it's a wormhole, like you say, wouldn't the wormhole just collapse or something? I read somewhere they collapse."

"This one doesn't."

"And it's in the *ground*?"

Laney laughed. "There's no reason why a wormhole couldn't be in the ground. This one happens to be. We can thank the aliens for that."

Off Ravel's blank stare, she continued. "You know those six-foot tall metal monoliths that started appearing during the pandemic, around the U.S.?"

"Oh yeah, I saw a picture of one."

"Do *you* know who left them?

"Um..."

"No one does, Ravel. We've determined this wormhole you're about to see formed around 1980."

"Nineteen-eighty?"

"Maybe '81. There are no reports of any strange sightings from that time, but that's not to say they didn't arrive and leave behind their mark with no one noticing. Here..."

Laney indicated the vast rocky terrain. "It's not easy to see right now," she said, "with the ice and snow covering most of the ground, so I'll show you some pics." She brought up her phone and scrolled past several photos until she landed on the ones she was willing to show Ravel, who leaned in.

"These were taken in September."

What Ravel saw on Laney's phone were a series of images depicting the Rambis Plateau in daylight, free from snow and ice. The images were taken from the sky; nearly the entire plateau had been captured. In the center of the plateau were a series of concentric circles carved into the ground, all leading to a central point. Strange symbols had also been carved around the circles' outer perimeter, and rocks had been arranged in odd shapes.

"It's been like that for four decades and no one noticed?"

"We doubt four decades. These flourishes were probably added in the last couple of years, during the pandemic. And since then Nicholas and the Bros have been working on the state of Colorado to secure the land. Make this area ours."

"Will the state actually sell?"

"If you know the right wheels to grease, yes. But a successful purchase is going to make Chronotrex's finances precarious.... He doesn't see the long game, financially and otherwise. Nicholas really is brilliant. The degrees, the awards, the publications.... But he has very little sense of how to run a company."

"Too bad. Look. Couldn't all this you're showing me be human-made? Like just a joke people left?"

"If it were," Laney countered, "the Chronoquantumogriphier wouldn't be able to do what it does. This spot, the center of those circles and all those symbols carved into the ground, and the stones all around in those shapes.... All that leads to the wormhole. When our machine is placed in that center there, it all comes together, and we can go back to any point from roughly 1981 to 1989."

"But only here in Colorado."

"We're working on expanding the Chronoquantumogri-phier's range through DOG."

"A dog?"

"Not *a* dog. *DOG.* D-O-G. Stands for Dimensional Otherworldly Guide. It's an AI system embedded in the Chronoquantumogriphier that makes the chrono-trek truly possible. Without DOG, you'd just be lost, never to return."

"What a comforting thought." Ravel took a deep breath and focused on what he assumed was the central point of the concentric circles, hidden under the snow. "How does it work? Do you just bring the Chronoquanto...uh..."

"Chronoquantumogriphier."

"Chronoquantumogriphier here and then it's all systems go from that spot over there?"

"We're obviously not going to bring out the Chronoquan-tumogriphier in broad daylight, with the chance of people seeing it. We're daring, Ravel, but we're not stupid."

"Of course. So..."

"So we bring it here at night, in the dead of night, when no one is around. Just us and these weird circles and symbols and stone formations. We uncover the entry point, drop the Chronoquantumogriphier in the ground and send whoever's going on their way."

"Simple as that."

"Not at all simple, Ravel." She handed him a pamphlet. Ravel opened it and began reading. All three sides were chock-a-block with text.

"Very informative," Ravel muttered.

"I could use your help with the writing and the layout," Laney said. "It's wordy, I know. I need to make it user-friendly."

In the pamphlet's pages the limits of time travel in the Chronoquantumogriphier were spelled out. Nothing too draconian, but rules existed that must be obeyed. It was impossible to be entirely free from all germs, bacteria, microbes when traveling to the past, but the chrono-trekker was nevertheless required to undergo an intense cleansing process with Chronotrex's very own 'debugger' before entering the Chronoquantumogriphier. The second rule: the traveler must agree to dress and look the part of the target time. Through a partnership with a prop company in Arvada, Chronotrex will aid in the appropriate clothing, hairstyle, eyewear (if needed), and all other accessories that will convince the actual people of the time traveled to that the traveler not only belongs there but has always been there. The third rule: to expand on the second point, the traveler must agree to take a crash—but thorough—course in the language, culture, history and people of the period being visited. The time traveler must always be sensitive to the surroundings—

At this point, Ravel stopped. "I thought this thing only went back to Colorado in the '80s. Sounds like this is for any time period, anywhere."

"This is for the future, Ravel. The future. I have dreams too, you know. Big hopes..."

Rule four: the traveler must agree not to stay longer than a time frame specified by Chronotrex. For safety reasons, Laney explained. "We don't want you *living there*," she added.

"Just passing through. A visitor," Ravel said.

"A *chrono-trekker*. Some of the Bros are trying to push for a twenty-four hour, one-day option, or longer, but Nicholas is holding firm."

The remaining rules: (5) the traveler must agree to not

take any physical item back from the period visited; (6) not reveal anything about the traveler's native time period when in the time period visited (this also goes for revealing anything about any time period that occurs after the time period visited); (7) not intentionally change the past in any way, no matter how supposedly insignificant. (8) Finally—and a point that was repeated several times at different places in the pamphlet—the chrono-trekker understands completely the risks taken by going back in time!

Ravel folded up the pamphlet and handed it back to Laney. "Unbelievable," he said. "But, you know, I'll believe it, for now."

"I thought you would. Kill those doubts about the possibility of time travel. It *is* possible. Hawking, despite the problems he has with the idea of traveling to the past, believes ultimately that the arrow of time emerges in the macro world, almost magically. Where does it come from, if it doesn't come from the particles we're built from? Hawking struggles with this idea that quantum mechanics doesn't care about forward or backward in time—time doesn't really mean anything to a particle—but somehow that arrow of time presents itself. Hawking's argument against time travel into the past is a philosophical, not a scientific one. Other scientists don't have the same opinion about traveling to the past. Einstein's general relativity ostensibly allows for it."

"Well if it's good enough for Einstein," said Ravel.

"Don't mock, Professor. I'm trying to teach you something. Put you at ease."

"I'm good on lectures, Laney. That really was the only one I needed. I do need to know something."

"What's that?"

"When I go back, if I go back, you don't want me to change anything."

"No. You're just observing this first time around."

"That means in the future…"

"In the future, Ravel, if it's safe, we'll see."

"Even though it says here I can't 'intentionally change the past in any way, no matter how supposedly insignificant'?"

"If it's Chronotrex-sanctioned…maybe."

Holy shit, thought Ravel. *This is it. My way in. My way in through a way out.* Aloud he said, "There's not going to be some kind of, I don't know, butterfly effect or something, right? Like if I throw a rock and hit something or someone in the past, it changes the future."

Again Laney laughed a little as she shook her head. "Why you'd want to throw a rock at someone is beyond me. But ease up a bit, Ravel. You have to be able to step on grass. You have to be able to breathe air, cough, climb steps, move around. Touch things. Speak to people. You have to allow yourself to *live* when you're in the past, even if it's only for a brief time."

"But is it true, the butterfly effect? I'm just curious."

Laney bare-handed a sizable rock and threw it at a patch of nearby ice. The first rock caused a crack, the second broke through, revealing water, a stream. Ravel dug his fists deeper into his coat's pockets. The wind had whipped up and the cold bit hard now, and Ravel had to wonder if this conversation wasn't in fact some sort of endurance test.

"You think that rock I just threw could have changed the future."

"Do you think it did?"

"Obviously there are limits," said Laney. "Rules. You certainly can't go back and meet your past self, even so much as be in the same dimension with them. That could...that could be very bad."

"I imagine it would be."

"Nicholas doesn't think much of the so-called 'butterfly effect.' I think there's some truth to it. I don't think a rock thrown when it hadn't been thrown before is going to cause future chaos. Make the space-time continuum go haywire. But if a chrono-trekker did something really big, something momentous, super-eventful.... Well then, it could do untold things, I think. Open up dimensions, alternate realities the chrono-trekker isn't prepared for."

"So I'm just hanging out. A voyeur."

"You're a fly on the wall, Ravel. This first time."

"You keep mentioning this is the first time. That means there'll be a second."

"If you work out, as I believe you will, then yes."

"And on the second time around, I could...do something?"

Laney looked Ravel over, as if he were hiding something. "We'll cross that bridge when we get to it, Professor," she said at last. "Oh. I should mention I'm starting my PhD in astrophysics at CU Boulder next fall."

"Oh shit. No shit. Congratulations, Laney!"

"You don't know this but I left MMC not long after you. I transferred to CU. Much much better math and physics programs. Anyway, do you have a time and place in mind at all?"

"For when I travel back? Well, I'm limited," said Ravel. "Anytime in the eighties in Colorado only?"

"For now. Don't think of it like that, though. Go for the experience of being in a time you never experienced, you never breathed—but it's all real. Actually real, not a movie, not a VR headset or Google glasses or any of that. It's a door opened onto the past that now exists in concrete space with all the accompanying sensory material that goes with it."

For the first time since nine that morning, Ravel turned to fully face his former student. "I put myself entirely in your hands."

"Don't put it that way, Professor."

"I hope it's not too gauche of me to ask about payment..."

"We're not paying you to do this, Ravel. The experience is payment enough."

"But will I be paying you?"

"Oh no," Laney exclaimed. "Absolutely not! We tapped you. It's our treat."

"Great. Because I should tell you.... Uh, I quit my job. Two days ago."

Laney folded her arms. "Oh," she said.

"I hope that's not a deal breaker."

"Why would it be? You're a real funny bunny, Ravel."

"Obviously you can still order parts from Maguffin-Shrift," Ravel said. "I just won't be there."

Within seconds Laney's bemused expression had returned to her formerly pensive demeanor. In the distance they could hear vehicles traveling past on the 119.

"This is where I accepted the job, if you can believe it," Laney said. "It was summer so I could see everything here, all the signs, all the markings. And it was the first year of the pandemic, and there was no one, just me. Nicholas told me to go here. He wanted me to see it for myself. He said he'd call with an offer. About thirty minutes after I got here, he did."

"You don't sound happy."

"I'm not."

"Is it because of him?"

"Largely. He wants to take Chronotrex in the wrong direction."

"How so?"

"Government. Military."

"He mentioned something about that, during the tour. Something about Chronotrex ending all war."

Laney hesitated before speaking. "Nicholas is thinking Chronotrex would best serve the country by partnering with the military."

"So time travel could be used as a, what, *a weapon*?"

"Yes. The weaponization of time travel."

"Wouldn't that be risky? Talk about going into the unknown."

"Risks don't concern Nicholas and the Bowtie Bros. Risk is what keeps them alive."

"But..." Ravel thought hard. "But using time travel as a weapon, that would, I think, destroy the world."

"Upend history," Laney said. "And the future. Intentional and unintentional consequences. Absolute chaos."

"Still," Ravel said, "you could cheat Fate."

"Do you believe in Fate?"

"I do. It's my Greek blood, I guess."

"What's that Greek word, the one where the person in a high position of power doesn't see the truth and remains ignorant—"

"Hubris."

"Hubris. That's what Nicholas has."

"And you're hoping to change him. With my help?"

"If I can. Not sure about you helping. Yet."

"Are you..." Ravel bit his lower lip and then went for it. "Are you seeing him?"

"Dating my boss? That's forward, Professor."

"Sorry if that's...but I've gathered—"

"We're only together in the work and the family sense. We're related by blood."

"Seriously?"

"Nicholas is my cousin on my father's side. My uncle's son."

"So he's French-African-American."

"My uncle went to France, fell in love with a woman from Ghana who'd emigrated to Paris when she was little, married her, and Nicholas is the result. That's hilarious you thought we were having sex."

"Um..."

"We're close, just not in that way. Nicholas is kind of all I have left. It's complicated."

"I bet."

"Nicholas is never going to fire me. He knows he needs me. But he can't admit that I know more than his bros about mathematics, astrophysics, quantum cosmology..."

"You do?"

"Damn, Ravel. Don't look so shocked. I'm not some dumb MMC blonde."

"No no, of course you're not. I just..."

"You just never bothered to get to know me, or any of your students, when you were teaching us."

Ravel felt heat rise in his cheeks. Conceding the point, he looked away. "I was pretty bad, wasn't I?"

"For me, you were fine. You *did* talk a lot about yourself when I visited you during office hours. But the other girls, they would shit-talk you to no end. I defended you! I tried to get them to see you were in your first year teaching and they should give you a break."

"Thanks."

"I'm surprised you're not teaching now," Laney said.

"I saw what it did to my mother," Ravel said. "And in turn what it did to me, having a teacher for a mother."

"I'm sorry."

"Don't be. I'm the one who's sorry when it comes to my mom. *That's* complicated. And I'm sorry I never knew you, and underestimated you, and, yeah, stereotyped you."

"Hey," Laney said. "Chill, dude. You let guilt get to you way too easily."

Ravel knew she was right, and yet despite feeling a sudden lightness in his chest, as if it had been cleaned out to make room for something new, he also felt a sterility, an airlessness that terrified him.

Ravel listened as Laney told him that all the men she had known, if she had ever really known any of them, had sorely underestimated her. They had held her down or kept her back, and that when she moved from Fort Collins to Boulder for the job at Chronotrex, she thought Nicholas would be different. She thought: Boulder, People's Republic, progressive, different than what she'd put up with at Mothers of the Merciful, and besides, Nicholas was family. He'd wanted her to interview, which at the time struck her as a sign of respect and only later as an insult. Why did she have to interview? Simply because her cousin had never seen her? And when he did see her, approve of her and all but give her the job, what did he do? Instead of sitting her down in his office and going over the specifics so that she could have a chance of negotiating, he sent her off to the Rambis Plateau. Nicholas knew Laney was having trouble finding a job; she had graduated at a terrible time, with the pandemic in full swing. The salary he offered put his cousin just above the poverty line. Laney wasn't surprised; when it came to women, this had always been her family's way.

"I got into MIT," Laney said, her voice quaking. "No way my parents were paying for that. Why acknowledge your daughter is brilliant in math and science, a budding physicist, an engineer, when you can send her to an all-girls Catholic college? It was always about the Mrs. degree, you know. And when I didn't marry my ex it was like, We want nothing to do with you."

Ravel recalled that day in class, at MMC, when he'd played Ani DeFranco's "New Foundations in Manhattan" in the wake of the 2016 election. Only one of his students had commented on the song: Laney, who had said, "I had no idea a woman could express herself like that." The comment had stuck with him all these years.

Laney tossed another stone. More ice shattered to reveal more of the stream. "I'm the best of them all at what they're doing, even Nicholas," she said. "I have ideas, blueprints, schematics, formulas they would kill for. I know DOG inside-out, and how to improve it. "

"Then break away," Ravel said. "Form your own company."

"That's the dream," said Laney. "A dream stalled. If I'm going to be stuck, I figure I might as well be stuck in the past, literally, physically. When I go back in the machine, whenever that'll be, maybe I just won't come back."

"That's scary. You'll come back."

"And you would? The way you talk about your…literary thing, I think you'd rather stay back there instead too. Why not hang out with the greats? You could get your voice heard then, way louder than now."

"You're suggesting we break one or more of your time travel rules."

"It's just talk," Laney said. "We can't, because of what would happen."

"But we don't know what would happen."

"When you go, Ravel, and we've got it to the point where we can push past the confines of the continuum and you can go back to most anywhere and anytime, you're going back for inspiration, to be around at least one great author and be inspired. That's all it should be."

"Of course," said Ravel. A stone could be tossed into the stream so that a minor ripple would undulate. To the unaware this stone, this ripple, was insignificant, but to Ravel it would work as a dam redirects a river. He had to drop that stone. He did not yet have it in his hand, but the sooner he got to work the sooner he would hold it. He checked his phone.

"You're sure you're ready," Laney said.

"Soon. Very soon."

"It's just a test run, remember. Nothing earth shattering." Laney looked at him, and in her look Ravel knew she hadn't meant the chrono-trek only. He watched her get into her jeep and pull out of the lot. For a while longer he stood facing the plateau. His gaze took in the symbols and circles. He was ready, he figured. He had to be.

DEBORAH WAS SETTING the table for four when Ravel walked in and set his satchel down. He noticed her dress: tasteful, not too much, it had been a gift on their last anniversary. *Four years. I've been married four years.* But then so had Tristan and Maggie Boppana. So had Spiros and Yoana Averof —four years before they divorced and Ravel's mother returned to her maiden name. Watching Deborah then, unable to deny that she was beautiful in that dress and in everything he had chosen for her and almost everything she had chosen for herself, Ravel understood how and why he had been married to her for this long. But another four, when he had nothing to show for his own aspirations? That's where his confidence mucked up.

They kissed and she finished setting the table while he poured them both glasses of white wine from the fridge. It was an important night, a night that could determine Deborah's future in the ivory tower. Her advisor and his wife would be dining at La Casa de Averof y Parker, and Ravel would have to be on his best behavior.

"Please stay at the table and talk this time, Rav. I promise I'll bring you into the conversation as much as possible. No hiding out in the office."

"You got it."

"Thank you." She clinked his glass. "To finishing this damn dissertation."

"To finishing it."

She leaned into him, and this time they kissed more deeply. One of his hands roamed down her back. He did like this dress on her.

"How was your hike?" she said.

This time he did not hesitate. "Good. I didn't go too far, just up into the foothills. Went a few miles."

When he and his mother were living together in the house in the San Diego Country Gems, Yoana would sometimes tell Ravel he wasn't a good liar. He believed her then, but he vowed to improve. He didn't improve—in fact, Ravel only turned more truthful as he aged. Yet this latest lie had slipped out effortlessly. *Perhaps*, Ravel thought, *it's Laney, and Chronotrex, something different, a new path.* This evening he had meant to tell Deborah he had quit his job, and that instead of hiking solo he had met up with a former student of his—a former and attractive female student of his—in a place where an honest-to-goodness time machine was used with great success. Tomorrow he would tell his wife the truth. Or the day after that he would tell her. And if he didn't, if he never did, he could get away with it, so long as the unemployment he'd applied for came through. With money deposited every two weeks, Ravel would be able to keep up the façade. And if his unemployment claim was denied, well, maybe Ravel would have to use the Chrono-quantomogriphier in ways he hadn't planned.

Less than half an hour later he was seated beside Deborah listening to his wife's advisor and the advisor's wife take turns talking about their travels to Guatemala, what they'd discovered in the way of indigenous folklore and customs. Ravel smiled and nodded. Then he felt the sudden urge to urinate. He excused himself and quick-walked down the hall. He made it to the toilet in time, but after zipping up he was shocked to feel the urge overtake him again, and his bladder let loose with what remained. "What the..." Ravel muttered. He stood before the bathroom mirror, a sizable dark spot soaked through his khakis. Even though he'd sensed the second urge before it hit, he'd been unable to stop it. *Must be an explanation*, Ravel thought. *My sphincter? Connected to my thirst?* He had guzzled close to two gallons of water over the course of the day, an unusual amount given he'd kept his sodium intake low and resisted exercise.

He returned to the table dressed in a fresh pair of khakis, and no one noticed the change. Deborah reached out and squeezed his thigh under the table. Her hand went down the inside of his thigh, where it stayed. For a moment Ravel tensed up. He had nothing to worry about now, he realized. His bladder had to be empty. He relaxed. He loved her. He didn't want to hurt her. But Ravel thought, instead of having attended grad school, he should've worked on a boat, or the docks, or been a train conductor, or picked cranberries in Maine, or patrolled the border in New Mexico, or led visitors on a tour of a National Park, or performed as a clown on a cruise ship, or bartended in Tahiti, or taught English overseas as Deborah had done, or, or, or, or.

FIVE

Again he was in the bookstore of his novel, *Your Great American Novel*. It could have been any bookstore; they were unanimous in their struggle to survive now. The same layout, with the better-selling books—the mass market fiction and the how-to-guides and the YA and the self-help tomes and the celebrity memoirs and cookbooks—in the center of the store, round tables and front-facing displays within easy reach of the toys and games and tchotchkes, while the literature and languages and reference books loomed in the back, watching with misty eyes.

In his pocket he fingered his phone. Around and around he turned the device, as if that would will Colorado's unemployment department to call. It had been three days since he'd filed his claim, described the incident that led to his leaving and why he felt he deserved to keep receiving paychecks, and since today was the Friday before New Year's weekend, Ravel was ready to ring in 2023 with some good news.

He stood not in the literature section with all the copies of Tristan Boppana's first two novels, or all his father's many muscular offerings. He stood in the poetry section, so slim, so sad, like the volumes it contained. Ravel was looking for even just one of his mother's books, expecting to find what he always found in these cookie-cutter bookstores: nothing in the way of any book written by a late-fifties Bulgarian émigré, certainly not a late-fifties Bulgarian émigré by the name of Yoana Kopecka. Ravel scanned and scanned, and he saw to his surprise a binding as thin as a straw bearing his mother's name. They had one! They had one of Yoana's books! Still not believing, forgetting his phone and the possibility of an imminent call, Ravel slid out the volume of poetry, *On the Threshold of Acceptance*, and admired the cover as only the poet's son could. A khaki-colored over, with the title and author's name enclosed in a border toward the top. Nothing else of note. No images, no blurbs. Just her. His mother. Ravel felt his pulse quicken as he flipped through the seventy or so pages. To think, this big-box bookstore in Lone Tree had his mother's work. The independent stores in Denver couldn't claim that, and he had checked so often. Ravel turned his mother's book over. His eyes jumped from the price of the book—fair, in his opinion—to his mother's author photo. In it Yoana, long gray hair swept back, bangs off her accusatory eyes, stared directly at the camera, her head tilted to one side as if she had a question. Ravel remembered the day that photo was taken. His mother had returned to the house in the Country Gems tired and irritable. Her son, who had flown to San Diego the day before, was waiting at the kitchen table. When he saw her come through the front door Ravel asked how it had gone, and Yoana replied by saying she shouldn't have done it.

"Should've let me drive you, Mom," Ravel had said, his

concern laid bare. "To go from teaching to a photo shoot.... Couldn't they have done it over the weekend?"

"I'm not exhausted, Ravel," Yoana said. "I'm sad. I am sad."

He watched her go to the fridge and take out an already open bottle of sparkling water. Yoana took a swig from the bottle while observing her son as if he were a stranger. In that moment Ravel considered the possibility that when his mother had said she shouldn't have done it, she hadn't meant the author photo shoot. Her movements, even the swigging, had slowed considerably since the last time he'd seen her. She appeared to have aged several years in the past few months. More than that: she was even thinner now, closer to a skeletal state. *Covid?* Ravel thought. *Can't be Covid. She got the vaccine.... Teaching then. Always that damn teaching.*

Looking at her, Ravel wanted to say, I can't keep doing this, Mom. I can't keep flying out here thinking you need help, thinking you're sick, and then you say you don't need help, you're not sick and you wonder why I'm even here. Instead he came out with "I'm just still upset they didn't drive out here and take it. They could've taken it in the backyard. Done you a favor."

"I am not an invalid, Ravel, not an old woman, yet," Yoana chided. "We all know I can drive there easy. They would never come to Anomar. They never have come to this little town. Such a drive from the city. And with the pandemic, it makes sense I go there."

"The pandemic is pretty much over, Mom. The vaccine's been available for months now."

"Ah. You really think so?"

"You've done *them* a favor by giving them your book to

publish. I just don't think you should do so much all the time. It's not like the publisher's giving you an insanely huge advance or anything."

His mother laughed. "Or any advance."

"Exactly. The least they could have—"

"*Ravel*," Yoana admonished. "Stop. It is over. It's the past now. You know I like my photographer. He's taken all my author pictures."

Yeah, all three of them, Ravel thought. That day the word *cancer* had not occurred to him. It would not occur to him until it was a reality five months later, when his mother was diagnosed as having less than that to live.

"He put it there, Mom."

"He what? Who?"

They were at the hospital then, waiting for the doctor to return. Ravel had once more flown out, this time for the end of their story.

"Spiros."

"Spiros..."

Yoana remained stretched out on the examining room table, her eyes closed, her hair disheveled, her body all but bones now. In those five months she hadn't described any of this wasting away to her son. None of it, and Ravel was sick with frustration and helplessness. He opened his mouth to speak but thought better and closed it. It was Dad, Mom, he wanted to say. Dad did this to you. You haven't lived with him in twenty-eight years and you're still smoking, even though I keep telling you.... I know Spiros didn't start you smoking when you were at the university together in Sofia, but he kept you going, that and the drugs, he introduced you to those, didn't he?

Ravel was certain Spiros's decision to abandon his toddler son had driven Yoana not only to seek a divorce but to smoke more cigarettes than she had before she'd met him. During those years, the nineties, the aughts in Anomar, the house in the San Diego Country Gems, Yoana's awareness of her ex-husband's success coupled with her difficulties getting published caused her to destroy her liver as well as her lungs.

Ravel was keenly aware of how much his mother, a single woman, a woman who spoke English only moderately well, struggled to raise her young son away from the city and all it had to offer. Inland San Diego North County. What friends Yoana did have at Anomar High School where she taught (German, not English literature as she had hoped) viewed her as an oddity, best to invite sparingly, and so how else was she expected to calm her nerves, face the blank page and her ex-husband's sky-rocketing success? Her son could play his video games—and play them he did; they were his form of entertainment and friendship. She never involved her son in her pain, Ravel was ashamed to admit. He had no idea just how much pain his mother had been in until she was nearly dead from it. Refusing to return to the hospital down the hill, her hair falling out as she lay on her back in bed, Yoana showed her son the pain he had always thought was fiction. And when she died in that house in Anomar, the San Diego Country Gems, he was ashamed she had not smoked around him, always taking her cigarettes outside instead. He was ashamed she had not drunk in front of him. He was ashamed she had not lashed out verbally or physically, had not struck him when he'd misbehaved. If she had he would have known, and he would have felt true pain too. With her death the insulation disintegrated, and Ravel could blame only himself and his father. He could only go on what little Yoana had told him about her marriage, Ravel's father's decision to leave when Ravel was only two—and all that Ravel could read between those words and surmise. He hated his father for driving his mother to death, just as he hated himself for not being more a part of that death.

Two of his mother's three publishers had folded. Only the one for this volume he held in his shaky hand was still kicking. He had this book of course—he had all three of his mother's books in his nightstand. But the book he held now was the only volume of which he had one copy. The other two were each three copies strong, spread out over the apartment, hidden away in secret places. What if, while he stood here dithering in this bookstore, the one copy of this volume he had at home burned in a fire, or an airplane crashed into the apartment, or burglars entered looking for volumes of poetry written by a late-fifties Bulgarian émigré? Ravel could buy *this* copy and ease his mind, rectify his failings to his mother a little more.

Ravel squawked as he felt his phone vibrate. He brought it out and gasped at the caller ID: unidentified. It was the Colorado unemployment department! He had to pick up, even though he was nowhere near an exit. He placed his mother's book back on the shelf and bolted for the front entrance. He had to pick up now. If he missed this call…

Just as he crossed the entrance and stepped outside Ravel hit the talk button and placed the phone to his ear. "Hello?"

"Mr. Averof?"

"Yes?"

"Did I pronounce that right?"

"Yes, you did. Thanks. Thanks for calling."

He talked with the female employee for close to ten minutes. In that time he relayed the truth: he was forced to leave Maguffin-Shrift because, due to an involuntary and wholly unfair move between departments, the working conditions became intolerable. True, Ravel had quit, but the nature of his sudden new line of work, and the attitude of his supervisors, were such that he could no longer stay. It was not a tolerant environment, Ravel explained. Not an environment in which he could adequately function. The changes in management, the constant employee turnover, the pressure to drive an even greater profit.... The woman from the unemployment department told Ravel that his was not the first complaint of this nature about Maguffin-Shrift.

"I'm not surprised," said Ravel. "I had to leave. A lot of us have had to."

A moment of silence ensued, as if both the state employee and the former private sector employee were paying their respects to all those who had called the unemployment department, successfully or not, before. Then Ravel's inquisitor, whose name was Tanya, asked a few more questions regarding discrepancies between the professed company profile, the description of the sales development associate position, and the true nature of the work. Ravel told Tanya what she needed to hear. He would like to have stayed on at Maguffin-Shrift, even at reduced hours in sales development if need be, but it was obvious he had been demoted without cause and so he could no longer carry out the duties for which he'd been hired. Ravel kept just enough in the dark so that Tanya would not be enticed to ask questions that probed too far, and when the call had ended Ravel was confident he would be receiving his first unemployment check in the mail by mid-January.

Ravel kissed his phone before reentering the bookstore. Elated now, he returned to the poetry section, only to find his mother's volume gone. Gone? Gone! *On the Threshold of Acceptance* was not in the spot he'd placed it. Ravel leaned in close to each of the shelves in the poetry section. He pulled out books and looked behind, in the back, the darkness. No Yoana Kopecka. He searched through the adjacent bookshelves—the drama section, the film and television section, the Shakespeare and visual art and even the literature section under K. Still no sign of his mother. He had lost her. She had been...taken. Somone in the store must have her! Ravel peered over the bookcases, hoping to see his mother's book in the hands of someone, anyone. Not seeing the volume in any patron's hands, he began walking around in an agitated state. He felt light-headed, dizzy. His thirst was more intense than it had ever been.

Ravel approached the sales counter intending to ask for help. Perhaps the store would reveal who'd purchased the book, and Ravel would then rush out to catch the person before they could drive away. An innocent mistake, one that could be corrected with whatever Ravel had in his wallet.

Then he saw it. As Ravel finished scanning the line of customers, his eyes stopped on the woman who had just stepped to the front. Admittedly, she looked like someone who might purchase and even read cover to cover a book of poetry by a late-fifties Bulgarian émigré: glasses, gloves, a heavy black coat that fell to her knees, an overabundance of lipstick and makeup, an unfashionable bowl-shaped haircut—but to Ravel the accuracy of the customer matched to the purchase did not matter. He had to have that book! He strode past all the customers and reached the head of the line, where the woman was just about to step forward. Ravel heard the standard "I can help you over here" repeated, and he turned to address the cashier. "Just a minute," he said, as politely as possible. He felt terribly light-headed now, but he managed to speak to the woman, who looked greatly displeased but who might understand if Ravel only explained the situation.

"Hi," Ravel said. His voice felt detached. "I hate to get in your way like this but that book you have there—yeah, that one—I had it first, you know. What I mean is I had it back there, in the poetry section, where I found it first, and I just had to take a call, a very important, life-important call, and so I left the book on the shelf in the poetry section, where I found it, because I didn't want to leave with the book as I took the call outside, because I was being respectful of this store and you and everyone in it, and I didn't want them to think I was stealing, and..." Ravel could feel himself slipping not just with this increasingly impatient customer but with himself as well. He was sweating; he never sweated in well-conditioned bookstores! Why did he feel as if he'd just gotten off a merry-go-round? Ravel now found it difficult to breathe. *Heart attack*, he thought. *Maybe?* The signs weren't there: no tingling in his jaw, no pain in his right or left arm, no chest pains whatsoever —just a severe shrinking of oxygen and lung capacity, and always that intense dizziness.

"...and the call took, it took..."

Two patrons had already passed the woman up, and a third was on his way. The woman, the last scrap of her patience having drifted into the incinerator, moved to circumvent Ravel, who stepped in front of her and put his hands out. "No!" he said. "You don't understand..."

"You're right about that." The woman made another

attempt to circumvent. Ravel, feeling as if he were about to pass out, grabbed for the book and succeeded in latching on.

"I need that book," he yelled. The woman screamed for help. Her struggles were in vain, for within seconds Ravel had torn his mother's book from the woman's hands and was fleeing toward the back of the store. "I'll pay for this!" he shouted. "I will pay!"

Could he lock himself in a bathroom stall and wait this disaster out? When all heads had cooled, when he spoke to the authorities, they would understand. He would be free to purchase his mother's book and leave the store in peace. But now he found someone close behind him. A man. A security guard. Trained. Ravel yelped as he was tackled. He hit the ground hard. The security guard pinned him, and although he was saying something, Ravel couldn't understand any of the words. It was gibberish to him. The whole world now was gibberish. It was fading from his sight. Whatever was wrong with him was ugly. The store spun, lights flashed and blurred. Ravel's head lolled, his body went slack. He looked beyond the security guard to the pantheon of great writers whose portraits had been etched in caricatures on the walls above. William Shakespeare, Zora Neale Hurston, William Faulkner, Jane Austen, Mark Twain. Ravel stopped on the face of a more recent, still-living author, that of Dalton Bryce, acknowledged the world over as the Emperor of Terror. Locking eyes with Mr. Bryce, Ravel felt a sudden warmth infuse his chest, a calm creep across his mind. Mr. Bryce smiled. He looked kind. He looked accessible, approachable, someone—

Ravel no longer thought. The world had left him.

AND THEN THE world was back, only this world was not the world he readily knew but rather a place he had once known. Dark all around him. He was heading into this darkness, and the farther he stepped forward the more the darkness enveloped him. Although he couldn't see his hands he knew he was intact, it was him, the thirty-year-old Ravel Averof. He was propelled forward by something behind him—some unseen force. Ravel did not resist; he wanted to go forward; behind him was cold and utterly dark, while ahead he now sensed warmth and light. He was leaving the smell of the ocean, the chilly sea breeze, faint salt spray in his nose. The seagulls faded. Ahead the light was stronger, as were the smells of this place, new but connected to what he had just left. Smells of coffee roasting, percolating, sounds of mugs on wood, a cash register opening and voices talking softly. The darkness opened out onto a lit area, and Ravel recognized the bookstore he was now in. It was an indie, one he hadn't patronized since he was young, his mother still healthy. His mother should have been around.... Ravel looked for her, but all he observed was the old familiar layout: dark wood every-where, the sagging, creaking floors, cramped rows of towering cases, books stretching to the ceiling, books stacked haphaz-ardly in aisles, nooks and crevices within nooks and crevices, places for a child to hide. And why did Ravel want to hide right now? He wasn't afraid. Ah, but he was ashamed! Such shame he felt then.

No surprise he couldn't find his mother: this place, which he knew now as the Upstart Crow in Seaport Village, San Diego, was empty except for him. And yet Ravel heard voices behind the counter where the cash register squatted as if it had never been used—as if time didn't exist here. Ravel touched the postcard carousel next to him. It spun just fine, even made the squeaking sound he remembered from long ago. He walked around the counter, noticed the empty coffee mugs yet smelled what was supposed to be in them, the display case stocked with cookies and brownies, but he had the impression that nothing had ever been eaten, let alone purchased or so much as admired.

Ravel heard a creaking above. The second floor. He didn't want to ascend; this kind of dream, provided it was a dream—scared him, but he knew that nothing he could see right now could be touched or retrieved, and how sad that was, how immeasurably sad, because he loved this place. He loved it more than anyone, save for his mother, knew.

The floorboards directly above creaked yet again, and Ravel found the foot of the stairs. He kept a hand on the railing as he took the steps one at a time—unusual for him, given the length of his legs. His strides were plodding, as if he were attempting to climb stairs deep beneath the ocean. He wanted to hurry up, for he sensed that whoever was on the second floor was growing impatient. Abruptly he was at the top of the stairs; he stood on the second floor, close to his favorite section. It was the section he would go to often, when his mother was off elsewhere and couldn't be bothered. Ravel turned from the sun-hazed window to the nook he remembered so well. In it there was a small table, only one chair, it really couldn't hold more than a single person. It was here Ravel would go to hide, here he would sit in that one chair and rake his eyesight across all the volumes on each shelf, this particular fiction section.

Ravel noted that the table and chair were empty. He surveyed the grand bookcase, the flow of all those paperbacks interrupted by the occasional hardcover. He recognized not a word on any of the bindings. Each time he strained to make out the titles and authors, the words eluded him. Curious more than upset, Ravel turned back to the table and chair, now occupied. Dalton Bryce sat in the chair, his back to the railing that looked out over the first floor. He was writing by hand what looked to be a letter. As Ravel moved closer, Mr. Bryce set down his pen and stared up at the younger man. Mr. Bryce himself was young, clean-shaven, without glasses, and his hair, parted in the middle, threw its straight bangs down either side of his forehead. He looked not unlike Ravel's father at a younger age.

Ravel felt as if Mr. Bryce was saying something, but no words could be heard. The voices, the sounds of the coffee and the mugs and the cash register—all had vacated the premises. All now was silence. Ravel felt he said, *Dalton. Mr. Bryce.* The true author, the successful one, said nothing. It was difficult to tell from his expression what he was thinking, if Ravel was bothering him or if he was happy to be found in his nook. Mr. Bryce appeared both serious and patient.

Ravel followed Dalton Bryce's gaze to a particular row, a certain book. Ravel thought he had the book, but he couldn't tell its title nor could he touch it when he reached for it. Stricken now, he looked to the Emperor of Terror for help. The true author, the successful one, remained seated. Now, however, the letter and pen had been replaced with a hardcover that engulfed much of the table's surface. As Ravel drew near, that book swiftly enlarged and consumed the space all around. It was a gargantuan book, a leviathan, well over a thousand pages, and Ravel, in the last throes of what he could see, knew exactly what it was.

NOW THE WORLD of unemployment checks and doctoral dissertations and endangered bookstores and traffic and rejection notices was back, and with it a hand holding his own.

"Ravel. Ravel…"

Above: Deborah's voice. His eyes opened and he knew from the intermittent beeping, the feel and smell of the thin blanket covering his body, that he was in a hospital, a fact confirmed once he'd opened his eyes to see his wife seated beside his bed, the monitor towering over the opposite side, a curtain separating his space from that of the next patient over.

He felt his hand squeezed tighter.

"Ravel. Say something, honey. I love you."

"I love you too." He winced at the sound of his voice. It was as if he were learning to speak all over again.

"Good," Deborah said, and her smile widened. "Good," she repeated, her smile still wide, encouraging, her eyes lit up with relief.

A nurse appeared in the doorway. She checked the monitor, then brought out a small square device and inserted a thin white strip into the top.

"What's that?" Ravel asked.

"Have to check your blood sugar," the nurse said.

"Why?"

"To see where you're at."

No further questions, the nurse's brusque demeanor warned. Ravel looked to Deborah for an answer, but his wife shook her head and shrugged. The nurse held Ravel's hand and touched the tip of a small plastic pen-like device to his index finger. He felt a quick sharp stab, and as he recoiled the nurse held his wrist firmly and touched the strip to the sizable bead of blood. The blood whisked across the top of the strip in a small thin line. The countdown had begun.

Afraid to speak, Ravel waited a few seconds until the result displayed on the device's screen. "Two-oh-seven," the nurse announced. "That's a lot better than your number when you came in."

"What was my number when I came in?"

"I believe it was close to nine hundred."

"Is that bad?"

"It is when you have what you have."

Ravel, his frustration rising, was about to engage the nurse in a tense volley, but at that moment the doctor, short and curt and slender, walked in. "Ravel Averof," she said. "I'm Dr. Usmani. You were in quite a state when you were admitted."

"Where is here?" Ravel said. "What hospital is this?"

Deborah answered before the doctor could speak. "You're in Denver," she said. "They called an ambulance at the bookstore, called me, and they took you here. Thank God you have great insurance."

At the words 'great insurance' both the nurse and the doctor glanced at each other. Deborah did not pick up on this, but Ravel did. *They know,* he thought. *How?* They would have to know, of course; at the end of 2022, no patient could be admitted without the hospital checking on their insurance coverage. Ravel had six months. He was safe until the end of June.

Ravel bit his lower lip and said, "What a way to spend New Year's, huh?"

Deborah nodded. Her eyes got watery, and Ravel took this as a sign of her disappointment in him.

"Deb, I'm sorry."

"Why are you sorry? I only want you well."

"I wish I knew what I have," Ravel said. He looked pointedly at the doctor, who cleared her throat and said, "I have bad news, Mr. Averof. Diabetes."

"Diabetes!?!"

"Yes, diabetes. You are a diabetic. Now whether that's type 1 or type 2 is still to be determined…"

"Diabetes…" Ravel rested his head on the pillow and closed his eyes. More than anything, he felt embarrassed. He could not look at anyone just then.

"You're sure?" Deborah said. "Ravel's healthy.… I mean, look at him."

Ravel heard the doctor say, "Unfortunately, a healthy BMI does not make someone immune to this disease. But your BMI, Mr. Averof, and your age would tell me this is diabetes mellitus type 1. Still, we can't rule out type 2…"

"Or a combination of one and two?" Deborah ventured.

Dr. Usmani ignored her comment. "In all cases I've seen, when a patient blacks out as you did, it's a case of hypoglycemic shock."

Ravel's eyes were open now. "Meaning…?" he said.

"Meaning the subject's blood sugar is too low. Far too low. That leads to seizures. Death is a very real possibility. But in your case, you blacked out when your blood sugar was terribly high. I suppose it could happen if there were extenuating factors, contributors.… Stress is often a major factor. I understand you were under extreme duress in the bookstore when you blacked out?"

Deborah held her husband's hand as she spoke for Ravel, who would not have divulged so much so easily. "My husband," said Deborah, "was in an altercation with another bookstore customer, and that must have led to a panic attack—he's had those before."

"What triggers these panic attacks?"

"Writing," Deborah said. "Always writing."

"Deb…"

"You know it's true, Ravel. You do! Ever since we met it's just been this pressure every day, all the time, in front of us or in the background, humming right along, and I think it just caught up to you finally. I hope this is the breaking point, your diagnosis. The bookstore people said you were…fighting over your mother's book."

Ravel groaned. "Not one of my better moments," he told Dr. Usmani.

"They said he was clutching the book when he passed out, even when he was unconscious he wouldn't let go. They had to pry it out of his hands."

"Your mother's a writer?" Dr. Usmani said.

"Was a writer," said Ravel. "She died earlier this year."

"What did she die of?"

"Cancer. She smoked every day, up until the very end."

"I'll note stress, anxiety on your chart," Dr. Usmani remarked. "Our behavioral health department will be of use to you."

"Jesus," Ravel muttered. To Deborah he asked if the woman at the bookstore had been given *On the Threshold of Acceptance* after all. "She should have it," he added. "She really should."

"I don't know if they gave it to her or not, Rav. I know she's not going to press charges, thankfully. You were such a sight when they took you out of that ambulance. On the phone I told the bookstore management about your, well, your mom and dad, that situation. They felt sorry for you. But I don't know what happened to the book."

"It wasn't worth it," Ravel told the curtain. "None of this was worth it." He gripped Deborah's hand. His other hand went to his throat. His eyes shot wide.

"Where is it?"

"Where's what?" Deborah said.

"My amulet. The amulet, Deb!"

"Your belongings are on the counter over there, Mr. Averof," Dr. Usmani said calmly. "The amulet, as you call it, is among your things. We had to run tests. Any jewelry had to be removed."

Deborah was teary-eyed again. "What are we doing?" she said to the air. "We both work too hard."

"We'll be fine, Deb," Ravel said. With the focus on his past, his neuroses and ambitions, he found a strength within to speak out and stand up for himself and all failing drifters everywhere. "We have to keep doing what we're doing."

"But you have diabetes."

"It's not cancer. Right, doctor? I mean, people with diabetes..."

"Can live quite a long time, if the disease is managed," Dr. Usmani assured.

"I'll take it seriously," Ravel said.

"Take it more seriously," Deborah said, "than your writing, okay? Please. For me?"

Ravel squeezed his wife's hand. "Could you get me my amulet, please?"

Dr. Usmani watched Deborah retrieve the necklace and

hand it to Ravel. "That must be very important to you," she observed.

"Yes," Ravel responded tersely. The amulet tied to the black leather string worked itself through his fingers.

"A gift from his mother," Deborah said.

"It *is* my mother," Ravel said. "It's really the only piece of her I have besides her books. There aren't many photos of her, we have so few pictures of the two of us together. Without this amulet..."

"Without it what?" Dr. Usmani's inquisitive eyes and slightly quivering mouth welcomed an answer. Even Deborah was leaning in. He'd never told her.

"Without it," Ravel said, "I think I'd lose her. The memory of her. I'd forget her."

"What of your father," said Dr. Usmani. "I'm aware of who he is. Pressure from him, no doubt."

"Indirect pressure," Deborah said. "He and Ravel haven't spoken in twenty years. But it's like the man's living with us every day of our lives."

"Larger than life."

"I don't have any of his books on my shelves," Ravel stated. "Have you read any of them? *The Epidermis of Malaise, Marsupial and Mastiff...*"

"I have read them," Dr. Usmani said. "They're quite good."

"Great. He's made the American Diamond Prize in Fiction shortlist for his latest, of course."

"All the more pressure, anxiety, stress and depression for you then."

"Depression?"

"Yes, Mr. Averof. I am going to go out on a branch here

and say you are likely depressed. I strongly urge you to connect with our behavioral health department. They will assist you with your family dynamic, and they'll also help you through your adjustment to a diabetic life."

Dr. Usmani explained the prescriptions that Ravel would be taking for the remainder of his life. In addition to the diabetes medications, Ravel was prescribed a pill for high blood pressure. Even if he did not have anxiety and hypertension, he would need to be on the medication to protect his kidneys. A major shift in thinking would now be required, Dr. Usmani said. A major change in lifestyle. Medicine alone would not keep Ravel alive.

"Behavioral health, Mr. Averof. They'll be contacting you soon."

"I can't believe I have diabetes," Ravel said.

"You last had your blood drawn for a physical four years ago, when you were twenty-six," Dr. Usmani said. "We just didn't have any test results for you in all that time."

Ravel would see Dr. Usmani in a week. He was to bring his glucometer, which he was required to use three times a day. He would also be enrolled in a diabetes education workshop, and depending on his early numbers, testing of his pancreas function might be necessary.

"Not to add more to your stress level, Ravel," Dr. Usmani said, using his first name now, "but time is of the essence. You'll want to get started on your medication, and the finger pricking, immediately. We'll put you in touch with a nutritionist, a diabetes educator. A month from now, we'll see where we stand. At this early stage we are going to feel out this disease and see if it is in fact diabetes mellitus type 2. If it is, your body should respond well to the Metformin. If not, then insulin will be necessary."

"Insulin. Jesus."

"In a few months, we'll check on your situation and see what you can do."

Dr. Usmani's last sentence left Deborah confused. Ravel navigated away from it until the hospital discharged him an hour later. At Mick's orders, Denver police officers had driven Ravel's vehicle from Lone Tree back to the Capitol Hill neighborhood. Deborah and Ravel were headed home.

Within minutes of pulling out of the hospital parking lot, Deborah said, "Something's going on, Ravel. Like the doctor knew. I swear the nurse knew something. What is it? What's going on?"

"Deb, I left my job."

"You *what*?"

"Maybe I shouldn't tell you this when you're driving."

"They *fired* you?"

"They didn't fire me. I quit."

To Ravel's surprise, Deborah said, "Maybe it's what you needed."

"You really think so?"

"Maybe.... Look at what you've just been diagnosed with. That job wasn't helping. But, God, Ravel, your health. Your insurance. It runs out when?"

"July first."

"Jesus."

Ravel delved into the particulars of his exit from Maguffin-Shrift. The transfer to the sales floor, the ultimatum. Deborah listened, nodded, never once took her eyes off the road. She understood his need to leave, Ravel thought. She knew he'd always hated working as a sales development associate, whatever that ever meant; she knew he could do better. It was unfortunate this move came now, in the wake of his diagnosis and Deborah still months away from finishing her dissertation and preparing for the oral defense. Ravel countered his wife's concerns with the news that he'd be receiving an unemployment check twice a month, starting in the middle of January.

"We can make it," he said.

"You need to start looking for work, Ravel. And figure all this other shit out, too."

All this other shit. His fading mother. His still-living father. What he had to prove, and to whom he had to prove it.

"Believe me, Deb, I'm going to be looking hard starting tomorrow, and I'm not going to quit until I've landed something suitable, something I like this time."

"Don't just like it, Ravel. Love it."

"I will."

Cautiously he rested his hand on her thigh, and she assuaged his fear by putting her hand on his. They held tightly. "I can see about the university's health plan, how much that costs. I can ask Dad about dipping into Mom's life insurance money…"

"Don't do that, Deb."

"Ravel. Seriously? You're thirty and you've just been diagnosed with *diabetes*. It's going to change your whole damn life. You know that. You're not in any position…"

Wisely, Ravel stood down.

"You have to work with behavioral health," Deborah said. "No resistance."

"Absolutely none. I promise."

"Promise me this also: I've heard about a support group, it's called Men Who Write Too Much."

"You're shitting me. Men Who Write Too Much? There's a support group for that?"

"It exists. It has members. A lot of members, from what I've read."

"I..."

"Do it, Ravel. For me. For you and for me. For us."

"Okay. I'll go."

"Maybe some famous writers are members. Like, uh, Dalton Bryce. You could get to meet him."

"I've already met Dalton Bryce, Deb."

Deborah waited for Ravel to continue, and when he did it was in a voice shaky and emotional. "I, uh, I experienced something, when I was unconscious."

"A dream?"

"It wasn't a dream, at least I hope it wasn't. I'd like to think of it more as a...a vision."

"A vision? Ravel..."

"No. Listen..." He related his vision to his wife. He started from the beginning, the darkness, the tunnel, the sounds of seagulls and smell of the ocean. He was certain it had been the Upstart Crow, shuttered now these past several years, only in his vision it was the nineties.

"The nineties? Really, Ravel? You could tell the decade?"

"It had to be the nineties. I was a boy. I might have looked like myself, but I *felt* like I was my young self, my child self when I was there in the vision. I had the feeling I had when I first went there with my Mom, in the mid-nineties."

"And she was there?"

"No. But Dalton Bryce was. I found him in my favorite

corner of the Upstart Crow, and if I stepped outside maybe I would have seen the rest of Seaport Village, the nineties, my mother alive. I don't know. I stayed in that corner where I huddled my first time ever there, when I was a kid, and I remember now that that was his section—Dalton Bryce's section, or the horror section anyway. Hang on, I can see it now.... I gotta write this down..."

Ravel tapped into the Notes app on his phone. "...or I'll lose it."

"Lose what?"

"What was in that book Bryce had. That big book. That..."

"What was in it?"

"Numbers. Maybe they mean something. Anyway, I have them down now."

Deborah asked if in the vision Ravel had spoken with Dalton Bryce. Ravel told her what had been said and she listened, worried. The writing. Worse: the writing without purpose, without assurance, no end in sight. It had always been this way with Ravel. Her husband's excitement burst as he talked. She worried what level his blood glucose was at now. Could his number, the one that mattered for his longevity, his life, be rising to an unacceptable level? Could elation over a vision involving Dalton Bryce alone do that? Dalton Bryce had wanted to tell Ravel something. They hadn't communicated in the usual way, with spoken words, but rather through a book, a monstrous book that swallowed Ravel whole, and that's when the vision had ended.

Behavioral health, Deborah thought. She said, "But you haven't read a Dalton Bryce book in years."

"I still own a few of them."

"Was this really saying something, or was it…"

"Just crazy? I don't think so, Deb. What I experienced was about the future. Bryce was telling me to do something."

"Write a horror novel? That can't help."

"Maybe writing got me into this," Ravel said. "But maybe writing can get me out."

They had been talking nearly nonstop since they'd started driving, and now the silence fell unnaturally.

"I don't know," Ravel said. "What do you think?"

"I think," Deborah said, "you need to come into the pharmacy with me, get your medications, your glucometer, and get in touch with behavioral health after New Year's Day." Ravel noticed they had pulled into the drug store parking lot. Deborah continued: "I know writing gives you meaning, but I think at the same time it's a curse for you, Ravel. You've just spent so many years banging your head against the keyboard, so to speak. Have you ever gotten past page five of that novel you've been trying to write?"

Slowly, Ravel shook his head.

Deborah found a spot and stopped the car. "I admire your drive so much," she said once she'd turned off the ignition. "I love your ambition. I'm glad we both aren't sitting on the couch popping Cheetos and drinking bad beer. But it's obvious this pressure having to do with writing has hurt your body now, and it's hurt me too. I need you to call that group. Message them."

"Men Who Write Too Much. They'll give me shock therapy. I'll end up lobotomized."

"Would that really be such a bad thing? Kidding, kidding."

"Ha ha. Funny. I will try it, for you."

"Try everything for me, Ravel. Everything you've been given."

Deborah looked at him then with such sincere concern that Ravel wanted to believe he would survive this. He was at last on the right path. For the first time in his life, he thought he could truly give up for good.

Six

As soon as Deborah left for DU, Ravel got to work looking for a job. It was the third of the new year, and Ravel felt duly optimistic. His optimism, however, gradually dissipated as the hours passed. He logged into his alumni accounts for the first time in years. He sent messages through social. He spent what little time was needed to update his meager resume. He wrote a new cover letter and sent it out to a few places. The job search had changed, he soon realized, and so too had he. When Ravel last searched for work, fresh out of grad school, he was gifted with patience. Deborah was in a less intense phase of her doctorate program. His mother was still alive and encouraging him from afar. Ravel landed the position at Maguffin-Shrift after only a few weeks on the hunt. This time around, over five years later, Ravel felt his aloneness acutely. He had no one. He did not begrudge Deborah anything; he could not expect her to hold off the writing and defense of her dissertation any longer, not for him or for anyone. This new job he truly had to find on his own.

At just past noon he stopped his search. He would take a lunch break, make some calls to health insurance companies, perhaps read a little, and then jump back into the pool. Unless he decided to spend the rest of the afternoon working on *Your Great American Novel*. But write? Really? In this situation, with his health the way it was?

He'd checked his blood sugar dutifully that morning and again just before lunch. Both numbers, though on the higher end, were within range. *Maybe type 2 after all*, he told himself. *Metformin's working. If I don't have to stick a needle in my belly, or go on an insulin pump...*

Instead of watching TV as he ate, he scanned the bookcase from his vantage point on the couch. Most of the books were his, and he had the heavy hitters: Joyce, Dostoyevsky, Kafka, Gaddis, Didion, Roth, Delillo, Mailer, McCarthy, Whitehead, Tolstoy, Pynchon, Egan, Krakauer, McEwan, Shteyngart, Sebald, James. While many of the volumes came close, only a couple—Mailer's *The Executioner's Song* and Tolstoy's *War and Peace*—topped a thousand pages. Ravel continued scanning, meat and bread churning in his mouth, and then his gaze stopped on the author he should have seen all along. Out of all the novels he owned, out of all the literature he'd amassed over the years, all the books bought new or used or just outright filched, he still held on to his far past, his childhood. He stood, swallowed and approached the bookcase. He leaned in and focused on the top shelf on the leftmost side, the Bs. He'd kept only three by Dalton Bryce: the collection of novellas titled *Strange Tastes* from 1993, and the novels *That* and *Bitter* from 1997 and 1998 respectively. All three were in paperback—*That*'s cover was the TV miniseries tie-in, Russ Goldweather as Fantabulous the Magician on the binding and the front.

That was big. *That* was over a thousand pages. *That* was the third and last novel of such gargantuan length in Ravel's collection.

These three were all that remained after years and years as a boy and then a teen reading every one of Bryce's books he could get his hands on. How Ravel and Yoana had fought over whether he could read them! The miniseries of *That* was about to premiere, Ravel remembered, and that had been the beginning. A week before the 2004 election, Ravel had opened to the back of the entertainment section of the *Union-Tribune* and seen the review for Part One, the picture of Russ Goldweather in full magician regalia—top hat, gloves, coattails, wand—and he'd asked his mother what *That* was about. Yoana had answered, "Oh, it's about a magician who makes children do terrible things."

Hearing her words, young Ravel couldn't turn away. He had to read *That*! But Yoana wouldn't let him. She had heard about *That*, and it was too many pages not to contain something objectionable. Ravel, knowing how his mother worked, tried a different tack: if he couldn't read *that* Dalton Bryce book, how about a different Dalton Bryce book? Yoana hesitated, but soon she relented. When Ravel came to her with *Goat's Grief*, she said she remembered it being not that bad, and so Ravel was off to the races with his first Dalton Bryce. When, a twelve-year-old momma's boy, he returned to Yoana to point out the curse word on the first page, first paragraph, first sentence, Yoana said a mere "Oh" and her eyes flashed with the recognition of the box she had opened. From there, after *Goat's Grief*, Ravel requested *The Fires Within*, then *Malcontents*, then *Dread Mind*, then *Janice*, then *Fagen's Place*, then *The Rush*. With the okay on each subsequent book

Yoana's powers of censorship further eroded. She had assumed that Bryce's early titles wouldn't be so bad, but from what her son was relating she was mistaken. Evidently Dalton Bryce had written disturbing sex-related scenes and gory deaths from the beginning of his career, and the eighties and early nineties were just as rife with rough material as the years following.

One after another, each book was bought, consumed and placed on young Ravel's bookcase to be opened again for an encore scene-immersion later. For two years, from age twelve to fourteen, the boy's only pleasure-reading outside of the books he was required to read for school consisted of Dalton Bryce. Yoana had delivered an unequivocal *no* to Ravel's request for the latest Bryce novel, *Martin's Gripe*, which had been released in the summer of 2006. She had anticipated this one; she had read the reviews, spoken with colleagues at the high school. She knew what gripe Martin nursed, and she would not, absolutely not, allow her almost-fourteen-year-old son to read it.

She had given Ravel her answer one morning while they were seated poolside at the Country Gems public swimming pool, the summer of the release. Ravel had argued, of course, but his words had little of the ferocity he would direct at her in the Anomar public library toward the end of that summer. Mother and son stood apart from each other then, she on her way out, while he stood defiantly holding back, a copy of *Martin's Gripe* in one hand. His concession to her was that he wouldn't *own* this latest Bryce novel, he didn't have to own this one, he would just read it and return it. If Yoana didn't want him spending money on this Bryce then he wouldn't. But, as Yoana made clear that day, she didn't care about the act of spending money, she cared about the content, and this was one book she forbade Ravel from devouring even a sentence. Ravel had shouted that day in the library. His mother had tricked him! Lied to him! She had let him read all those previous Dalton Bryce books—he was all caught up now. He had read *The Other Side*, *Little Ones*, *Things that Go Bang in the Night*, *Bitter*, *The Amulet*. He had read *That* in one week, holed up in his room for hours after school until he finished. Why now, after all those, this emphatic *no*? When none of his words worked, impassioned and aggressive as they were, Ravel resorted to tears. In the library, in front of his mother and fellow Anomarans, he had cried (and if his father had been there...). Not one of his better moments.

Ravel looked now at his personal library, the collection he'd carted around with each move, and pulled *That* off the shelf. He really had read this behemoth in a week, averaging two hundred pages and four to five hours a day. He had spoken very little to anyone that week. He thought of speaking to Yoana now, of apologizing for how he'd behaved that day in the library, at an age at which he should have been able to control himself, but it was too late. On his mother's last day on earth, Ravel had started to apologize for other things, but Yoana would hear none of it. She wanted only to die.

Ravel turned *That* over in his hands. He felt its immense heft, flipped the pages quickly, his nostrils close. The book smelled of a recent purchase, a modern bookstore. Where had he purchased this copy? Not the Upstart Crow. Strange that after so many years, so many moves, the copy he held should retain that new book smell.

He opened to the copyright page, the Library of Congress catalog data, the specifics on the publisher and its subsidiaries in different countries. This novel would last, if not on Ravel's shelf, centuries after he was gone, then in the public record. *That* wouldn't go away, not like some half-assed opening to a novel never finished, stored for years after its author passed only to be deleted from the computer, torn up and thrown into the recycling bin, put out of its misery. Ravel's children would perhaps wait a decade, maybe even two, before ridding themselves of their father's paltry effort. One of them would perhaps try to finish the novel, possibly even succeed at what his father could not. The thought wasn't any true comfort. Ravel would not be around to experience such success. Even if he was aware, a specter floating above his future bloodline, he doubted he would feel pride. Envy he would feel. Anger. *Your Great American Novel* was *his* novel, after all. It could have been his novel, anyway.

And that was it. That did it. These musings on the future, his place in the afterlife, his legacy, had led to a connection to the past—not Ravel's past but the past of the novel he held in his hands. How it had come into existence—not just the actual writing of it but its inception. Ravel smiled. *That* could have been his novel. *That* could have been anyone's novel, really. *That* ended up Dalton Bryce's, but did it have to be? Could *That* be Ravel's?

Laney answered on the fourth buzz.

"Now's the time," Ravel said.

"I was hoping you'd agree to now."

"I need to do it, as soon as possible. Can you send me off?"

"As long as you follow the rules."

"I promise. I'll give you my severance check and my first unemployment payment—"

"Payment's not necessary for this trek, Ravel. We established that earlier, remember?"

"Oh. Yeah. Thanks."

"We wouldn't do that to you. I wouldn't do that to you."

"Okay..." He heard Laney fumbling with something on her end of the line.

"It's tough that it's early January," she said, "but so be it. The weather.... It needs to be clear if it's going to work, and it needs to be night, like, early early morning night, and it needs to be over the weekend."

"This weekend then," said Ravel.

"Pray for no snow."

"Saturday the seventh," Ravel said. "The lucky seventh."

"All right. The lucky seventh it is then. I gotta go, Ravel." No sooner had Laney spoken then she'd ended the call, leaving Ravel with a steady thumping beat in his brain. He brought his phone to his lips, tapped his mouth twice, and set the phone on top of the bookcase. The mammoth paperback still in one hand, he went into the office and sat in front of the computer. He moved the mouse to kill the screensaver, then brought up a new blank word processing document, the first he'd opened in months. He set *That* to the side of the keyboard and opened to the first page. He hadn't remembered the font being so small, the lines so close together. So many words.... It had taken him a week to read them all when he was a boy—how long would it take him now to write those words? And if he were to do that, would what he had in mind work?

It didn't seem logical. If he went back in time and succeeded at doing what he was considering doing, then the novel he had beside him would not exist, which meant that if it existed now, as it did, it meant he had failed. If Ravel had succeeded in his plan the book would not exist *now*—but then how was he going to make it his before going back?

Overthinking it, Ravel thought. *Just do it and see*. He thought, faintly, of what Laney had said of the butterfly effect, the opening of new, possibly hellish dimensions and alternate realities. Chaos on the continuum. Yet there had to be a way...

His phone rang. A startled Ravel yelped and sprang in his seat. He watched his device, unsure if he should answer. Better not. If it was job-related, better to let the employer think Ravel was at an interview or otherwise pounding the pavement in search of a job.

An actual message was left. Ravel placed his phone to his ear and listened.

"This message is for Ravel Averof. Ravel, my name is Bruce Bednarik and I'm with Men Who Write Too Much. I believe you're aware of our organization, but I'm not sure you're familiar with what it can do for you..."

Bednarik. A Slovakian name. Or Czech. Did Deborah know Bednarik from the time she taught in Eastern Europe? This Bruce Bednarik sounded older, gruffer. Ravel imagined a big man with a full beard.

"...and we're certainly hoping you'll give us a call, or if you'd like to cut to the chase you can show at our meeting, next Monday night at eight in the Wash Park rec center. So if you're interested, show up at the meeting or give me a call at—"

Ravel silenced the rest of the message. He couldn't go to a group whose purpose was to drive the desire to write out of him—certainly not now. Bednarik could only have gotten Ravel's number from Deborah. Only looking out for her husband's best interests, she would say. Just helping. Ravel understood she needed to do this, that Deborah had made the call because she didn't trust him to contact the support group himself. With writing she did not trust him. They trusted each other with so much, but when it came to writing…. Deborah knew Ravel would do anything when it came to writing, perhaps something foolish or even dangerous. When it came to Ravel Averof's writing aspirations, he was capable of anything. *And soon*, Ravel thought, *I'll even be capable of* That.

THAT NIGHT over dinner Deborah asked him why he was so quiet, and Ravel revealed that Bruce Bednarik of Men Who Write Too Much had called.

"I thought he'd at least wait a day," Deborah said.

"Do you know him?"

"Not too well, no. He put flyers around campus last year. First day of the semester we had to take them down from the department, but I kept one."

"I just wish you wouldn't have gone around me like that, Deb."

"Were you really going to call them? I mean really?"

Ravel kept his eyes on his cobb-ish salad. Lots of salads from now on. Lots of beans too, apparently. Low carb, the right carbs. He took a bite and swallowed. What he wouldn't give to be a doctor right now. A doctor without diabetes. He felt not so much angry as tired, as if he had just finished defending his own dissertation. Deborah reached out, some-what cautiously, perhaps fearful of his anger, and touched her husband's free hand. He grasped her hand and caressed it.

"I love you," she said. "I want you to live a long time."

"I do too."

"I hope so. I just want you to take your diabetes seriously."

"I am, Deb. I'm on the medication, I'm eating this, I'm

pricking my finger, checking my blood. It's looking all right so far."

"I've been reading up on it, Rav. It's awful, if you don't get ahead of it."

"I'll keep ahead of it. I'm pretty sure I'm ahead of it now. I might be type 2, you know."

"That would be great if you are. If you can just deal with it using Metformin..."

"And not the needles, not the pump."

"Have you been taking breaks from the job search to get up and stretch and walk around?"

"Some. I'm looking into gym memberships too."

"We need to order a treadmill."

"Where are we going to put it?"

"Or an exercise bike. Something. The gym is good, but it would be great to have something you can jump on at home without having to drive anywhere."

"If I have to I'll go for a walk—out there. I'll just bundle up and put on the Yaktrax."

Since the day of their wedding Ravel had known that he would die first. Deborah's mother had died relatively young from Covid, but that was a freak death considering the longevity of all her other family members. Deborah would outlive him even if he hadn't been diagnosed with diabetes at age thirty. Still, he had to keep going for as long as he could— for her if not for himself.

"I'm changing, Deborah," he said. A bit of anger had infiltrated his voice. "I will cut down on writing, but I can't give it up completely. If you're asking me to do that, if I'm forced to do that, that would be the end of me, I think."

"But, Ravel, honey. How much do you really write?"

There it was: What he didn't want to admit: the truth. Ravel really didn't write all that much; it was far more the *thought* of writing that kept him up at night, kept him tense and fidgety when he should have been free.

Knowing her question had gone deep, Deborah backed off. "I'm sorry," she said.

"No, you're right. Writing is not good for my health. I admit that. I'll go."

"You mean you'll go to their meeting?"

"It's next Monday. I'll go. It's at eight. It can't hurt to go and check it out."

"It can't." Deborah kissed him, smiled and returned to eating. Ravel stuffed more salad into his maw. She had gone around him, but then wasn't he going around her as well?

THOUGH HE WAS BORN after the eighties ended, Ravel preferred the music from that decade to that of any other. He had a soft spot for the music of the nineties, the decade of his childhood, but the eighties sound carried an irresistible air of mystery. As he streamed his Ultimate '80s Playlist in the car, Ravel imagined the year, the month, and sometimes even the day in which each song was released, the lives of the people who first heard the song on the air, or on cassette or vinyl or early compact disc, people he didn't know. What were they doing when they heard this song? What event that would later worm its way into a high school history textbook was occurring at the same time as this song's release? Was this song in their minds—any of their minds—at the moment of death?

At this awful hour in the early morning, going on four decades after the initial releases, heading up the I-25 to connect to the 36 that would take him to meet Laney and his destiny, Ravel noticed police lights flashing in his rearview mirror. As it was nearing two a.m. and the freeway was almost entirely devoid of vehicles, the word that surfaced in Ravel's mind was *Odd*. He was just below the speed limit and should have had nothing to fear.

The police car was right behind him. Its lights continued to flash and now its horn was blaring short and dull. Ravel, already in the rightmost lane, pulled to the shoulder and came to a stop. Seeing the police car pull up behind him, he killed the engine and muttered "Unbelievable" while shaking his head. He looked in the rearview again and took a couple of breaths. The lights had not stopped flashing. Ravel looked to the left and saw a semi-truck blow by at well over the speed limit.

The doors to the police car opened and out stepped Mick Parker. Ravel would have recognized that build, that swagger, that gun from a far greater distance in an even deader night. His father-in-law, who had been riding shotgun, kept his gun holstered but held what looked to be a ream of paper. To Mick's side was his good buddy Godwin whom Ravel had met at a barbeque when he arrived in Denver years ago and hadn't seen much since then. But he remembered Godwin well. Unlike Mick, this officer was a little less of a vigilante, more respectful and level-headed. Still, he was Mick's compadre, so Ravel wasn't about to let his guard down.

Ravel had rolled his windows down by the time the officers leaned in from either side. Chill sliced into his car in a wide arc. Ravel zipped up his coat and found Mick on his left.

"Hey there, Ravel," Mick said. "Wonderful night we're having, isn't it?"

"I suppose so."

"You remember Godwin."

"I do. Hey."

Godwin nodded and raised a hand while leaning through the passenger window.

"Mind if we get in? It's cold out here at this God-awful hour."

Godwin took the passenger seat while Mick slid in behind Ravel. *A hit*, Ravel thought. *Murdered by my own father-in-law. The Denver PD got me.*

Mick plopped the heavy ream of paper into Ravel's lap. Before he saw the first page, Ravel knew what it was. He'd done it. His father-in-law had finally birthed his baby.

"I could ask a whole lot of questions right now, Rav," Mick went on. "Like, why is my son-in-law, married to my daughter, out on the I-25 at two in the morning on a Friday?"

"Saturday now," Godwin corrected.

"Saturday now, whatever," Mick said. "But why is he driving at this time? Where is he going? Does Debbie know? Is she supposed to know? Should she know? Should I tell her? Or is that a secret my son-in-law doesn't want revealed?"

Ravel knew better than to say, *I'm not cheating on your daughter, Mick.* What a stupid thing to say, Mick would think; Ravel would think the same. His father-in-law would respect him much more, even if just a little, if Ravel kept his mouth shut. Strength in silence.

"So there's a lot I could do with this right now," Mick was saying, "but I don't think I'm going to do anything with it. Yet. An ace I'll keep up my sleeve, right, Godwin?"

"Affirmative, Mick."

"We were young men once, young as Ravel here. We did some questionable things in our day..."

"That we did," said Godwin.

"And we appreciated when our secrets weren't spilled. We'd like to do the same courtesy for Ravel here. But if we scratch his back, he's going to have to scratch ours."

Ravel shifted in his seat so that the formidable weight of the dead-tree doorstop went from one thigh to the other. The screenplay, three-hole-punched, bound with brads twice over, rubber-banded for extra measure, seemed to taunt him from his lap.

"*Freedom Freeway*," Ravel read off the title page.

"We thought it'd be the right call to give it to you here."

"How'd you even know I was here?"

"Ravel, Rav.... After more than four years, you don't think I keep tabs on you and Debbie occasionally?"

"Just occasionally? Or all the time?"

"Not all the time, Ravel. That would be too intense, even for an overprotective dad like me."

"Creepy," Godwin uttered.

"You just happened to leave the apartment at a questionable time, which raised the red flag, and we tailed you from there."

"Great..."

"But you're in luck, Rav. I'm not going to ask any questions. I won't bring you into the station. I'm going to let you go wherever you're headed. I trust you."

Thank...you...? Ravel thought.

"But you gotta scratch our backs. Give it to your agent."

"I've said many times, Mick—"

"I know. She's not your agent. But you can still reach her. You have an in."

"It's very...long," Ravel said. "For a screenplay."

"I told you!" Godwin said. "That McKee guy—"

"Shut it," Mick cut in. "No doubts. Let him read it. Then let him give it to *her*."

Ravel, for all he had done well in his life, had also done quite a few things wrong, and not being up front with his father-in-law about his tenuous connection to Maxine was one of them. Maybe if Mick hadn't intimidated him every time Ravel saw him with the gun, or reminded Ravel of the bullies he'd put up with when he was younger, he would have told him he and Maxine no longer spoke; in fact, Ravel was certain that if he tried to contact his former non-paying employer now he would be met with a thudding non-response. *Mick*, Ravel would have said, *that agent I worked for had so many unpaid gophers running around I'll be floored if she remembers even three of them.* Maxine would remember perhaps two, but Ravel would not be among that number.

Mick said, "It could be a couple pages—maybe three pages —too long. I know what the seminars and books say but..."

"We poured our hearts and souls into that thing," Godwin insisted.

Ravel nodded. He could tell his father-in-law the truth of his connection to Maxine. And then he would quite likely be arrested, or, worse, news of this middle-of-the-night excursion would make its way to his wife. Then Ravel would have *a ton* of explaining to do, and his plan, his future, would be in jeopardy.

Ravel thought, *A gatekeeper without a gate.* He hefted the

ream. Easily three hundred pages. Cardstock. They'd printed the damn thing on cardstock.

"I'll make sure she takes a look," Ravel found himself saying.

"We want more than just a look, Rav. We want her to *give it a read*."

"I'll do my very best."

"That's what we want to hear. How long will it take to hear back?"

"A while, Mick. That's the honest truth."

"We'll wait," Mick said. "I'm not dying any time soon. What could go wrong?"

"Nothing," Godwin said.

"Nothing after this." Mick tapped the script in Ravel's lap. He opened his door but halted on his way out. "Seeing someone in the People's Republic, Rav?"

"Mayor must be safe tonight," Ravel said. He held his father-in-law's gaze. Mick's smile dissipated.

"He's got you there, Mick buddy!"

"He in your trunk?" Mick said, his eyes still locked with Ravel's.

Ravel laughed. His phone alarm waking him at that awful hour, the pull-over on the side of the I-25 at two in the morning, the absurd paperweight of a script in his lap, his father-in-law literally breathing down his neck—all of it combined to send him into peals of laughter, which must have been contagious, because Mick soon broke into his own guffaws.

"You're on to something," said Godwin. "Not the mayor but *somebody*. Perfect time of night. Headed to the foothills. I bet there's a shovel in the back along with the remains."

This escalated Ravel's fit into near-hysteria. Godwin caught the bug as well. Soon all three were cracking up.

"...I do like you, Ravel. You're real lucky," said Mick. "You're quite a character..." Swiftly he gripped his son-in-law's shoulder, silencing laughter on all sides. "You're all right, but if I find you're cheating on my daughter, you'll be in a trunk on the way to the foothills. Got that?"

Ravel nodded.

"Mick," Godwin bemoaned. "What happened to 'we were young once too?' Don't snitches get stitches?"

"Wherever you're going," Mick said, "you be careful, Ravel. Come on, Godwin."

A shot in the dark as both doors slammed simultaneously. Ravel startled in his seat. He set aside *Freedom Freeway* and watched Mick and Godwin return to their unmarked DPD SUV. He knew better than to wait for them to leave first. They would not leave first. They were waiting for him to make the first move. Ravel pulled back onto the I-25 and left his father-in-law and company in the distance. This time as he drove he kept the music off. Silence. He had a lot to think about, and he didn't want any distractions.

SEVEN

Laney was setting up when Ravel pulled into the parking lot at Rambis Plateau. The sky's intense darkness had not altered one bit since he'd disengaged from Mick and Godwin. If anything, he felt as if the darkness was encroaching on him now, engulfing him like a wave. He saw it everywhere now, his life, and the January stars peppering the sky did little to make him optimistic. *What am I doing?* Ravel thought. *Dead of night in the foothills with a former student, former female student, going back in time in a freakin' time machine...What am I thinking?* Had his life really descended to this depth? Could he lower himself any further?

"Cold enough for you?" Laney jibed. Her eyes shone wide. "How's your coffee intake?"

"Plenty," said Ravel. "You?"

"Positively wired. It was a pain getting this out of the basement level." She gestured to the truck and attached trailer behind her.

"Where's Nicholas?"

"Couldn't make it. Or didn't want to. Leaves the heavy lifting to me, right?"

Laney's demeanor was in some way off. Ravel couldn't place it. He sensed she was holding back.

"Laney…. Is all this on the up and up?"

Laney's smile faltered. "If you want to do this, Ravel, don't push it, okay? Help me unload the machine."

Together they opened the trailer and rolled out the Chronoquantumogriphier, which had been secured to a wheeled platform. In the freezing wind they pushed the machine across the plateau into the area of the concentric circles. Laney's headlamp lit the way.

"This spot," she said. "Right in the center."

"I figured. Does it work any time we want?"

"Let's hope."

"You mean you don't know?"

"Hey," Laney snapped. "I'm doing you a favor here, remember? It should work, but we've never done it in, you know, uh, the freezing cold like this. Only you and I are crazy enough to freeze our asses off at three in the morning. Cross your fingers, okay?"

He had always done what was expected. Being there for his mother, marrying, getting a job and making money. He'd never anticipated what any of his choices might do to him. He'd been in denial of another path for far too long.

"So," Ravel said, "Colorado. The eighties. Do I just tell you exactly when and where I want to land there and you punch in the coordinates?"

"First we have to prep you. That means the debugging process. That takes a little time. The lab is in the trailer."

"What does the lab do?"

"Cleanse you—within reason, of course. It won't remove everything, there are plenty of good germs in the human body too. We don't want to kill you! But the idea here is not to bring any illnesses from the 2020s back to the 1980s. You don't feel sick at all? No fever?"

"No and no."

"Ever have Covid?"

"No. I lucked out."

"I had it. It sucked. Covid in the '80s I imagine would be the Second Coming of the bubonic plague times five hundred."

"They'll make an '80s version of that Bruegel painting, *The Triumph of Death*," Ravel said. "An eight-bit version. Nintendo-style."

Shivering, Laney managed a half-smile. "Your mind sometimes, Ravel. Anyway, as much as you want to call the shots as to where you're going, this first time around I need you to go where *I* want you to go."

"Why's that?"

"Number one reason: It's safer. Number two: I take it you didn't come prepared with any of the clothing from the time you're planning to travel to."

"Oh. Dang. Forgot about that."

"It's okay. I got you covered. Remember I told you this is just a test run. I've got clothes genuinely made in the eighties waiting for you in the trailer."

"Warm clothes, I hope."

"An eighties winter outfit. Only the finest. Now you honestly didn't take a single breath of life in any of the 1980s?"

"I'm thirty. I was born in 1992. If it helps, my wife, who's from here, she was born in 1990."

"All right. I'm assuming you had no family living in Colorado in the year 1989."

"That year my parents were living in LA. I'm sure they wanted nothing to do with Colorado."

"Good. Then 1989 Colorado. Rocky Mountain National Park."

"Really, Laney? RMNP, which I've been to like eight times already? How am I going to even know it's 1989?"

"Baby steps, Ravel. Do this test run and the next chrono-trek is all yours."

"Okay," Ravel said, swallowing some of his impatience.

"Before you go, you need to sign this." Laney held up a clipboard clamped down on a contract. In the meager light from Laney's headlamp, Ravel could make little sense of the dense miniscule print.

"That's a lot of legalese, Laney."

"You're smart enough to have expected this, Ravel."

"I might die."

"You might. But you're willing to take that chance, unless I got you all wrong..."

"You didn't get me wrong." Ravel flipped through the several pages, scanned only in places, and then signed and initialed the necessary lines. Laney took the pen and clipboard.

"Apparently a few conversations about my regrets, my burning desire to do things over again, go back in time if I could—that's all it took," said Ravel.

"It was more than that, Professor," Laney said. "Every day in class, you just seemed like the exact person who would do this without hesitation. When Nicholas asked for an outsider—"

"I was the first one who came to mind."

"You were the *only* one who came to mind," Laney corrected.

"And then you proceeded to stalk me.... For how long exactly?"

"Months."

"The psychometrics, or whatever?"

"Profiling a person who puts themselves out there as much as you do on social, the internet, all those apps, it's not so difficult."

"I'm embarrassed I'm that much of an open book," said Ravel.

"You're not alone," Laney consoled. "But you're soon to be unique. The only one who's ever—"

She caught her next words, wouldn't release them. Ravel's brow furrowed.

"What was that, Laney?"

"Nothing," she said. "Just: remember the rules. No potentially future-altering actions."

"Only watching," Ravel assured her. "An observer. Fly on the wall. Or a fly in the snow."

"I'm not going to send you back in the dead of winter. I'll send you back to late spring of that year. Still, early morning in RMNP is going to be cold. Let's go for Sunday, May 7th, 1989. Lucky seventh, right?"

"Right," Ravel said. "Can I get started already? I can't feel my face anymore."

"Change and debug first."

Inside the trailer, Ravel swapped clothes. He put on

underwear he never would have worn in the 2020s (whitey tighties), stiff jeans and a polo shirt. Additional layers consisted of a garish sweater seemingly knitted by a grandmother who got run over by a reindeer, an Adidas brand pullover, and, to top it off, a puffy blue ski parka. Ravel switched out his heavy socks for equally heavy socks, apparently manufactured in the '80s, and snow boots that looked like they were worn in that early '80s movie *Tron*. Ravel took a deep breath and looked himself over using his phone. He looked out of time, which was the whole point. Soon he would be in time, a new yet older time.

The debugging consisted of standing in a cylindrical chamber, breathing deeply yet calmly as tiny drones went to work scrubbing skin, hair, nails, clothing. Shots were administered. A painless laser beam washed over Ravel from head to foot. He had been ordered not to blink.

"Leave your phone," Laney told him when he emerged.

Ravel handed his device over. "I'm not going to end up phased into a tree or anything, right?"

"No, Ravel. Without DOG, that would be a distinct threat, but since you have your AI copilot you're going to arrive safely."

Laney accompanied Ravel to the Chronoquantumogriphier, which was now hovering directly over the massive uncovered hole at the center of the concentric circles. Laney pushed some buttons on a remote and the hatch to the Chronoquantumogriphier lifted to allow Ravel access. He looked in.

At first he thought someone was already in the machine. Then he saw what he mistook for a body was in fact a spacesuit of some kind. *Time suit*? thought Ravel. It was open on the sides like a beetle's carapace, waiting for him to fit inside.

"Um, what's with the suit, Laney?"

"That's the only way to enter the past, Ravel. With that suit. We need everything, of course. The wormhole is what sends us into the past, the Chronoquantumogriphier is the vessel, the ship we travel in, DOG is the navigator, the compass, the guide, and this suit is your only way of touching down safely." Laney saw Ravel's blank stare and continued. "When you reach the place and the point in time DOG has approved, you detach from the Chronoquantumogriphier."

"Detach like, what, a spacewalk?"

"You could think of it like that, sure. A time walk."

"So I arrive in the suit, not the machine?"

"You arrive in neither. You arrive as you're dressed, suitless."

"*How?*"

"At the moment of impact, the point of arrival, DOG will essentially launch your atomical structure out of the Chrono-quantumogriphier and the suit also at the last possible point in time and space."

"Sounds like I'm going to die, Laney."

"Without the suit, you would. This is like armor that keeps your structure intact, safe."

"And what about getting back? How the hell am I going to find the suit, the machine, if I don't land with them?"

"Again, DOG. DOG will find you, signal you. You'll know it's there when you see a crackling energy field in the air. It won't be too big, so don't miss it. Go to that field. The suit will be just beyond, back through the slip portal. Once you're through, the suit will close automatically around you again,

DOG will yank you back into the Chronoquantumogriphier and—"

"Laney, please tell me you're not making this shit up."

"Ravel, just go, okay? It's exhausting to explain all this to a novice."

With one last glance at Laney, Ravel got in. Just as she said, the suit he settled into closed instantly around him. He was encased, unable to move. Through his helmet Ravel saw the machine's interior in a dim orange light. The Chronoquantumogriphier's interior was free of any buttons or levers. Ravel found the seat comfortable. Laney told him to strap in. "It may be a bit bumpy," she added.

Ravel locked in the two separate seat belts, each running across his chest and into his lap like bandoliers. "Snug," he said. "No windows in this thing."

"DOG's all you need," Laney said. Ravel looked at the screen before him. It was wide and chock-a-block full of numbers, formulas, data. A Quantum Quilt. Ravel watched fluctuating patterns and wavelengths in a green-on-black color, reminding him of an EKG. Laney explained that these patterns and wavelengths monitored the life of both his suit and the Chronoquantumogriphier, and they had never been in better health.

"I hope my health stays all right," muttered Ravel. Briefly he thought of his blood sugar, his numbers. His kidney function, his blood pressure, his heart.

Instead of reacting verbally to Ravel's concern, Laney nodded and stepped back. "Trust in DOG," she said. "He'll get you there."

"So DOG is in front of me, this screen?"

"He's embedded throughout the Chronoquantumogriphier. He essentially *is* the Chronoquantumogriphier. Please don't try to speak to him—he won't answer. He only answers to us."

"I trust you, Laney."

"And we trust you, Ravel. This is all about trust, you know. Remember: no deviations from the limits whatsoever. Remember the brochure."

"Aye-aye, captain. Send me on my way already."

"To make it official, I have to say this: Do you, Ravel Averof, solemnly swear to abide by each and every one of the rules as they are laid out and explained in the contract you signed?"

"I do."

"Do you fully understand everything you read in that contract?"

"Uh, yes. I definitely do."

"Do you understand that going against any of these rules, even just one, could lead to consequences, dire consequences, that not even Chronotrex may be able to reverse, and in such a case Chronotrex is in no way to be held liable?"

She didn't have to say all this. Ravel knew the rules. He had read, signed and initialed each page of that contract. Besides, it wasn't as if this time around he was planning on disobeying.

"Yes. I understand and I'll obey it all."

"Then tesser well, Ravel."

"What's that? Tesser..."

"Tesser well. It's not the same thing really, but it's close enough, and I've wanted to say those words ever since I read *A*—"

"*A Wrinkle in Time.*"

"Right. *A Wrinkle in Time.*"

A jolt of memory struck Ravel then: he, five years old, accompanying his mother at night through the University of California Santa Barbara campus. He had the UCSB bookstore receipt still. The date was February 7, 1998, and author Madeline L'Engle was on campus to give a reading. Yoana had driven up from LA, where she and Ravel were living at the time in the wake of Spiros abandoning them and absconding to New York when Ravel was only two. Ravel remembered nothing of the reading itself, but he would never forget meeting L'Engle at the table where she sat ready to sign his paperback copy of *A Wrinkle in Time*. Above her name she had written the words *for Ravel—Tesser well.*

"Ravel, are you okay?"

"I'm fine. Just remembered something, that's all."

"I have your phone," Laney said, "your keys, your wallet, your glucometer, your wedding ring.... Oh shit, what about that necklace you wear all the time? Let me have it now."

"It's an amulet, Laney. Not a necklace. And no, I have to have it with me."

"I can't send you, Ravel, if you don't give up *everything*."

"Not this," Ravel said. "I can guarantee it was made before May 7, 1989."

"You swear by that?"

"I swear on my mother's grave."

Laney twisted her mouth and narrowed her eyes. She took a moment to consider. At last she gave Ravel the okay.

"Thank you."

"Okay, DOG," Laney said to the Chronoquantumogriphier's interior, "time to unleash."

The previously blank and dark panels surrounding Ravel

lit up and flashed in various patterns and at different degrees of intensity.

"I'm closing the hatch now," said Laney. "Give me a moment to set the coordinates. This works sort of like a control tower at an airport. With the help of DOG, I can tell where objects and structures and people and animals are, and also where there's open space to phase in the traveler. We can only guess what the physical matter is, but with DOG steering, your coordinates won't overlap with that matter. No instantaneous death."

"Or any death, I hope."

"I'll be here when you return."

"How much time is going to pass here compared to there?"

"If Chronotrex's formulas are correct, nearly no time at all."

"Really? Even if I spend a ton of time in the past?"

"I strongly urge you not to do that, Ravel. That could be extremely dangerous. You might not come back. Remember: in and out. You're just there to observe. Take the past in. I've set the Chronoquantumogriphier for ten minutes. Go to that shimmering energy field and worm your way into it before your time is up."

"What if someone sees the energy field? The shimmering of the slip portal or whatever?"

"They won't, according to DOG. Not with where I'm placing you."

Laney used her remote to lower the hatch. Before he lost sight of her, Ravel gave a thumbs up, and she did the same. Then: darkness save for the dim orange light seen through his helmet and the flashes from the control screen and the panels on either side. A moment of doubt seized Ravel, a gut-punch that threatened to empty his bowels. *Okay*, he thought. *Aliens, or whoever put this here, don't let me down.*

"Ravel, I'm about to launch you."

He shot to attention at Laney's voice in the compartment. He gripped his thighs. "Ready," he said.

"Then here we go. We'll lose contact with each other until the time I bring you back. During the chrono-trek you're probably going to feel some bumping and tossing associated with the time bends and chrono-vortex continuum, I can imagine. If you feel like you need to throw up, do it in your helmet. Your vomit will be sucked away. The helmet's made for that." A slight but noticeable pause. "Relax and remain calm. Have a good time. See you in ten minutes."

The data on the control screen began to scroll at a rapid pace. The panel lights flashed wildly in alternating patterns, and a soft but unmistakable whirring ensued. Rather than scared, Ravel felt enthused. *It's going to work*, he thought. *I'm going to—*

The lights dimmed to an ominous glow. The whirring continued, punctuated by louder whooping that sounded like an AI-generated bird crying for its AI-generated young. Then Ravel felt his actual body lifted in the seat. Through the helmet the lights flared and presented themselves as droplets running down his line of sight. The droplets ran into one another like quicksilver and then, when enough had combined, started to swirl like the contents of an ice cream maker. Ravel closed his eyes but realized they were already closed, and when he opened them he knew they were already open. He had never dropped acid or eaten shrooms or done Ecstasy, and he supposed that something like this might have been experienced by someone on any one or a combination of those substances. But would a shroom-eater, an Ecstasy tab-taker, an acid dropper, feel her or his or their body bounced around as if flying through the South Pacific storm that claimed Amelia Earhart and her non-AI copilot? Would those consumers of drugs have felt their skin tingling to the point where they'd rather have the entire epidermal encasement flayed from their physical form? Or had they ever felt their fingernails peeled back, layer by miniscule layer, or their nose hairs lengthening to the point where those hairs touched their lips? So far—and Ravel was sure he had experienced all this in only the first thirty seconds of travel—the extraterrestrials' wormhole and accompanying time bend continuum were not kind to those seeking passage, and Ravel, for a moment, wondered if this was the way to go after all.

And then, as if he had been stabbed back to consciousness with a syringe through his breastplate, he saw a boom of bright colorless light and he rocketed through to stand outside. His brain feeling as if he'd just downed ten scoops of ice cream in the span of three seconds, he blinked his eyes and reached out to steady himself against something solid. Cold. Rough. Wood. Bark. His eyes returned to him. He faced the tree he was leaning against. *Close*, Ravel thought. His body stung all over, as if he'd suffered thousands of miniscule internal paper cuts. *Atomical structure*, he thought. *Rearranging my atoms?* His raging headache had thankfully begun to recede. He blinked several times, still facing the tree. *One more millimeter over, he thought. One more and I'd be phased in. Dead. Thank DOG it worked.* Another minute passed before he was his full, painless self again, all his senses having returned. He no longer felt like retching. *How much longer?* he thought. *I'm already down how many minutes?*

He did not see any energy field, shimmering or crackling. Ravel looked around. He stood amongst trees, and just beyond the one he was leaning against he could see an open field sloping downward toward a road in the distance. Vehicles were backed up on the road, and people had emerged. It was early morning, the sun halfway risen. Ravel saw his breath in front of him. He couldn't identify the cause of the backup, and with the acute awareness that his clock was ticking he decided to leave the stand of trees and head down the slope. As he drew closer to the vehicles he saw that none of them were from the 21st century. Many older models from the eighties and seventies, perhaps even one from the sixties. The people standing by their vehicles were dressed much like he was: in warm clothing that in the early 2020s would be called 'retro.' No one—not a single human—held a phone.

A few excited cries issued from those who'd emerged. Ravel followed their line of sight across the road from where he stood. Something was on the other side, farther down the continuing slope. Ravel walked across the road, weaved past vehicles and people, avoided making eye contact. Amazing how people looked at him and smiled. Smiled! They acknowledged him with nods; a couple even said hello. Ravel's reticence didn't phase them. They were content, unplugged, unwired, parked on a road in Rocky Mountain National Park as the sun rose fully on the morning of Sunday, May 7th, 1989.

Ravel reached the guardrail and looked down. The slope leveled out a hundred or so feet below, where a large animal drank from a pond. A dense thicket of trees lay beyond. The sight, with the sun nearly at full force for the day, the pond water sparkling, the large animal dipping its head, was breathtaking. More national park patrons gathered at the guardrail on either side of Ravel. Their already excited voices rose in volume. Several pointed. Ravel shook his head. "No," he whispered.

The large animal drinking from the pond was an elk—a giant elk, its antlers as intricate and regal as a crown. It was the most magnificent creature Ravel had ever seen. The elk was not the problem. The problem was the tourist approaching it. An Asian man, a large camera slung over his neck, slim and older, inched closer to the great elk. He wore a heavy coat, the fuzzy hood falling back to reveal his thinning hair. He lifted the expensive-looking camera as he drew within a few feet of the beautiful beast. What a shot! "No," Ravel whispered again. "No." Not one of his fellow witnesses said anything now. All was quiet. Ravel spotted what could have been the man's family—his wife, his children—standing farther up the slope.

The eager man shuffled up to the elk, which turned. Now standing eye to eye, elk and man shared a moment. The elk's mouth moved, as if it were chewing cud. Now a few shouts of warning rose up from those gathered at the guardrail. The man's family remained silent. The man ignored the shouts from above. He stood resolute and raised the camera to his eye.

All witnesses hushed. A tableau, the scene suspended in time. The tourist must have snapped pictures, because now he reached out to touch the elk's nose. His fingers stretching, the elderly man closed the gap fast, but the elk was faster. It bellowed, a terrifying sound that stretched into a roar, and it reared up, its massive hooves punching out. Those front hooves landed on the hapless tourist's head. The man went down in a shocking geyser of blood. The man's family—if it was his family—screamed and retreated. The crowd gathered at the guardrail convulsed. People turned and fled to their vehicles. Engines started, horns blared. Ravel took one more look at the scene of the elk stomping on the tourist's body at the edge of the pond, the dead man's family running up the slope, away from the carnage, and took off. He was met with a sweaty mustached face, almost a headbutt, and the words "move move" in his ears and the smell of pungent cologne up his nostrils. He too joined the crowd in fleeing. A mullet, so many mullets. Ravel dodged a lurching sedan. He leap-frogged across the road and landed in grass. Gathering himself, he ran up the slope toward the stand of trees where he'd arrived. It had to be there. His time was almost up and the energy field had to be there. He did not want to be stuck here, in Rocky Mountain National Park, in 1989, to experience more bloodshed and bad haircuts. No internet. No social. How did anybody find anything? How did they gain knowledge? How did they kill time? How did time kill them?

Ravel looked wildly from tree to tree. Nothing. Where was it? Where—

He sensed it before seeing it. The energy current, the field, suspended in midair between two trunks. A barely perceptible crackling that would be missed unless you knew to look for it. Ravel reached out to touch the small circular band of wavering light.

He pushed his hand through the field, then his arm, then his head and upper abdomen. He felt himself yanked forward, sucked through like a particle in a vacuum. The forest fell away and it was only him, in darkness, spinning and churning, the lights bursting like solar flares on all sides. He felt as if he were forced into a cylinder two sizes too small, his body still spinning, his blood sugar surely spiking or crashing or both. His migraine and those internal paper cuts had returned; it was as if every synapse and nerve ending was on fire. Through the flames he could see writhing faces he did not recognize, faces he feared he would see forever. Where was the time suit, Chronoquantumogriphier, DOG, the control panel he couldn't control? Without the time suit and its helmet he would surely go blind, why was he able to see now, hurtling as he was through the flaring outskirts of time? Now that he was exposed, Ravel expected his insides at any moment to implode, and although he might have appeared fine on the outside, his body intact, floating serenely through the time-space continuum, his insides would be upended, ravaged and rearranged. He saw the stars all around yet out of reach as he hurtled, the constant flares rising every few seconds, and ultimately, just ahead and approaching fast, the sun. The sun was bigger than he'd ever seen it before. It continued to come at him—or he at it—bigger and bigger, faster and faster, enlarged and engorged, and the heat grew unbearable. He couldn't turn from his fate. It wasn't so horrid—he knew this even as he screamed.

He snapped to in the seat of the Chronoquantumogriphier, encased in the suit, the helmet secured. Instantly the extreme ice cream headache was back and he had to purge his stomach. If he didn't vomit now then whatever was in him would become a permanent part of him, to remain even with his remains. Seeing the congealing flares before him, seemingly within the Chronoquantumogriphier, glowing and pulsing in the vortex of the chrono-continuum, he upchucked into his helmet. True to Laney's word, Ravel's puke was purged immediately through a vacuum-like tube near his mouth. Ravel's retching lasted an astounding five minutes during which time his lids were closed but his eyes still witnessed. The Chronoquantumogriphier was being battered around badly. Along with that an increase in speed, in the sense of urgency associated with the return trip, as if whoever or whatever was controlling this contraption knew that the traveler might not make it.

And then, as if coming out of unconsciousness for the second time in a week, Ravel found himself out of the wormhole, out of the slip portal and into the present. The Chronoquantumogriphier had settled. In desperation Ravel tried to wrench the helmet off. Impossible: the helmet was part of the suit itself. He would have to wait until the hatch opened. He took in deep breaths to help ease his maddening heart. The feel of the amulet against his chest, near his heart, helped as well.

The latch slowly lifted, and Ravel was met by Laney, the Rambis Plateau, and the sun breaking on the horizon like an eye opening. Laney looked afraid. She offered Ravel a hand.

"Holy Christ," he wheezed. "Jesus, Laney."

Laney, her best face forward, exited Ravel's view. Ravel remained in the Chronoquantumogriphier, taking deep breaths, holding then exhaling. He had calmed down considerably by the time Laney returned. His suit opened, the helmet disengaged, and she helped him out. On terra firma now, Ravel let go of his former student's hand—a mistake too late as he crumpled. He mustered enough strength to get to his knees, then swung himself back to sit so that his knees were drawn to his chest and he could hug for warmth.

"You made it," said Laney. "I almost didn't think—"

"I think I've gone crazy," Ravel said, his voice clearer now.

"What I saw—everything. Not just in that place I went to, but the other places, the places I had to get through…"

"I need to know what it's like, Ravel. I need you to describe it to me, as much as you can."

"Didn't they tell you when they came back? Was it all that much different than what I went through?"

Uncomfortable now, Laney looked away. At the edge of Ravel's mind was a realization, crawling in on all fours.

"Laney…. I trusted you. I still want to trust you. What—"

"He made me swear not to tell," Laney said. "We needed someone who would go along with it all so easily, someone who *needed* this more than we needed them to do it."

"Why…"

"Because, Ravel, you're the first. The *very* first. And Nicholas, and the Bowtie Bros, they didn't want to…"

"They didn't go," Ravel said. "They never went. None of them went. Not even Nicholas."

Laney faced Ravel. She didn't even have to nod.

"Oh my fucking God." Ravel rolled onto his side. "Oh Jesus. You—Christ, Laney, you tricked me. You tricked me! You didn't tell me I was going to be the first, *that's* why you needed me, *that's* why you made this so easy for me…. I was your *fucking guinea pig*! You couldn't get some other sucker to do this—"

"Believe me, Ravel, we tried."

"There were others before me?"

"Several others, yes. For months we tried. Each outsider got to the point where they were in the Chronoquantumogriphier about to launch—and then they couldn't do it. They dipped. They weren't…desperate enough."

"And I was." Ravel laughed bitterly. "You kept me in mind

for all those years, knowing I would fall right into this because I'm me."

"I *remembered* you. I *knew* you."

"You knew me as a sucker. So you made me your space monkey, a dog you shot out into the wormhole to the past not knowing if I'd ever come back! And if I didn't, well, I signed some papers and you're not legally responsible, are you? Are you?" Ravel's anger had gone from zero to six hundred as he spoke. He brought himself to his knees again, then, wobbly, foal-like, got to his feet and stayed there. He straightened up, his chest heaving, and touched his forehead. The migraine was nowhere near at the severe intensity it had been during the chrono-trek—but it lingered.

"I understand why you're upset—"

"I'm way more than upset, Laney." Ravel laughed again harshly. "I'm *hurt*. I feel.... I was going to *die*."

"You would have if DOG hadn't located you when you pushed through. There was an unanticipated delay in suiting back up."

"I feel like I'm older now."

"You are older now," Laney said. "I've calculated—"

"Oh no..."

"That chrono-trek took some time off your life."

"How much time?" Ravel cried out.

"Not much, from what I can determine."

"*From what you can determine?*"

"Otherwise you would look much older than you do now."

"How old do I look now?"

"Really, Ravel," assured Laney. "There's no difference."

"This is what you call trust, Laney? I can't believe..."

"You wanted this, Ravel. You signed—"

"The super-fine print, of course."

"I need your input," Laney pressed. "Tell me everything."

"Not a chance." Ravel stepped away from Laney and the Chronoquantumogriphier. "I don't trust you. You knew that elk was going to be there. You knew what it did to that guy would cause a stampede. You put me there to die!"

"Apparently," Laney said to herself, "paranoia is a side effect."

Ravel turned and kicked the Chronoquantumogriphier. His foot clanged off the side. "Oh my God," he said, his eyes widening. "That's why you needed that part. You sent this thing back in time without anyone in it, and when it returned the side had blown out."

"Close, Ravel," said Laney. "Can you be honest with yourself?"

"Huh?"

"You would've still done this. If I'd told you anything about the chrono-trek, or pointed you to anything in the contract's fine print, you still would have gone. You're that desperate."

Ravel nodded. "I had to go," he admitted. "And now that I have, I'm not going again. I'll die if I go again, and I'll be damned if I'm going to die. I have a wife I love, and I have a life, and...and..."

"Anything else, Ravel?"

"I guess not."

"All right then."

"This has been a real trip, Laney, a real trip and a half. But the vomiting, the headaches, I could live with those. But the aging? That's where I draw the line. That's where, when you start taking time off a person's life.... I know what I want, but even I don't want it that bad, enough to lose my life."

"Understood."

"I need my glucometer. I'm afraid what my number is right now. And I need my phone, and my clothes."

"The trailer's yours."

Ravel changed quickly. He tested: his number was high, but not dangerously so. *Not again,* he thought. *Only thirty and I have to go the distance with this disease. Can't let it win.* He checked the time on his phone. It occurred to him that more time had passed here on Earth than it had in the past time-space of Rocky Mountain National Park in the early morning of May 7, 1989. Mid-morning now, and he was older than he should have been.

Laney couldn't look at him as he got into his vehicle. Her face tight, she stood before the Chronoquantumogriphier, remote in hand. Ravel wondered how she was going to get the machine back in the trailer on her own. Feeling something then, an emotion, he rolled down his window. "Hey," he shouted.

"What."

"I'm sorry. Laney. About how I reacted just now."

"None of us could know, Ravel. The past is the future. Maybe sometime soon you'll be willing to talk."

"Yeah," Ravel said.

"Good luck, okay?"

"Good luck to you too."

Laney nodded, her lips pursed, eyes downcast. Ravel rolled his window up, started his vehicle and pulled out of the Rambis Plateau parking lot.

EIGHT

I f Ravel had not been so shaken, still so sick and so scared, perusing his face in the rearview every few seconds, he might have picked up on the announcement sooner. As it happened he caught only the tail-end of his favorite literary podcast—but heard enough to cry out:

"Motherfather!"

He had done it. His father, Spiros Averof, had just been announced the winner of the ADPiF—the American Diamond Prize in Fiction—the latest—and so far financially greatest—prize created for those who dared to write beyond the first few pages.

The podcast's host chided any listeners who found it a surprise that this Greek émigré, at age 58 author of twelve novels, nearly all of them a winner of some kind of award and many of them bestsellers, had won the ADPiF—who else would they have chosen? the host said.

There's Tristan Boppana, Ravel thought. *There's me.*

The award was such a momentous honor it would not be given until late August, in New York, allowing for several months of publicity and sales. *I could be there*, Ravel thought. *I could show up*. He had only to make an excuse, tell Deborah he had a big job interview in Manhattan that day. Or, if he wished to be invited to the award ceremony, he could take his second chrono-trek after all.

But the thought of using Chronotrex in any way after what he'd just experienced did not sit well with him. He had half a mind to call his father-in-law and have the police shut the whole operation down, if for no other reason than to head off further disaster. Laney and company were a bunch of crackpots. They gave the appearance of knowing what they were doing, but in reality they were groping through the dark, nowhere near the light. They'd gotten lucky discovering that wormhole on Rambis Plateau, a gift from some alien species, but it was obvious now they had little understanding of their own power. To think: a company having to dupe outsiders, U.S. citizens, into thinking the chrono-trek was harmless so they could rope them into their time machine, then blast the poor hapless saps off down the wormhole—and how many would be lucky enough, like Ravel, to return? How many of those travelers—mothers and fathers and children and grand-parents—would return intact, sane and whole? By shutting down Chronotrex Ravel would be decapitating the monster before it had a chance to fully grow. He would be doing Laney and Nicholas and the rest of humanity a favor. They were only going to get themselves in trouble with this, and if the U.S. military got a hold of the Chronoquantumogriphier, well.

To hell with whatever he'd signed. Legit contract or not, surely there was some law in Boulder County if not in all of Colorado that forbade nutjobs from inventing and then exper-imenting with a time machine in an otherwise reputable and well-meaning business park and an otherwise serene nature setting in the foothills. Ravel pictured the raid and smiled. He imagined cops, dressed in Prohibition-era extra-long navy coats and big buttons, sharp caps and with billy clubs swinging, descending on the basement-level lab. Nicholas and his bros would put up little resistance. Perhaps one officer would get taken out with a Molotov Bunsen burner, but not before one of the Bowtie Bros had his skull split open right down his symmetrical butt-cut part. With what the law would find on the premises, any signed contract would be considered null and void.

Ravel saw himself breaking open Nicholas's desk with a crowbar, retrieving the original of his contract and setting it on fire as the boss-man, handcuffed, watched with an officer on either side. Perhaps Mick Parker would lead the raid, if the mayor had another detail at that time.

Ravel would laugh—laugh!—as he watched Nicholas shoved into the back of the police SUV, his hands behind his back so that he couldn't shield his face from the news cameras. Laney, an accomplice and therefore also arrested, would look at Ravel with such venom—and he wouldn't care. He would return to Denver, the apartment in Capitol Hill, Deborah, his future, whatever that was, never to travel back in time again. Never again would he even consider it. His future was another office job, an office job he could live with until retirement, a child or two, a renewal of vows, celebrations of birthdays, anniversaries, graduations, then actual retirement, grandchildren, decline, funerals (finally his own), and at last: forgotten.

Forgotten. That one word was what he feared most, feared more than death, for what did it matter if he died as long as he was remembered? And not remembered in some trite way such as with a park bench or a plaque on the wall of some office building lobby—but with thoughts, words, a conversation with the future. With his published work entrenched, he would never truly die. Shakespeare had never died. Melville had never died. Baldwin had never died. Wiesel had never died. Didion had never died. Twain had never died, nor had Homer, Milton, Cervantes, Rumi, Dickinson, Poe, or Lady Murasaki. Had any of them thought, while still alive in their time, that the work they were doing—dabbling for some, bleeding for others—would open a doorway, build a bridge, their time leading to all times after, and that they would comfort so many in need of something to do, someone to speak to? Did Cervantes know that four hundred years from his last day on earth, that fateful day in April, millions of people worldwide would be reading his great work and laughing uproariously?

The Greats. The Titans. The Transcendent. Hopeful but not delusional, Ravel did not expect to join their ranks, but he did believe he deserved at least one well-received novel in the Library of Congress. Just one would ensure some small degree of immortality. If that didn't happen and Ravel was forgotten, as the outcome appeared to be now, what could he possibly look forward to? Life, certainly, all that he had and could associate with staying married, having children, grandchildren, working, providing, supporting, loving—but what would his life be to him without the assurance that *he*—it didn't have to be his image, just his name and his work, his words—would *never* be forgotten? That his writing, his contemplations, characters, scenarios, imagination—and therefore him—would *always* be digested and discussed?

Deborah was in the kitchen when he arrived home. "Where were you?" she asked. "You left early."

His thoughts still consumed by the news of his father having won the American Diamond Prize in Fiction, Ravel did not immediately respond, which heightened Deborah's suspicion. "Well, Ravel?" she demanded.

"Thought I'd get a walk in before I ate. Drove over to Cheesman."

Deborah assessed her husband's truthfulness. At last her eyes released him. She carried on making breakfast. Ravel offered to help, and, after a tense several seconds of hesitation, she accepted. The sharpness of her tone should not have surprised him. Still, he was troubled. Deborah's suspicion was marching toward disbelief and hurt, and Ravel wasn't sure he could reveal the truth to stop it from happening. He had signed that contract; from what little he had read, he knew he could be taken to court if he reneged on the non-disclosure clause. Their kitchen that morning was tense. Each time Ravel moved toward his wife, Deborah either falsely anticipated by giving him an item he did not need—without a word—or she cut him off by stepping out of his way so that he was left fumbling for an item he didn't need to justify his advances. It reminded Ravel of tag, only he seemed to be playing with a ghost.

"My father texted me."

Ravel stood shock-still, unable to breathe.

"He says he gave you his script this morning."

"Oh. Yeah. He did. It's in the car still—"

"He gave it to you in Cheesman Park, right?"

Deborah's eyes locked with Ravel's. "Right," he said, making certain not to blink.

"I mean, that's where he'd have to give it to you, if you say you went there to walk."

"I did. That's where we ran into each other. Or, really, he's keeping tabs on me. He admitted that. Even now, after all these years.... Anyway, I'll go get the script."

"He wants you to go early Monday morning and deliver it to the agent."

"Monday?"

"The holidays are over. She should be back in the office, right? Dad didn't think you'd be doing anything. *Will* you be doing something?"

Looking into his wife's eyes—skeptical now, not accusatory as he'd expected—Ravel realized that Mick, for all his hangups, remained a man of his word. He had not divulged all the details of the early morning run-in on I-25. Ravel also realized then that if he refused to go to Maxine on Monday and hand over Mick's script his father-in-law would tell Deborah everything. Was Mick Parker willing to make Ravel's marriage miserable, perhaps even end it, just to push that script through? Of course. Mick Parker was, if nothing else, a man of the people.

"Count on me," said Ravel, "to give that script to Maxine on Monday morning, first thing."

"Dad said giving his script to that agent should be very important to you now. What does he mean by that?"

Ravel paused for an appropriate length of time, during which he appeared appropriately pensive. "I'm not sure," he said. "He might want to give me a share of the profits if the script gets picked up?"

Deborah laughed. "Where were you really this morning?" Though her eyes were bright, they shone for the wrong reasons. To Ravel, they glistened.

"I've told you the truth, Deb. Ask your dad if you still

don't believe me."

His challenge worked. Deborah softened considerably. "Next time," she said, "text me, okay, Rav?"

"Absolutely."

For the rest of the weekend Deborah did not press her husband. They carried on as they always had, as if the morning's inquisition had never happened. To Ravel's surprise and mild, muted concern, Deborah Parker was excessively pleasant.

WALKING along downtown Denver's Wazee Street after having successfully bypassed it for the past five years gave Ravel a feeling of alienation. He couldn't be bitter—not now that his former boss Maxine Dein had been gracious enough to respond to his email and set aside some time for a Monday morning meeting. It was now up to Ravel to find that same degree of graciousness within himself. He had to let go of Maxine's dismissiveness of his writing, her prejudice against anyone with a graduate degree that wasn't an MBA or a JD, and concede that he was groveling before her again after so long not for himself but for his father-in-law—and present himself as gregarious and positive as possible. *Away, cynicism,* Ravel thought as he entered the building housing Maxine's literary agency. *Away, bitterness. Away, ghosts.*

In the elevator he glanced again at the cover page of Mick & Company's script. *Freedom Freeway.* Ravel shook his head. He had a hunch his father-in-law's nascent writing career wasn't going to survive to MLK Jr. Day. Maxine wasn't a fan of anything she had read too often before—and this script was everything she had read before and then some. Mick would have to accept the pass and content himself with the acknowledgment that his loyal, faithful son-in-law had done all he could. By that time this absurd blackmail would be at an end.

The door to Maxine's office was closed and a loud voice—frighteningly familiar—could be heard issuing excited exclamations behind it. Ravel stood across the hallway from that door, just inside the open threshold of the interns' office, and tried not to pick up on too much. It was difficult, given the thinness of Maxine's door. Her voice, so excited, was unmistakable, but then there was another voice, deep and guttural, that Ravel knew. He had heard this voice before, perhaps as an intern for this exact agency. The current intern taking charge of the office opposite Maxine's was a young woman who looked to still be in college. At least she had sense enough not to be on her phone; rather, she was going through Maxine's voluminous stacks of files, most of which concerned projects she had rejected over the years. As Ravel recalled, Maxine would every so often send interns into those old files, none of which were ever thrown away, to search out manuscripts that might now amount to something after all.

The current intern glanced up at Ravel and flashed him a harried, insincere smile. Ravel quipped about looking for a diamond in the rough; the intern seemed not to have heard him. When she did give him what little attention she could muster he explained that he had an appointment, Maxine was expecting him.

"I'm not sure when she'll be out," the intern said. "They've been in there a while. They've really hit it off."

Ravel dared to ask with whom Maxine might be speaking. The intern shook her head, said that was private information. She wouldn't give the name of this new client, but she did reveal that the man was older, wealthy-looking and "kind of snobby-sounding, maybe from another country?" Ravel remained standing as the intern alternated between sifting through files, keeping an eye on any new messages Maxine might be receiving, and checking the progress of image uploads for the agent's forthcoming website.

Ravel smiled and said, "When she gets through with whoever's in there, tell her I just went down the hall, okay? I'll be back soon."

On his way out of the interns' office, Ravel heard little from behind Maxine's door. She and her new client were still talking—but low now. Ravel walked to the end of the hallway and entered the restroom.

Inside, on the john to take a break from standing rather than to do any legit business, Ravel thought of what he had heard from behind the closed door. The names of production companies, cities (New York, LA, Miami, San Francisco, Boston) and publishers bandied about—almost entirely in that deep, guttural, foreign-accented voice. Seated on the toilet's lid, Ravel swore he had encountered that voice up close before—but when? If he couldn't readily recall then obviously the person wasn't that important, and since the client didn't matter, Ravel waited minutes longer before getting up.

As he emerged he caught sight of a shadow, long and thin as a spear, slipping away down the stairwell. He heard footsteps, soft shoes on stone, and thought briefly of descending the stairs just to see at least the back of Maxine's new client. Ravel controlled that impulse as well, and he returned to stand in front of Maxine's now open doorway.

The agent, tanned and stunning, stood up when she saw her former intern. "Ah, Ravel," she said, holding out her hand. "Did you run into him?"

"Run into who?"

Ravel had never witnessed Maxine swallow her words before, but she did so now. Her eyes broke from his. To the former intern's surprise, she looked uncomfortable.

"Maxine?"

"You must have just missed crossing paths."

Maxine's arm remained outstretched. Ravel shook her hand. Maxine noticed the mammoth manuscript he was carrying under his left arm.

"Don't tell me, Rav," she said. "You finished it."

"Finished what," Ravel said dumbly.

"Your novel! *Your Great American Novel.* Isn't that the title?"

"Oh this..." Ravel held *Freedom Freeway* now in both hands. "This isn't mine—well, it is, sort of. It's my father-in-law's."

Maxine pointed, her mouth twisted into what might have broken into a laugh at any moment. "He write all that?"

"With his buddies. I think...yeah, there are three of them all together, including Mick."

"Mick?"

"Mick Parker. My father-in-law."

"Take a seat, Ravel. Let's talk."

Ravel seated himself across from Maxine. She did not offer to take *Freedom Freeway,* so Ravel continued to hold the doorstop in his lap. Maxine asked what Ravel was doing these days, and he answered with "Sales development," a term that seemed to have no effect on the agent whatsoever. She asked him if he had married that girlfriend of his—what was her name?—and Ravel responded with pride that he had. "Best decision I made," he added. In the lull that followed, Ravel's eyes flitted from Maxine to the stack of books on her desk. Around a dozen, and all of them bore one name: Spiros Averof. Ravel stared. All except the top tome was in paperback, the top tome the latest release, the novel that had just won the American Diamond Prize in Fiction. The stack was arranged with care; looking at it, Ravel knew who had been in this office, seated in this very chair, shortly before he'd claimed it. Ravel knew who had descended those stairs, whose voice was deep, guttural, foreign-accented. He knew, and it was this knowledge, striking like the smell from a public toilet that hasn't been flushed in weeks, that caused him to keel over and retch.

"Ravel! Please!"

"I'm sorry." Ravel gasped as he came up. With his sleeve he wiped spittle. "It's nothing, nothing's there in me. Just some dry heaves."

"Nothing on the floor?"

"Nothing on the floor."

Maxine leaned back and assessed this former intern with penetrating eyes. Upon exhaling quite audibly she said, "I didn't expect your father to be here this morning. He dropped in without notice. You'll understand why I had to take the meeting."

Ravel nodded and finished wiping. He'd put together what had transpired in this office. The great author living now in the greatest city in the United States, if not the world, had swooped in to drop off all his great works and to see if Maxine Dein, still a powerhouse Hollywood agent at age 65, who had nevertheless grown tired of LA and moved to, of all cities, Denver, in the early 2010s so she could enjoy the outdoors and her family, would be so brilliant as to make the calls, work the connections, draw up the contracts, set up the meetings so that all of Averof's oeuvre could find its way onto the screen. Maxine could barely remember her interns' first names let alone their last ones, but she could not forget the name Ravel Averof, and she had made the connection between father and son early on. That connection was one of the reasons she'd welcomed Ravel so readily to the internship; it was also the reason she'd been eager to read Ravel's work. The son of Spiros Averof! Surely the son would follow in *those* footsteps!

"It's only business, Ravel. You understand."

"I do. Yes." After a moment Ravel added, "All his novels are going to be turned into movies?"

"We're certainly going to try for that. Some of these.... I'm not sure. Hollywood's been scratching its head over his writing for decades."

"But."

"But if anyone can get these on the screen, it's me. The ADPiF win helps substantially. We'll start with this latest, go from there." Maxine stared hard at Ravel, who had composed himself well enough by now. "I do apologize for the awkwardness," the agent said.

Precious little of Maxine's goodwill remained, judging from the way her jaw clenched. Ravel was familiar with that clenching, and he knew he had only a short time in which to stoke the home fires. The air the former intern exhaled in a whoosh seemed to be sucked through Maxine's nostrils and forced through the agent's constricting internal passages. In this office, this hallway, this building, time was as much a currency as looks or money or signatures or phone calls or emails or text messages or video calls, and the more Ravel delayed the more he was seen to be stealing what to Maxine was the most precious currency, the currency that held the key to all others. The agent could sympathize with her former intern's personal family drama for only so long before it was time to turn to the business at hand.

Ravel held up *Freedom Freeway* and said, "Will you take this?"

"Heft it over."

Maxine lingered on the cover page. "*Freedom Freeway*.... Cute. Alliteration irks me to no end."

"He, uh, pulled me over on the I-25 to give me this."

"Who did?"

"He did. Mick Parker. My father-in-law's a police officer."

"A cop, huh."

Maxine flipped through to the end of the leviathan paper mound, took note of the final page number, and simultaneously raised her eyebrows and whistled consternation through puckered lips.

"I don't know how long," Ravel commiserated, "they took to write it."

"You've read it?"

"Most of it. I couldn't devote all my time to it this weekend."

"So I have to take the bullet, is that it?"

Ravel's heart withered at the words. His fear and shame subsided when he heard Maxine laugh generously. "I'm kidding, Ravel. You look like somebody died."

"Oh, you know."

"You know I can't promise anything—"

"Of course," Ravel said quickly.

"It has to go through the interns, the usual channels."

"Absolutely."

"But I'll get to it, as big as it is."

"Don't spend too much time with it."

"I'll find something useful to do with it."

"I'm sure you will. Thanks, Maxine. You're doing me a really big favor, getting him off my back. If he knows I gave it to you and you at least gave it a read, I'll be okay."

Maxine flashed her obsessively maintained whites. "I certainly wouldn't want you to be pulled over again."

"He wants the truth as much as me, whenever you can get to this."

"All right." Maxine placed *Freedom Freeway* next to the stack of Spiros Averof's novels. "As you can see, I have a lot of reading ahead of me."

The threat of retching, of the dry heaves, had returned—only a threat at this point.

"He wants to adapt these himself. Can you believe that?"

Before his bowels could get involved, Ravel strained in his seat and said, "Maxine—I'm sorry. I have to split, unfortunately."

"I can see that. It was good you stopped by, Ravel. I'll let you know about the script."

Ravel, already out of his chair, said thanks, shook Maxine's hand, smiled and headed for the door. As soon as he was in the hallway and clear, he bolted.

On his way home he thought back to the last time—really the only time—he'd seen Spiros Averof. For so long Ravel had fooled himself into believing that deep down he didn't give a damn about his famous father, when in reality he cared so much, too much; in fact, the nonchalance he presented to others was a mere front, a posture that was now eroding, so much sand swept away to uncover a tablet inscribed with a crucial axiom.

He remembered a boy of almost nine years old reading the latest issue of *Nintendo Power* in his bedroom. It was early September and muggy, the house in the San Diego Country Gems devoid of effective air circulation. The fan on Ravel's dresser swiveled to blow warm air just above his head. The ragged bottom edges of his Kobe Bryant poster rippled every several seconds. Young Ravel turned the page and flipped over to lay again on his back, the top of his head aimed at his closed door.

The door opened and his mother, who never knocked due to having grown up in a two-bedroom apartment with four siblings and a grandparent in a high rise in Burgas, entered. Yoana looked her son over sternly, and for the first minute or two Ravel thought he had done something wrong. It became apparent soon enough that he was not to blame, at least not in any direct way.

He saw in her hand a piece of paper—a letter, typewritten, with what looked like an official letterhead. Had the President written? Was Yoana going to have to leave the country? Ravel knew the word for that, though he couldn't think of it now. His mother had spoken the word before. He watched as she folded the letter without looking at it and said, "Your father wants to see you."

Ravel bolted to a sitting position as if electrified. He set *Nintendo Power* aside and held out his hands for the letter. Yoana informed him that the letter was short, didn't say much other than a lot of legalese. It would be of no interest to him. Ravel suspected that his mother might be lying but knew enough not to press her. He knew that his father had left him and his mother when Ravel was two, in Los Angeles, a year after Spiros had published his debut novel to sharp critical acclaim and mediocre sales. In the fall of 1994 Spiros had struck off for New York, and Yoana had reverted to her maiden name, Kopecka. When he was six, Ravel and his mother had moved south to San Diego's North County, to the little town of Anomar, because it was cheap and Yoana had secured a teaching position at Anomar High School. Since he could remember, Ravel had only seen pictures of his father, in his novels, in literary magazines, online. Yoana spoke so little of Spiros Averof it was as if the man was a ghost. Ravel felt the animosity his mother harbored toward his father, and early on he knew she would lie to him concerning Spiros. He was certain she was lying to him this September day, but that did not matter to Ravel. He was going to see his father in the flesh!

Ravel would never know the intricacies of the arrangements; he knew only that the following week, on a Tuesday morning, his ninth birthday, instead of taking the school bus he was allowed to wait at the window looking out on the driveway. At any moment his father would arrive and take him away for a birthday breakfast, as Yoana claimed the letter had promised. Ravel must not expect more than that. Spiros had arrived in San Diego to read from his work at several bookstores, and he could not be expected to spend more than a few hours with his son. Ravel understood. He watched and waited.

The sight of the unfamiliar car, when it did pull into the driveway, was the antithesis of Ravel's life up to that point. Every night his mother spent cooking for him, caring for him, reading to him in her thick accent that would never Americanize no matter how many years she taught at the high school —those nights had never occurred. Here was his father, in a disorienting reversal of night to early morning, coming home from work, as fathers were supposed to do. Spiros would be just like any father, he would be *the* father, ready to wrestle with Ravel, play video games, coach his son's sports teams in which Ravel was struggling, and read to him from one of the books Spiros had written. Ravel could not have known then that this was precisely the effect his father hoped to have on him—and Yoana—by pulling into that driveway as if he had always lived with his wife and son. It was a brazen action characteristic of the man, an action young Ravel took little note of but which the older Ravel, the thirty-year-old Ravel, picked apart.

He remembered how his father had waited in the car as young Ravel had waited for Spiros to get out and go to the front door, again, as if he lived there. Ravel waited until Yoana had come up behind him and told him to go, his father wasn't going any further.

Young Ravel ran out to the driveway, his backpack swinging heavy off one shoulder against his stomach. That backpack contained all he intended to show his father: the Nintendo 64 cartridges, the latest *Nintendo Power* with Mario Kart Super Circuit on the cover, his autographed copy of *A Wrinkle in Time*, and the book he'd written and illustrated in his second grade class the previous year. Ravel had so much to show Spiros, he had so much to tell him. Gone was any lingering anxiety; in its place was a love that should have been.

The interior of Spiros Averof's car—a newer, luxury make and model, though not the sports car young Ravel had pictured—smelled as if it needed no cleaning, ever. Yoana vacuumed the interior of her older vehicle every few months, but she never took it to be professionally cleaned. Why would I pay a person to clean my car, she once questioned Ravel, when I have the vacuum in the house and the hose in the front yard? To Ravel, having grown up knowing his mother's—and by extension his own—financial situation, that Yoana had invested a great deal of her money into securing and maintaining this house in a slightly more upscale area of Anomar because, in her words, she did not want her son growing up in an apartment, this point of financial conservatism made sense. Still, the boy liked the smell of a newly cleaned car, or, in this case, a car that never needed to be cleaned, ever, the way he liked the smell of a newly purchased video game or book. Situating himself in the passenger's seat spurred Ravel to think of shopping at Horton Plaza, that one day leading up to Christmas when his mother would take him around the multi-leveled, multi-colored outdoor mall on the hunt for acceptable presents to send back to her remaining family in Bulgaria. Would Spiros take him to Horton Plaza, perhaps to buy a video game or a book for his birthday? His hands hidden under his thighs, Ravel crossed his fingers.

Without a word or a glance at his son, Spiros backed out of the driveway. At that time, two decades ago, Ravel remembered his father blessed with a great dark-blond mane that brought to the boy's mind a predator on the savannah. That September day Spiros wore sunglasses, his nails were manicured, his skin lightly tanned and his short nose pressed in a bit like a Persian cat's. His smile curved like a scimitar when he spoke.

"Today is really your birthday, is it?"

"It is, yeah."

"Happy birthday."

"Thank you. I'm nine."

"And that would mean I'm thirty-seven. But my birthday isn't today, of course."

"When is it—" Ravel stopped himself before he could say 'Dad.' He wasn't sure if he could call his father 'Dad,' or anything yet. His father had yet to use Ravel's name.

"Oh, earlier in the year. Spring. May. But this isn't about me, Ravel. It's about you, and *your* birthday."

He had used Ravel's name! The boy felt giddy. The tightness throughout his body lessened.

"For your birthday we'll drive through your town and look at the sights. I hear they have a museum of Anomar."

"Uh..."

"I only tease, Ravel. We'll go to the city, to downtown."

As he drove Spiros asked his son about Anomar, whether the boy liked it. Ravel answered by saying it was okay. He liked San Diego better.

"Who wouldn't?" Spiros said. "America's finest city, it calls itself, though I'm certain many American cities call themselves the same."

Spiros spoke of his city, New York, the only city he could call home. He had lived only in cities: Athens, where he was born, then Sofia where he had been a student (and where, Ravel would learn a few years later, Spiros Averof had met Yoana Kopecka), then to San Francisco and soon after that to Los Angeles. "New York is it for me," Spiros said. "My terminus."

"Would you ever get an apartment in Anomar?"

"No, Ravel. It would have to be a real city. The City."

By the time they reached downtown, fifty minutes after

they'd left the Country Gems, they had established that they both liked the ocean, they both liked to read and write, and they both liked movies. When Ravel asked why his father couldn't stay longer, Spiros made it clear that he had time only for Ravel and the bookstore readings.

"That's why my publisher gave me this car."

"This isn't your own car?"

"I don't have a car, Ravel. I have no need of such a thing in New York!"

"Wow," said Ravel. "No car..." His southern California sensibilities would not allow him to make sense of this fact. "It must be nice to publish a book."

"I've published five."

"When can I read them?"

"You're nine? Not now. When you're older."

To change the subject—and to deflect some of the embarrassment over having asked stupid questions—Ravel asked about the readings that his father was exuberant to discuss. Apparently Spiros did more than just read aloud—he also answered questions and signed autographs in copies of his books purchased by those who'd come to listen. "It's a good experience, Ravel. You see who your readers are." Spiros had a copy of his new book for Ravel, and he would sign it for his son when they were through. "Just remember," he said, "wait until you are older to read it." Spiros then asked, as he turned the corner onto 44th Street, narrowly missing a homeless woman, where Ravel would like to go.

"How about...Horton Plaza?"

"Ah yes, the mall. I must read tomorrow, at Bretano's. I'm hoping to avoid it before then. But there is a bookstore I am not reading at and I have not been to."

In Seaport Village they meandered along the empty pathways. While it was still morning and a Tuesday, Ravel had expected there to be more people out and about. Plenty of shops and restaurants had opened, yet the area looked like a ghost town by the sea. They neared a Mexican restaurant, and Ravel saw people crowded inside. He looked to his father, but Spiros was already headed in. Ravel followed, and immediately upon entering saw the source of all the commotion. On the TV screens above the bar were images of the World Trade Center, the twin towers, burning. As Ravel watched, CNN replayed the footage of each tower being taken out by a separate commercial airliner. He heard his father speaking in a low voice to a group of men close by. Spiros gathered the details, then took Ravel aside and explained to him what had happened. Then Spiros insisted they eat.

"I'm not really hungry."

"Don't be ridiculous. You will not starve yourself on your birthday for this."

"Look, Dad."

"Yes. I see. But we must eat."

The waiter seated father and son in one of the many available booths. All eyes, including Spiros Averof's, were upturned to the TV screens in the bar. Though at a considerable distance, the author honed in on the images and the closed captions as if he were reading a densely written book. Occasionally he glanced at Ravel and ate snatches of his food once it had arrived, but mostly he remained focused on the tragedy in his city.

"I'm sorry," Ravel said at last.

"Why are you sorry?"

"It's just that..." Ravel saw the bemused look on his

father's face and felt a hot stab of anger for the first time that morning. He quickly suppressed the unbecoming emotion and said, "I'm sorry for all the people there...who died. There must've been a lot who died..."

"Thousands," Spiros said.

"On my birthday."

"On *my* birthday," Spiros said, "when I turned sixteen, two tragedies happened on the same day."

"Really? Here?"

"One in this country and the other in England. The volcano Mount Saint Helens exploded, or *erupted* I should say, and the singer for Joy Division chose to end his life."

"Joy Division?"

"A band. I believe you would like them, when you're older."

Ravel picked at his food, not sure what to say. His father filled the silence. "Tragedies occur every day, Ravel. They are always occurring. But then so too are comedies, and birthdays as well."

After breakfast they continued through Seaport Village. When Spiros offered to buy Ravel a cookie, the boy accepted without guilt. If the tragedy in his city had affected him, Spiros was not showing it. He appeared immensely at ease, as if swept up by a lightness beneath his feet. Why should his father feel at all bad, Ravel thought, when the man was *loaded*. Ravel's eyes were drawn to Spiros's wallet every time he took it out. Ravel wasn't thick like that wallet; he knew his father made money off his writing and that his mother made nothing off hers. Ravel had read some of Yoana's poems, and dutifully he had said he liked them, they were good. Most of her poetry Yoana would not show her son. In the presence of his father, Ravel was beginning to understand why.

This was only Ravel's third time in the Upstart Crow. His mother was not a fan of Seaport Village and any shop on the premises. "Like Nesebar on the worst of the tourist days," she once said of the place. Tourist traps in foreign countries Ravel understood a little, but Seaport Village and the Upstart Crow? He'd taken to the bookstore the moment his feet passed from the light of the entryway into the dark pungent interior. Drifting along the off-kilter aisles, up and down stairs, hearing those creaks and percolating coffee pots had made him want to read more than even his mother did. Ravel was happy when he saw that his father felt the same way. He remained close to Spiros as the author moved with a purpose. His father, upon entering the Upstart Crow, seemed to have forgotten his son. Spiros carried himself with a demeanor that rivaled that of those shocked by the World Trade Center attacks, which had expanded to include the Pentagon and a plane in Pennsylvania. Grim, determined, Spiros had one goal in this bookstore: the father must show the son the novels he'd so far published. Spiros and Ravel faced a corner of the large bookcase marked Literature, and to Ravel it seemed as if the man next to him might say a prayer. Spiros pointed to each of his novels, four in paperback, one in hardcover, a couple copies each. He did not take any of his work off the shelf but said rather, "What do you want to be, Ravel?"

"Uh..." Ravel's eyes took in all the books they could. So many! He would never be able to read them all. "An author?" he said, more a question than an answer.

"To be an author," Spiros lectured, "you must have discipline, courage, talent, luck."

"That's a lot."

"You may have that all someday. You may not. It all comes down to this." Spiros held up a coin, which he flipped. He caught the coin and pressed it to his forearm. He then uncovered the coin and announced, "Heads." He handed the coin to his son. Ravel accepted the quarter, a 2000 New Hampshire, as if it were magic. LIVE FREE OR DIE, Ravel read.

Spiros Averof would be unaware that five years from that day in Seaport Village, his son would compile a report for his freshman English class at Anomar High on the career in which he was most interested—that of a book author. Ravel's report covered the likes of Dalton Bryce, Gilda Mooring (she of the popular vampire and witch novels) and Sam Bourgeois, the lawyer-turned-legal thriller author, and focused on where they lived and how much they earned. Nowhere in the pages of that report—so naïve, so idealistic—was there even a mention of Spiros Averof. The father never saw his son again after that September day in Seaport Village, the day the towers fell, the day of Ravel's ninth birthday. Yet they appeared to be at ease then. In the Upstart Crow they breathed in books for almost two hours, during which time they remained apart. Spiros was never where Ravel expected him to be, and the one time his father did chance upon the son in the upstairs nook the boy loved so much his father all but ignored him and the horror fiction on the shelves behind. A cursory glance, a slight nod of acknowledgement, but the man was no longer approachable. Ravel began to fear, as he left his beloved nook and twisted through aisles on both floors, that his father would leave him the way Yoana had left him in a dream he'd once had.

To young Ravel's relief, Spiros eventually found his son in the humor section poring over a collection of Far Side comic strips, and to Ravel's surprise his father bought the book for him. "For your birthday," Spiros said.

As soon as they had put several paces between themselves and the Upstart Crow, Spiros's mood lightened. They walked along the ocean's edge and the man spoke of his father, a great sea captain who ended his career ferrying tourists around the islands. Ravel asked if he would ever get to meet his grandfather and grandmother, and Spiros answered, "No, Ravel. They are dead. They died not long ago."

Ravel remembered thinking then that he could have met his paternal grandfather and grandmother, if Spiros had been in his life.

Over lunch at a restaurant on the ocean's edge Spiros asked Ravel about his school, his interests, his friends and enemies—especially his enemies.

"I don't have any enemies," said Ravel.

"You must."

"You mean like in the movies? Like a villain?"

"A real enemy is not someone who looks or acts like a movie villain. Life is not a cartoon, or a movie or a TV show. But someone who causes you hurt, at school perhaps."

Ravel thought about it. He hadn't really been bullied in the past years at Gordon Lawrence Elementary. Most every kid left him alone. Who hurt him the most? *Ravel* hurt himself the most, Ravel figured. He was always worrying if he would make his mother proud, help her out, care for her, provide for her, be there for her in the way his father wasn't. The pressure he put on himself every day was the bully. That bully was Ravel.

"There's really no one," Ravel told his father.

"That will change soon enough," Spiros said. "When it

does change, and you know your bully, you must beat him any way necessary."

"Beat him? Like hit him?"

"If necessary. But somehow you must win. However you do so. Crush your enemies. You must."

In silence Ravel picked at his food. He could feel his father's head turn. When he looked up he saw Spiros staring at a waitress, an attractive woman who reminded Ravel of the star of the lifeguard show on TV, *Baywatch*. Ravel watched his father watch the waitress, until she left the room and Spiros's attention was again directed at his son.

"I am," the author said with gravity, "single, as your mother is."

It was the first time any mention of the woman between them had come up. Ravel opened his mouth but stopped short of saying what he had on his mind. Spiros did not press him for it. Toward the end of their meal he announced he would be taking Ravel home. From Anomar he would go to his readings in La Jolla and Del Mar. He would end the day late at Bretano's in Horton Plaza.

Ravel thought about asking if he could come to at least one of the readings, but he knew what Spiros's response would be. Too much driving, too many people to meet and greet, too many hours—and on a school night! Given what had happened that day in New York and Washington and Pennsylvania, who knew how the readings would play out? His father, the author, could not have a boy with him. Ravel's silence showed he understood.

In the driveway of Yoana's house Spiros reached underneath his seat and brought out a small brown paper bag. From out of this bag he took a copy of his latest novel, opened to the title page and asked if Ravel wanted anything written there besides his father's signature.

"I don't know," said Ravel. "You choose something."

What he got was *To Ravel—may this day, your ninth birthday, serve as your crucible, the tragedy your comedy, this book your inspiration. – Spiros Averof*

"Remember," Ravel's father said, "wait to read this novel when you're ready. You'll know when that is."

"I'll have to hide it from Mom."

"Why is that?"

"She won't let me read any of your books, even when I'm older, she says."

Spiros laughed heartily. "She has always been..." He did not finish his sentence. Instead, he began anew: "You would be brave to read that book, someday. You would stand up then."

"I will."

But Ravel hadn't stood up. He had hidden the book under his bed until his mother had found it while cleaning a few weeks later. Ravel had read none of the book except his father's inscription, and when Yoana held it up for Ravel to see the boy said he understood, he would read it when she wanted him to read it. Yoana had not punished him but instead taken the book away to where it would be discovered years later buried in the bottom dresser of her walk-in closet. Ravel read the novel then. He still had the book—the only one of his father's he owned. He hadn't held it since the day after his mother's death when he'd thought of burning it. Burial under the bed had made more sense then, but now as he turned off Colfax and onto his street in Capitol Hill, Ravel felt the intense urge to bring it back, to bring all of it back.

NINE

Nearing eight o'clock that Monday, January 9th, Ravel arrived at the Wash Park recreation center already unimpressed with Men Who Write Too Much. The cursory research he'd conducted had turned up little in the way of a social media presence, and no authors worth their ink would deign to blurb such a harebrained organization. No authors, period, would dare even mention MeWWToM (the group's official acronym). Yet Ravel, an author in his own mind if in no other, had arrived in person. He had sunk to his lowest depth—or so he believed that night.

When he walked into the center's main room he was amazed: there, filling row after row of folding chairs, were men of all ages and races and ethnicities. More men lined the walls, which offered the only open spots. Ravel had thought he would simply walk in, take any of several open seats, and be done in twenty minutes or fewer, but this, he soon realized, was *war*. He continued to survey the scene, shocked at the sight of boys as young as eight or nine seated on the floor next to men ten times their age. Ravel found one of the few available spots against the leftward wall, in between two older men, one of whom presented as meek, wore glasses and rocked a mullet like it was the early '90s again, while the other man, taller, stockier, wore jeans, boots, lightly shaded sunglasses and a trucker cap in the style of a John Deere that read *Deere John*. They returned Ravel's nod. Leaning against the wall, Ravel heard the man on his left, the Deere John, say, "Must be your first time."

"How'd you figure that?"

"First-timers never show up early."

"I thought I was showing up early," Ravel said.

Deere John shook his head. "You're not early. I've been here for the past forty-five minutes."

"An hour and fifteen." The meek man on Ravel's other side stuck a thumb into his own chest, puffed with pride.

"Now *that's* early," Deere John affirmed.

"I had no idea. Is it always like this?"

"Always," the meek man said. "Only this is the most we've seen yet. It's really catching on. The flyers are working."

"Old ways are still the best ways," Deere John opined.

From out of his satchel Ravel took a pen and his current little black notebook.

"Oh," the meek man said. "We don't use those here."

"What?"

"Can't have 'em," Deere John enforced. "Not allowed."

"Really? You gotta be kidding me."

"He'll confiscate both of those, no foolin'."

Ravel muttered the word 'unbelievable' but put away his pen and notebook. He believed what these men said. As he again looked around, he saw that no one, not the eight-year-olds or the eighty-year-olds, had anything with or on which to write. No pens, no pencils, no notebooks, legal pad or those old-school composition books. No laptops or tablets either, and nary a phone was in sight. Downright *creepy*, thought Ravel. How could this be? Who was this man who forbade the use of all writing implements? Rather than keep that last question in his head, Ravel posed a paraphrased version of it to Deere John.

"The head of all this? That'd be Bruce."

"Bednarik," the meek man said. "This is his baby. Talk to him if you absolutely have to write something during the meeting."

"Be sure you ask first," said Deere John. "If he sees you writing without his permission, ooh boy watch out!"

"Shhh..." The meek man hushed his compatriot. "He's starting."

At first Ravel could see no one at the front of the room, where the attention of all those gathered was now focused. Then, upon closer inspection, Ravel realized someone had appeared at the front of the room, only it was again not what he had expected. Bruce Bednarik did indeed stand there, but he was short—*very* short. He was, in fact, a little person, standing no more than four feet eight inches at most. Ravel caught sight of the large heavy boots Bednarik wore.

The crowd, already quiet, hushed to a point of near-religious reverence as Bruce, holding a cordless mike, stepped forward. He turned on the mike and tapped its top. The sound of his finger tapping sounded loud and clear.

"Can everybody see me?" Bruce said, to which the crowd

responded with laughter. "I know, I know. I'm just waiting for someone to tell me that's getting old. Anyway, it's incredible to see so many new faces as well as the returnees, the usual suspects..."

As Ravel listened, he connected Bruce's deep, accented voice to the voice heard on his phone. So this was the man who would save Ravel from writing too much. This was the man who had spoken with Deborah, who knew Ravel's wife on a friendly level.

"Now as usual," Bruce was saying, "we at MeWWToM like to start out by introducing the noobs to everyone. And just this week a certain man came to my attention..."

Oh no, thought Ravel. *Oh no oh shit oh no.*

"...just like you and me, works a mind-numbing job, has dreams of making it big with his writing, but it's seriously bringing down his health, as many of you are familiar with..."

Several 'amen's and 'say it brother's could be heard throughout the room. Panicked, Ravel saw a young boy looking at him directly and nodding. That boy knew! They all knew!

"...give a big warm welcome to—you're not gonna believe this—Ravel *Averof*!"

The applause broke immediately on the first syllable of Ravel's surname, and the author's son was overwhelmed, not unlike the time he was plowed underwater by a La Jolla wave and found himself struggling, drowning, dying if not for his boogie board. All eyes were now on him, the crowd had parted like two magically compelled waves, and through that opening Bruce stood at the end, craning his neck and pointing at Ravel and shouting into the mike for the author's son to come on up before the men of MeWWToM dragged him there.

Ravel, a sheepish half-smile forming, his eyes avoiding everyone, rushed through the parted crowd as if both sides would close on him any millisecond. At six-two, Ravel stood beside Bruce and, the author's son assumed, made for an odd-looking pair. But if the audience had that impression they made no indication of it. Ravel swayed a bit, bathed in the applause and whoops, the light brighter and harsher here at the front. So many men! So many older men, younger men, mere boys, men wearing glasses, men who'd never needed glasses, men who had perfect teeth, men whose teeth were beyond bad, men who wore wrist braces, men who weren't wearing deodorant, men who had no hair, men who had too much hair, men, men, men! Ravel felt faint looking at them all, for now he could not turn from them, his future.

Bednarik quieted the crowd with a throat-slashing motion. He turned to Ravel and said, "Ravel, I'm not going to say it. I want you to say it."

Ravel stared at Brednarik blankly.

"Your last name..." Bruce prompted.

"Oh yes." Ravel snapped to attention and went on autopilot. "Averof. My father is Spiros Averof. I'm his son. Well, his first son."

"He has another son?"

"A young one. From his second wife."

"And how does that make you *feel*?"

"Uh..."

"Never mind that question. Scratch that question. Tell us why you're here. Tell us about yourself, something besides the fact you're the son of a famous author."

Ravel stared at the mike as if it were an alien object. Bruce smiled and thrust it farther into his face. When he was about to kiss it Ravel recoiled and blurted out, "My father that's why I'm here."

The crowd waited. Ravel wanted to run, but all avenues of escape had been cut off. His audience was assembled before him as one large mass that had metastasized to all corners and nooks of the room. No spot was unoccupied. *Gotta be a fire hazard*, Ravel thought. He said, "I'm not sure how many of you are the son of a famous novelist..."

From the back a man, possibly Deere John, shouted, "None of us but you!"

"You'd think," Ravel said, "that it would be great. I'd have all these connections, these ins, you know, but it's not like that. It really actually sucks, if you think about it."

Again the murmurs of 'amen' and 'say it brother,' in addition to some 'speak the truth's and 'I hear ya's could be heard. Ravel paused, his head bowed, and when he looked up he said, "But honestly I'm not here because of my dad. I'm not here because of Spiros Averof. I'm really here because of my wife. She's very concerned about me. Just recently I, well, I got a diagnosis, I found out writing put this stress on my body, among other things, and.... Anyway, she loves me, and I don't want to let her down. But I don't want to give up writing either. I can't. So I don't know what to do."

"Change your name?" someone offered.

Ravel shot in the speaker's direction a stare that could have withered the hardiest weed. He waited for the words. He felt that if he said the wrong words the crowd would pounce. They were expecting a certain script, one he had no conscious hand in writing. Or had he? It was possible Ravel had been writing this script his entire life without knowing it.

"My mother," Ravel said suddenly. "My mother's the one

I should talk about. She was a writer too, a poet, and the writing killed her, and I don't want to go that way."

He could say nothing else. He held the mike out to Bruce, who took it and patted Ravel's hand. "That's fine, Ravel. For now, that's fine. No need to talk your heart out tonight. Just an introduction is enough. Thanks so much for sharing."

The applause, the cheers, the adoration that followed was what Ravel had always hoped for—just in a different context. Perhaps he did need this. Perhaps these were the fans meant for him, the extended family that would care for him. Above all, perhaps this would be the way he would finally finish his story—not by writing it, but by telling it to those who would listen.

Outside the rec center Ravel hurried to his car through the swirling snow. He was about to slide in when he heard Bruce's voice behind him. Turning, Ravel saw the leader of Men Who Write Too Much standing close by with his arms outstretched. Despite the snow and steadily increasing freezation, Bednarik wore jeans and a leather jacket. Ravel, feeling self-conscious in his heavy coat, wool cap and gloves, bent down a bit and shook Bruce's bare hand.

"What you did in there," said Bednarik, "took guts. Real courage. Seeing as where you come from, what you come from."

"I don't know if I want to talk about it all yet. She died just last year."

"I'm sorry, and I understand if you need time, but from what I saw tonight I don't think you need too much time, Ravel. You shouldn't take too much time. The more you share, the sooner you share it, the sooner you'll be on the path to recovery."

Ravel mumbled a thanks, his mind on home and Deborah now.

Bednarik clasped his hands in front of his body as he spoke. "I'm going to be insistent, Ravel, really. I hope you won't mind. That's the way I've always been, and it's just that your story's so unique compared to everyone else's, even mine. When you speak, we all know you got something there. We need to hear it, and you need to hear it especially."

Bruce extended his hand again, and Ravel shook once more.

"See you next week."

"Next week it is," Ravel said.

"And hey."

"Yeah?"

"Go Nuggets."

Ravel watched Bruce walk off, both skeptical of and hopeful for what was to come.

BY THE TIME Ravel arrived home that night, skepticism had won out. Bruce Bednarik and MeWWToM could not truly support him to the point where he no longer cared to pick up a pen or rain fingers on a keyboard. No possible way. During the meeting, after he'd taken a seat that one of the front-rowers had offered upon completion of his introduction, Ravel heard about the eleven-step program ("We don't need as many as AA," Bruce had joked). He learned the most impor-tant step of all: The Cleanse. The Cleanse comprised of thor-oughly divesting oneself of all writerly ambitions as presented on social media. This detox also meant deleting all self-publishing accounts, taking all books off-sale and, if possible, destroying all evidence of ever having published in the first place. Of course, it helped if one had never hit the self-publish button. In Ravel's case, he was lucky. Bruce believed his new recruit had less of a fight ahead of him.

Still, Ravel doubted. He'd heard perhaps the youngest boy in the crowd talk about how he used to only feel comfortable communicating through the written word, he'd even self-published a book that had gone nowhere but down down down in the rankings, but now with the help of Men Who Write Too Much he was engaged in sports, had joined his elementary school science team, and even had a girlfriend. All great, Ravel thought, except the need to write would always be there, in that boy and in every man gathered there that night. You could not kill the drive to write. It was either in you or it wasn't, and if it was in you, you could not rid yourself of it unless you rid the world of yourself.

He arrived home to a dark and quiet apartment. Deborah was asleep, exhausted from her twelve-hour day of researching, writing, and TA-ing. They had just missed each other, she coming home right after he'd left for the MeWWToM meeting. She had left a note on Ravel's laptop that read *Hope it went well and you don't want to open this! P.S. Don't forget to check your number before bed!*

Instead of opening his laptop, Ravel locked in on his phone. Not something he could use to write, even if he'd wanted to; tonight's meeting had sapped him at least temporarily of any desire. He was simply going to scroll.

He didn't like what he was doing—the scrolling, but also giving in to MeWWToM. Joining this silly support group was tantamount to admitting defeat, admitting he was a failure. Perhaps he'd always been a failure, and he was at the point now where he needed to acknowledge that fact and never more, after tonight, look up his rival, his contemporary, the writer he compared himself to in all aspects.

The entry for Tristan Boppana had been updated since the last time Ravel checked (a few days ago). He'd anticipated it would be, as he did every time he checked, but the anticipation did nothing to help him focus on the words. Ravel squinted at the screen, sucked in the update, and then looked at something else in the darkened office, the clock that had actual hands and not numbers. Of course it was true what he had read: Tristan's second novel, longer, more involved and apparently better than his bestselling first, had topped the *New York Times* bestseller list and was in development. Ravel could see a vast flood of cash filling up Tristan's multi-million-dollar penthouse as he and Maggie two-back-beasted on top of all those rising Benjamins.

But the worst update was yet to be seen, and when Ravel saw it, he momentarily stopped breathing: Maggie too had a book, her debut work, accepted for publication. She would be publishing in early summer.

And then, underneath that little ditty, the entry's final slap in Ravel's face: *They live with their child in Brooklyn.*

A child. *Jesus*, thought Ravel. *A child. Must be an infant. Maggie twenty-eight now, just had a baby, Jesus why did I look.*

He knew why he'd looked, and why he'd looked steadily for years. He wanted to see their marriage, their lives, end badly. He wanted to find out they'd divorced or died or were cheating on one another. He wanted to know if Maggie had turned out to be just a failed housewife, just the wife of a famous writer. But none of that was going to happen, and the more Ravel hoped it would, the more he searched for his schadenfreude, their hoped-for downfall, the more he ensured his own irrecoverable tailspin.

A child, Ravel thought. And then, out loud: "She did it. She did both." The knowledge that Maggie, at an earlier age than he, had won their competition, that she had managed to give birth to both a child and a book before the age of thirty, made Ravel both sick and resolute. Sick that he'd failed, but resolute with the belief that he did not have to let his failure stand. That idea he'd had—he could attempt it after all. He could go for it and see where it took him. He did not have to be afraid now. He'd been afraid of so many things for so long: afraid of his mother abandoning him, his father outliving him, Maggie not needing him, not caring about him, his sentences not spooling out perfectly on the page, every individual who'd ever known him forgetting Ravel Averof had at one point in history existed, Deborah coming to her senses and seeing her husband for what he was: all mulling and rumination and no action, a weakling who'd allowed his past to control both his present and his future and divorcing him over it, not having children, never finishing a single manuscript of any length, of any substance, of any words.

But that was the old Ravel, the fearful Ravel. This new Ravel, backed by a plan outlandish enough to work, no longer had cause to be afraid. Of *That* or anything.

THE NEXT AFTERNOON, when the front door to the apartment banged open like the sky releasing a thunderstrike, Ravel was on the john mulling over how best to start in on his idea—and get back in with Laney and Chronotrex. He bolted up, even though he was not yet finished, and looked for something, anything with which to defend himself. A home invasion at last! The stomping of feet, heavy boots in the front entryway, on the kitchen tile. More banging—this time the cupboards and the fridge. They were after...Deborah's stockpile of frozen chicken thighs? The ten pounds of pork shoulder blade she was planning to use for her carne adobada recipe over the weekend? Ravel stood and grabbed his electric toothbrush. It would be, if anything, a distraction, something to throw before he ran. Why had he not taken his phone with him to the toilet? He was trying to be good, to detox—and now this! Ravel gripped the electric toothbrush tighter, ready to turn it on for added effect. Then he opened the bathroom door, careful to make not a sound.

He crept down the hallway, hugging the wall as he went. The front door was just around the corner to his left—he could make it, especially since the intruders were still in the kitchen, preoccupied, it sounded, with pouring liquid into a container.

What the? Ravel thought. He turned the corner—and just about tripped over three pairs of boots haphazardly thrown in front of the closed door. He recognized one pair, but he could not yet sigh with relief. Still holding the toothbrush, Ravel, looser now but not having dropped his guard entirely, entered the kitchen to find Mick, Godwin and Russell, whose name also appeared on the cover page of *Freedom Freeway*, gathered at the kitchen counter, two twenty-four count cartons of domestic beer between them. They'd broken open one of the boxes, popped open a few cans and poured their contents into the German-style beer steins Deb and Ravel had received as wedding gifts. Ravel noticed that a fourth ice-laden glass had not been claimed.

"Ravel!" the men cheered and raised their glasses to him.

"Oh shit." For Ravel, the realization had just hit home.

Mick, holding out Ravel's glass, approached his son-in-law, the widest grin Ravel had ever seen breaking across his face.

"I took my shoes off—did you notice?" Mick handed the glass to Ravel who nodded, bewildered.

Now the other two officers were closing in, not for the kill but for the congratulations and compliments, and Ravel wondered if he might not have had another hyperglycemic blackout in the bathroom and this was another of his visions. But the officers were real. He could smell their sweat and breath, could feel the cool tall glass in his hand. No way this could be a vision.

For whatever reason, for the execution of some cruel joke perhaps, Maxine Dein had signed these guys. *Real world,* Ravel thought. *Salt of the earth. Experience. Age before wisdom. Shit.*

"Sorry," Ravel said, sensing Mick about to propose a toast. "I'll be right back. You guys kinda caught me..."

"With your pants down? Oh we heard," Russell said.

"Thanks. Be right back."

He didn't return to the toilet but instead stood before the mirror. It had happened. From Tristan Boppana and Spiros Averof making deals with Hollywood to Maggie announcing the release of her debut work to his father winning the ADPiF to Mick & Company hitting the jackpot with Maxine, it was obvious how it had gotten to be this way: Ravel had allowed it to be this way. It wasn't *his* fault, wasn't that he was some talentless *hack*; Ravel Averof had *plenty* of talent, so much talent, in fact, he'd been *wise* to save up his solid golden words year after year, waiting until the time was perfect, inspiration had struck him at last and allowed him to finally, finally, finally pour those solid golden words across so many pages.

But he'd held back a tad too long. He'd allowed them to take advantage of his greatness, Ravel's swollen fruit that had just now, finally, fallen.

In those moments of shaking himself down, of not breathing and of feeling as if a vein in his head had burst, Ravel knew that it did not after all have to be this way. He did not have to take this. He did not have to take this sitting in Maxine's office, nor did he have to take this drinking a lukewarm domestic beer handed to him by his gun-toting father-in-law, and he certainly did not have to take this standing in front of the mirror in his own bathroom with the door closed as if he were at a party years ago embarrassed to emerge. Far from embarrassed, Ravel was now fully convinced that the plan he'd conceived was the correct one, and it was not too late for its execution. He only had to go back. He would not be able to change their fortunes—not even, ultimately, that of the one he hoped to pursue—but that had never been the point. The point had been to change the fortunes of Ravel Averof, and the rest could stay as they were.

The sooner Mick and his cowriters left the sooner Ravel could get to work. Ravel knew that showing any sign of impatience to Mick would make his father-in-law stay longer to twist the knife so that his son-in-law did not get what he wanted. Rather than tap his foot, sigh and drum his fingers on the counter, Ravel helped himself to the beer Mick had poured for him. Ravel reminded those gathered that as a diabetic on Metformin, he'd been warned by his doctor to watch it with alcohol. To Ravel's surprise, the officers understood. If they'd wanted to razz him about his recent diagnosis, they were doing an admirable job controlling their impulses. Instead, they chatted about "the industry," "the biz," as if they'd worked in Hollywood since they were child actors and each had thirty-odd spec scripts under his belt.

At last, an hour later, they left. As soon as the door had closed on the back of Denver's finest, Ravel turned from the front entryway and entered the living room. The time for second-guessing had gone out the door with Mick & Company, and in its place was action. Without hesitating, Ravel took *That* off the shelf and carried it with him to the office. The massive book felt old and alive, like a pet that was at last going to be put down. He did put *That* down—on the clear workspace to the right of his laptop. The face of actor Russ Goldweather as Fantabulous the Magician stared up at him from the cover. For a time Ravel stood above *That*, staring down and finishing off his one beer. *All right*, he thought. *You and me. You're mine now, all a thousand-plus pages of you.*

He sat before the screen and took his last swig while thumbing through the first few pages, the blurbs from newspapers that had since stopped reviewing books. "An epic horror novel, the greatest the genre has ever had," proclaimed the *Los Angeles Beat*. "Bryce had the devil at his back when he wrote this!" crowed the *San Jose Sentinel*. From there Ravel turned to Bryce's bibliography, then to the copyright and dedication pages, and he did not feel bad reading any of them. Dalton Bryce already had so much—what did Ravel Averof have? Nothing but the previous desire to quit, to which even

Bryce could relate. Surely the emperor could grant a little something to one of his most ardent subjects.

On to the ubiquitous epigraph page of song lyrics, the table of contents and another page of poetry and song excerpts. As Ravel flipped and skimmed, turned and scanned he felt himself stepping back, not forward, and that scared him more than anything Dalton Bryce, the Emperor of Terror, had ever written.

The first page, the first sentence—the first paragraph. Ravel read that one-sentence paragraph again and again. Finally he put the book aside, opened a new word processing document and began to type. He wrote from memory, and what he ended up with was highly similar to the first sentence of Bryce's own novel. One of the original words had gone missing, another word had moved to a different position, but it was not the same sentence; of that Ravel was certain. It was his sentence now—not a sentence written by Dalton Bryce in Massachusetts but rather by Ravel Averof in Colorado, three decades later. Ravel's sentence contained all the elements of the original—the rain, the years, the little toy battlecraft headed down the creek—but that sentence now belonged to Ravel. He owned it. Or, rather, he would own it, free and clear, once he'd gone back and succeeded in his plan. After he'd made the call, asked for forgiveness and another go-around in the suit, the machine. To be even safer, and especially seeing as it was the first sentence of his new novel, Ravel deleted another word and changed the arrangement of the introductory clause. Now the sentence was even more his own, paraphrased to the point that Bryce's style had been subsumed.

Ravel checked the time. It had taken about three minutes

to write the first sentence. How many sentences were there altogether? How many minutes did he have for this project, his new, his first novel? True, it would take him a while to finish, but he had no doubt he would. That was the first part of a two-part plan, the pulsation, and all Ravel had now was time.

TEN

Again a vision—or rather a dream, since he was asleep when it began.

He was walking down a dirt path in the early morning. It wasn't too cold out. The air was crisp, the sky clear. All around him he saw giant rock formations rising at odd angles like arms and legs. The occasional tree or bush he passed signaled life with its chirping or rustling. He was dressed differently—clothes from an earlier time, before he was born.

Ravel sped up his pace. He had the feeling he was supposed to do something here, soon. He rounded a boulder and nearly tripped over a body laid out across the path. A man. As Ravel inspected he took a step back and cried out. It was Dalton Bryce, dead, for how could he be alive with that hunting knife stuck in his chest?

No blood, Ravel noticed. No blood at all. The Emperor of Terror's eyes were open—not dead open but alive open. Bryce's chest rose and fell evenly. The hunting knife continued to stand straight up.

Hey there, Dalton Bryce said.

Who did this to you? asked Ravel.

You did, Bryce answered.

How could I? Ravel said. I was just walking.

I can't go any farther, Bryce said. You'll have to take my place.

What am I supposed to do?

However you do it, it'll be okay. Keep going. You'll see it. It'll be your book. Take it. Remember it. When you write that novel, it'll never have existed before. You'll kill mine when you create yours.

But—

Get going or you'll lose it! Bryce shrieked, and now blood spurted from his mouth.

Ravel stepped over the Emperor of Terror and ran along the path. More boulders, bushes, trees. Then he saw it: nestled under the craggy overhang of a twisted rock formation, a makeshift tent, its flap open, its entrance inviting. Ravel stepped off the path and approached the tent. All dark inside, and yet someone (something) lived there. Ravel reached into the tent and was jolted by a bloody scream.

He awoke. He could tell it was later in the morning by the strength of the sun edging the curtains. Deborah had vacated the bed and left for campus long before.

Dream or vision—or maybe both, Ravel thought. Bryce had again spoken to him; he had given the struggling writer permission to take *That*. Hemming and hawing over the logical impossibility of the plan was pointless. Ravel had the go-ahead now, he had his memory. It didn't matter that the novel existed *now* with Bryce's name on the cover. Didn't mean Ravel was going to fail. If it took opening a new dimension and living as a successful author on an alternate time-path, Ravel would gladly write over a thousand *That*s without shame.

And so the great work began. By the end of the first week of work on his new novel, that third week of January, Ravel had completed a good seventy pages without having sacrificed his health or sanity.

Each day after seeing Deborah off and going to the gym, working out for no more than an hour, he would return home and to the kitchen where he would first check his blood sugar. Most always it was within range, to Ravel's relief. He feared his number would only rise as he continued to sit and write for so long each day, for hadn't his sedentary lifestyle contributed to his diabetes? Genetics played a major part, his doctor assured him, but just who in Ravel's family had suffered, or still suffered, from diabetes would remain a mystery. Ravel had not spoken to Yoana's side of the family since he was a teenager, and he had never communicated with anyone on his father's side. Even if he knew, what would it have mattered, really? He would still have to deal with the disease. It was comfort enough to know he was ahead of the anticipated rise in glucose as he carried his copy of Dalton Bryce's *That* with him to the office. There he flipped, skimmed, marked, chunked, synthesized and wrote. He wrote his own sentences, or for the most part his own sentences, for four hours uninterrupted. After breaking for lunch, he would return to the great work and produce more pages he knew were his own. On Friday afternoon, seeing the healthy length of the document on his laptop, he kicked back at his desk and laced his fingers behind his head. Lost in his thoughts, he nearly missed the call on his phone. Seeing who it was, he let it go to voicemail.

"Ravel. It's Bruce here. Bruce Bednarik. I noticed you weren't at this week's meeting. You missed quite a time. A lot of guys opened up, a lot of guys bared their blood-spattered fingers and souls. Anyway, you can miss one meeting, I understand, but I'll expect you at the next, and I hope you'll share then. See you soon."

Ravel deleted the message and hopped on the internet without another thought of Men Who Write Too Much. It was job search time from now until Deborah arrived home. When she did she found him hard at work, his eyes red and raw from looking at the screen so much. She asked about his blood sugar, his number, and he said it was all right and he had made sure to get up and move around every so often.

"I'm sorry you've been searching all day," she said.

Feeling low, Ravel had trouble meeting his wife's eyes.

"Let's go out to eat," she said.

The snow and the worse of the cold that day had subsided, and as they drove over to Park Hill they had their windows rolled down so they could breathe in the pure Denver air.

To Ravel's question of how her day had been, Deborah answered that she had had a breakthrough with the dissertation, and now that the most significant writing was underway she'd have to spend even more time in the small secluded library room she'd claimed as her own.

"More weekends?" ventured Ravel.

"Every weekend." Deborah sighed. "Until I'm done, Rav. Get the draft out, my adviser says. I can't stop now. Have to push through."

"To the other side."

"I'm sorry, Ravel."

"I love you, D."

She seemed startled at this abrupt sentiment, but soon she smiled and rested her hand on his thigh. "We don't say that enough," she said as she squeezed. "When I'm hooded and I land that tenure-track position, then there'll be no excuse for us not to say it all the time."

"I'm here for you. I just want you to know that."

"I know. I wish I could be here more. I guess I'll always feel somewhat guilty."

"Don't be. I'm getting a lot done. Making a lot of headway. You saw me. Every day I get closer to landing something. Something that matters."

"I'm so happy to hear that," she said.

"I've really gotten into it. It's big, too. I'm pursuing it aggressively. Passionately, I'd say."

"Well, good. So what is it?"

Ravel considered before saying, "I don't really want to say until I have it. You understand that, right?"

"I understand but. You shouldn't be superstitious."

Again she squeezed, and Ravel covered her hand with his own.

Much later that night, after Deborah had gone to bed and fallen fast asleep, Ravel returned to his laptop with his copy of *That* marked on page 99 ("Early Darkness: James Godfrey Swallows His Pride"). He hadn't quite achieved a satisfactory word count for the day. He'd only made ten paperback pages of *That* his own. His goal, which he'd had in sight all that week until it hiccupped that Friday, was to make fifteen pages his own each day of the week—including weekends. If he could make it to the top of page 104 or perhaps even 110, the start of a new section ("Geoff Dahl Swallows His Prejudice") he could rest. Reaching page 110 meant he could push even farther on Saturday. It was late now, but that mattered little. Ravel needed only to start rewriting sentences, changing any newly encountered names, injecting his style into what was already there—all in the next five pages. What Deborah had said was true—they would say they loved each other more often in the future, once they were both settled professionally and raking in the respectable pay, she as a tenured professor and he as a bestselling author. What Ravel had said in the car on the way to dinner had not necessarily been a lie. By writing his novel, *That*, he was auditioning for the only career he'd ever wanted, and he had to be ready for when the call came.

Far from abating, the great work only intensified as the weeks turned to months. From the beginning of February to the end of April Ravel finished over half of *That*, the first 586 pages, the first three parts including the two Hallowsbury interludes. His daily page goal jumped from fifteen to twenty, and on really productive days, when he was certain Deborah wouldn't be back until very late, he was able to push the count to as many as twenty-five. Once, Ravel churned out close to thirty. He was buoyed by the bi-monthly unemployment checks, which he promptly deposited and kept a portion for the final stage of his plan. The first part of his two-part plan was a beast, though. Some days Ravel doubted himself, other days he wanted to shred many pages he'd written. It was Bryce himself who checked Ravel before the younger writer wrecked himself. In the published pages of an author Ravel had once read voraciously and still secretly admired, the apprentice at last found his voice. Ravel's voice was not unlike Bryce's: each author had the tendency to use em-dashes in places where a comma would have worked just as well; both authors liked to set off characters' thoughts in italics and shouting dialogue in all caps; both authors were qualmless when it came to breaking out suddenly with lengthy stream of consciousness-infused paragraphs. Since their styles were so similar, Ravel reasoned, he had to be right in what he was doing. That similarity in styles, more than anything, affirmed the great work. *That* as it currently read could very well have been written and published by Ravel Averof from the very beginning, and now it *would* be written and published by Ravel Averof from the very beginning. Ravel never thought of it as plagiarism. It was more like emulation, a reimagining.

Dates in the novel changed so that instead of the youthful sections taking place in the mid-sixties, when Bryce was a boy, those sections now took place in the early 2000s, when Ravel had been the same youthful age. He had to be careful, as there had already been two screen adaptations, the latter updating the youthful sections to the late eighties, when the showrunners had been young, while the present-day scenes took place in the mid-2010s. For the passages of his novel involving the characters as adults, Ravel set the time during the pandemic. The characters were in their late twenties and facing a two-pronged terror: Covid-19 and the creature known only as That.

Gone from Ravel's novel was the inclusion of any pop culture from the time before its author was born; in its place were the music, movies, videos, social media, ads and the like with which Ravel was familiar. Instead of epigraphs featuring song lyrics from mid-sixties hits, Ravel's *That* placed front and center lyrics penned by artists from the early to mid-aughts. Many of the monsters—if not always the scenes they originally appeared in—stayed. Ravel felt it safe enough to keep the Werewolf, Dracula, the Mummy, the Creature from the Black Lagoon. Such monsters were universal and eternal, and as long as they fit the fears of Ravel's characters he didn't see a problem with reusing them. Other, more obscure creatures from horror movies of the sixties, seventies and eighties had to be replaced with those that terrified Ravel's generation when they were adolescents: Ghostface, whatever showed itself at the end of *The Blair Witch Project*, torturers and terrorists and mass-murdering school shooters, the girl from *The Ring*. Ravel included all he could think of, aware that by his generation the monsters had changed to the point that they didn't appear to be monsters any longer. Many of them were people.

Ravel pushed onward, for the first time confident in his abilities, his powers of perception and observation. As he transformed Dalton Bryce's words into his own—or mostly his own—he found that entire chunks of prose fell away. Ravel's *That* would remain an epic, but it would be fewer pages than the original. Never once did Ravel feel any guilt. This was his novel now. *That* by Ravel Averof.

At the end of April, Deborah sat him down for a talk. It was a Sunday, the last of the month, and spring was particularly fickle, even for Colorado. Outside the wind whipped up the rain. Ravel was seated at the dining table, his mind occupied by the great work that awaited him late that night. Deborah approached him from the kitchen. Ravel couldn't understand why she looked so concerned. His A1C had dropped somewhat—remarkably, for how many uninterrupted hours he'd been sitting in the office each day the past few months. The Metformin was doing its job; if catastrophe awaited Ravel's health down the line, it was still too far off for him to fret. Why should he worry? He was close, so close he could feel his novel in his hands, published in hardcover. He'd successfully ghosted Bruce Bednarik, who by the end of March had ceased calling. If anyone asked Ravel point-blank he would say he was happy in the extreme; he'd never felt better. His wife looked the opposite.

As Deborah rounded the high-walled kitchen counter, two cups of tea and a small ramekin in her hands, Ravel smiled. This Deborah returned, though her smile was wan and forced. She set the cups and ramekin down, pushed a cup toward Ravel and then raised hers to her lips to blow on the contents. She seemed warm but sad, a countenance Ravel had not seen since 2021, the year after her mother died. He wondered, briefly, if he should bolt.

"First off," Deborah said, "I want you to know I love you, Ravel."

"And I love you, Deb. Do you think I don't?"

"I know you do. It's just…"

"You're worried."

Deborah scrunched her face up—a look Ravel had never seen before. He realized what it was: disappointment. His wife was disappointed in him. She pitied him, he was certain of it.

"Oh yes. A whole lot of worry. Ravel, it's been four months and you're *still* unemployed. I know that sounds harsh, and I don't want it to, but it's the truth and you have to hear the truth because no one else is going to tell it to you. You're here all alone, day after day—"

"What about you?" Ravel tried to keep his rising anger in check. He would not be pitied. He would not be seen as pathetic, a disappointment, a loser. He was about to be one of the greats! "You're all alone too, D, in that little room of yours, in the library. Day after day…"

"But I've produced something, Ravel. I'm finished."

"You…are?"

"Yes. I didn't want to bring it up now because of your situation—"

"No, that's great, Deb, so great. I'm so happy for you. Wow."

"Thank you. So, Rav, please don't put this on me. This has to be about you now. You've got to find a job. If it's a career, great, but at this point, you have to take *something*. Anything."

"But it's not like we're not getting any money."

"Money that's going to run out in two months, Ravel."

Ravel gathered himself before speaking. "I know I'll have it before they stop the checks."

"What is 'it,' Ravel? Last month you were telling me you were so close. So close to landing a job, possibly having a new career…"

"I got very close. It just didn't pan out. I was one of two finalists, and they chose the other candidate. You know as long as we're getting the same amount of money I was making at Maguffin-Shrift—"

"It's not just about the money, Ravel!" Deborah withdrew her hands. "That's never been the most important thing. It's always been about you, first and foremost. You. Your well-being. I want you to live a long time—"

"So do I."

"And I don't think you can do that if you don't feel worthy and alive and confident."

"You don't think I'm those things?"

Slowly, Deborah shook her head. "Your diabetes…"

"I'm managing it all right."

"For now, yes. You've been doing great. But you heard what the doctor said: it's progressive. A progressive disease, and if you're not fulfilled in your other areas of life, like work, it could get out of hand. It could turn into type 1. It might be type 1 and we don't know it yet. You have to keep moving forward."

Ravel took a moment to sip his tea; Deborah, feeling sheepish about the chiding, did the same. At last Ravel said, "I am telling the truth when I say I feel more confident, more alive and more worthy than I have in a long time."

"That job was killing you."

"And I will not go back to the same thing, okay?"

"I understand that, Ravel. But with our bills and, you know..."

He knew. Neither of them wanted to mention the child that would have to arrive.

"...I can't support us alone." Deborah finished.

"Just give me till June. Please."

Deborah laughed. "You're just suddenly one day going to wake up and find the job you want has landed in your lap? It doesn't work like—"

"I'm finally doing what I want to do, Deb! I—"

Ravel jumped in his seat as Deborah slapped her palm on the table. He had never seen such anger and uncertainty in her eyes before, and he realized he would have to let her into his world, if only a little.

"There it is," she said. "At last. What do you do all day here, Ravel? What. Do. You. Do. I love you, I do, but if you're...Are you...?"

"I'm not cheating on you," Ravel said adamantly. "Why would I?"

"Because you're not getting enough. Because you…"

"What?"

"Because you want someone who has more time, someone who…who's younger, who doesn't have to think about having a child right now. Or maybe someone who doesn't even want to have children."

There. She'd said it, and she'd said it without any apparent weakness. Her lips did not quiver, her eyes remained dry and she'd looked at him directly as she spoke. He realized then that the reason he'd always assumed their marriage could end was not in fact the right reason.

"Deb," he said. "Your age has nothing to do with anything. You're only two years older than me."

"Thirty-two is getting up there to have children, Ravel."

"It's really not. Look at…. I want a child too. I really do. It's not your schedule either or anything like that. I love you. I love you more than any woman I've ever known. And you know me by now to know I don't need a whole lot. What we have is fine. I love being with you, when I can be with you, and I'm content with that."

"Be honest. You must be watching porn at least a little each day."

"I'm actually not. I swear to you I'm not. I'm using the time I have each day. Using it really well. It's like I've been reborn."

Deborah leaned back, crossed her arms and stared at him, her mouth tight. "That's what I need to know," she said. "What you do all day."

"I told you—the gym and—"

"And what? I don't believe you're doing all day what you say you're doing. If it's not porn and it's not the job search all the time, then what? Seriously, Ravel, someone as smart and resourceful and handsome as you should have *something* by now. Unless..."

Ravel downed the rest of his tea even though it was still too hot.

"Unless..." The realization struck her, and she covered her mouth with one hand. "Oh Jesus. You're writing, aren't you?"

"I swear when I finish what I'm working on, I am going to make it. Make it *big*. We both are."

"What are you writing, Ravel?"

"I can't really say—"

The palm against the table's surface again. "Say it!"

"A novel. And I swear, Deb, when it's done, and it will be done in June, you'll see. It will bring me the satisfaction I've always been seeking. And it'll sell so many copies. Just, please, give me the remainder of my time."

His wife exhaled audibly for some seconds. "All right," she said. "Okay. So the job search never even happened? Never started?"

"I have been searching. Just...not a lot."

"You lied to me, Ravel. Every day lying to me."

"I'm sorry, Deb. Please forgive me, and please understand this is my one last chance."

For several sickening seconds Deborah Parker seemed suspended in time, hovering above a knife's edge. At last, when Ravel felt faint from holding his breath, she spoke:

"If you think, if you think this is the one, the breakthrough, I'm going to believe you."

Ravel reached across for Deborah's hands, but she would

give him neither. "I want you to believe me, Deb. The way you did when we first met."

"I'll give you this," she said. "I will believe you."

"Thank you."

"I take it you haven't been going to that support group, the men..."

"Men Who Write Too Much. MeWWToM. I can't. It's just too sad. I don't want to be sad, Deb. I want to be a success. I deserve that."

"You honestly believe you deserve it?"

"For so long I've only wanted to make it as a novelist, and this is my last chance. I'll make it my last chance. I promise—I promise you that if it doesn't happen for me, I'll go into something else, something I can live with for the rest of my life."

"That's a promise," said Deborah. "I'm holding you to it."

"Of course."

She leaned forward and stabbed him in the chest with her pointer finger. "Then do it. Finish it."

FINISH IT HE DID. By the end of May he had pushed well into the final section, "Part Five: The Séance of Sarcophagi." He debated for a longer time than usual as to what the final monster would be in Ravel Averof's *That*. In the original, That's true form was that of a gargantuan scorpion, and even if Ravel did successfully alter the past event in which the point of conception occurred, the lynchpin to his plan succeeding, and the future was successfully thrown off, Bryce's well-known fear of scorpions might raise suspicion. Playing it safe, Ravel changed That's final form to that of a giant earwig. Comical to some, merely disgusting to others, earwigs terrified

Ravel, and so too would they terrify the protagonists of his *That*.

He had to stop referring to his creation as 'his *That*.' It wasn't his *That*—it was just *That*, written by Ravel Averof. Soon enough, it would be.

He screened all calls during the last leg of the great work, didn't see anyone except Deborah during that last month and a half. Winning approval from Deborah had released him to drop any pretense of conducting a job search and to hit the gym only intermittently. During the last leg of the great work Deborah kept out of Ravel's way. It could have been that she was angry, upset, scared by the idea of her husband giving up months of his life, almost half a year, to accomplish something he had already tried and failed at—but the signs that were there, the sighs, the shifting, closed doors, Ravel did not pick up on, and the great work continued at a record pace. His confidence got to be so great toward the end that he returned to earlier sections and revised them further, making them even more his. Always, though, was page 1,178 in mind. Always, a good hour before Deborah returned home, would Ravel start to unwind so that he was ready for what his wife wanted, now that she had granted him the time he'd always desired.

He was an ethereal being, out of body, unheard of to his previous self, and in mid-June, on the day the Nuggets held their championship parade through downtown Denver, a day when Deborah was at the library, he reached page 1,178 in the paperback version of Dalton Bryce's *That* and the corresponding page 1,090 in the manuscript version of his own novel, which was now and always would be the only *That* known to the world.

He stared for some time at the screen, the final twisting

sentence that had once been Bryce's. Ravel was tempted to write at the bottom of the page the exact dates on which he'd started and ended *That*, but such a flourish would have been far too close to Bryce's method. Instead Ravel wrote END at the bottom and threw both arms over his head in triumph. In celebration he turned to the music on his computer and blasted The Lumineers. He jumped and danced in the office, careful not to swing his arms too wide. Then he opened a drawer and took out several thumb drives. He'd kept these relics knowing they would be of use someday. Now Ravel, the music blaring, plugged in each thumb drive and copied over the document containing the completed *That*. When he had *That* on each of the thumb drives, he deleted the original file from his laptop. An act of lunacy, everyone would say. No backing up to email or an external hard drive or the drive or the cloud. But to Ravel his decision made sense: he did not trust the drive, did not trust the cloud or his email service provider. Did not trust the internet. He had to go old school. And even his computer had to be free of *That*. He feared Deborah or some stranger going into his laptop and finding his novel; he knew of no other way to keep it on his person only. He could not be carrying around over a thousand physical manuscript pages. But with so many thumb drives on his person, it would be impossible, Ravel figured, for all of them to malfunction. No way would he lose his manuscript. It was his manuscript, and it was perfect. *That* was vintage Ravel Averof.

When Deborah arrived home that evening she found a dining table laid out nicely, and on that dining table was a vase of calla lilies with her name on it. She set down her own hefty manuscript, which she had just finished proofing, and flipped up the card. *Thank you*, it read. Sensing movement she turned in time to see her husband launch himself at her. In one hand he held an unopened bottle of champagne, which he kept pressed to her back as he went at her in a way he rarely had before. More from relief and the realization of what this initiation meant, Deborah returned the kisses and groping in equal measure.

Later, after sex and toasting and dinner and, much to their amazement, more sex, they lay in bed, close. Deborah's hand rested on Ravel's stomach; she pinched at the flab around his waist.

"I admit I didn't work out half as much toward the end."

"At least you got through it. It's over."

"Yeah," said Ravel, pensive.

"What's it called? What's the title?"

"Um...right now I'm still debating. For now I'm just calling it 'Untitled.'"

"I'll help choose a title, if you let me read it."

"Ah, okay..."

"You will let me read it, right? Or do you not want me to? What, am I in it?"

"No you're not. Just let me. Let me proof it first."

"I hope you've written something I can read, Ravel."

"I can guarantee you, Deb, that you and so many millions of people are going to want to read this novel."

"How do you know? Can you see into the future or something?"

"Not the future..." *The past*, Ravel nearly said—but stopped himself. "Give me...how about three days."

"You're being mysterious again."

"There's nothing mysterious about it. We both should

take some time from it. Let it percolate, or whatever. Then I'll let you have first crack at it."

"Three days, okay," Deborah said. "But no more."

"No more. You got it."

He slept through the night and into the early morning, but sometime before dawn he awoke with a start. Something was wrong. Deborah slept beside him, but something was going to be wrong. This was the novel he'd chosen.

In the office he opened his laptop and plugged in each of the thumb drives. None of the devices malfunctioned. *That* was on each one. The other novel, the impostor, had been returned to the shelf to await its fate. Ravel touched the screen, the cover page of *That*, about 300,000 words, and deflected a spike of fear. He got online. A quick search for Chronoflex brought up nothing, not even the old site under construction. A search for Chronotrex turned up the same.

"Shit," Ravel said. "Oh no. Oh man."

He scrolled through his list of contacts. Of course Laney wasn't there—what if Deborah had decided to use his phone to call someone when he wasn't around? Panicked now, muttering curse words and other interjections, Ravel ran through his list of missed, dialed and received calls. He hoped, he hoped....

There it was: Laney's number in the missed calls folder, showing only once, just before the cutoff when the operating system deleted data after months of numbers piling up.

A sharp quiet sound of joy escaped from Ravel's mouth. His thumb hovered over Laney's number, but he hesitated. If he called her now, at this awful hour of the morning, he'd be forced to explain, to blab, and she could easily cut him off, block his number—provided she even still had her same number and was still working for Chronotrex, which no longer appeared to be operating. It was looking likely that the intense groveling Ravel had intended to perform before Nicholas and the Bowtie Bros would not need to be done.

He had to be sure. Traffic would be nonexistent at this time. Deborah would understand. It was for the novel, their future. Ravel pocketed each of the thumb drives and brought out the other items and articles of clothing he'd collected in his months of writing his first novel. Then, after penning a short sweet note for his wife, he headed out.

Eleven

The longer he remained parked in front of what had once been the home of Chronotrex, the more he felt homeless. He'd entered, exited and reentered the building five times since arriving a half an hour earlier. Each time he'd gone in expecting to be proven wrong, his eyesight proven faulty. What he saw was true: the door at the end of the hallway that had once opened to Chronotrex now opened to nothing. It didn't even open. Ravel had peered through the window to the side of the door, blinked several times, but still he could see only a bare floor, bare walls, nothing. No front desk, no coffee table, no plants, no magazines, no reception area of any kind. Each time he peered through hoping to see Laney or Nicholas or any of the Bowtie Bros in their white lab coats emerging from the hallway at the back with a box or two cradled in their arms. At least let them be in the process of closing, at least let Ravel have the chance to speak to someone in person. But by the eighth peek into the vacant space Ravel had to admit that unless he called Laney now, he was seriously screwed.

Now he regretted not checking in on Chronotrex in all the months he'd been writing *That*. He'd felt ashamed by the hissy-fit he'd pitched upon returning from the chrono-trek to RMNP '89, so ashamed he couldn't bear to walk into the Boulder building let alone place a call to Laney and apologize. The better move, Ravel had reasoned, was to let time go by, emotions cool down: anger muted if not forgotten. He had become so immersed in writing his novel that he never once considered that Chronotrex might go out of business.

The sun was spreading and he no longer cared if he woke her or if she didn't answer or if he reeked of desperation.

Just as he was about to make the call his phone rang. Deborah. Ravel watched his wife's name and number on his screen for five rings before silencing the call and letting it go to voicemail. When it did Ravel ran through the missed calls, past those belonging to his wife, and tapped the appropriate line. Laney picked up on the very first ring.

"Hello?"

"Oh..."

Taken aback by the speed at which she'd answered, he ended the call, then closed his eyes as inevitable embarrassment took hold, made all the more acute by the certainty that she wasn't going to call him back. Ridiculous. He was a thirty-year-old husband and eventual father who had just completed a great novel—perhaps *The* great novel—and had to go back in time to solidify his hold on it! He had the power here. It took Laney longer to pick up the second time. Before she could say anything Ravel had launched in with "Laney it's Ravel remember me?"

"You're still in my list of contacts, Ravel." Her voice

sounded cool but not hostile as he had expected. "What can I do for you?"

"What can you do for me? You can bring back Chronotrex for starters!"

"Chronotrex is here."

"Chronotrex is not here. It's out of business, Laney. I've been standing outside the door to the company and inside it's all dark and bad and blank. It's all bare inside, okay? Explain that."

He had not expected Laney's laughter either. "Chronotrex is *way* in business, Ravel. We've just moved."

"Moved?"

"Right on the spot. You know."

"Oh. So…"

"So you'll see us, if you drive out that way. Take the 119 into the foothills and you can't miss us. You'll be impressed. A lot's changed since you left."

"Oh wow, um…"

"You're still interested in chrono-trekking, I take it. Why else would you call?"

"Uh…"

"Come in today and we'll set you up."

"Laney, what happened—"

"That's enough out of me, Ravel. They're probably listening. And work calls."

"You go to work this early?"

"Like I said: a lot's changed since you bowed out. You'll see."

Ravel scoured the maps app on his phone. He zoomed in hyper-close along the 119. No sign of a business, a building, even a Porta Potty. Next to Rambis Plateau: nothing but the digital green signifying wilderness terrain.

"Okay, okay..." Ravel muttered. "She's not messing with me. She wouldn't do that."

Or would she?

Before pulling out of the lot he checked for voicemail. Deborah hadn't left anything, not even so much as a text. Not a good sign, but also not a situation with which he could concern himself. Before heading out to Chronotrex, Ravel had to run through his plan one more time.

LANEY WAS RIGHT, of course: no way could Ravel have missed sighting the oblong-shaped biodome that had been set down on the Rambis Plateau like a conquering spaceship. As he turned off the 119 and pulled into the visitor's lot, now the parking lot for Chronotrex, Ravel noted that the wormhole had been covered over by the company building, which in the strengthening sun gave off the appearance of a gargantuan scaly slug. Where were the windows? Where, for that matter, was the front entrance? Ravel got out and took a deep breath before slipping his hiking backpack over one shoulder and striding toward what he supposed was the way in. As he drew near he made out the faint outline of an oval-shaped doorway. No knob, no panel to input a keycode. Who was allowed inside was controlled completely from within.

Ravel jumped when he heard Laney's voice on an intercom. He wasn't sure of the location of this intercom, he only knew her voice was loud, as if she were standing beside him.

"I see you're already dressed."

"I want more control this time," Ravel said, then added: "If that's okay."

"As long as those clothes you're wearing weren't made later than the '80s."

"They're from the late '70s, I'm pretty sure. I spent months scouring the vintage clothing stores. I'm wearing a hundred percent rayon."

"That's dedication. Nothing else on you from after the '80s?"

"Search me already," Ravel challenged. He hoped to God his voice didn't sound as anxious and on edge as he felt.

"We haven't gotten to that point yet."

"Because you haven't had any other clients since me?"

A pause. Then Laney said, "No, Ravel. We've had a few. Our backers. But there's still a special place for you at Chronotrex, despite January's antics. I knew you'd be back."

The oval-shaped entryway slid open to reveal a dark interior. Laney commanded Ravel to enter.

He saw her approaching from down a long ultralit hallway. As always, she looked good.

"What's with the suit?" Ravel asked.

"Girlboss wears the pantsuits. Didn't you know?"

"What's that?" Ravel felt old. "Did you say—"

"Girlboss, Ravel. Means I'm the boss." At that Laney turned and high-heeled it back the way she came. Ravel trailed at what he hoped was a respectful distance. A camera was embedded in the ceiling every ten feet. At the end of the hall, under an infrared light, Laney scanned her eyes across a glowing panel in the door, which then buzzed and slid open.

"You're *the boss*? Of the whole company? Since when?"

"Since Nicholas passed."

He followed her into the inner sanctum. The lights came on and Ravel was met with an immaculately clean and comfortable reception area, complete with plush sofas, chairs, an ornate oak coffee table stocked with magazines, a water cooler, a coffee-maker, and exotic-looking foliage in the corners. A massive aquarium stocked with colorful tropical fish provided the grand reception desk with a dramatic backdrop. Overhead, faint through an intercom, one eighties hit ended and another began.

"Passed?"

"He died. Of a rare blood disease. Apparently it skipped a couple generations and got him. He told me about his genetic line once..." Laney paused, her look contemplative, almost wistful.

"That's...awful, Laney."

"In April he was driving along 28th in Boulder when he got the attack. He started having these seizures, the first sign it's over. He knew. He made a right turn onto this quiet street, like he didn't want anyone to see him. He stopped the car and even set the parking brake, which I find funny. They got him to the hospital but by then it was too late."

"Dang."

"Official cause was an aneurysm, most certainly brought about by the, you know, the blood. It's strange and sad that he's gone, of course, but.... I was positioned well by then, and I made my move. Kind of ruthless if you really want to know."

"What about the Bowtie Bros?"

"Those who didn't bend the knee were dismissed. Nearly all of them. They wouldn't work under a woman—not in that way, at least. Shall we?"

Laney led Ravel around the reception counter and

through another set of doors that required her eyes to be scanned.

"You're the boss and you're opening this place?"

"I'm here for you, Ravel. When I got your call this morning, I just knew. I have a good feeling I know what you want to happen today."

Beyond the counter was an expansive open-plan office layout not unlike the bull pit at Maguffin-Shrift. The sight of rows and rows of low-walled workstations spanning the remainder of the floor brought Ravel back to his days of employment, and he didn't like it.

"Sales, Laney? Really?"

"Advising. Now when clients come in they'll meet with one of our experts here to assure they get exactly what they want out of the Chronotrex experience. Nicholas was well-meaning, but let's face it: he would never have gotten up the nerve to go public."

"You've gone public?"

"We're going to. By summer '24, if projections are accurate. Investors have flooded the coffers."

"What about the military?"

"That's a sore spot for them. They didn't expect me to be in charge."

Laney's office, its walls lined with large screens depicting every area and level of Chronotrex's headquarters, was spacious enough to have fit inside two if not three of Maguffin-Shrift's managerial rooms. Ravel sat across from Laney, careful to keep his hidden items from falling out.

"So," she said, "I take it you're ready."

"I am. I want to go today. This morning, if possible."

"Oh it's possible. As long as you have the money."

"This isn't free?"

"Ravel..."

"I don't suppose it would be given my reaction the last time. The first time, really. No wonder you were so eager to open for me. It's all about money now with you."

"And you?"

Ravel felt a lead weight drop into his stomach. "What do you mean?" he asked.

Laney's laugh was like a bird's chirp. "Come on, Ravel. You want to go back this time for *something*, right? To *do* something?"

"Um..."

"It has to be small, of course. Nothing earth-shattering, like I said in the beginning. But that's going to cost you."

"How...how much?"

Laney wrote a figure down on a notepad and pushed the pad across to Ravel. The number opened his eyes wide.

"If you can't pay all of it today, we do have a payment plan."

"Paid out till the end of my life! You're like the Blue Origin of time travel!"

"My intention exactly. Thank you. I take that as a compliment." Laney watched Ravel stare at the number. "How badly do you want it, Ravel?"

"Beyond anything."

"Anything? Do you really mean *anything*?"

Ravel nodded.

"Then you'll pay this. No free rides this time. You'll be happy to know the conditions and effects of the chrono-trek have vastly improved under my watch."

"That's a relief."

"So you're really paying for the best, the most top-notch experience. You just have to follow the rules. Those are solidly in place now. So…. What do you want to do exactly?"

"I just want to go back in time, Laney. Have you expanded the Chronoquantumogriphier's range at all?"

"Afraid not. Not yet. You're still stuck anytime in the '80s in Colorado. Nowhere else and no time else, unfortunately. Is that going to work for you?"

"Yes. Believe it or not."

"So my question stands: What are you going to do exactly, when you're back there?"

"I want to go back to check out someone. A writer, of course."

"Not a younger version of your dad."

"Yug. You know me better than that. And besides he wasn't in Colorado at all then."

"All right." Laney placed her hands behind her head and leaned back. Her eyes had changed to steel. *All those scans*, he thought.

"Leave behind your medication, your glucometer, phone, wallet, keys, anything else—and I do mean *anything* else—that was made after the wormhole formed. I assume you have to take that amulet with you…"

"You assume correctly."

"But *nothing* else. Remember the time limit—same rules apply, and they *are* enforced."

"Got it. But I can…talk with this writer, right?"

"Yes. You may talk to the writer, whoever it is, whose name I'm assuming you're not going to reveal."

"You again assume correctly."

"Ravel. You have to be careful. Nothing else but talk. No

mention of now, 2023, the pandemic, your parents, the last several presidents, the—"

"Laney, I know all this. Please don't lecture me."

"If you go over the forty minutes…"

"Forty now?"

"Yes, forty. You're paying for it, of course."

"That's nice, if expensive."

"The cost must be worth it to you. But, seriously, Professor, if you go over those forty minutes by even one millisecond…"

"I won't come back."

"Worse than that: you'll be stuck in the wormhole, in between time."

"I know exactly what I'm doing, Laney. I hope you do too."

Laney folded her arms. "You don't have to hide anything from me, Ravel. I'm going to have to find out more about your trek if I'm going to send you back."

"You don't need to know who, only where and when, right?"

Laney looked at Ravel with a coldness he'd never seen in her. She struck him then as older than Ravel Averof, she the professor and he the awkward student, their roles reversed. She was indeed the boss now, and he shivered under her gaze. He smoothed out his vintage late '70s coat, feeling the thumb drives resting in its pockets.

"Have a heart, Laney. Let me just check out this writer and talk a bit, please."

Laney took a moment before reaching into her desk. "I have a heart, Ravel. I've wanted to help you for a long time."

Ravel detected pity. He did not despise Laney for it. He

welcomed it. He flashed to a day when he again stumbled through whatever he thought was teaching in that classroom at Mothers of the Merciful, how Laney and the other young women had looked at him: with pity. They had all pitied him. They knew they would go on to do great things, while he was just some awkward Colorado State grad student the university had made a mistake in hiring for their freshman year.

A long time, Laney had said. What did she mean by that?

Laney sighed. "Where and when. That's all I need to know."

Of the *where* there could be no doubt: Colorado Springs. Even more specifically: Garden of the Gods. Of the *when* Ravel would have been far less certain if not for the vision. Without the vision he'd had before waking up in the hospital a diabetic, he would be lost. Dalton Bryce's own site listed the event as having occurred in 1983, but all other evidence from Bryce biographies and compendiums pointed to 1982, when the Emperor of Terror was still living with his family in The Springs. Ravel had searched so many sites and read so many books and still he could only make an educated guess. Then one day he was going through the Notes app on his phone and saw the one note he'd made the day he left the hospital. A memory overtook him then, so sharp and powerful it was as if he were reliving it. His first vision: Dalton Bryce and Seaport Village, the mammoth book that had blotted everything out, and on that book had been a series of numbers spread across the pages. The numbers had made no sense then; Ravel had typed them into his Notes app, remembering the numbers repeated line by line by line. It occurred to him the numbers were a date and a time: the exact date and time of when the event had occurred in Garden of the Gods, Colorado Springs,

Colorado. Dalton Bryce, or whatever spirit or devil or alien was working with or against Ravel, had reached across the chasm of consciousness to hand the aspirant the key.

Ravel brought out his phone and opened the Notes app. He gave Laney the date and time. "Any reason why you need to be there right then?" she asked.

"The writer's going to leave right after. I have to time this right if I'm going to..."

"Going to what, Ravel?"

"Meet him when he's in the right frame of mind, Laney."

"So it's a he."

Ravel kicked himself internally. After biting his lip, he chose his next words carefully.

"This writer has a process. Always has. Commune with nature, here in Colorado. Inspiration. I want to see if I can emulate, learn from him."

"You writers," Laney said.

"I'm playing by the rules."

"I'll believe you."

Ravel handed Laney his personal credit card and signed on the dotted line of every page.

SURVEILLANCE WAS as tight as the hall through which they traveled. Cameras blinked from their nests in the ceiling and along the walls. Drones weaved between and around the two humans. The click of Laney's heels rang out from the slick metal floor as she led Ravel to a final imposing set of doors. Again the scan of the eyes and they were in. What Ravel saw through those doors dropped his jaw. The center of the facility was devoted to the wormhole. In the center of the cavern was the hole itself, circled by a floor-to-ceiling electrical field. Ravel could feel the energy pulsating through his body.

The Chronoquantumogriphier stood upright on a launch pad above the wormhole. Framing the cavern were computer consoles, wires and hydraulics and cords snaking around the walls. All of it looked to be connected to both the energy field and the Chronoquantumogriphier.

"Laney..." eked out an awestruck Ravel. "You've been busy."

"A lot of this we purchased through Maguffin-Shrift."

"You really turned this place around, Laney. I knew you could do it."

"Did you," she said. "Did you really?"

"Yes of course," Ravel shot back quickly, but her back was already to him.

He watched as Laney took a seat at a console and ran through the screens. The Chronoquantumogriphier awoke.

"So outside of your backers, as you call them, I'm still the only civilian to have tried this."

"Sadly, yes. The investors are in, but no actual bites from the outside yet."

"No unending well of desperation, I take it."

Laney smiled. Her eyes lingered on Ravel's coat. "That's going to make for a tight fit in the Chronoquantumogriphier. Sure you don't want to leave it behind?"

"It's fine, Laney. You know the day I'm going back to. Early morning. I'd rather not freeze while I'm there."

"You'll hardly freeze, Ravel. It would make for a more comfortable chrono-trek."

"Comfort is secondary," said Ravel.

"To your mission."

"If you want to call it that."

"Just don't be surprised if DOG complains. You'll have to put up with his protests."

"Just as long as he doesn't kill me, I'm good."

Laney gave a slight smile and shook her head as she turned back to her screens. The Chronoquantumogriphier continued to hum and crackle.

From out of his coat and jeans Ravel removed his medication, glucometer, phone, wallet and keys. These items he placed on a nearby table.

"All right," he said. "Beam me up."

"Aye, captain," a bemused Laney said.

"I need to debug, right? That's still part of it."

"You bet."

In a chamber off the main room Ravel let the debugging drones do their work. He had by this time, out of fear that the robots were equipped with cameras showing Laney exactly what was in his coat and jeans, stuffed all the thumb drives and the ski-mask into his early '80s whitey-tighties. So that he didn't bleed out from his groin, the knife remained concealed in his snow boot, taped to his ankle underneath his heavy wool sock. Seated as the drones swept over him with their lasers and atomizers, Ravel felt deeply uncomfortable. At last the debugging was over, and he emerged to see the girlboss standing in front of the open Chronoquantumogriphier.

"Ready, Ravel?"

"As ready as I'll ever be."

He got in. The suit closed around him, the helmet secured, the orange light flooding his vision. Laney returned to the command console and keyed in several codes and formulas. Her fingers moved in a blur. Ravel, uncomfortably tight inside the Chronoquantumogriphier, heard the machine whir and rumble. DOG beeped and bopped noises Ravel had never heard: complaints. Laney continued punching and typing like a mad composer from an earlier century.

Ravel felt himself rise as the Chronoquantomogriphier lifted off the platform, or perhaps the platform had given way and the time machine remained suspended above the wormhole.

"Laney. Don't kill me, okay?"

"Only you can kill you, Professor."

The door closed. He couldn't see the wormhole below him, but he knew he faced it. The darkness, the void he would now fill. The Chronoquantumogriphier rocketed forward, Ravel's head dug back into the seat and sudden panic swarmed his mind.

Worse than not coming back, worse than dying: failure. If he failed—

But he wouldn't fail. That vision had saved him. Dalton Bryce had saved him. Never had Ravel felt so confident.

IF IT HADN'T BEEN such early morning, with only the crack of dawn to guide him, perhaps he could have better negotiated the craggy footholds and crevices of the massive rock formation he now descended. Above and behind him he heard the lingering crackle of the energy field. Laney had improved the chrono-trek: unlike before, Ravel's head did not ache nearly as much, nor did his stomach feel quite as queasy. His atomic structure had held together better.

Even after he'd reached solid ground he still had to work his way through heavy vegetation, and the sense that a wild animal might jump him at any moment did not abate until he'd finally reached a well-worn trail. The clock ticked loudly in Ravel's mind. No phone or watch with which to tell time, but doing so would only have slowed down the mission. Each second counted more than the last.

The sun rose from behind the dramatic rock formations. Ravel, the vision in mind, was certain the path he jogged was the very same path Mr. Dalton Gerald Bryce was about to trod —then and now.

Thus far he'd journeyed through the Garden without seeing a soul. Ravel knew, however, that just around the next corner would be Dalton Bryce's impetus for *That*: a small and crudely constructed tent in which lay sleeping a homeless man who, as the Emperor of Terror had described on his site and so many other sites and books had parroted, had given the author the idea for Fantabulous the Magician, and therefore the means of opening Bryce's mind to the great work that he would finally complete a decade later. *That*. That homeless man, whose name Dalton Bryce had never learned, had awoken just as Bryce passed by, alone, on one of his dawn walks that he would often take to mull over ideas. The hobo had spoken with Dalton, sat with him for a while and shared several stories. He had also, Dalton Bryce and so many other sources explained, shown the Emperor of Terror magic tricks, after which the author, already a publishing industry force with two books under his belt, had the seed of a new novel, a grand work, the grandest horror book of them all, in his mind.

Ravel turned the corner and, as expected, saw the crudely constructed tent wedged in a crevasse of a towering formation. Careful not to make any noise, but also knowing that the homeless man was too drunk to wake up easily, Ravel backtracked along the trail, then took the path that headed toward the parking lot. In the distance, just past thick bushes and more formations, he could see a 1981 Chevy Scottsdale pull in and park, the only vehicle to have done so since the Garden had closed the day before. Ravel crouched. Like a soldier, he crawled to where he was just off the path and out of sight, snug behind a tree and a boulder. This was the path Bryce would take, and in a little while longer, that homeless man in the tent would pack up and move on to avoid the crowds and the authorities. Conversing with just one person, Dalton Bryce, would be enough social awkwardness for one day.

But that conversation would never happen.

The leaves along the path startled and skipped in the rising wind. The silhouette of Pike's Peak stood stark against the sky's radioactive-like glow.

Most important day of my life, thought Ravel, *and I haven't been born yet.*

Down the path he made out a ghostly figure, only an outline at this point. Bryce was approaching. It was him, heavy beard and glasses and all. The Emperor of Terror was by now fewer than twenty paces from Ravel's hiding place, perhaps another sixty or seventy paces from the homeless man, the impetus, the catalyst for *That*, and if Bryce set even one eye on that tent or one foot in the hobo's area, all the money and time and energy Ravel had put into his surefire hit, his massively popular, bestselling novel, would be wasted.

"Yoana, forgive me," Ravel whispered before he dug deep down past his jeans into his whitey-tighties, pulled out a dark ski mask, surely manufactured and originally purchased before 1982, and put it on. He then pulled from his snow boot the stiletto knife he'd been told dated to the late seventies. Ravel grasped the handle with his left hand, pushed the button so that the long blade shot out, took an agonized breath, and then with a terrifying bellow leapt out to face his master.

Dalton Bryce was only five feet from the twist in the path when he saw the knife-wielding, ski mask-wearing assailant stagger from behind the bushes and boulder and brandish the menacing weapon.

"What the—" Bryce shouted and stumbled backward. He fell to the ground and, using his heels, propelled himself away from Ravel, who advanced with the stiletto pointed out.

"What do you want?" Bryce said, his voice thin. "You want my money? Here—" He dug his wallet out and threw it at the assailant's feet. Ravel stepped over the wallet. The knife lowered a bit. "What then?" Bryce said. "You want an autograph, psycho?"

The masked assailant paused to consider the offer. After a moment, he shook his head.

"What then?"

Gesturing with his knife, Ravel indicated that Bryce was to turn back instead of continuing farther along the trail. Ravel even mimed turning a key and steering a wheel to help the Emperor of Terror get the message.

"What are you—some kind of anti-walker?" Bryce said. "This place is open to everyone." After getting to his feet, Bryce stepped toward Ravel. "Let me through," the famous author demanded. "This joke's gone far enough."

The masked assailant raised the knife and lunged. Bryce cried out, backpedaled and stumbled again. This time he was able to stop himself from falling by planting one hand in the dirt. The knife-wielding psycho continued to advance, forcing Bryce back the way he'd come.

"If I find out who you are..." Bryce threatened, his face flush and his forehead and the back of his neck glistening. He looked back at the masked psycho who hovered not far behind, the knife still raised. Then Dalton Bryce headed down the path, parking lot-bound. The mysterious Garden of the Gods gatekeeper remained, immovable. Never once did the Emperor of Terror deviate from the path back, and the mysterious knife-wielder, through the rocks and bushes, watched as the author got into his car, keyed the ignition, and drove away. Within seconds, the Scottsdale was gone.

If Bryce had taken his chances, said to hell with it, he would have seen that his assailant was in tears. He would have been able to disarm the masked man and drag him by the scruff of the neck to the police. Ravel was that weak, that sick by the time the Emperor of Terror reached his vehicle. The struggling writer sat heavily in the dirt and leaves, took off the ski mask and dabbed his eyes and blew his nose with it. He pressed his mother's amulet hard against his sternum. Gradually, as Ravel rocked himself, he regained a shred of his former composure. He ceased rocking and looked up into the searing sky. It had to be done. He knew what would happen next, but it had to be done.

She didn't ask questions, only helped him to his feet, handed back his wedding ring and other belongings, directed him to the elevator and her office, finalized his payment and wished him luck on his way out. Had Laney demanded that Ravel undress before her, or if she or any of her robot underlings would have searched him, patted him down, she would have found the ski mask and stiletto knife, all the thumb drives, and then the interrogation would have had every right to begin. But instead she swiped her client's credit card, smiled and reminded him of the contract he'd signed that forbade him from uttering even one word about Chronotrex until the company had presented itself to the world.

On his way back to Denver adrenaline continued to pulse through Ravel. Nearing three in the afternoon he returned to the apartment, stashed away the ski mask and knife, and entered the living room. Noticing Deborah's absence he glanced at his phone for the first time since leaving Chronotrex. He had voicemail. Rather than listen now Ravel stood before the bookcase and scanned the titles the way he'd done periodically all his life. All the titles of all the books that had been written—only now one book had not been written. Ravel's eyes stopped on the small section of Dalton Bryce books he'd chosen to keep. *That* was no longer there. Not only was *That* no longer on the shelf, but there was no indication it had been taken off the shelf, loaned out. Ravel could find no gap, slight or large, indicating that a book belonged between *Strange Tastes* and *Bitter*. Both he and Deborah always made a point to keep the space created by a removed book open, just to remind them what needed to be returned. But on this particular shelf, in this particular bookcase, no tome by Dalton Bryce had been removed.

His throat feeling now like a throbbing heart, Ravel took *Bitter* off the shelf. It looked the same as it had that morning: the original paperback edition, the one with the fictional harlequin romance novelist Tom Grafton on the cover tied to a chair in a corner by a window overlooking the ocean. The shadow of his tormentor, Bernadette Ames, rises to darken much of the room. The silhouette of an old-fashioned whaling harpoon juts from her figure. This edition of *Bitter* contained the same inside cover mocking a typical harlequin romance novel, with Dalton Bryce himself in the role of the passion-igniter. "*Bitter's Back* — Tom Grafton." But when Ravel turned to the "Also by Dalton Bryce" page he gave a cry of joy: under Bryce's bibliography, *Malcontents* preceded *Strange Tastes* preceded *Goat's Grief* preceded *The Fires Within*, but above *The Fires Within* where *That* had been listed that morning, only *The Amulet* (with fellow horror novelist Stenson Juniper) took up that space.

His hands now shaking, still unsure if it had actually happened, Ravel shelved *Bitter* and checked his phone. He searched both Dalton Bryce and *That* together as well as the words separately. Nowhere on the Emperor of Terror's website could he find any link, mention of or reference to a novel titled *That*. Bryce's anecdote describing how he'd hit upon the idea to write *That* was nonexistent. No mention whatsoever of encountering a hobo while walking at dawn through Garden of the Gods. Just as with the physical version of *Bitter*, all online bibliographies on both Bryce's official site and retail outlets listed the publications chronologically as *Janice, Fagen's Place, The Rush, The Line Drawn, Dread Mind, Malcontents, Strange Tastes, Goat's Grief, The Fires Within, The Amulet* (with Stenson Juniper), *Bitter, Things that Go Bang in the Night, The Other Side, Little Ones, Martin's Gripe*, and so on right up to Bryce's latest, *Off the Archipelago*. Nowhere in any of the lists of works, of the novels, collections, nonfiction books, books written under Bryce's pseudonym Michael Zircon, screenplays, teleplays, ebooks, novellas was there any indication that Bryce had ever published anything titled *That*. If *That* had been a short story then Ravel would have caught that too—but when he typed in Fantabulous and Ben Bradstreet and the other characters in his novel he found almost nothing. Ben Bradstreet, the protagonist of *That*, did appear as a character in a story by Bryce, published as "Turning Back" in the 1993 *Malcontents* collection. In this story a debut novelist on his way to run an errand for his wife seeks to cross a bridge but is accosted by a man dressed as the devil. The assailant calls himself Faustabulous, a name that recalls for Ben a mess of childhood memories, his friends he no longer talks to, the pressure he put on himself as a young man, and at the end of the story, after all the flashbacks and trauma have been revealed, the implication is that Ben did in fact meet the devil and gave up his soul not to cross the bridge and complete the errand for his wife. Instead, Ben returns home empty-handed except for the devil's guarantee that he will have continued success as an author.

What's in a name, Ravel thought as he read the summary of "Turning Back." Names can easily be changed. Aside from a couple of names, "Turning Back" posed no threat to Ravel's imminent success, it was nothing like his own novel. In the office Ravel opened his laptop and plugged in each of the thumb drives. *That* was still there. He opened each of the file copies just to make sure they ran the same word count, no inadvertent changes brought about by his action in the early '80s. Ravel found none. *That* was exactly as he had written it, and he again kissed the screen that displayed the cover page. It was his, truly his and his alone. That vision, however it had originated (from the same aliens who'd left the wormhole? from an alternate Bryce?), had both guided and saved him.

Hours later Deborah arrived home to the sight of the table once again set, the smells of cooking and wine already poured.

"You better damn well have a job," she said as Ravel hugged her.

"Something better," he said. "Peace of mind."

"Does 'peace of mind' mean a steady paycheck?"

"You bet."

"Good. I'd hate to learn you had to split at six this morning for the typical, non-remunerative peace of mind. I'd hate for it to have been peace of mind from *me*."

"From you? Hardly." Ravel scoffed. He went to kiss his wife and did not look hurt when she pulled away. "It's nothing about you, D. Seriously. I love you and I'm so grateful you supported me to the end."

"So where were you."

"Went for a long walk, then to the library to do some final fact checking and polish up the last pages."

Given how tired she was and the fact that her husband was again cooking one of her favorite meals, Deborah chose not to press. *Why fight now?* she thought. *He's happy, these months have done him some good. Let him have his dream.* That night, unburdened, complete, Ravel initiated sex, and a surprised Deborah accepted. Now that his novel was at last ready to send out, Ravel promised her more nights like this one. To that promise Deborah could only think *Well—*

COLFAX WAS loud as usual that night, but in an alley off the main drag Ravel was sure he could get the job done without anyone noticing. He had seen unhoused people gathered around flaming steel barrels in movies but never in reality. From out of a large black garbage bag, stashed for the past several hours in the trunk of his car, he took his vintage ski mask and dropped it into the barrel. The coat, rayon long-sleeved shirt, jeans and whitey-tighties followed. Then he took out a container of lighter fluid, squirted enough so that the items were soaked through, struck the match and dropped it. Instantly a great fire shot up and Ravel recoiled. He held the stiletto knife, that Bryce terrorizer, close to the belching, smacking flames and pushed the button to release the long lethal blade. Would it burn sufficiently? At least his finger-prints would be erased.

"Cool knife."

A boy of about fourteen stood near Ravel, as did an equally waifish girl of around the same age. Both boy and girl held skateboards covered in stickers none of which Ravel recognized in the flickering light. The kids held their skateboards vertically over their stomachs and groins as if they were shields.

"Did you kill someone?"

This from the girl, a voice infinitely laconic.

"Me? No. I wouldn't do that."

"Why are you burning your stuff then? You know breathing all that in gives you cancer."

"Shouldn't you be on your phones?" Ravel said.

The boy and girl cackled, the sound of a mammalian species yet to be discovered. "I bet you did kill someone with that knife," the boy said. "Go ahead. Throw it in. We won't tell."

"No. Look—I would never. I'm a writer."

The boy and girl looked at each other with dubious expressions.

"I've written a novel," Ravel said, feeling a kind of pressure not experienced since working at Maguffin-Shrift. "And it's really good, so..."

"Why'd you do that?"

"Do what?"

"Write a novel."

"You could've cured cancer," said the girl.

Ravel stared into the flames. "I don't think I could have," he said. "You kids are depressing. Don't you have homes?"

"If we did," the boy said, "think we'd be here talking to you?"

"Come on," the girl said to her counterpart, and she turned to leave.

The boy lingered. "Yeah?" Ravel said, a challenge.

"I'll take that knife off your hands."

"And then kill me with it?"

"I think you're the killer," the boy said before spinning around and following his companion down the alley.

Ravel shook his head at the flames. He still held the knife, the last of the evidence. He had to get rid of it tonight or risk being found out, he was sure of it.

Screw details, Ravel thought. He dropped the knife into the barrel and took off.

Ravel couldn't believe it. Of all the agents he'd approached first—and this one had proven him wrong.

He sat across from Maxine Dein in Maxine's office, the same seat, same office in which years earlier Ravel had received the disheartening decision on the work he'd amassed at that point, the same seat and office in which only a few months earlier Ravel had submitted his father-in-law's screenplay to Mick Parker's great fortune. When Ravel drove to Maxine's agency a couple days after burning the evidence he knew that by handing his former non-paying employer his novel he would meet with some resistance—the manuscript was, after all, 1,090 pages, far longer than anything ever submitted to Maxine. Still, given the path taken to reach this point and the proven quality of the work under consideration, Ravel had expected only one outcome. But what he got—

"It's quite gripping at times," Maxine said, her eyes poring over the pages quickly—never a good sign. "I'd even say it's quite horrific. I mean this creature that runs a kind of sideshow encampment in this small town in what, San Diego?"

"San Diego County," Ravel said thinly. "A small town in San Diego's North County, outside the city."

"And it changes shape into all sorts of celebrities and movie monsters depending on what impresses or frightens the kid or the adult it's going to make do awful things, or just eat. Great idea, really. It has echoes of…"

Ravel stopped breathing.

"…what was it, Bradbury. *Something Wicked This Way Comes*. That's it."

Ravel exhaled.

"But it's just too damn long, Ravel."

"It was a lot longer before, believe me."

"I'm sure you went through a lot of drafts, and I really did try to get over the length, but for a debut novel, in this day and age…it's not the 1800s anymore, kid."

"Or the '90s," added Ravel.

"I know you've got a lot to prove. I know you're thinking *this is an epic*. It may well be. But for my tastes…. Remember what I said about *Ordinary People*?"

"Too many characters," Ravel said, his eyes closed.

"Look at *Ordinary People*. Four characters. No, three. Only three characters, and here in this monstrosity you have..."

"I know," Ravel said, "but I can't change it."

Maxine stared at Ravel as if he'd said something far worse. "That's poison, Ravel."

"Maxine, I mean...maybe you just don't like horror."

"I don't believe even horror fans would go for this."

"Seriously?"

"I can't sell this to a publisher because they'll know they can't sell it to the public. People aren't going to pay money to read something of this insane length. Not now." With that, Maxine plunked all 1,090 pages into the box and slid it to Ravel.

For a moment, he didn't want to take it. *Leave it*, he thought. *At least I tried*. What Maxine said next both incensed and spurred him to action.

"Can you at least change the title?"

"What?"

"*That*. I don't like it. I see why you chose it, given what I read of this but.... If I were looking to buy a book, a horror novel, and I saw a one thousand-plus page hardcover or paperback with *That* as its title, I'd pass. I just would."

"Okay."

"Think about it, Ravel. You might as well call it *The* or *A*." Observing Ravel's darkening reaction, Maxine added, "I'm only helping you."

"Unfrickin-believable," Ravel whispered, aware of the dangers of shouting the words he wanted to shout while he was still in the building. By now he'd made it to the bottom of the stairs. Once he was out the front entrance he could curse above a whisper. So Maxine had found it in her heart to take on Mick & Company's gargantuan screenplay, *Freedom Freeway*, close to two hundred pages over the acceptable commonsense length for that format, but she wouldn't give more than a few minutes to a novel that had already sold millions upon millions of copies, already been turned into a successful TV miniseries and, later, a two-part movie, already gone through so many printings, been picked up by so many libraries and changed hands in so many countries—if only Ravel could show Maxine all that proof! But that proof no longer existed—the sales records, the printings, the publicity, the book tours, the filming—all that had never happened. Ravel's vision had made certain of it.

It all had yet to happen. Maxine was only one agent. Ravel knew of another.

Seated in his vehicle, Ravel got on his phone. Bing, whom Ravel had met in grad school, was still at the Manhattan-based literary agency he'd interned at after receiving his master's. Bing had done well for himself. He'd left the junior agent title behind and now boasted an impressive list of clients, awards, acquisitions and sales records. Ravel spent a considerable amount of time on Bing's agency photo and bio. They hadn't communicated in a while, but Ravel was certain Bing would remember him, bypass the gatekeepers and give *That* a personal read. Surely success was only one manuscript submission away.

Twelve

His life had until this point been a near-constant game of catch. He would be thrown a ball in the form of an opportunity; sometimes he would catch it, most other times he would miss. Every time he did make a successful catch he would eventually drop that ball, that opportunity. So many drops, all those fumbles. Just what he had been trying to hold on to—fame, wealth, some form of immortality—had always been within reach, there for the taking. He had come of age in a time when it seemed widely possible, tantalizingly easy, to make it big, whether success was through the internet or social media or sports or entertainment. There was the economy to consider, the Great Recession that had hit when Ravel was in high school, but even then he'd had the impression, as so many his age had, that with an A for effort, a little luck and intelligence and, if it happened to be hanging around, talent, one could realize The Dream. In his twenties, however, propelled out of the sheltering cannon of college and graduate school and into the working world, Ravel, like so many his age at this time, was hit with the reality of financial necessities, hardships remembered, a dull yet constant throb of responsibility. Yet through it all, that drifting dream remained.

Once again Ravel held the ball in his hands. This time he would not drop it. Today he felt he might, though. Today he felt unsettled. It wasn't just that Mick and his co-writers had invited Ravel and Deborah to lunch at one of Denver's swankiest establishments, it wasn't that Maxine also was at the meal, seated on Mick's left, not even a mention of *That* on her mind. It wasn't just this surreal sight of his father-in-law, who only in the past year or so had revealed screenwriterly aspirations, clinking glasses with the agent Ravel had once thought his—it was a feeling that something was about to happen. A tornado was always possible, but Ravel suspected it had something to do with his submission, and the likelihood that the ball would again be dropped.

It was the last day of July, and Ravel had been miserable for most of the month. He'd sent off the entire manuscript—all 1,090 pages of *That*—to Bing along with a highly personalized, at times nostalgic cover letter that spanned three full pages. He'd neglected to follow the agency's submission guidelines, and when Bing hadn't responded enthusiastically after two weeks Ravel mentally kicked himself for not obeying the directive of submitting only the first three chapters, a brief synopsis, cover letter and marketing plan. By the end of the third week he had turned moody and sour, driving Deborah out of the apartment for more days and longer hours and increasing her insistence that now that he had finished the damn thing he needed to get out, get a job and get on with his life. Heading into the fourth week a sharp sense of helplessness struck—if not within the month, then never, and if not

Maxine, if not Bing, the only agents to whom Ravel had a personal connection, then what agent could he approach? Dalton Bryce hadn't even approached an agent with his first novel—it had been a blind submission, a shot in the dark that hit its target, legendary Bentworth editor Stanley Swenson, the launchpad to the Emperor of Terror's career.

Seated next to Deborah, their feet and hands and legs not touching as they usually did during a meal, as he picked at his expensive food and listened to Mick go on about how he and his buddies had come up with the idea for *Freedom Freeway* and how they had plenty of other wicked ideas for sequels, prequels, franchises, toys, lunch boxes, Ravel wondered if he had made a mistake by writing the wrong novel into a new existence. Couldn't he have pursued *Janice* instead, gone back in time to that awful cramped and rented trailer in Holyoke, Massachusetts in 1979, stopped Farrah Bryce from finding the early pages of her husband's first successful full-length manuscript, and waited for the trash to be taken away—and with it Dalton Bryce's subsequent forty-four years of wealth, fame and knowledge of his guaranteed immortality? Shouldn't Ravel have made *Janice*, a novel of barely 200 pages, his own instead of *That*? Wasn't *That* a poor choice compared to *Janice*? He should have written *Janice*, not *That*! *Janice*! How could he have chosen one of Bryce's longest novels?

Most upsetting was the fact that Ravel could not go back again, could not travel back to Massachusetts in '79, distract Farrah long enough for the garbage to be disposed of or simply take the manuscript out of the trashcan himself when she wasn't looking and destroy it, thus consigning Dalton Bryce to a life of teaching and elevating Ravel Averof to the title of Emperor of Terror. He could do it—he could take *Janice*, then

Fagen's Place, *The Rush*, *The Line Drawn*, *Dread Mind*, he could take them all, rewrite them as his before going back in time to tear up those pages fished from the trashcan—and he would *become* Dalton Bryce. He might be forty by the time he made all of them his, but then he would have no more work to do for the rest of his renowned life, and no matter how many of those ideas for novels Bryce had written out he would never get any of them published; whenever a publisher wanted a new work, Ravel would simply hand over a new manuscript, beating Bryce to the quick. Would you look at this? I've got another one right here, ready to go! I call this one *The Fires Within*, this manuscript *Little Ones*, this *Phobia*, this *Consternation*, *Implants*, *The Creeping Path*, *Fairchild's Tale*, *Off the Archipelago*. Why had Ravel settled only for *That*? Why was one novel enough? Why not take the man's entire body of work? Why not take his life?

Money. Ravel did not have enough of it to go back again. He would either find success with *That* and fund future chrono-treks, or he would fail and be forgotten by all but his wife, whose marriage to him moving forward would be in doubt.

"What I wanted to do most today," Mick was saying, "was show my appreciation to my son-in-law, Ravel. Without you, Rav, I wouldn't have found Maxine—"

"More like I wouldn't have found *you*," Maxine said. Ravel swore she made eyes at his father-in-law then, and he wondered if something far more intimate might exist between them.

"And I'm just so happy our hard work and dreams came true." Mick looked directly at Ravel as he said this, as if his 'our' included Ravel. "If only my wife were here. Cassie..."

Deborah inspected her utensils and Ravel placed a hand on hers. She did not pull away.

"But we're beyond that now. The pandemic is over, right?" Mick raised his glass for what might have been the tenth time (Ravel had lost count). "My wife would've been so happy you're my son-in-law, Ravel. Here's to you!"

"To Ravel!" Those gathered raised their glasses and bottles and clinked. Ravel touched glass with all those he saw, but he couldn't look anyone in the eyes.

The feeling that something (a rejection email sent during lunch) was about to happen hadn't left by the time they were on Broadway headed to Colfax. Deborah drove and Ravel leaned out the window like a dog in the wind.

"I still can't believe my dad landed a Netflix deal," said Deborah. "It makes sense it's being turned into a mini-series, the script is so long and involved. But it's in the right hands. Can you believe they got that director? *Freedom Freeway*'s actually similar to the one he did a while back—you know that one..."

"What one?"

"That movie he made back in...oh, I don't know what year it was, but it's definitely similar to *Freedom Freeway*."

"Familiarity breeds monsters," Ravel told the wind.

He pulled himself back inside. "All those scripts I read for Maxine, all those scripts I passed on, and she agreed with me—scripts just like your dad's!"

"Jealous much, Rav?"

"I'm more astounded than I am jealous. Just...floored."

"Well obviously Maxine saw something special," Deborah snapped. "And not just an agent, but a producer, no, three producers, the head of the studio, and now of all directors..."

Silence accompanied them from the car to their apartment. Upon entering, Ravel made a beeline for the bathroom. All that wine had worked against his stomach's better instincts. Perhaps *that's* what he should have gone back in time for—to scare his younger, college self out of the desire to pursue a career as a novelist—and really flout Chronotrex's rules that way.

Ravel got on his knees, his head over the toilet bowl. His phone buzzed on the counter. Ravel ignored it. He felt terrible, yet nothing, not even dry heaves, came up. He got unsteadily up, turned and sat on the john. To think: what he needed wasn't for Dalton Bryce's past to change—he needed *his own* past to change. That would have been the gift worth going back in time for.

His phone burped a short loud buzz to signal a voicemail. Ravel picked up and for a moment ceased to breathe. Area code 646. Manhattan.

Just another scam call. Ravel had gotten plenty bearing NYC numbers. Even so, his hand shook a little as he placed the phone to his ear.

"Oh Jesus Deborah Jesus!"

Ravel toppled off the toilet, the phone glued to his ear. Through the voice recording he heard Deborah banging on the bathroom door. "Ravel! Ravel, what is it? Are you okay?"

"It's *That*! The agent I sent it to, Bing, he left a message! A message!"

"Oh my God really? Can I open the door?"

"Yes!"

The door opened just as Ravel reached it. He and Deborah stood staring at one another. To Deborah, her husband looked crazed. Crazed but ecstatic.

"He's not on the phone now, is he?"

"Voicemail. A message, an actual message from an agent. And it says..." He tapped the speaker function and together they listened.

"This message is for Ravel Averof. Ravel, this is Bing Ganzorig with Martin Matthews Literistic. I've read your novel, *That*, and I'd like to pursue this further with you. You may reach me here..."

The rest of Bing's message was drowned out. Deborah was screaming. Ravel was screaming. He grabbed his wife and pulled her to him. He kissed her with such force that his face could have melded into hers.

"Does this mean it's going to be published?"

"It's the start," said Ravel. "It's the furthest I've ever gotten. This call right here, it's a triumph, what I've been waiting for, what I deserve. What we deserve."

"I'm so proud of you, Ravel."

He saw then that she spoke the truth—she *was* proud of him. Her face had taken on a new look, a look he had rarely seen. Deborah's face was flush with pride in her husband, genuine, open, unquestioning pride. He kissed her again, knowing now would be a good time to go further with her—if he didn't have to return Bing's call right then. It was just before two-thirty Mountain time; Bing had said he would be in the office until five. With one last kiss, Ravel disengaged from Deborah, entered their office and returned the call.

WITH THAT PHONE call the stasis of July gave way to the intensity of August. A usually quick-to-reject intern was confused by the length of Ravel's cover letter, as well as the leviathan-sized manuscript that accompanied it. Another intern suggested rejecting the submission outright; the length alone spoke ill of the author. This Ravel Averof was obviously a lunatic seeking to torture all those who worked at Martin Matthews Literistic by daring them to read even a third of this 1,090 page behemoth. And the title—*That*? Come on.... Who would title their novel *That*?

Caution prevailed. The owner of the first pair of eyes sent the submission to Bing, who thanked the intern for noting the grad school connection in the cover letter and said he would deal with this submission himself. Ready to reject outright, Bing read the letter that morning. While personal, it was also excessively nostalgic and self-conscious. How could Bing have forgotten Ravel, who'd given him a couple stories to critique in their master's program. Not an especially good writer, Bing had thought then, but he did see in Ravel a drive, a determined ambition, that few their age could match.

Of course, this submission didn't sit well with Bing. The title alone was grounds enough for an outright rejection. *That*? Talk about a throwaway title better suited for a work in progress. Bing sighed as he scrolled through the seemingly endless document. He expected the novel to be, like the cover letter, rambling and self-conscious, an uneditable, unworkable, unreadable mess.

How Ravel proved him wrong! From the first page, as the toy amphibious assault vehicle sped down the swollen creek toward the tent encampment of Oodlelolly the Magician, Bing could not turn his eyes away. He did something he reserved only for those rare submissions that showed promise: he printed out pages. Then he read. And read. And read. He took breaks, but in a record week—six days to be exact—reading five to six hours a day, he completed *That*, and when he turned the page over on the last scene in which Bob Delaney and Justine Stradler ride together down the street on Bob's childhood electric scooter, he knew he had himself a winner. He contacted editors at a trio of publishing houses and felt them out on their interest in a horror epic that was really about so much more. Horror's just the hook, Bing pressed. This is *the* novel of my generation, really the novel of every generation, and I can't begin to count the millions and millions who are going to eat this book up.

Within a week he had interest from one editor who'd blown through the manuscript, and by the end of the third week he had interest from two more. Bing knew he had to gauge interest before calling Ravel, who had obviously put years of his life into this novel and deserved not to have his hopes falsely elevated. When he was certain they would go to auction, Bing made the call to the author of *That*.

"It's amazing," Bing told Ravel over the phone. "How'd you do it? Wait—forget that. I just never would have expected you had something like this in you."

"It was a long time coming. A lot of work."

"The evidence is all over. These characters, and the scenes you create, so vivid, so alive right off the page. Summers in San Diego County in the early aughts, post-9/11 but before social really fucked us all up."

"The last true childhood."

"That's it. The last true childhood. Ravel, this is huge!"

Bing was especially impressed with the Palestinian-American narrator of the Interlude sections—and one of the seven members of the Down-and-Outers Club—Ahmed Hassan. "This guy really spoke to me," Bing said. "A true representative of the underdog. You really get it, Ravel. You get what it's like to be all of us."

Bing had never said to a new client what he said to Ravel that late afternoon: the manuscript, as gargantuan and complex as it was, needed very little editing work done on it, in his opinion. "That's just unheard of," Bing said. "It's like this story was already floating around, and you caught it in your head and just wrote it all out, like Mozart or something." He needed Ravel to sign soon, as an offer—in fact several offers—could be imminent. "They were concerned about the length of course," Bing continued, "and you'll have to be prepared to cut some. But I've talked with them, I've convinced them this can sell phenomenally well." The competing editors thought so, too. Since giving *That* a read—also in a week or so—they had been coming up with ideas on how to market this monster of a novel most effectively. To call *That* an epic in the vein of Gilda Mooring's *Toil and Trouble* and Dalton Bryce's *The Line Drawn* was a start, but those books sat squarely in the horror genre while *That* went beyond. "Not only are all horror fans going to pay for it," said Bing, "but I believe a great swath of the more literary-minded are going to connect with it as well. What few professional book critics are left out there aren't going to fight it. It'll be like a tidal wave washing over the entire publishing scene."

"I don't want to sound immodest," said Ravel, "but I knew it was a slam dunk."

"Reading it's like eating an unending bag of potato chips. And we're not changing the title. No way."

Ravel had to be prepared for not as large an advance as he'd been expecting. "I know you were hoping for high six-figures, even low seven," Bing said. "We still hear these stories of some hot shot out of the gate getting a million dollar advance. So rare now, you have to realize. This isn't the same environment as it was even before the pandemic. The houses that matter are more risk-adverse than they ever were. Seven-figures would be an act of God. If they do offer you a six-figure advance, it'll be at the lower end. I know that sounds disappointing for how much work you put into this, but believe me: they know and I know it's a sure-fire bestseller, and if we negotiate right you'll be making so much more once it hits the shelves and the online stores. You'll earn out easily. The advance'll seem miniscule comparatively."

"Even approaching six-figures would be great," said Ravel.

"We're not dealing with the small publishers here. These are the biggest houses. They'll play tough, but then so will I."

Bing needed Ravel to sign the necessary documents as soon as possible. When Ravel said he would start looking at flights immediately, Bing laughed. "No need for us to meet in person, Ravel. I mean yeah, eventually. But face-to-face isn't necessary at this early stage. I'm just going to send you a Docu-Sign link."

"I'd like to be there, soon, in New York."

"That's your prerogative. We can definitely meet in person. But you don't have to. It's, you know, 2023 now. Alternatives to the face-to-face do exist."

"I just need to be in New York," Ravel admitted. "Soon."

His agent said, "I'm working weekends on this—it's that important. You're at the pinnacle of my list now, Ravel."

Bing ended the call by congratulating Ravel, who planned to fly to New York within the next few weeks to meet the editing and marketing teams of whichever publisher won the bidding war.

After ending the call, Ravel left the office but could not find Deborah. Often, when she was home, she worked at the dining table or in the living room, but she was in neither place, nor was she in the kitchen or the bathroom. He found her at last in, of all places, the bedroom, lying on the bed, naked. He went to her, shedding clothes like old skin.

Afterwards they held each other and Deborah told him he must do whatever he had to do. When Ravel brought up the job search Deborah shooshed him and said not to worry, she certainly wouldn't.

"The advance is going to be more money than I've ever seen," said Ravel, "but still, it's not going to take all the pressure off. The cost of everything now, and, well..."

"Well what?"

"If we want to have, you know, kids..."

"Kids? As in *plural* child? *Children*? Oh Ravel!"

She pressed herself into him. He could feel her warmth and passion and femininity. The intensity he so admired in her. She was most intense when she was above him, as she had been only minutes ago. He thought of children, nameless, faceless blobs hovering in the room, watching their parents like ghosts.

"You really want them?"

"I do. Of course I do. They cost money though. From birth till..."

She shooshed him. A kiss followed.

"I'm just saying, even with the advance it's going to be a rough start. But Bing, my agent Bing, he's confident I'm going to earn out—"

"What does 'earn out' mean?"

"Something having to do with when I've sold enough

copies of my book to cover the advance they gave me, I get additional money."

"Like royalties?"

"Maybe. I'm not clear on all of it, actually. But I will be. Bing was talking about earn-out bonuses, option deals, foreign rights in so many territories, audio rights, mixed media rights.... Apparently, these are all part of the deal in publishing, and they're all going to be in my wheelhouse."

"I'm so proud of you, Ravel. July sucked, you know. Your health insurance running out, your attitude.... I know you didn't like leaning on my father—"

"I'm going to pay him back."

"We know you will."

"It'll be a bestseller. Without question."

"Then we're fine."

Ravel nodded, his eyes closed.

AUGUST PITCHED him into the arms he had always hoped would welcome him. Every day Bing kept him updated on the progress *That* was making through the New York publishing circuit; not a day went by in which Ravel's agent did not call. Bing never asked Ravel to tweak more than a couple of paragraphs in a few sections—*That* was, indeed, ready to go, as if it had already been vetted and published.

Starting in mid-August, Bing began to hear back. The first word was a rejection from the most prestigious house that while praising the novel cited the length as ultimately cost-prohibitive. "The economy, the economy, the economy," Bing griped. "Inflation, shrinkflation, supply chain concerns that still haven't cleared up since the pandemic ended, blah blah blah *blech*. But we have to respect their decision."

It would happen, Bing assured his number one client, and soon enough it did. On a Monday morning in mid-August Ravel awoke to find that an intense bidding war for *That* had begun. Three major houses were ready with their offers, the highest of which came from Stalwart. For the next hour Bing called Ravel back with updates every ten minutes or so. They were at $150,000, but the agent was certain he could get them to go higher. Ten minutes later it was at $250,000, and after another ten minutes it had jumped to $300,000.

"Still a chance to push it."

"Bing, maybe we should, you know, quit while we're ahead. I don't want to lose it."

"We won't lose it," Bing assured. "There's no backing down with something so important as your advance. My take is fifteen percent, remember."

By the end of that hour—the giddiest, most adrenaline-fueled hour Ravel had experienced since the hour leading up to his confrontation with Dalton Bryce—a deal had been finalized, and Stalwart stood alone. For $400,000, the company had agreed to publish Ravel Averof's debut novel *That*.

"That's just the beginning of what you're going to make," Bing crowed. "And they have no problem with the title. Absolutely none."

Four hundred thousand! After his agent's cut Ravel was left with more money than he'd ever thought possible for a failed writer such as himself. *A* former *failed writer*, he corrected.

"In our current climate, this is a phenomenal advance for a

first-time author. Dalton Bryce never got anything like this for his early novels, even adjusting for infla—"

"Dalton Bryce?"

"Yeah," Bing said. "What's wrong?"

"Nothing. It's just.... I've been hearing you on the phone and in your emails, and it's not the first time you've brought him up," a wary Ravel said. "I was wondering why the focus on him."

"Isn't it obvious?"

The pause on the line just about stopped Ravel's heart. Bing laughed to alleviate the awkwardness. "They're calling you the next Dalton Bryce, Ravel. In all these phone conversations, this communication with the publishers, and the publisher who took you on and is paying you handsomely, I'm seeing and hearing things like 'echoes of Dalton Bryce'...'reminiscent of Dalton Bryce, in his heyday, pre-9/11.' That sort of thing. You think a publisher is going to pass up the chance to make a comparison like that?"

Ravel hung up wondering just what it was he'd done. What he had done was simple: a $400,000 advance is what he'd done, a far greater sum than his father, the great Spiros Averof, had received for his first novel, even when adjusted for inflation. Still, the comparison to Bryce unsettled him. It was as if the past had not actually not happened after all. Ravel checked online and then his shelves again. No sign of *That* anywhere.

That night he and Deborah dined at the Capital Grille in Larimer Square, the most expensive meal they'd ever consumed. For once money was not a character in their play, it waited backstage, gussying itself up to make its grand entrance on a palanquin carried by lesser writers who had not the tenacity or the good fortune of Ravel Averof.

"I need to go to New York."

"I assumed you needed to, Rav. This isn't a dream, though it feels like one, doesn't it?"

Ravel nodded. "I hope you're happy," he said.

"I am. And you have to be.... Is something wrong?"

Ravel's shrug shed only a little of his uneasiness. "Nothing," he said.

"I'll join you," said Deborah, "after your meetings and all that hoopla. If you don't mind."

"You're okay taking time away from the dissertation?"

"Revisions are almost done. I'm close. So close.... But yes, I can take a little time. I'm okay now that you're okay. Oh, Ravel, it's been so long!"

"It has," he said, gripping her hand. "Too long."

Thirteen

To him the city spoke of success. New York harbored no true failures. If you were here, even downtrodden, you were still in the greatest city. You could go to the New York Public Library or to Central Park. Not all avenues of experience demanded money. Not all avenues of experience led to utter and abject failure.

Bing had laughed when Ravel announced he would take the subway from JFK. "You don't have to, Ravel. In fact, we'd prefer you didn't. We're paying for the Uber."

His ride let him off in front of his hotel near the intersection of Waverly and Avenue of the Americas. Ravel tipped the driver generously and made his way to the front counter, where he was greeted as if he was already known as the best-selling debut novelist of *That*. Maybe the concierge did know. Perhaps Bing had tipped him off.

Once settled in his room, Ravel searched for two addresses: the one for where the inaugural American Diamond Prize in Fiction would be awarded, and the other for the main office of the iconic magazine where she worked. As much as he wanted to show up at that office now, he knew doing so would be unwise. His agent was expecting a call—and lunch.

In a tasteful French restaurant on Prince Street named— what else?—The Little Prince, the two met. Bing had not changed much in the years since graduate school. Still the same watery, saturnine eyes masked partly by large brows and heavy lids, still the same pursed mouth and slender face. When he stood to shake Ravel's hand the author saw that his agent had grown thinner than he remembered, a certain sharpness in the shoulders, the elbows, the hips and knees, as if Ravel could be cut if he touched the wrong places.

"Escargot?"

"Pardon?"

"Snails," Bing said.

"Oh, yeah, that's right. Um.... I'm not a fan."

"You've had them before."

"My, uh, mother made them once. They came in what looked like a tennis ball container, in some kind of liquid. She cooked them, but they were rubbery and..."

"Gross," Bing finished for him. "They do them much better here."

The agent insisted, the client acquiesced. When the wine was poured Bing raised his glass. "Here's to you, Ravel. You made it..."

"Thanks. You sound like you wanted to say more."

"'Without your dad,' I was going to say. You know that's going to come up when *That* releases."

"I'd like to use a different last name."

"Oh, really?"

"If that's okay."

"It's what you want. You could slap the name God on your novel—but I wouldn't recommend that. There must have been a lot of pressure over the years..."

"Since I committed to writing," said Ravel.

"How old were you?"

"Twelve. That's when I knew."

Ruminating over the wine he'd just sipped, Bing said, "In a few days Spiros Averof is going to be awarded—"

"The Diamond Prize in Fiction. Believe me, I know."

"I'm attending the ceremony, Ravel, and if you'd like to accompany me..."

"Really? I was going to see if I could crash it."

Bing laughed thinly. "You can't crash something like that. But my partner is unavailable that night. You're welcome to join me. Just, please, if you do confront him..."

"I'll be good," Ravel said.

As they drank and ate, the conversation turned to topics ranging from the personal—Ravel talked no more about his father but much about Deborah, the married life and Colorado, though Bing revealed nothing on these subjects— to, eventually, the literary yet again.

"Bryce must be an influence, no?"

"Somewhat," Ravel hedged. "I mean I grew up reading him.... Who didn't, right?"

"I for one didn't," Bing said. "Not a lot of Bryce in translation in Ulaanbaatar. It took me years after my family emigrated to pick up something by him, I think it was *Dread Mind*. Never connected with him, but I can see the appeal. I can see why he sells. You obviously picked up on that. Took a page from Dalton Bryce, so to speak. You okay?"

Ravel downed the last of his wine in a single substantial swig. "Fine," he said. "Is it okay if I make a request, Bing?"

"Anything."

"The comparisons to Bryce..."

"Too much?"

"I want to be my own writer. I am my own writer. I'm me, not Dalton Bryce."

"I get it," Bing said. "No more comparisons to Bryce, at least from me. At least until *That* publishes and the public has at it."

Under the table, Ravel picked at a flap of skin on his thumb enough to draw blood.

Aware of the tone the conversation had taken, Bing brought up the meetings Ravel would be having with the team at Stalwart. "I get you to myself today, but tomorrow they corral you. I mean that in the sanest way possible. They're going to lob all sorts of ideas at you. Just know: you're in control, you have final say. Yes, they are giving you a lot of money up front, and you should have compromise in mind, but this is *your* novel, *your* hard work, *your* heart and soul. Remember that, always."

They finished eating and Bing insisted on paying for the meal. Ravel didn't argue. From the restaurant he and Bing walked down Prince Street and turned on Greene. "Just think of Graham," Bing said. Up ahead, on the right, was the building that housed Martin Matthews Literistic. Once inside the office, Ravel met most of the other agents and interns. Everyone there had either read or was currently reading *That*. "It's that big," one agent said. "I stopped reading one of my client's manuscripts when I read the first page of yours. Finally she called and asked what was going on. By then I was just about finished with *That* and I couldn't put it down. She just about fired me."

Throughout the agency hummed a palpable energy and enthusiasm, proof that Bing's new client would be a success for them all, indeed for all those who adored the written word. Even the senior agents seemed deferential to the debut novelist who had produced this masterpiece of horror, so reminiscent of the early work of Dalton Bryce.

Each time Bryce's name was brought up in conversation, Ravel demurred. Bing did his best to steer the other agents and interns away from the comparison, but the other employees of Martin Matthews Literistic were insistent. Didn't Ravel *want* to be compared to the Emperor of Terror? It was good publishing practice to talk up comparisons to the already famous. Sales often shot through the roof this way.

Bing, ever-perceptive to his client's needs, assured Ravel that the comparisons were praise and the praise was genuine. "You are your own writer, and you want to know why?"

"Why, Bing."

"You're *literary*. Horror with a literary bent. Once *That* hits, we're going to position you. The biggest literary magazines. *Harper's. Granta. The Paris Review. The New Yorker*."

"Seriously?"

"You're going to be your own brand, Ravel. Stand on your own feet, separate from Dalton Bryce."

Alone now in Bing's office, the door closed, the agent asked his new client when he could expect more material. "I'll read anything, Ravel—even what you were writing back in grad school. You may think it's unpublishable, but with a novel like *That* coming out you'd be surprised what we can push through. We'll place pieces in the big-time magazines like I mentioned, get together a collection for your second book, unless a second novel is in the works already..."

"I, uh..." Ravel was surprised at how similar Bing's office was to Maxine's. If only he could avoid this conversation altogether by switching topics to the Bauhaus décor. "I have some things," he acknowledged. "It's not much."

"I understand," said Bing. "But you have to understand they're going to want to publish *That* quickly, as early as next spring, and when that happens the public, everyone, is going to want more. If you can get into a rhythm of a book a year, like—" Bing caught himself. "Like some authors do now, you'll be solid gold."

"I'll find something worth your time. It's just I have been working on *That* for kind of forever."

They spoke for half an hour longer about future projects. Ravel, under unexpected duress, realizing he was not prepared for such probing and likely would not be prepared for tomorrow's meetings, tossed out ideas to appease his agent. The ideas were Ravel's own, and Bing at least appeared satisfied. They could work with these, he claimed. Ideas that Ravel had seen as jejune—a new take on the Romeo and Juliet story, set during the Holocaust, a future world where the Pope is the supreme ruler and all the people of all countries practice Catholicism—could now see the published page. *That* had made it possible. His first novel. His.

Nearing four-thirty Ravel was at last set free from his obligation to Bing and Martin Matthews Literistic. He wasn't sure he would make it before the magazine's main office closed. If he arrived even a minute past five he would miss his chance.

He hoofed it through Soho, glancing up just enough from his phone's maps app to avoid a collision, then pounded down the stairs of the appropriate subway entrance. He didn't have long to wait for a train to take him north. He caught the N, crushed in with a surge of bodies, and hoped that when the doors opened at 34th and 6th, Herald Square, he would not squirm and claw his way out only to see her waiting for a southbound train on the other side and so miss her.

When the doors did open and he fought to emerge, he felt as he imagined Deborah must have felt when she traveled on the Paris metro and accidentally bumped her traveling backpack against a high-end woman who lowered her sunglasses and glared at Ravel's future wife as if she were about to commit murder. The memory of Deborah relating that tense moment brought to mind his wife, whom he would be seeing in a couple days, and Ravel felt only slight guilt as he broke free of the press and dodged through the ranks of those who walked ahead, through the gates, up the stairs and out into open midtown. At the corner of 32nd and 6th he paused and took cover in the doorway of a building that wasn't hemorrhaging workers. Three or four doors down, and in the crowd of twenty- and thirty-somethings, well-dressed, many of them bespectacled and nearly all of them attractive, he could not identify her. Had she left work a few minutes early, or not shown up at all that day, he would be crushed. Tomorrow would be even less reliable, given all that he had to do with Stalwart. The day after: Deborah.

Then she emerged abruptly from the building three or four doors down. She wore a short-sleeved blouse and tasteful skirt, high-heeled boots and her dark hair up in a bun. She walked alongside a fellow assistant editor, also female and dressed as professionally as possible in the sweltering cauldron that was New York on this late-August day. As Ravel had hoped, both women turned left out of the building and headed up Sixth in the direction of Herald Square and Ravel.

He stepped out of the doorway. They were twenty paces away, heads bowed, complicit in some secret. They remained this way with ten paces left, and Ravel feared that, having lived in a city of so many people for so long, they would pass him by. He considered putting his hand up and saying something ridiculous like *halt*, but she saw him before he could make a fool of himself again before her. She recognized him. Within the span of a couple seconds her shock had been replaced with annoyance.

"This is creepy," she said.

"Maggie," Ravel said.

"You could've emailed. I'm on the masthead."

Maggie's companion was looking back and forth between the former couple, expecting, it appeared, to be introduced.

"Lauren. This is Ravel."

"Ravel..." Lauren did not find this name familiar.

"He's visiting or living?"

"Visiting," said Ravel. "Maybe living, soon."

Maggie arched one of her slim striking eyebrows, a sudden stab of memory. "I suppose you want to talk."

Ravel flashed what he hoped was a sheepish, disarming grin. He thumbed in the direction he hoped was correct. "I'm headed to the subway, if that's where you're going."

They—including Lauren—took the F southbound. Ravel made sure to not sit directly across from either young woman but rather at an angle, his head tilted away while talking, the appearance, he thought, of nonchalance. Neither Maggie or Lauren seemed terribly enthusiastic, but they did converse with him, answered his questions and asked some of their own. Lauren revealed she'd been working at the magazine longer than Maggie (four years) and was about to be promoted.

"Associate editor," said Ravel. "Congratulations." To Maggie he said, "I don't suppose you're gunning for the same?"

"I'm not 'gunning,' Ravel. I have other plans. You must have read about them, if you came all this way to stalk me."

"Not stalking, Maggie. Just catching up. Anyway, your book. Congratulations to you too."

"You didn't come all this way from California to tell me congratulations, Ravel."

"I didn't fly in from California. Colorado."

"Oh." His ex-girlfriend, four years younger than Deborah, turned to Lauren and exchanged a haughty look: *fly-over state*. Ravel felt the flush in his face.

"I wanted to tell you my good news. I had to tell you in person," he said.

Maggie waited. Lauren looked from one ex to the other.

"I'm here to see my agent and publisher."

"Your agent?"

"And publisher."

Agent, the word a weapon on Ravel's lips, and this time both of Maggie's immaculate eyebrows arched—a good sign for his intentions.

"Yeah." Ravel continued to shovel dirt into the void. "He's over at Martin Matthews Literistic, in Soho." He grinned.

Here he was, on the F train telling his ex his good fortune, dropping names and neighborhoods as if he called the city home.

"So you did it."

In that moment of Maggie saying those four words Ravel caught a glimpse of his former girlfriend as she had been to him: motivator, muse, competitor, admirer. Her volatility, always on the edge of cruelty at the end of their time together, was for a few seconds at least replaced with the warmth he'd once felt from her, in the beginning. "You have something," she finished.

"A lot more than something. An epic. *That*. That's the title."

"*That*?"

To Maggie Lauren said, "You can't title a book *That*, can you?"

"I could call it The King James Bible if I wanted," Ravel said.

"*That*," Maggie mused, a smile at last pushing its way through her uneasiness. As Ravel talked up his debut novel, she remained quiet, reminiscent of how she'd been toward him in the beginning, before they were together, when *she* had been the stalker.

He assumed that when the doors opened at York Street, the first stop in Brooklyn, and Lauren rose, Maggie would follow her. But instead the coworkers said goodbye. Ravel cocked his head, his puzzlement genuine. Maggie shifted so that she sat directly opposite him and said that he could see her to her place in Park Slope, as she assumed he wanted. Ravel nodded.

"What does your wife do?"

"She's almost earned her PhD. Finished with the dissertation and about to give the oral defense."

"So a professorship."

"You got it."

"I'm happy for you, Ravel."

But not proud of me, Ravel thought. For the rest of the ride they stared at each other with such intensity neither seemed willing to blink. He was again twenty and she eighteen, a freshman seeking an upperclassmen with literary ambitions, someone she could write inscriptions to in the books she gifted. She had found that upperclassman, graduate of another college, who had given her what she'd wanted most, a dedication page bearing her name in his first and bestselling novel.

She had done it, too. Ravel thought of asking what her book was about, but the truth was he already knew. His phone had told him what he needed to know. A slim, snarky collection of essays that would sell modestly, it did not have the titanic appeal of Ravel's debut novel, which would be translated into countless languages, even Mongolian, and hit the shelves of every bookstore and library the world over.

When the doors opened at 15th Street/Prospect Park Maggie got up and, without saying a word, Ravel followed her out. She never once turned around as she passed through the gate, followed the signs for Prospect Park West, reached the above ground exit and ascended the steps. They emerged into the late summer dusk. She ignored the roundabout and continued walking north, along the park's edge, and Ravel, like a dog that needed an owner, obediently trailed.

He stood beside her at the intersection of 12th and Prospect Park West. They waited for the traffic to pass. Maggie still had not acknowledged him. She would not until she'd reached her walkup a block and a half away.

Inside the dwelling, Ravel observed what might have been his. In the center of the living room, on the hardwood floor, lay an intricately woven Turkish rug. To his right against the wall a glass case contained several artifacts recognizable to Ravel. He remembered Maggie having brought these items back from the European trips she would often take with her family. She and Tristan had gone beyond: shelves displayed souvenirs and mementos from Japan, Vietnam, India, Cambodia. A claw of some great animal rested on the ledge just below a Noh mask.

Unsurprisingly, no TV was present anywhere in the living room or adjacent kitchen and dining room, but surprisingly the sound of an infant boy or girl was not present either.

"Is your...child sleeping now?"

"She's with my aunt in New Rochelle."

"A daughter," Ravel said to himself. He asked Maggie for the child's name.

"Why do you need to know that, Ravel? For your next novel?"

She left him alone in the living room. When she reemerged her blouse was already partway open. She approached Ravel, her intense, sharp eyes on him, her flush face expressionless. She was close enough for Ravel to reach out and hold her now. He asked what she was doing.

"What does it look like?" Another button through. He could see the edge of her bra. Lace. Scarlet. "Isn't this what you wanted?"

"No," Ravel said.

He surprised himself with that word. He meant it.

Maggie stopped, her fingers fiddling with the second-to-last button down. Her bra was now fully revealed, and Ravel's memory was a heartache and a curse. It was time to kill it. It was time to kill *that*.

He had not often seen Maggie surprised—certainly, on the last day he'd seen her in person, ten years earlier, she'd been surprised when he'd made no indication that he wanted even so much as to remain friends. The look she gave him now was similar to that look—only more annoyed.

"Okay..." she said in that tone indicating Ravel was stupid. "Now this is just weird. Why *did* you come here?"

"To tell you I made it. And to say goodbye, for good. That's all."

"*That's* all? *That's* all?" Maggie's face turned the color of her bra. He recalled her rage.

"You think *that's* what I wanted. That I came here for *that*? No, Mag. Just: no."

"Yeah, right." Maggie laughed harshly, but for once it appeared she believed Ravel.

"I was hoping Tristan would be here so I could tell my success to him, too."

"Fuck you, Ravel. I see through you now. I so see through you."

"What do you see?"

"It's always been your writing you get off on. *That's* your love. That. It was never about me. I..."

"What?"

"Get out."

He knew he had done her wrong. He *had* put his writing above her, he had rarely been the boyfriend she'd anticipated he would be. She had not asked for much, love and affection and attention, adoration, but even the role of a baseline boyfriend was too distracting for a focused, driven, navel-gazing Ravel. And so she'd felt used. And now here was her ex glibly rubbing in the fact that he'd moved on.

Confidence and joy, backed by a protective blindness, coursed through Ravel. Just as he had rarely seen surprise on Maggie's face in the time they had dated in college, so too had she rarely seen confidence or happiness in him. She was seeing an abundance of both now, and the knowledge of his trajectory hurt her.

"Get out *now*."

Outside the sun was succumbing to darkness. To Ravel it seemed he could run to that spot at the end of Maggie's street where the shadows were encroaching and be transported to another world, another time, a time before he'd met Maggie, when he still had the chance to pull back from his literary ambitions. A heartache and a curse.

He took a lengthy walk through Prospect Park, mapless, as-yet-companionless, unsure of where he was heading but also not caring. The people he passed, mostly well-to-do couples, some with children, paid no attention to this soon-to-be megaselling novelist, this man of ambition and nerve.

It had been a good day, Ravel decided. A lot had happened in his favor. His days would be eventful from now on—he had made sure of that. No longer would one day be as the next, that simple. Wasn't eventfulness, in the end, what everyone sought?

SHE HAD BEEN TO EGYPT, Turkey, Morocco, Spain, Portugal, most of the rest of Western Europe and Eastern

Europe, where she had lived while teaching at a language school in Hungary. But Deborah had never been to New York, except once in the airport on the way to Prague. Airports don't count, her husband had once said, in typical Ravel fashion. They're non-places.

They met at JFK, she unaware that a move to the greatest city in the world was on her partner's mind. Exiting the terminal, Ravel commented that now Deborah could say she had visited New York. "You're here," he said, "where we belong."

"You think this should be our city? Our new home?"

"I'd like it to be. Because of *That*, we can make it happen. Even with children. What's left for us in Denver, now that your oral defense is over? You're going to be hooded. There are so many universities here, one of them has to take you on. Wouldn't it be great to raise a family here, or just outside the city, take the train in, the museums, the concerts, the sports, the—"

"The Nuggets win the championship and you bail for the Knicks? You've got a long wait, Rav."

"Just think about it," Ravel said, and they kissed.

He loved Deborah most of all for her no-frills realism. She'd been no bridezilla, they'd had a remarkably modest wedding in the foothills outside Denver, without church and elaborate reception hall, attended by fifty or so people—more friends than family. But she had to know, as Ravel had always known about himself, that she'd married a high-end man. If they were to make NYC their permanent home, he'd demand modesty be tossed out the window and replaced with an excess neither of them had experienced before: social gatherings every week, trips to Europe on the fly, gifts of jewelry she'd never thought to wear and rare first editions they'd never seen themselves owning. Just as Ravel was changing, so too would Deborah eventually give in to The Dream.

"Promise me," she said, as they rode the subway into Manhattan, "you won't go over-the-top with all that's happening."

"Define 'over-the-top.'"

"No yachts, no third Bentley, no second mansion."

"What about a second *home* somewhere?"

"Possibly. I can see you living like Dalton Bryce."

Ravel's breath ceased for a moment. "What?" he half-gasped.

"Are you okay?"

"Uh yeah, I'm—what do you mean?"

"I mean Dalton Bryce has a mansion, he's a bazillionaire, but he's still pretty down to earth, right?"

"He has a place in South Carolina, along with the first home in Massachusetts."

"Fine: get a second home somewhere—maybe Denver? I like Denver, you like it too. My point is Dalton Bryce isn't flashing his money everywhere."

Ravel nodded, tense. Picking up on his demeanor, Deborah pressed herself against him and kissed him on the cheek, then took his head in her hands and kissed him on the lips.

"Of course," she said, "some flashiness is expected."

"I'm going to make a lot, Deb. A ton, really. We're negotiating all those rights I mentioned, the royalties, overseas rights, all the translations, there's already so much interest from foreign publishers. I don't know much about how the numbers all work, the percentages, but I'm learning. Bing is doing most of it. I'm just there to be in on the conference calls and shake a lot of hands."

"They better give you all that you deserve," Deborah said.

"The paperback rights are going to sell for some insane amount not seen in a long, long time."

"How long before it's published?"

"Not long. Usually it's a year, but Stalwart's so sure they have a hit on their hands they're pushing it through ahead of everything else on their plate. April."

"April!"

"Early April. I'm actually going to have an honest-to-God book tour in the spring."

"I can't believe it, Ravel. I mean I can...but to think, the entire time I've known you, when I thought you weren't writing, just staring at the screen, or something else on the screen besides an empty doc, you were working on *That*. Honey, you should've told me."

"And break the creative tension? No way."

Smiling, Ravel held his wife's hand until Deborah said, "Before it's published, I'd like to read it."

"Before it's published?"

"What's wrong? I'm not looking for anything—"

"—I know—"

"—in particular. Or if I did find something, you know, about me, I wouldn't demand to change it. I can take it. I won't censor you."

"You won't find anything about you."

"Nothing at all?" He was surprised that Deborah sounded a little hurt.

"Uh, you won't find anyone you know in it, not even me."

"Are you serious, not even you? How can that be, when you've written 1,000 pages."

"That's just how it is, Deb. It's pure fiction. Honestly."

"You're saying you don't have any of yourself or anyone you know, or anyone I know, or me, in *That* at all?"

"That's what I'm saying. I achieved The Dream. I finally exorcised my demons."

Deborah turned her husband's last statement over in her mind. At last she said, "All right. So if this one's safe for me to read, let me read it."

"I will. Can you wait for the galleys?"

"Sure. So exciting." She squeezed his hand.

"I think," said Ravel, leaning in to her, "you and I both live a lot in the future, or the past, and it's not right. Let's just enjoy what we have. Only what we have right now. Let's give ourselves the gift of the present."

Deborah smiled and said, "I like that. The gift of the present. Sounds like the title of something."

"Maybe it is," said Ravel. "Maybe it could be."

He reiterated his desire to move to the city. Deborah said nothing but also did not let go of his hand.

"I know how close you are to your dad, and Colorado..."

"You really have to live here, Ravel? Really live here? Have you looked around? There's a reason why so many people have left New York."

"But we'll have the money."

"You can't just look at it as a playground, an entertainment center."

"It's going to be where we raise our children. The best schools—"

"I'll consider it, Ravel. I will."

"That's all I ask." He hugged her to him. He was aware Deborah might well discover the most pressing reason why he wanted to move to New York after she questioned him upon his return from the ceremony for the American Diamond Prize in Fiction. If she did find out, so be it. The discovery would not change the direction in which they were inevitably being pulled. Indeed nothing, Ravel felt then, could change the sudden sparkling course of their history.

Fourteen

His mother had owned only two cars while living in Anomar, and they were in the first one now, a sedan from the eighties that sounded as if at any moment the transmission would bottom out. Ravel would drive the car in high school, when his mother broke down and bought herself a sports car she'd squeeze into like a sardine. For now though he was eight and eager to head into town. Yoana, her hair the same straight it would be until her death two decades later, pulled toward the stop sign at the end of their street. Her sunglasses sat big and heavy on her nose, and out of her window dangled the arm that held the cigarette she had only just lit. Her knees steadied the wheel. On loud was a male Bulgarian singer whose name Ravel could no longer recall.

There had been no argument, not as there would be at the end of the decade—only a single mother and her only child going on an outing in town, the first day they both had off from school. It had been Yoana's first year as a full-time teacher; ever since their move to Anomar, she had subbed to give herself the flexibility she needed to write. Ravel remembered as a young child the days when he would hear the phone ring at five-thirty in the morning and wait anxiously to hear if his mother would accept that day's assignment or not. Many mornings she would not, and when Ravel was very young and not in school for the entire day he was always glad his mother would be there for him. As he got older though he began to see his mother's lack of commitment as laziness, a nuisance to him—and unfair. Why did he have to go to school and she didn't? Yoana told him she didn't take every sub job because of her writing, something very important to her (but not more important than her son, Ravel was assured). And certainly when one of his mother's poems was published they celebrated by going out, and Ravel was proud then, but the publications happened so infrequently, the magazines in which the poems appeared were so piddly, that teaching seemed to Ravel the better option. He did not understand when he was young his mother's compulsion, did not realize it lay dormant in him.

He was never happier than on the day his mother came home wearing a nice dress and announced that she was going to be working full-time from then on. Later Ravel would understand the sacrifice Yoana had made—the trade-off, financial security for her art. With her son college-bound and their savings running low, Yoana knew she needed an actual income. But an older, teenage Ravel wondered if another reason his mother had gone full-time at Anomar High was because her writing career had not gone as well as she had hoped. She had published a slim volume with a small press, true, but it had sold hardly any copies, and Yoana's efforts to secure a teaching position at a nearby community college fell flat. She had begun working on a novel, she claimed, but she never showed Ravel any pages, never sent out any excerpt for publication. A teenage Ravel, nearing graduation from AHS, called out his mother on her posturing one night. It turned into one of their bitterest arguments that devolved into Ravel slinging mud on the medium of poetry itself. Of all the awful things he ever said to his mother, his degradation of poetry as an art form hurt her the most. He had no idea then that he had followed in the footsteps of his father, who had spoken similar words to his wife when Ravel was an infant. Yoana's tears told her son to back off, and he did.

For now though, in this specific memory, Ravel was not concerned with the differences between poetry and prose. He did not even know yet that he wanted to pursue writing. He was just eight, and today they were going to eat at the best Mexican restaurant in Anomar, on Main Street, and then check out the little museum that covered the town's history.

Yoana turned right onto Vincenzo, the road that would wind them a mile or two into town. Ravel looked out his window at the small corner strip mall: the dentist, a real estate agent, the video rental store, and of course the small grocery and deli they frequented on weekends when his mother didn't feel like making anything for lunch. The video store looked busy, maybe later they would—

Ravel turned sharply at the sound of Yoana cursing in Bulgarian, one of the many words the meaning of which she would not reveal to him. He saw her staring into her rearview mirror, and he felt the car slowing down and pulling to the side. He'd seen enough shows to know why. Seated on his hands he pushed himself up straight and twisted around. The lights above the police car were flashing and the officer, big boots, trim form, was almost to Yoana's window. Yoana brought her arm into the car, and Ravel saw that she no longer held her cigarette. She did not look at him, only waited with her head turned toward her open window. Ravel's dread spiked when the officer's frame filled the window.

The officer leaned in so that he was at Yoana's level. His sunglasses were almost as big as hers. He looked younger than his mother by a lot, and Ravel hoped he would be kind.

"Do you know why you've been pulled over, ma'am?" A clean voice, like sparkling water.

"I'm sorry, I don't."

The officer took a moment to register the response. It was impossible to tell what he was thinking, planning. His eyes were absent, his mouth a thin line. At last he said, "I caught you going past the stop sign at the corner without stopping."

"I did stop."

"Not completely. If you want to argue this..."

Yoana did not want to argue. She waited, jaw clenched, face forward, still not having looked at her son, as the officer wrote her a ticket. After the officer had driven around them and shot off down Vincenzo, Ravel expected them to get going as well. But his mother did not start the car, nor did she look at him. Ravel grew worried. His mother muttered something in Bulgarian, two words Ravel understood. He'd heard them before. "This country," Yoana said, and then she took her sunglasses off and wiped her eyes. Ravel watched as his mother, thirty-five years old, began to sob quietly. He had thought then that she cried because of the ticket, the embarrassment it had caused, and there was certainly that, but there was more as well, and he wanted to share that moment, that memory—as well as so many others—with the man who had never known about it and needed to.

There was the man now, rising from the spotlit table at the head of the grand ballroom. He had taken off his Herringbone flat cap and carried it at his hip, his head bowed as if in humility. *Like a man like that could ever be humble*, Ravel thought. He would be humbled tonight—but not by the award he was about to receive. Ravel sat at the back of the ballroom, Bing just in front and to his left at their own circular table, and watched as his father, Spiros Averof, head bowed still, walking with a sprightly but (Ravel was convinced) affected limp, took to the dais. The woman who had introduced him, a fellow author and contemporary living in the city, was not aware that the man she was now applauding then hugging had abandoned a wife and child—and had spent considerable amounts of money over the decades to keep the details of that decision in the dark.

Ravel's gaze flicked from his father, who was just now settling in behind the podium, to his father's son, Ravel's half-brother, ten years old. The boy, whose name Ravel had encountered once online and promptly and decisively forgotten, was seated next to his mother, a brunette sculpture in her early thirties. Ravel knew so little about this woman; unlike with his half-brother, he could not remember ever coming across her name on any screen or in any printed matter. His father had married a woman at least twenty years his junior, which meant Spiros was—Ravel shuddered—old enough to be her father.

Ravel gave the lightest golf clap as the rest of the audience, Bing included, whacked their palms together over and over as if flaying the skin from their hands. Spiros waited for too long a time, in Ravel's opinion, as the roar washed over him, the cameras flashed and he put his hands up and pronounced calm. When calm finally did settle in Spiros again waited a prolonged time in which he smiled and seemed to acknowledge every one of those gathered. He lingered on his wife and son, the former mouthing something to her husband. When he spoke, Spiros's accent was thick, but his voice was strong and to Ravel he sounded younger, the same age as his second wife. The youth in that voice surprised Ravel, who wondered what medication his father took.

"Friends, colleagues, family," Spiros began. "Thank you all. I came to this country an immigrant, in the year 1984, having published only a handful of stories in small periodicals in Greece and Bulgaria. But why reach an audience of only a few million when I could reach an audience of many millions? So in Los Angeles I lived and wrote and studied English. I took the language classes. I read the books, many books, the Los Angeles public library my home for more days and nights than I care to count. In Los Angeles in the '80s I found writers like me, and we banded together, exchanged our work, and some of us would go on to immense recognition and wealth. The Literary Brat Pack. But I stood apart. My success took a while longer. I knew I could succeed—I would succeed—but factors conspired to delay that success and distract from it. The greatest decision I made was to leave Los Angeles and move here. This city saved me, made the year 1994 my rebirth, my debut at 30, and allows me to stand here now, almost thirty years later, and say to you I am not only a New Yorker, a New York author, but a diamond, a diamond once in the rough, but always a diamond!"

As the great author's admirers rose and applauded more

wildly than before, Ravel tapped Bing and leaned in. "I'm going for it. Now."

Bing, face still forward and smiling, nodded. "Just remember," he said through gritted teeth, "your debut's set to come out. Any waves made tonight—"

"No waves," said Ravel. "Smooth sailing only."

The applause and cheers and shouts of "Spiros! Spiros!" still going strong, Ravel's father stepped from behind the podium to accept the diamond-studded trophy now being handed to him by an official-looking elderly gentleman. Spiros and this man exchanged warm words and smiles, their free hands gripping each other's elbows. Holding the award, Spiros turned to face the audience. Cameras like lightning created a strobe effect. Ravel, his emotions at their peak, watched his father descend from the dais into a crowd of congratulations. In the manner of a religious leader or football quarterback who had just brought those gathered to Jesus or the Big Win, the New Yorker reached out and clasped hands. Those gathered pushed and pressed and stepped hard, and Spiros, award tucked under an arm, made no move to retreat. He locked eyes with each fan to prove here was an author unafraid of the public. For a man of 59 who wrote so much, he was surprisingly fit, strong, energetic. *He could live to be 90,* Ravel thought. *He could live to be 100, 110. He could outlive me.*

Considerable time passed before Spiros was able to reach his wife and son, but when he at last touched them it appeared as if he'd been saving his greatest degree of affection for them. He wrapped himself around his wife and buried his nostrils in her hair. He lifted her a little. The true lifting, though, was for the boy who seemed not in the least embarrassed by his father picking him up and raising him as if he were a newborn. The boy had expected this, it seemed to Ravel, who thought all their affection choreographed, calculated.

Along with his anger and jealousy and guilt, Ravel quelled his cynicism as best he could. He was by now a mere seven or so feet from his father, though a great many people separated them yet. Ravel had to at least appear calm for the confrontation. With Bing's voice in his head, Ravel waited. Before long the crowd had thinned enough for him to make an acceptable move forward. At last Ravel Averof stood before his father, who at the moment was speaking with the woman who had introduced him. Ravel stared, expecting his father to turn and see him at any moment. He honed in. The crowd fell away. It was now just him, his father, his father's second (and favored) son, and his father's literary contemporary.

When Spiros finally caught sight of his first son, his initial glance was one of cursory interest, but on second look, perhaps startled by the intensity of this younger man's stare, he returned, this time showing recognition.

The female literary contemporary, sensing Spiros had made a connection beyond a simple meet-and-greet, bowed into the background, leaving Ravel alone with his father and half-brother. The surrounding voices faded into white noise, and all Ravel heard were his father's words.

"Hello," Spiros said as his first son stepped closer. "It's been a long time."

"Twenty-two years," said Ravel.

The boy looked confused. *Not in the script*, Ravel thought —and smiled.

"How were you invited?"

"My debut novel's being published," Ravel answered, "in April."

"Must be one of the big publishers to get you in here."

"It is. The advance wasn't too shabby, not too shabby at all. The novel's going to sell millions. They know it. I know it."

Spiros averted his gaze while grinning and shaking his head. "Millions," he said. "Such confidence! Using your name to your advantage, I see."

"Not your name," Ravel said. "*My* name. Rav Kopecka."

"Your pseudonym?"

"It's not a pseudonym. It's my name now. It's what the novel will be published under."

Spiros looked from his second son to his first.

"I expected this," the father said. "Sometime it would happen. You want to talk."

"Not here. We can go somewhere close, though."

"Dad..."

Spiros placed a hand on the boy's head. "This is someone important to me," he said. "Very important."

Ravel scoffed. The boy looked at his father in alarm.

"Be civil," said Spiros.

"I am civil. I just want to talk, just for a little while, tonight only."

"Spiros—" His second wife turned the trio into a quartet but stopped short of extending a hand to Ravel. "Is this..." she began.

"You're not so different from me, are you?" To his wife Spiros said, "I'll return. Don't wait for me. I'll call Dimitri when I'm through."

He kissed his wife—a sight that turned Ravel's stomach—and hugged his second son.

"We'll finish the story tonight," he told the boy.

Two decades and four presidents later, they were again seated across from one another. This time it was a bar serving shrinkflation spirits. Despite the exorbitant prices, Ravel insisted he pay. Hearing this, Spiros did not look at Ravel but instead bade the server wipe the table's already clean surface.

"Pay if you like," Spiros said after the server had departed.

They waited in silence, Ravel suddenly not so confident. When the drinks arrived Spiros picked up his Scotch, sipped and said, "This is the point, isn't it?"

"What is."

"The point of you paying. To show you can pay for my expensive drink, yes?"

Not only was Spiros Averof an award-winning, bestselling author—he was a mind reader too. "Yes," said Ravel, his own drink of sudden acute interest to him.

"If I had known I would see you again," Spiros said, "I would have been prepared."

"You mean a script, like what you essentially read from at that ceremony?"

"What I said, I said from who I have always been." Spiros pushed his glass forward as if to offer his son a sip. He pulled the glass back toward him. He did this a few times as he spoke. "Your anger is your right, it is your birthright. But direct it at me, not my wife and child."

Ravel pursed his lips and shook his head. "I don't know why I'm doing this," he said.

"Because we never had our—what is the word for it? There is no word for it. We never had our *conflict*."

"We've been having our conflict all right. You just haven't been aware of it."

Spiros looked at Ravel as one would a troublesome

employee whose axing had come. Ravel, drink in hand, pitched forward, causing a startled Spiros to draw back.

"Your wife? Your child?" the son said. "What about your *wife*? Your *child*? Your son..."

"My first son. I understand the implication, Ravel."

"Do you know what it did to her when she saw you on TV in that interview and didn't hear you mention us. Forget us— she wanted you to mention *me*. That would have been enough to save her—just the mention of her son by way of you. Instead you killed her, by not acknowledging either of us."

"*I* killed her?"

"Tore her heart out. You could've left her at least that much."

Spiros knocked back his Scotch then signaled for another.

"You know nothing of value of your mother."

"Oh yeah?" Ravel signaled for a second drink as well, even though he was not yet halfway done with his first. "Tell me, because I'd really like to know from a guy who knew her for less years than I did."

"Fewer," said Spiros. Off Ravel's blank look he continued. "*Fewer* years. That's correct."

"Speaking of *that*," Ravel spat. "You use *that* too much in your writing."

"Is that so?"

"Most of the time *that* isn't necessary as a connecting word."

"A connecting word."

"Just leave it out already. You don't need it."

The drinks arrived, delivered quickly by the server who felt the tension. Father and son waited, and when the man had cleared out Spiros took another sip, seemingly calm.

Ravel hesitated on his second drink. His doctor had warned him one per day should be his absolute limit. If he imbibed too much at one time hypoglycemia could take hold of him, he could go into shock, lapse into a coma, and die. Ravel raised his glass to his lips.

"Do you have a gun, Ravel?"

"No."

"Good. You look like you'll shoot me. I will survive these petty criticisms of my writing, but a bullet?"

Ravel did his best not to blink.

"Your mother is me," said Spiros. "A woman so self-absorbed she did not want to have children—"

"Bullshit."

"Allow me to finish. I'll tell you what I know, which is the truth, and you may decide from there. But not before."

Ravel imagined his tongue tacked to the table. The image did not stop him from listening.

"It's the truth your mother didn't want children—neither of us did. I had more of a mind for it than she, but not before—"

"You made it."

"I achieved success, yes. Your mother, when she was twenty-six, decided to have a child—you. Her absence of belief in herself and her work, her knowledge that I would succeed, led her to you. She had you by way of me to keep me, to control me and stop the success I would achieve regardless."

Ravel's bloody tongue was now twisting on the table. Yet he listened.

"It did not work. It's true I wanted a child—a son—but not in this way, not with that pretense. You'll not understand,

I'm sure, why I then left for these reasons, but surely you will remember your mother's bitterness, directed at you."

Ravel, sensing Spiros had allowed him an opening, said, "She loved me. She was there for me."

"She had to love you. She had to be there for you. It was not what she wanted."

"Well aren't you lucky," Ravel just about shouted. "You played your cards right, didn't you? Got the attention, the affection, the cooking, the cleaning, the *sex* you wanted, and when it came time to truly commit *for life*, you fled. You used her, and you used me."

Spiros smiled and once more shook his head.

"No way you can deny that. No way."

"Your mother never cooked. She made, perhaps, one edible thing from nothing. She did clean..."

Ravel banged his fist on the table. The drinks jumped.

"You killed her, you fucker! You want to know what it was like to watch her die, when she was only fifty-seven? Are you going to have the guts to watch your new wife die—oh, but that's right, you won't, you've made sure of that. You won't be around to see her go. This time you won't even have to pack your bags. You'll just die." Ravel was beginning to weep, of all things, and he couldn't stop. Not a loud sobbing, but it was an outpouring of all he'd been feeling toward his father and—he now realized—his mother for the past many years. Spiros took a deep breath and watched. He indicated Ravel's napkin, which the son used to wipe his eyes.

"And if she hadn't," Ravel continued, relatively composed now, "and if she hadn't been under so much pressure to raise me, alone, no support from you—and don't say money, I know she got money from you, I'm talking about something else, something more—if she hadn't had to do all that she wouldn't have smoked so much, drank, lived unhealthy with the hate of you."

"Your mother did not hate me." Spiros's voice rose. "She was angry with me, just as she was angry with you. But what she felt toward us wasn't as strong as what she felt toward herself. She hated herself. *Herself*. She did not hate anything but her own mediocrity."

Ravel seized the butter knife that lay next to the basket of untouched bread and brandished it. Spiros looked from the knife to Ravel.

"What are you doing?" he said.

"I don't know yet," said Ravel.

"With that knife?" Spiros smiled. "Son," he said. "Put it down."

The word *son* caught Ravel. He had never heard a man direct it to him before. The butter knife lowered.

"I would be grateful," said Spiros, "if I did not come to harm tonight. My family would be grateful."

Ravel set the knife down. "She died of cancer, you know. Three different kinds, all over her body. She was one big tumor in the end, her hair falling out, the blinds drawn, lying on her bed in the house she wouldn't leave. And I was the only one there for her."

"I know you were. I heard. And I felt. But I must remember your mother as she was in life, not as she was in death. Sharp. Fierce. Fierce toward us, toward men."

"Can't you just say her name?"

"She never had another man, did she?"

"You can't do it." Ravel sat back. "Everything else I can believe, but I can't believe that. That you can't say her name."

"I know her name."

"Then say it."

"I know her name, so why say it?"

"Because…" Ravel, his jaw slack, blanked. He thought of trying again, but he had no words left.

"Because this is the point in our story that demands it?" Spiros asked. "But there is a distinction to be made here. This is *your* story, not mine. Only your story."

After his father had left, Ravel remained seated, his index finger rimming his second glass. He felt his blood sugar low and knew he should eat something. What his father had said about his mother was true: she *had* been angry with him many times while he was growing up, and hadn't that anger in turn intensified his need for—and hatred of—the absent Spiros Averof?

He could recall many times his mother shutting herself away in the office at the end of the house. She made it clear by that closed door she was not to be disturbed. As Ravel entered his teen years and made friends, his mother's sequestering did not matter as much, but early, when he was five, six, seven, he felt the lack of attention acutely, equating the absence of her body to an absence of love. He was giving in to his usual histrionics again, though. Her neglect could not have been so extreme. She must have shown love for him, must have. In a way, she had always been there for him, if only in the background. His mother a presence, a force, without being present, the hugs and kisses infrequent. As a teenager he had accused her of keeping him homebound out of spite more than parental caution. He remembered shouting at her that he didn't want her life, he didn't want to be *her*. When Yoana called him on the fact that he wanted to be a writer he replied, harshly, he didn't want to be *that* kind of writer. He didn't want to be her kind of writer. His kind of writer needed to be around people, in the public eye, driving down the hill at night to gather material. A few minutes past curfew served his higher purpose.

"Mom, I'm building a foundation," he'd said one of those after-midnights. "What I'm doing now is going to last me... forever."

"You are becoming your father," she'd said.

In all their years living under the same roof together without anyone else entering their lives save for the rare visit from one of Yoana's relatives from Bulgaria, his mother had hardly ever mentioned his father. A few times when Ravel was young and pestering, and then of course his father's actual visit on his ninth birthday, but into the aughts any mention of Spiros Averof on Yoana Kopecka's part seemed unnecessary, as Ravel was old enough to answer his own questions by then.

As soon as the words had left her mouth she knew what she'd said was wrong—not that it wasn't correct, in her eyes her son *was* becoming his father—but it was wrong she'd said it then, that night when they were both so exhausted and overheated.

Ravel's overheated engine sparked that post-midnight hour. He unleashed on his mother a torrent of adolescent accusations: she did not want him to have his own life, she took a sick pleasure in stifling his friendships because it made her feel better about not having any true friendships of her own, she was being overly cautious, nervous, borderline paranoid, a foreigner still. Did she want them to move to Bulgaria so Ravel could work under her watchful eye at some tourist resort on the Black Sea? He stopped short of questioning why his mother had not remarried, why she had not so much as gone out on a date in all the time he could remember. The move to Anomar, this unincorporated town far outside San Diego, was not to blame. Men Yoana's age lived here. She knew several of them through the high school, the district, and yet she refused to know any of them intimately, beyond a quick drink in a group setting. That night Ravel stopped short of saying Why are *you* not building a foundation? Don't you see what you're doing? You're killing yourself!

He saw it then, in the way his mother coughed far more frequently than she had in the nineties. How she would drop everything in the middle of a lesson and race out to her two-seater Mazda Miata in the staff lot, leaving the class laughing and chattering about crazy Ms. Kopecka—but also embarrassing her son, one of her students, who sat in the front row.

How her doctor visits had increased in frequency, how she would rarely tell him anything of substance from these visits. By the late 2000s and the night of that argument, Ravel could see the deterioration in his mother's face and her scarecrow frame. The cigarettes had aged her, sunk her eyes in, withered her lips. It pained him to witness her self-destruction. As loudly as he was shouting at her, he also loved her, he needed her, she was all he had and he wouldn't know who to turn to without her.

Maybe she should go back to Bulgaria, he thought later that night after their argument had petered out. I can stay here, she can go. This country is killing her. (I'm killing her.)

That night was the first he'd been aware of his mother dying. He feared she would not be alive to see him graduate. But she did better than that: not only was Yoana there for Ravel's high school graduation, she was present for his college graduation as well, that day the greatest of them all, his mother truly, righteously happy for him, and the words she'd written in the card were not in the form of a poem but in the form he knew best and respected:

> Ravel, you have talked about building a foundation. You have here the cornerstone, the brick that can never be removed. Continue to build, my son, my dearest love. May it be a house you will welcome all into.
> Love always,
> Your mother Yoana

He had not done drugs as she had feared, he had not hung out with any bad crowd, broken any laws, drunk himself into oblivion for his art, for his father. He had stood up and stood apart, and when Yoana hugged him at the end of the college ceremony in May of 2014 he felt an unfamiliar force from her, a strength and a love that told him his mother was at last letting him go.

She had appeared healthier then, healthier than she had since he'd entered college, and her appearance, what proved to be a façade, continued as he entered graduate school, left California for Colorado. When he returned with both his master's degree and a girlfriend named Deborah Parker, Yoana had seemed fine. The day he returned was the day he felt the most love for his mother: he had approached her as she reclined on the back patio in the sun. Here in the backyard the early June light was strong, the bees loud in the heavy willow tree, the smell of flowers pungent.

Yoana motioned for Ravel to pull up a chair. She wore sunglasses and a ridiculously large straw hat. Together they watched the backyard for a time in silence, the only sounds the bees and the sprinklers watering the newly verdant lawn and the fruit trees in the distance.

"I'm not staying for long, Mom."

"I know. I understand."

"Deb has a lead on a job for me, an office job in Denver."

"That sounds promising."

"I don't want to teach. It didn't work out at that Mothers of the Merciful College. I know you think I should but..."

"The classroom will always be there, Ravel. It's all right to do something else."

"I'm just going to get some dumb job and work on my writing until I make it. I thought something would happen by now but..."

Yoana returned to observing the willow tree. She kept her hands folded.

"You have always put so much pressure on yourself, Ravel. So much, ever since you were young. I know why: me, your father..."

Just knowing he's out there, Ravel thought. *Succeeding.*

"It's okay to not be that person, you know. It's okay to follow a new path."

She touched his hand gently, as she had when he was very young, his first memory, and held it. "I believe in you," she said to him directly. "You must believe in you as well."

With her hat tilted back she leaned in and kissed him on the cheek. Ravel closed his eyes and put one arm, then the other, around her. He would be glad he did not cry that day.

To cry over something like that, when his mother was in fact dying, and would be dead in only five more years.

"Sir?"

Ravel looked up. The server, younger than him, stood expectantly.

"Just the check, please."

Ravel took the amulet out from under his shirt. His fingers turned it over and over. Then he put it back in place, polished off the last of the bread and pricked his finger. Back at an acceptable level, for now. He checked his phone. Deborah had left voicemail and a text during his time alone. He turned up the volume and prepared to call her. Time to be getting back. Time for the house to be finished.

FIFTEEN

L ooking out on the crowd that had gathered to hear him and only him, Ravel massaged his throat. An attendant had promised water a while ago. The author gulped and attempted to work up a swell of saliva. No good. *So many people*, he thought. *So many....* He would never be able to sign all those copies they clutched! Could Rav Kopecka switch to his off-hand when the pain reached its apex? What did Dalton Bryce do at book signings?

Don't think of him, Ravel thought. *Don't think—*

The first bookstore, the first reading, the launch of Stalwart's promotional blitz, and it was only April 11th. *That* had been published two days earlier, and rather than wait for all the reviews to filter in, let the judgments percolate, the good words spread, the publisher had chosen to put Ravel out there now.

"You're not a bad-looking guy," Stalwart's publisher and CEO Dennis Midriff had said. "No sense in hiding a handsome face when we don't have to."

Truth be told, Ravel was none too excited about starting

his book tour earlier than expected. He and Deborah were on their ninth house under consideration in Westchester County; half their belongings were in storage and the other half were scattered around the Queens apartment they'd been renting for the past two months; Deborah had a lead on a tenure-track position at a research university in the Bronx; and he and his wife were looking into adopting a puppy. Until they settled down into a suitable and permanent home, Ravel reasoned, any action taken toward the creation of a child would have to wait.

That wasn't all of it, though. Ravel had another reason that he withheld from his wife. A house of cards in his mind, always there. *That.*

He momentarily lost sight of that mental image as he began to read. The march toward fame and immortality, the media and soirees and awards and figures both numeric and human was now officially underway. This was his book launch, his novel, damn it, he'd worked so hard to get it to where he could call it his own. For his first-ever public reading, Ravel chose the opening of *That* in which Bob Delaney's kid brother Bruce chases his toy amphibious assault vehicle along the swollen creek's edge. The toy disappears just as it passes by a shoddy-looking campsite, and Bruce approaches the crudely constructed tent, its interior dark and foreboding. Seeing a smiling face inside, the boy reaches an arm out.... And what came next only Ravel knew—knew even before he'd written the scene. He glanced up and observed his captivated, hushed audience, most of whom were holding the novel for not the first time. They waited, unable to breathe. Ravel smiled wickedly then plunged in with his—Bryce's but now *his*—description of Oodlelolly the Magician's entrance, how the monster offered to give the toy back if only the boy would enter the tent and converse, discover what the magician had to offer....

When the description of the offer and Bruce's acceptance of its terms was read, most in the crowd gasped, and Ravel continued with the subsequent visceral scene without fear of what anyone would think. None of them would turn back. *They all read Dalton Bryce*, mused Ravel, *so what's the difference?*

As Ravel, his performance intense now, his voice rising and shifting in all the appropriate places, his mouth shooting the proper spittle, his hands shaking the lectern with the passion of the prose, read two more gory monster-laden scenes, he saw himself as Dalton Bryce—or at least as how he imagined Mr. Bryce had looked and felt the first time he had given a professional reading. In all his youthful obsession, all his reading of the work and research on the man, Ravel had never learned anything of the first time Dalton Bryce had stood in front of a crowd and read from the just-published *Janice*. Perhaps someday soon the younger novelist would learn about that time by meeting with Mr. Bryce and discussing their respective work.

During the autograph portion, Ravel watched the line about as often as he bowed his head to scribble. He watched not for the line's length so much as for who was queuing up. Heading into this evening Ravel had pictured everyone he had ever known shuffling forward dutifully, cradling their just-purchased copy. They had all descended on New York just for him. Even his former co-workers and bosses from Maguffin-Shrift had flown in from Denver. We wouldn't miss it, Ravel!

Ravel, you should've told us! We always knew you were more than just a sales development associate!

All those Ravel had ever loved and ever harmed would be there for his autograph, registering and storing every word he spoke as they hung over him like Death.

The actualization of this grand vision was not to be. For the first half of the signing Ravel recognized no one. No elementary school bullies singing their *mea maxima culpas*, no distant family members who'd always doubted he would achieve any success. Not even his father. While the greatest would have been for Spiros Averof to show up, head bowed, arms hoisting *That* reverentially, Ravel was realistic enough to know that would never happen. But not even a former classmate from high school or college? Someone from his master's program now living in New York must have heard of Rav Kopecka's book launch and, jealous, gone to this bookstore to snicker and shake his head and refuse to buy *That* on principle. But not even the dregs of Ravel's past could be found in line.

It wasn't until Ravel had signed well over a hundred copies that the patrons began to look familiar. The author observed them more closely. They were all...men, and Ravel swore he had seen them before. The man approaching him now was big, wore lightly tinted sunglasses and a cap in the style of John Deere that read Deere John.

"No," Ravel whispered. "Oh no."

"Hiya," the burly man wearing the Deere John cap said. He placed his copy of *That* on the table. "Name's Reggie by the way. Behind me's Clark..."

The shorter, meeker man Ravel recognized from the Wash Park rec center peeked around Reggie's frame and waved.

"I remember you," Ravel said. "Men Who Write Too Much."

Reggie turned to Clark. "He remembers us!"

Past these two men queued so many more, all of them attendants at that meeting over a year ago in Wash Park. Boys as young as eight waved and smiled, and Ravel returned their camaraderie.

"But I gotta say," Reggie said, "we're not all here. Not everyone's happy with this."

"Why not?"

"You wrote too much," Clark piped up from behind Reggie.

"Bruce says you betrayed the group. I don't believe him, but he does have followers. There was a kind of split when we found out your book was gonna get published."

"A rift," Clark added. "A fracture. But," he added quickly, "we're not fascists."

"We're not fascists *yet*," corrected Reggie. "I do gotta tell you...Bruce is here."

"He's here? At this bookstore? In line?"

"Nah," Reggie said. "He refused to show his face here. All these words, he said. But he's in the city, somewhere. And he ain't happy."

"Is he..." Ravel's gaze fell upon a nearby window, expecting Bruce Bednarik to be pressed up against it, grinning maniacally at the sell-out author. "...tailing me? You don't think he's going to, you know, do something, do you?"

"Can't say for sure," admitted Reggie. "I'm taking too much of everyone's time. Could you just make it out to Sue. That's my sweetie."

Members of Men Who Write Too Much who'd broken

with Bruce Bednarik and his faction kept the crowd heavy, and through it all—the scribbling, chatting, snapping of photos— Bing, whom Ravel spotted leaning against a nearby shelf, made not a sound nor a move, preferring instead to keep his arms crossed and his lips pursed. Ravel, who by the four-hundredth-and-something fan, had loosened up to where he was laughing, did not recognize the look on his super-agent's face until the very last patron hovered over the table. Bing still had not moved from his frighteningly singular position. Sensing something was up, Ravel rushed the final autograph of the evening and waited for doom to descend.

"We gotta talk," said Bing. "Just not here."

Half an hour later, Ravel plunged into what amounted to a catatonic state. If he had looked straight into That's grave-lights he couldn't have been more overcome with shock. Across from him sat his agent, ever patient, alarmingly protec-tive, and around him buzzed and banged the sights and sounds of this latest restaurant. Initially, upon taking his seat, the sounds had been strong, the sights bold, but as Bing's purpose became clear those sights and sounds faded until all around hung a dullness like a well-worn blade. Only Bing's voice was the point that hurt.

"I'm doing my best to calm them down, but they're in a panic. Not yet apoplectic, but they'll be there soon. They're not assigning you blame—yet. But heads are definitely going to roll. Whoever was in charge of fact-checking, vetting. Hell, whoever was involved in any way who's seen as expendable. I just...don't know how this could've happened."

In all honesty and after months of living the life to which he had always aspired, Ravel could not believe it either. At times, such as during his first-ever reading and book signing, it had been at the forefront of his mind, but he'd assumed his fears were overblown. His plan had gone so well, and yet the possibility remained. Now that possibility was reality.

Had Dalton Bryce really read *That* in three days, gotten on the phone with his agent and editors, friends and colleagues, and decried parts of the novel as plagiarized? Apparently, he had. And with the Emperor of Terror's call to arms many others—critics, amateur reviewers, social media meticulosos, and some group calling itself Men Who Seek the Truth About Rav Kopecka (MeWSTARK)—had taken up the cause. Already more than a few sites had posted passages from *That* alongside passages from some of Dalton Bryce's stories and novels. Ravel's passages bore an unsettling similarity to those of Mr. Bryce's. The characters names had all been changed, the ages and locations and time periods altered, but some of the situations, the deaths and dismemberments, and in a few cases some of the actual sentences remained the same.

"The word order," Bing had said as if he was delivering news of stage four. "There's one sentence—I've checked it myself—it's on page 634 and it's almost the exact same except for the character's name. Almost the exact same words, Ravel..."

The exact same words. But how? How when he had been so very careful in those five months of writing—writing that, he had to admit now, had only been *rewriting*. The more Bing revealed the more Ravel also had to admit internally that he might not have been so careful. With many, many passages he had been, but the novel was so gargantuan that only an AI superbot or the honest original creator could not have messed it up.

Of particular concern were the childhood scenes—these,

apparently, were the closest, if not the exact same, to what Dalton Bryce had written into his own stories dating as far back as 1985. The story "To Eat His Own," published in *Playboy* in 1987 and collected in *Malcontents*, contained the situation with the walk-in freezer and presented itself halfway through Rav Kopecka's *That*—complete with near-exact replicas of dialogue, description and deaths. Just one of a few examples, the list of which was growing by the minute.

"I can't believe it," Ravel said. "If that's really the case, why didn't Stalwart..."

"Catch these things? Jesus, Ravel. They weren't supposed to have to catch these things. But the book is so massive, and these parts and passages, they're all from earlier Bryce works, a lot of different works, it's like they were in one big thing originally and then one day thirty years ago they suddenly got broken up and scattered around."

"There's no going back," intoned Ravel.

"This thing's snowballing. They're talking lawsuits. Bryce feels betrayed. All those comparisons Stalwart made in the marketing campaign haven't helped."

But it had worked! He'd checked to see if Dalton Bryce had published *That* after he'd been driven away from the hobo, never to meet the homeless man, hear his stories, learn his magic tricks, and the proof was all over the internet, all over social media, in libraries and bookstores. No *That*. No *That* by Dalton Bryce whatsoever.

But what Ravel, in his rush to achieve the suddenly achievable, had failed to consider, failed to latch on to for even so much as a second, was that simply because Dalton Bryce never encountered that hobo in Garden of the Gods in the early eighties did not mean he would never write anything from

That. The novel itself may not have come together due to the lack of the inciting incident, the impetus, but that did not mean the idea to write about the bullies from Bryce's childhood, the monsters that could destroy those bullies and the friends who were privy to their demise was attached solely to some homeless person's stories and tricks. Certain ideas, scenarios, characters were always going to be written by Dalton Bryce regardless of whether or not he encountered the model for That's most famous form, and the only way Ravel could not have been caught, the hack realized now, was to have gone through *all* of Dalton Bryce's work *before and after* going back in time, read every word of everything ever published, committed all those words to memory in his vision as he had *That*, and made sure that *none* of Bryce's writing from anywhere made it into Rav Kopecka's *That*, which was now no longer Ravel's novel. It was now no one's novel.

"Say something."

When Ravel looked away, tears threatening to show, Bing pressed. "Speak up for yourself. I gotta know, before it ends now: did you or did you not willingly go through certain of Dalton Bryce's works and put certain material into your own novel? Tell me the truth, Ravel, because right now I'm your only buffer, the only guardrail keeping you from them. Believe me, you don't want to be talking to Dennis before you talk to me." He took a breath, exhaled audibly. "I need to know I can trust you."

The time had come for Ravel Averof to sink or flounder. He could reveal everything that happened—Chronotrex, the uncollapsible wormhole, time travel, the five-month long haphazard writing that was actually just rewriting—to a person willing to trust him, not believe him and likely punch him in the mouth, or he could tread water for at least a little while longer while the sharks circled closer. For Ravel, the decision was obvious.

"Whatever happened was not done willingly," he said.

"So you had no awareness you were plagiarizing."

Ravel, remembering what Mick had said about lying, looked Bing directly in the eyes and said clearly, calmly, "I had no knowledge I was plagiarizing anything of Dalton Bryce's. I swear."

"A subconscious act then."

"A subconscious act, purely coincidental. I'm a huge fan— at least I was when I was younger. Huge. The biggest. I don't even have those books, those stories, but I read them when I was like twelve or thirteen. I just had no idea…"

"I'll be with you there tomorrow," said Bing, "but you're going to have to do the talking. I can't speak for you on this one. Tell them what you told me, just now, and we'll work on putting out the fire."

As he was walking down the hall of his apartment building, Ravel's phone buzzed a 970 area code. He recognized the number, though he had not used it in over a year. Laney. Ravel put his phone on silent and unlocked the door.

Deborah was on the couch, one arm thrown over her closed eyes.

"Any better?"

"The fever's gone down a little. I'm sorry I couldn't be there, Rav. I'll be there for the next one. I promise."

"If there is a next one."

Deborah, who'd scooted over but still lay curled on the couch, sat up. "What do you mean? Didn't it go well? You were gone long enough."

"I was."

"So, what then?"

"Uh…" It had to happen. He had to have made that slip in his speech, the chink in his armor, just as Dalton Bryce had to have read his novel—Dalton Bryce's novel—and send the ax swinging. Ravel was beginning to see one thing, though, that did not have to happen. It was this most of all he was debating telling his wife. "Um…" he struggled. She watched, patient in the screen's glow that had become her own.

"They hated it?"

"They love it. I signed so many…. But afterwards Bing was there, he needed to see me, it was urgent."

Deborah waited, no longer patient.

"Apparently," Ravel proceeded, "there are some rumors going around claiming that parts—small parts—of my novel are already in certain stories by Dalton Bryce."

"Really? Oh Ravel…"

"I didn't know."

"Of course you didn't know!"

"I didn't know it would happen when I…"

"When you were writing it? Sure! Who does? You take a big chance putting yourself out there like that. I know you loved Dalton Bryce when you were younger, and your novel's so big, so full of so many wonderful things, true about all of us —when I read *That* I felt like I was reading something like a Dalton Bryce book—but not an actual Dalton Bryce book."

"Did you?"

"Ravel, it's *your* novel. Just because you were subconsciously influenced a little by all you read in the past doesn't mean it's suddenly not your book. Dalton Bryce doesn't suddenly own it. Jesus, who owns anything anymore?"

"It may be more than a little—the influence, I mean."

"But that's all that happened," Deborah probed. "You had no idea your work was going to be influenced like that."

In her eyes Ravel saw that she wanted to believe, and if he was going to be honest with himself there was still a part of him that wanted to believe as well. If he could perhaps go back in time and stop Dalton Bryce from reading *That*—but how would such an action be possible now that Laney was calling, no doubt aware the rules had been broken? It was better to ignore and to believe. By ignoring and adhering steadfast to one's belief, the situation would have to work itself out.

"That is all that happened," Ravel said, "and tomorrow I'm going to take care of it when I meet with Dennis Midriff and his gang at Stalwart."

"They pushed the Dalton Bryce comparisons way too hard. They rushed it."

"I know, but they believed. It's my job tomorrow to get them to believe again."

Deborah blew him a kiss, which he caught before sending his own.

"You're still a great success," she said.

Overcome with the truth, Ravel bowed his head.

"But most of it's yours, right?"

"Yes," said an increasingly exasperated Ravel.

"How much would you say? Ninety-eight percent? Ninety-five..."

Like Deborah, Dennis Midriff, president and publisher of Stalwart, wanted to believe, but unlike Deborah there would be no kisses blown. The grilling had only intensified, and

Ravel dared not look at his phone. Bing was at his side, but as the super-agent had explained the night before, he could say little during this meeting. And this meeting was shaping up to be something other than circling the wagons. This meeting was clearly going to decide whether Ravel Averof—Rav Kopecka—would stay seated or if he would be thrown out onto the street.

"I'd say...ninety-seven percent."

Ravel's answer appeared to pass some muster. The president and publisher, who had previously been gripping the edges of his desk, relaxed somewhat. He looked to the heads of legal, editing and marketing, then to Bing, then again to Ravel.

"Ninety-seven percent," he said. "I was hoping for ninety-nine. Hell, *one hundred percent* was what it should have been from the beginning. But ninety-seven percent..."

"Dennis," one of the editors broke in, "if I may.... You know it's a deal killer. In this day and age, anything, even a sentence..."

Midriff scoffed. "With so many authors relying on AI now? The heavies hiring out ghostwriters, slapping their name on a book written entirely by their co-writer? We all know it's not humanly possible for Dalton Bryce to churn out two massive novels a year. And yet that's what we have. No, Ty, I can live with ninety-seven percent. We've invested so much in *That*, it would be a shame to kill it. A shame."

"Bryce is not going to back down," legal revealed. "He's going for our jugular, Dennis."

"That is a problem. You want me to do the right thing. I hate to do the right thing, but you want me to do it and I have to do it, don't I? Christ, hasn't anyone here read a lot of Dalton Bryce?"

Everyone in the room, including Bing and Ravel, hung their heads in response to Midriff's question.

"You'd think," Dennis continued, "someone here would have caught these things, you'd think during the editorial rounds, the first pass, the second, the third pass, said to themselves, 'You know, this reminds me of this one part in this Dalton Bryce story!' and mentioned it in the damn edit letter maybe. Someone at *your* agency..."

Bing held up his hands in self-defense.

"I wanted to believe too, Dennis, just like you."

Dennis looked at Ravel, stone-faced. In the silence that followed Ravel expected the man to say, Notice how we said we believe in the book, not that we believe in you—but instead what came out was "You'd better do a lot more than this. You'd better kiss our asses and give half your earnings to your agent who made sure I was much calmer now than I was before. Do you know what betrayal feels like?"

"No, sir."

"Well I do. I believe most of us who work here do. We did before and we do now."

"It's a betrayal I can work with," Bing said abruptly, and such was the calm strength in his voice that no one stopped him from continuing. "Whether or not it was intentional—I believe it was not, as I think some of you do here as well—whether or not that's the case doesn't change the fact that we must deal with it immediately."

"We damn well better," said Dennis. "We managed to stop the next run, recall as many as we could from as many places as we could. There's still a lot out there."

"In the last twenty-four hours," marketing said, "two more passages have come out..."

"Still want to go with ninety-seven?"

Ravel's voice was as calm and strong as his agent's. "I will defend my work. I do not believe every accused passage is plagiarized."

"There does seem to be some let-up, at least a little let-up, in the accusations," the same editor who'd spoken before said. "They may have run out of passages."

"And," marketing said, "there are some who are actually coming out in defense of *That*. They're not many, but they are at least opening up a debate that may be to our advantage. Can this book really be considered plagiarized? Could it be considered more of a homage, a pastiche, a—"

"A pastiche? A *pastiche*?" Midriff's face darkened blood red. "Stalwart does not publish—"

"—I didn't mean—"

"—*pastiches*!" Stalwart's president and publisher leaned back and ran his hands over his face. When he withdrew his hands, he spoke in hammerfalls. "We're not going there, and yet I see where this is going. I have to head it off. It's up to me to avoid tying the noose. I'll tell you why this stinks to high heaven: I don't care what any of you want to call it, but *I* at least can call it out for what it is: laziness. Let the other houses publish their ghostwriters under the big names, let them go to AI to churn out their content, but not Stalwart. This company doesn't publish *brands*. This company doesn't publish lazy authors. This company publishes *real* authors, hard-working *writers* who sweat and *bleed*." With his next words, Dennis Midriff spoke straight to *That*'s author. "Now I believe you put a lot of work into this, a hell of a lot, and I don't want to see that go. You have a stay of execution. It's a short stay, believe me. What I need from you is your honest explanation of how you think you can get out of this. I need your ideas, your confession. We might be able to spin that. We positioned you before, we can position you again. Start with telling me each and every part, paragraph and word that is not altogether yours, and I need you to do this by this time tomorrow or—" Grave resentment seething from him, he paused and surveyed the room. "I need go no further. You have twenty-four hours. Be here tomorrow at eight. Bing, you can be here, but I expect you to take the same role you're taking now."

"Of course."

Through the halls and entryways, in the elevator and out on the street, author and agent remained silent. At last, as he was about to cut away, Bing said, "I'm sorry, Ravel."

"I'll get it done today."

"The best we can hope for is going to be a reissue. It's possible to overcome this, but it's going to be extremely difficult."

"I know. I'm thankful you're here with me. I hope you'll be with me after this."

Bing's smile was thin. "Deal with this first. Then we'll see."

Ravel had intended to offer his hand, but his agent had already turned.

Sixteen

At least the puppy loved him. A dachshund, it squirmed its ten-month-old tube-like body around like a spinning sausage. It kept licking Ravel too, its little tongue darting out to softly strike his hands.

Passing the hallway's floor-to-ceiling mirror, Ravel avoided his reflection. He did not want to see a thirty-one-year-old man and a thirty-three-year-old woman, husband and wife for coming on six years now, bringing home a wiener dog. It wasn't a baby—what they should be bringing home now. An actual baby brought home to an actual home.

Deborah inserted the key into the lock and pushed open the door. As she stepped over the threshold she screamed before backing into Ravel, who nearly dropped the wriggling dachshund.

"What?" he shouted. Then he saw them, through the open doorway, getting up from the couch and stepping over the boxes on their way to the front door. Two men, forties or fifties, wearing track suits for jogging or committing mafia-style murders. Both men also wore sunglasses and kept their hands in the pockets of their windbreakers as they approached.

"Run," said Ravel, shielding the dog while pushing Deborah with his hip. "Run!"

Deborah turned into him and he shoved the puppy into her arms.

"Ms. Parker, please!"

Deborah hesitated. Ravel thought again of shouting at her to run but knew his wife wouldn't budge. They remained in the doorway, the dachshund nose-whistling now.

"What is it?" Deborah said as she faced her husband. "This is about the book, isn't it? This is about *That*."

"This is about the book, Ms. Parker. We need to speak to your husband. It's urgent."

"Are you here to...to protect us? Bodyguards?"

Both men shook their heads.

"Dalton Bryce sent you. Don't you dare do anything to us..." Deborah reached into her coat pocket.

"We're not working for Dalton Bryce," the shorter man said.

"We were hired by Chronotrex," his partner stated.

"Chrono-what?"

"Oh shit," Ravel muttered. Deborah stared at him sharply. The puppy was merely curious.

"What's going on, Ravel? You know these—"

"With all respect, Ms. Parker, you don't need to be a part of this."

First the taller man then the shorter pushed past Deborah. The men crowded Ravel into the hallway and backed him against the mega-mirror.

"You should've answered Laney's calls."

"She's been calling every half hour."

"I was going to call her back," said Ravel. "I swear I was. I've just been really busy."

"Let's go."

From either side they grabbed Ravel and yanked the struggling novelist down the hall. Before they'd taken more than five steps Deborah cried out for them to stop. All three men turned to see her phone raised.

"Let him go and I won't call the police. Let him go now!"

"Lady," the shorter man said. "A lawsuit's pending against your husband that could bankrupt him."

"And probably you too," his partner said. "You both could lose everything."

"Ravel, tell me what's going on. You know this.... What's Chronotrex? Who's Laney? Why's she been calling you?"

The taller man released his hold on Ravel and gestured to Deborah and the apartment. "We can do this here, if you'd like. Tell your wife the whole story in the comfort of this place. We can give her the papers, the video footage, a copy of the lawsuit if you like."

"Video footage?" Ravel looked from the taller Chronotrex thug to his wife standing in the doorway with a quizzical-looking dachshund cradled in one arm and her other arm slowly lowering the phone. That he had betrayed her was evident in her widening eyes, her slack mouth. Whatever had happened, he had betrayed her.

"D..."

She put her phone away and stood aside, offering them entrance. It took Ravel time and strength to say, "Not here. I'll go with you guys. Just.... Deb, I'm sorry."

"Ravel, what did you do?"

"I'll fix it. I'll take care of it."

He was whirled around and forced down the hall, hands on his shoulders and pressed against his lower back. These he shook off and continued walking. "I'm going, okay?" If he'd looked back he would have seen the anxiety rampant on his wife's face, the mistrust manifested in her eyes, and the tears falling—as if she knew.

"What did you do?" he heard her shout, and then he was in the elevator descending. With him and the two thugs was an elderly woman, and Ravel thought of escaping somehow, of using this woman somehow to his advantage. But he couldn't, he was out of ideas—if he'd even had any to begin with. He turned to the taller thug. "This is seriously your guys' get-up?"

"We went jogging in the park before we came over," the shorter thug dead-panned.

They moved swiftly out of the building. Idling at the curb was a black unmarked sedan, but in front of that, standing in their path, was Bruce Bednarik and another man of about Ravel's height. Bruce and his bald companion smiled as they moved forward.

"Hey, Rav Kopecka! Ravel!" Bruce said. "Finally found you, you traitor!"

The leader of Men Who Write Too Much was removing something from his jacket pocket.

"Official business, bud," the shorter Chronotrex thug said.

"Official business my butt," Bruce said. From out of his jacket pocket he drew a handful of eggs—three, four, Ravel couldn't tell the exact number. He didn't have time to count, for Bruce was hurling them at the literary fraud. Ravel ducked as best he could, but the thug's hands held him firm, and all but one of the eggs missed. The eggs' stench sent Ravel's senses reeling into unfamiliar territory. He gagged, and his eyes welled up.

"Rotten writer!" Bruce Bednarik taunted. "Rotten writer! Rotten writer!"

"Shut it," the shorter Chronotrex thug said. He placed his sneaker into Bruce's chest and sent the leader of Men Who Write Too Much flying to the curb. The taller Chronotrex thug growled at Bruce's companion, who backed off. Ravel's handlers rushed him toward the now open door of the unmarked sedan.

"I never joined your group!" Ravel yelled just before the door slammed shut. He was between the two thugs, and ahead the darkened screen allowed no view of the driver.

"This is kidnapping."

"Not when you had your chance it's not."

"Didn't you read the contract?" the shorter thug said. "And I quote from memory: 'In the event the undersigned client breaks contract for any of the above reasons, including but not limited to being dishonest about the nature and purpose of his or her or their time traveling trip, Chronotrex reserves the right to seek out and acquire the client in question.' End quote."

"It *was* the fine print," the taller thug said to his partner.

"Jesus.... Guys, there's a coffee shop around the corner."

"Too late for that, I'm afraid."

"But I stink!"

"We know you stink. What's new?"

"No, I mean are you really not going to let me change or clean up in anyway?"

"Bingo," the thugs said at nearly the same time.

Minutes later they'd jumped on the Lincoln Expressway headed east.

"Okay, what is this? Where are we going?"

"Denver International," said the shorter thug.

"No way. No fucking way."

"Call your wife from the plane. Tell her you're taking care of it."

"But I have to work today. I have to gather evidence. I have an eight a.m. meeting tomorrow!"

"Yeah, we heard about that. Like you were actually going to pull that off?"

"I was!"

"Kids these days." The taller thug grimaced as if he were passing a kidney stone.

"Uh, guys…" Ravel tried. "You're really going to sit with me on this flight to Denver while I smell like *this*? Really?"

"*Really*. We've smelled worse."

"You sure the flight's not booked already? I mean, this *is* last-minute. Unless you bought a ticket for me ahead of time, which I guess…"

The thugs looked at one another before turning to Ravel. "You think we fly commercial?" The taller of the two joined his partner in ascending laughter.

He could have done anything, really. He could have saved his mother from an early death by going into the girl's bathroom on the fourth floor of the college prep academy in Burgas and, when her fifteen-year-old self wasn't looking, placed a worm inside the pack of cigs so that when she opened the pack she would forever associate the worm with the cig and so never reach for the latter again. He could have stopped his father from making it, perhaps by sneaking into the room on the day he finished typing out his first successful novel, taking the completed manuscript, at the time the only copy, from where it lay next to the typewriter and setting it on fire just outside the apartment as his father went about his business in the bathroom and his pre-pregnant mother napped.

He could have done more, so much more, to help or to hinder, but no matter what he did it would have forced him back here to Laney's office, somewhat stench-free, to be placed across from her by the two goons who, at some point during the four-hour flight, revealed their names to be Bradford (the taller) and Dunning (the shorter). The goons had left, the doors had closed, and Laney continued to stare so hard that Ravel felt the need to flinch. Instead he concentrated on the desk, which had papers scattered across it, photos interspersed —all evidence of what he had agreed to and what he had done to break that agreement.

Laney, powerful in her pantsuit, had said nothing to Ravel so far, opting instead to address the hired help only. How long would she make her culpable client squirm? Ravel, still reeling from the abduction, the flight and the rushed ride from DIA to the back entrance of the Chronotrex headquarters in the foothills—all at around eleven at night—felt like a fifth grader who'd been brought before his mother by the school principal. He knew what he'd done, and worst of all she knew as well.

Within minutes of the goons' dismissal, Ravel's strength showed itself. If he had to be the one to speak first in this situation, well then let it be him.

"You should've had me killed."

"Because you feel so terrible right now you wish you were dead?"

"Hardly. Because I'm going to sink this company. I'm going to make sure this company goes under. You want to go public, right? What will the public think when they find out you're kidnapping clients?"

Laney formed her hands into a steeple and touched the tip of her nose to the top. "Why didn't you answer your phone?"

"I was *going* to call you back. I was going to call you back *tomorrow morning* after I met with my publisher."

"And you convinced them everything not yours in Ravel Averof's *That* was unintentionally written, all part of some subconscious influence."

"It happens more often than you think," said Ravel. "And my author's name is Rav Kopecka—got it?"

"Look at you," Laney said. "You're nothing like you were before."

"How I was before, huh? Because I'm no different than I was the day you walked into that class eight years ago late. This has always been in me, waiting to get out."

"I don't like it."

"Tough. You know what I don't like? Being brought back here to apologize for something you damn well knew I was going to do."

"I didn't know you were going to do *this*."

"It was up to you to know. You're the boss, for Christ's sake. Anyway, I thought you were going to cut me some slack, Laney. I thought..."

"You thought I was just going to let this one slide, just this one? You broke the rules, Ravel. It's as plain as the lie on your face."

"Good luck finding out the truth, Laney. I'm the only one who knows what I did."

"Chronotrex knows, Ravel. And there's someone else, too: Dalton Bryce."

Ravel froze. Laney continued: "I am certain Mr. Bryce will remember a certain incident that occurred when he was living in Colorado Springs in the early '80s. We've scoured the interviews, the essays—it's something he hasn't wanted to make public. But I think now he'll be convinced. And if you think this publicity you've given us is going to sink us, well, Ravel, it's a good thing you're not a businessman."

The next day Chronotrex's lawyers would meet with Dalton Bryce and his counsel. At this meeting Chronotrex would announce that it was willing to aid Mr. Bryce in pursuit of legal action against Ravel Averof, Rav Kopecka, should Mr. Bryce wish to do so. After Bryce met with Chronotrex, Laney was confident the Emperor of Terror would take that route.

"This *That*," Laney said. "It's his, isn't it? It was Dalton Bryce's, before you went back in time and changed something that made it yours."

Under the table, out of Laney's sight, Ravel picked his fingers, something he had last done while stealing *That*.

He nodded. His throat hitched. "Dalton Bryce," he said quietly.

"The logistics of it mystify me," Laney said. "If you went back in time to make *That* yours, then *That* would be yours in the current time, *before* you went back. But how could you have written, or I guess rewritten, *That* in the first place then? How'd you have Bryce's novel?"

"I had some help," Ravel said.

"You enlisted the help of someone else? Who?"

"Only me. Call it divine intervention, Laney. The writer god came to me in a vision."

"Okay.... Whatever that means. Your divergence succeeded somehow, which means this is an alternate path you're on. At least tell me you changed the title. Tell me at least that much is yours."

"All of it's mine," Ravel said, and now tears were in his eyes. "All of it."

"Ravel..."

"It became mine as I wrote it. I found my novel in it."

For once Laney's edge dulled. She leaned forward and pushed the box of tissues toward Ravel, who waved them off and instead dabbed his eyes with his sleeve. She watched as he regained his composure. Minutes passed, neither ready to speak. At last Laney said, "I don't understand..."

"You wouldn't understand. You're not a part of this... *thing*."

"What thing?"

Ravel sighed and said, "What do you want me to do, Laney?"

"I want you to tell me what *you* want, what you realistically want. What do you want that's *realistic*? Then I want you to come with me."

ON THE WAY down he had time to think. He hadn't been doing much of it, he realized.

Laney was right. She couldn't see his past clearly, but she could see his future. Ravel's future was a morning meeting at which he failed to make amends with his publisher, who had made the decision not to keep him as soon as the scandal had broken. Ravel could go the whole day poring over his manuscript, but none of it would matter—Dennis Midriff had already decided to drop him and his work regardless. The future was reneging on the contract, a dismissal of future earnings and an order to return those earnings not yet spent and pay back those that already had. The future was legal action regardless of Dalton Bryce's or Chronotrex's involvement. The future was the utter ruination of a reputation that needed nurturing, needed marketing and promotion, needed *positioning*—of days then weeks then months of unreturned messages placed to Bing and every other legitimate agency. The future was Deborah leaving him, so shocked and overcome with revulsion that the husband she had thought she knew so well was in fact a fraud, a despicable plagiarist who couldn't even come up with one idea of his own. She would take the dog too, along with the earnings from her newly acquired professorship, and find an honest man who cared for her enough not to keep things from her.

Ravel was headed for that future—unless he acted now.

The inner sanctum, the holding tank for the Chronoquantumogriphier, was staffed by several drones hovering like bumblebees, and cameras in every nook made sure not to leave their human targets. Except for the inclusion of a small camera on the dashboard, the time machine itself appeared unmodified. Ravel seated himself. He buckled up then looked to Laney who was finishing feeding the coordinates to DOG.

"I thought this wasn't possible, Laney."

"Why wouldn't it be? You're still going to that same point in time in the past, Ravel. Early eighties Colorado Springs."

"I know but...I thought I couldn't go to a point in time

when I'm alive. I mean alive in the past my present self is going to."

"We've done a lot of work on DOG since you last chrono-trekked. It *should* work. When you did what you did in the past, Ravel, you changed course when you returned. You're on a different path. Think of this, the life you have now, as an alternate dimension. If you return to the previous dimension, the previous path, you can get back on track, or…"

"Or what?"

"Or go on a new-new path. Yet another alternate dimension."

"Oh great."

"Hey. *I* didn't alter history."

Ravel turned to the dashboard, took a deep breath and exhaled. "Tell me you've had a client do this before successfully."

"I'm not going to lie to you, Ravel."

"Not even one client?"

"One, yes."

"Really? That's great."

"I used a key word," said Laney, grim. "*Successful.*"

"So someone wasn't?"

"They weren't."

"So…what happened?"

"We're still dealing with this one, Ravel. Suffice it to say we're still looking for them, in the wormhole."

"Oh shit."

"Good luck." Laney smiled and patted Ravel's shoulder.

"This is going to be so surreal," Ravel said. "I'm not sure I can convince him."

"You're going to have to."

"Thanks."

"Tesser well," said Laney, and then she retreated to the command console.

Ravel's suit had encased him. He could feel his amulet pressed tight to his chest. The door lowered, and within seconds he was rocketing down the wormhole one last time.

WHEN HE WAS at last aware of his surroundings as a physical, concrete reality, he knew he'd been here before. He could tell from the early morning sky, nearly cloudless, the crisp and biting cold, the sight of the sun eking out over the Flatirons. Ravel rose to his feet. The trees' scent was strong, as were the sounds of the leaves rustling and of a small animal scurrying into the underbrush nearby. Past the trees, bushes and boulders, discernible now in the distance, was a trail that led to a massive rock formation, and Ravel knew he had been down that trail, too.

He had already made his move—and yet he hadn't. Not yet. Ravel looked up and saw another towering rock formation, this one rising at a gentle angle and continuing to finish at an acrophobia-inducing pointed tip. From already having climbed down and up this formation, Ravel knew that it looked similar to a kind of launching platform, the kind daredevil motocross racers jump their bikes off. It was at that highest point where he'd touched down the last time.

He could hear footsteps coming closer down the anvil-like rock formation. He could not yet see the figure but knew who it was. Ravel took a deep breath and ran up the formation's slope. Careful in the dawning light not to put his feet in any crevices or holes, he kept his head bowed while pounding forward like a bull. At one point he stopped and listened. The footsteps above had ceased. All was quiet. The sun shone bright enough now for him to see shadows in amongst the rocks. Ravel moved not one millimeter. Finally the footsteps above started up again, and Ravel remained in place. For a moment he thought of hiding—behind one of the many boulders lying along this path—but decided instead to wait. Why hide? It wasn't as if Dalton Bryce was coming down, wasn't as if he didn't already know about the chrono-trek. This time Ravel would see himself—and not back away.

It was him, after all, the slightly younger Ravel Averof taking the treacherous path in stride. He wore the late seventies get-up and had his head down so as to make sure he did not stumble. Upon seeing his younger self, the self of only a year earlier, Ravel's breathing ceased for a second. Is this what it was like? Had Laney been wrong—or worse, had she always known and this was in fact her way to get rid of him, negate the present with the past? Would the younger Ravel, upon seeing his older self, merge into that older self? Would they simply cancel one another out, the two of them, upon making eye contact, going *poof*, vanishing, never to reappear?

None of that would happen, for the younger Ravel had just sighted the older Ravel on the path ahead. The younger stopped, startled, and stumbled back. The older self did not budge. They remained alive, present in the past.

"Holy shit," said the younger Ravel. "This is..."

"Messed up, I know, but—"

"You can't be a ghost..."

"I'm your older self. And I know what's going to happen, if you do what you plan on doing."

"And you're here to warn me."

"I'm here to stop you."

The younger Ravel scoffed and shook his head. He reached down the front of his jeans, in plain sight of his older self, rooted around, immodesty just a memory, and came up with all the thumb drives containing *That*. These he turned over in his hands and spoke without looking up. "It's that bad, huh? This is so freaking ridiculous…"

"It is bad."

"So what happens, huh?"

"You don't succeed. You fail."

"I have to succeed. Or…. I have to try at least."

"No, you don't," Ravel said. "You don't have to. You certainly don't have to succeed, and you don't even have to try."

"It can't be that bad. Who do I hurt? Who do I kill?"

"No one killed. But hurt. Lots and lots of people hurt. You lie, you betray…"

"If no one's killed," said his younger self, "then what's the harm?"

"Seriously?" Ravel said. "Harm has been done. Harm is enough. Hurt is enough. I'm here to head that off."

"You backed down, you coward," the younger Ravel snarled. "You didn't give it a chance."

"Please. Go back. Don't do this. Let me have the future I deserve."

"Yeah?" his smiling younger self said. He held up the thumb drives in one clenched fist. "*This* is the future *I* deserve—the future *we* deserve."

"It's not the future that was meant for you, or me, or us. Believe me."

The younger Ravel dropped to one knee, the thumb drives

still clenched in one fist. He looked as if he was about to pray. Instead he exclaimed, "And look at you! Your hairline's receded even more!"

The older Ravel, already unbalanced by the vehemence issuing from his younger self and not expecting such a comment, reached up to touch his scalp. As he did the younger Ravel whipped the stiletto out of his boot. He pressed the button and the blade shot out. The younger Ravel, an unsettling smile overtaking his lips, leapt at his older self, brandishing the weapon with pseudo-expertise.

"Oh Jesus…"

"I kill you," the younger Ravel said, "and I'm still alive. It's not like the other way around. I have nothing to lose. You have your life to lose."

Now the older Ravel took a step back. His younger self was no more than a few feet away. "This is a nightmare," he said. "Laney was right. It's a different path—"

"So if it's a nightmare, then if I cut you you'll wake up, right? Let's see!"

The knife stabbed out, its tip dangerously close to the older Ravel, who stumbled but managed to keep his balance. "This is not real. It's not how it's— Something happened when we met right now."

"Like we can't share the same space, the same time, huh?"

"Another path—"

"We can't be here together. One of us has to go." Again the stiletto blade flashed and sliced.

"Jesus, you're no killer! *I'm* no killer!"

The older Ravel remembered what Laney had told him. Don't let him pass. If he passes then the wrong future is irrevocable. You can't go back again. You can't keep trying.

But Laney had neglected to say that his past self would be a monster reflecting the worst Ravel had never acknowledged was in him.

"She leaves me, okay?" he said to his younger, steadily advancing self. "She leaves you. Deborah leaves you, you sick fuck. That's what happens, one of the things that happens. Don't you care?"

A moment passed in which it seemed as if the younger Ravel did; but it was only a moment, and after it had passed the older Ravel realized *he* had not cared about that possible future scenario at the time *he* landed at the top of this particular rock formation in Garden of the Gods to change Dalton Bryce's trajectory. He had not cared because the book was more important. More than important, the novel and all that went with it was the only goal then, just as it was the only goal now to his younger self, who was inches and seconds away from driving a stiletto blade into his older self's chest.

"Last warning..."

But if his younger self could threaten like this, so could he. And if his younger self had the passion and intensity that came with wanting to achieve a feat so desperately, then he had the wisdom and strength that came with knowing what to expect.

So when the younger Ravel gave a semi-startling warrior-like cry and drove forward with the knife outstretched, the older self was already one step ahead in anticipation—and that one step, a pivot on the ball of his right foot—saved his life and his future.

The stiletto pierced his shirt and nicked his pectoral. As the point caught on the fabric and the pullover began to rip, Ravel, in the time it takes to blink, grabbed hold of his younger self's weapon arm and forced the attacker forward.

Still holding fast to that arm, the older Ravel fought to wrench the knife free. The younger Ravel, fueled by fury, twisted the stiletto so that the blade was aimed at his older self and proceeded to push. The point of the knife edged closer to the older Ravel's throat.

With youth comes strength, but with age comes desperation, a desperation different from the curse that possessed the younger Ravel. When faced with death flying in on the screaming tip of a blade, there was no better tactic than to resort to baser instincts. Rather than shy away from the knife, Ravel leaned toward it, surprising his younger self, who relaxed for just a moment. In that moment the older, wiser Ravel turned the blade just enough so that it avoided his throat.

The younger Ravel yelped and cursed as the older Ravel bit hard into the hand holding the knife. Ravel had never bitten into anything so deeply. His teeth broke skin, hit tendon. He tasted blood, sensed the hand loosening its grip. With his fist he struck upward, connected with the weapon hand, and the knife popped free. Having anticipated this, the older Ravel snatched the stiletto's handle in the second it hung in the air, and he came away with it. Instead of disengaging, he stabbed the younger Ravel's fist. The younger Ravel shrieked and his fist opened. The thumb drives fell.

"No! Ah fuck no! Not my work!"

"It's not your work," the older Ravel said. He trained the knife on his younger self while feeling around on the rock for the thumb drives. As he gathered each one he counted: *that's one, that's two, three....* When he reached the lucky number seven he knew he had them all.

Witnessing the theft, his younger self did not retreat. A

wounded animal now, still dangerous and even more desperate.

"You'll have to kill me," his younger self said. He stepped forward. "That means killing you."

"I'm better than that now," Ravel said, and he turned and ran up the mini-mountain.

"What the— Stop! What are you doing? You're not taking *my* way back!"

Ravel kept his eyes on the path ahead. One missed step, a trip over a rock, a foot plunging into a hole—and it would be over. He knew his younger self was chasing him; he just hoped he had enough strength left to make it to the top.

His breath was ragged. On either side the boulders and rocky ground were giving way to air, nothing but air and the distance below. As he ran he snapped one thumb drive after another into two pieces, breaking off the metal insertion point. He flung the pieces into the crevices and over the sides. Behind him he heard his younger self screaming not to do it, not to destroy any more of *That*. Ravel broke apart the last thumb drive and tossed that too. The scream turned into a wail. The ground ahead continued to slope upward and narrow. He was close, and so was his younger self. He could hear his voice, whining, pleading, cajoling: pathetic. Was that him? Had he really been like that?

He saw the shimmering traces of the Chronoquanumogriphier that had previously expelled him into this place and time, separate from the shimmering traces below that had just recently brought him here. Just past the younger Ravel's way back was a crop of boulders; he dashed between these so fast he almost fell off the edge that opened before him. A drop of a hundred feet perhaps, and his acrophobia was kicking in. But before it could kick in all the way he had hurled the stiletto knife off the cliff.

No dramatic cry of rage issued from the younger Ravel, who stood a short distance behind, amongst the boulders. His younger self looked nothing but exhausted now, older than either of them could ever be. The younger Ravel leaned against rock, panting and wheezing. The older Ravel, stepping cautiously away from the edge, approached his would-be killer.

"You ruined everything," the younger self said.

"I saved you."

Ravel placed a hand on his younger self's shoulder.

"Look at me."

The younger Ravel looked up, took another deep breath, wiped his mouth with his forearm and rose to his full height. "So it's over," he said.

Ravel nodded.

"I suppose I won't be needing this." The younger Ravel dug around in his jeans and whitey-tighties and retrieved the ski mask. He offered this to his older self, who begged off.

"If you don't mind," the older Ravel said. "You do the honor."

His younger self moved to the edge. He sighed before chucking the ski mask over. Turning back to his older self, he said, "What am I going to do?"

"You're going to go back to your time, to Chronotrex, and you'll be me. That'll be our path."

"I hope this is the right decision."

"It's the only decision that matters."

The younger Ravel appeared to accept that answer. He

glanced at his older self, then looked at him directly without shame. Neither Ravel spoke, but they understood.

Ravel gestured to the path between the boulders. His younger self bowed his head and took the lead. Ravel walked close behind. At the hovering, crackling energy field the younger Ravel inserted an arm. Ravel raised a hand in good-bye, and his younger self nodded. He stuck more of himself through the field. Ravel watched his younger self consumed by the shimmering light as he returned to 2023 and whatever path awaited.

Sun had spread over the boulders and along the ground. The air was warmer. Ravel unzipped his pullover, checked to make sure the blood from his chest wound had slowed to a near stop, then continued down the path to home.

SEVENTEEN

The door opened and he slid out. Laney was standing close by.

"God Ravel that looks nasty. I'll get a compress."

"No need. The bleeding's stopped."

"At least let's put something on it to make sure it doesn't get infected."

"Fine." He waited while Laney retrieved the medicinal ointment, which she handed to him and he applied through his sliced shirt.

"I take it he resisted."

"You could say that. But I did it."

"You did. More than you know."

"What do you mean?"

"A new path has opened. And you're on it."

"This is...what, another dimension? The right one this time?"

"You have to see for yourself. You be the judge. I hope you accept this life, Ravel."

"I just need to know what to do now. Where to go next. I feel…. I feel lost."

"That's understandable." Laney, her eyes warm, held out something for Ravel to take. A slip of paper, folded in half. Ravel opened it and read.

"What's at this address?"

"Go there. Your car's waiting outside. Drive."

"I don't…"

"It took some time, but I found you. I found your life, Ravel."

"Laney, what did you do?"

She smiled then, and in her generosity Ravel detected a sly streak he had to trust.

"You did everything, Ravel. I just gave you the keys."

Ravel looked over the address once more.

"You think you can find it?"

"I'll find it. So…are we, uh, cool?"

"Yes, Ravel Averof. We are cool. Do you want to bump fists or something?"

"A handshake would be nice."

Laney's hand, like her entire demeanor now, was gentle.

"You did well," she said.

"I hope you're not hurt if I say I'm never coming back here again."

Laney laughed. "That's all right. We're going to be very careful with our clients. All eyes are on us now."

"Not on me."

"Are you sad?"

Ravel was already turning. "No," he said, and then he waved goodbye.

HE DROVE, and as he connected to the I-25 and headed south, as the sun broke open along the Front Range and more vehicles joined him this Saturday in mid-April, Ravel could sense the future becoming his present. He was catching up, although to what exactly he did not yet know.

The house, a simple one-story tract home, was in a neighborhood bordering the University of Colorado – Colorado Springs campus. Ravel pulled into the driveway. He sat there with the engine idling, his hands on the wheel, debating. *One more time*, he thought. *One more time back in time to—*

He killed the thought, annihilated it. Just: no more.

He turned off the engine and, after taking a deep breath, got out. He reached the front door within seconds, his throat drying then tightening as if he were about to go on his first date. He knocked on the door, and when there was no answer after half a minute he tried the knob. The door was unlocked.

He recognized the smell of the interior—it was the smell of his last interior dwelling, the apartment in Queens. It was Deborah's smell. But where was she? He could feel her presence—not a ghost but a living being.

He walked past all their old things—the framed paintings on the wall, their couch and recliner and coffee table. The kitchen contained their microwave, air fryer, coffee maker. Their dishes, a wedding gift, stood upright in the drying rack. Everything was there, and as Ravel walked from living room to kitchen and then down the hallway toward the back of the house, he realized all these things he'd known were not so old, not old at all. They had simply been moved, and he had been gone for only a little while, perhaps a day, perhaps only hours, or minutes, or seconds, and perhaps he'd never been gone at all.

Through the hallway he passed framed photos he recognized and others he didn't. Older photos of Deborah's parents were familiar, as were those photos he remembered taking of his wife, or his wife and him together. But he did not remember an apparently recent picture of Deborah and him at a fancy Mexican restaurant with a mariachi band in the background. In the photo Ravel wore a giant colorful sombrero—and when had he ever put something like that on? For that matter, when was the last time he and Deborah had dined at a restaurant of that caliber?

As he pondered, Ravel began to see himself there, with his wife in that restaurant, and as the scene turned real he remembered. He *had* been there, just as he had been in Manitou Springs and at the U.S. Air Force Academy taking a tour. By inspecting each photo, he allowed the feelings and sensations to return, and he believed.

At the back of the house were four doors, three of which were wide open. Ravel approached the first, the one immediately to his left. In this room he saw two desks arranged at opposite ends, laptops resting on both. Bookcases took up the rest of the wall space. Ravel stepped into the office and approached the nearest desk. On it were an assortment of books concerning folklore and cultural anthropology, as well as a stack of student papers in need of grading. Above the desk hung framed degrees, one of which was Deborah's PhD.

On the other desk were books, papers and notes—but these pertained to education and teaching. The laptop on this second desk was on. Ravel moved the cursor and awoke the screen. His breath caught when he saw the document on the screen: a lesson plan, his name at the top. He recognized his handwriting on the legal pads, his annotations in the text-books that covered classroom management and K-12 pedagogy.

He could not find any other kind of work—writing or reading—not related to the fields of education and teaching. No fiction. No manuscripts. This was his desk, and he was done. He was truly done. He remembered that now, too.

He checked each of the bookcases, which did contain some fiction—but no Dalton Bryce. Dalton Bryce? He knew of the author, but he didn't care much for him. He had certainly never read anything by him. Why Bryce had popped up in Ravel's mind just now was unclear. He moved on.

The room across from the office was bare except for a stack of boxes, unmarked and unopened, in the center. Sunlight shone through the open blinds. Eager now to find her, Ravel left this room and passed the bathroom to stand in front of the last door. It was not entirely closed. He pushed it open. Before him was their sun-streaked bed, the rumpled covers, his wife just turning to look at him.

"Hey," she said.

"Hey…"

The headboard, the dressers, the nightstands—all the same. Something about her though was different. He stepped toward her.

"How long have you been up?" she said.

"A while. Feels like a long time."

Deborah sat up, revealing her collegiate shirt covering a round belly. Ravel gasped.

"What?"

"Nothing."

"Did you go for a walk?"

"Kind of. Just around. I was...thinking."

"What's on your mind? Come here."

He sat on the spot where Deborah had indicated. She didn't look concerned—only sleepy. His eyes were again on her belly.

"You made the right decision," she said.

"I did. I..."

Deborah held his hand, leaned in and kissed him on the cheek. "I could use a walk."

"Really? You just woke up."

"I need to get up and get moving. Lots to do today."

"What about..."

"Silly," said Deborah. "It's fine. The doctor said, remember? Let me put on shorts and we'll go."

He watched her in her shirt and underwear search the dresser. She was the most beautiful he had ever seen her, his Deborah, the woman he'd married. The birthmark on the back of her right knee had not disappeared.

Having found a suitable pair, Deborah turned. "What?" she said. "Am I even bigger?"

"I'm going to be a teacher."

"You are. I thought you weren't having any doubts. You're more than halfway through the credential program."

"I don't have doubts. I just..."

Deborah slid on the shorts and picked a light jacket out of the closet. She came over to him.

"What's wrong? What happened? Is your glucose okay?" She hugged him close.

"I think it's okay. I should check, I know, but I feel all right."

"You've been doing really well lately. Your A1C's stayed level. Don't you remember Dr. Craston saying you're a 'very stable diabetic'?"

"I do," said Ravel. He closed his eyes, calmed himself, waited. "I remember now. I remember. Are you ready?"

Down the hall she called out a name: "Sabre! Sabre!" Ravel followed Deborah into the kitchen where she opened the fridge and took out a small can with aluminum foil covering the open top. He watched as she took up a small metal bowl from a corner in the dining room.

"Sabre! You must have really been out of it this morning. You're usually so good about feeding her."

Deborah scooped the rest of the can's mashed contents into the bowl then hit the small spoon against the side. On cue a cat of about a year old strutted and stretched into the kitchen. A tuxedo cat: black with a white chest and nose. The cat went to the bowl and ate while Deborah stroked.

"Sabre..."

"Rav. I'm worried. Are you sure you're okay? You need to check your blood sugar now, just in case."

Ravel found his glucometer and pricked his finger. He was fine. He'd never, in fact, felt better.

As they walked across the street Deborah held his hand. She led him past the houses opposite theirs into a lightly wooded area. The strengthening sun cut through the shade and warmed them as they walked. At last Ravel stopped. "Unbelievable," he said.

"What?"

"That we live *here*."

"You're a broken record, honey. You've been saying that pretty much every day since we got here."

"In January."

"Yes. When I started teaching and you started the credential program. Remember?"

He did remember. He remembered so much now: the happiness they'd both felt when Deborah called him in November to say she'd been offered a position with the anthropology department at UCCS, and how on the day they'd moved into the house in early January, the snow holding off for just a little while, he took her to their bed, the only item they'd properly set up then, and made love to her with more sincerity and trust and strength than he had in all the time he'd known himself. And how, a short time later...

Ravel pulled Deborah close and put his hand on her stomach. "Can you feel him yet?"

Deborah nestled into the crook between his chest and chin. "A little," she said.

"I can feel him."

"Them. I think there are two."

"Really? Two..."

"Boys. You're sure of it, aren't you."

"Not a hundred precent positive but..."

Deborah drew back to appraise him.

"You know," she said.

Ravel nodded. That was all he needed. He could no longer remember what that was, but he knew he would walk this path, with or without his wife, with or without his sons, and think of the time and the people he'd known. Absently, he touched his chest through his sweater and shirt. His smile faltered. Something had been there, against his chest, his heart. The memory of someone. But when he reached underneath and felt for it, it was gone.

ACKNOWLEDGMENTS

Writing a novel is an act of faith; some call it an act of prayer. I have put my faith in my friend Jeffrey Bard, who has helped steer me through the publication of four books now. It's not hyperbole when I write that without Jeffrey's notes, our phone calls, his encouragement and tough love taken to my writing, the books I've published would be nowhere near as readable as they are. I've known Jeffrey for quite a long time. May I know him for quite a long time more.

For holding my feet to the fire at an impressionable age, for helping to keep my literary life alive, thanks go to author and fellow grad school survivor Stuart Ross.

This novel is dedicated to my wife, Emily, who has seen me through the highest highs and the lowest lows of a writer's life. Without her I would be a shadow of the man I am today. I thank her and my sons every day for the wonderful life they have given me.

About the Author

David Ewald is the author of the novels *The Book of Stan* and *He Who Shall Remain Shameless*, as well as the collection *The Fallible: Stories*. He is a graduate of the College of Creative Studies at the University of California Santa Barbara and the MFA creative writing program at the University of Notre Dame. He writes, teaches and parents in California's Central Valley.

facebook.com/davidewaldauthor

x.com/David_M_Ewald

instagram.com/davidewaldauthor

www.ingramcontent.com/pod-product-compliance
Lightning Source LLC
Chambersburg PA
CBHW020245010826
48973CB00006B/1658